A HALLOWEEN READER

A HALLOWEEN READER

Poems, Stories, and Plays from Halloweens Past

Edited by
Lesley Pratt Bannatyne

PELICAN PUBLISHING COMPANY
Gretna 2004

Excerpts from "The Feast of Samhain" reprinted with permission of the Society of Authors as literary representative of the estate of James Stephens.

"A Halloween Chant—the Midnight Flitting of the Corpse and Tomás MacGahan," from *Irish Poems: From Cromwell to the Famine. A Miscellany,* 1977, reprinted with permission of Associated University Presses.

The word "Pelican" and the depiction of a pelican are trademarks of Pelican Publishing Company, Inc., and are registered in the U.S. Patent and Trademark Office.

Library of Congress Cataloging-in-Publication Data

A Halloween reader : poems, stories, and plays from Halloween past / edited by Lesley Pratt Banntyne.
    p. cm.
  Includes bibliographical reference.
  ISBN 1-58980-176-8 (pbk. : alk. paper)
 1. Halloween—Literary collections. 2. American literature. 3. English literature. I. Bannatyne, Lesley Pratt.

  PS509.H29H35 2004
  810.8'0334—dc22

                                2004014559

Printed in Canada
Published by Pelican Publishing Company, Inc.
1000 Burmaster Street, Gretna, Louisiana 70053

for Gary

CONTENTS

IT HAPPENED ONE HALLOWEEN . . .

FUN AND GAMES: LIGHT VERSE

Part II. Stories

THE STORYTELLERS' ART

GAY, GHASTLY HOLIDAY

Part III. Plays

ILLUSTRATIONS

Page 25
Death in a top hat. Illustration by K.M. Skeaping for *Told After Supper* by Jerome K. Jerome (1891).

Page 28
Portrait of Sir Walter Scott. Frontispiece to *Waverley: or 'Tis Sixty Years Since* (1855).

Page 56
"The hands stretched forth appealingly." Illustration by F. Phineas Annin for "The Legend of All-Hallow Eve" in *Harper's Magazine* (November 1879).

Page 75
Death always catches up with you. Illustration by K.M. Skeaping, *Told After Supper* by Jerome K. Jerome (1891).

Page 89
"All Hallowe'en." Illustration by T.G.C. Dakley for *Godey's Lady's Book* (October, 1879).

Page 102
"Kings May Be Blest." Illustration by J.E. Christie for *The Songs & Poems of Robert Burns* (1913).

Page 137
The Kirkyard. Illustration from *Harper's Monthly Magazine* (October 1910).

Page 212
"'Tis now the very Witching Hour." Illustration by K.M. Skeaping for *Told After Supper* by Jerome K. Jerome (1891).

Page 236
"Hallow e'en party." Stereocard, 1909. The Universal Photo Art Co., C.H. Graves, Philadelphia.

Page 247
"The Witch's Ride." Illustration by J. Copland from *Witchcraft and the Superstitious Record in the South-western District of Scotland* (1911).

ACKNOWLEDGMENTS

I owe a large debt of gratitude to the Harvard Libraries—primarily the Theater Collection, Widener, Lamont, and Schlesinger libraries—and to all their excellent staff. My thanks go also to the Harvard Music Department, especially Nancy Shafman and Tom Kelly, for the flexibility they gave me to work on this project.

I would like to acknowledge Elizabeth Gray and Stephen Mitchell for letting me audit their courses so I could better understand the cultures in which many of these stories and poems were written, and the staff at the Library of Congress, particularly Alice Lotvin Birney, for assistance tracking down work by unpublished writers.

I am also grateful to Associated University Presses for permission to reprint "A Halloween Chant"; to S. T. Joshi for "Hallowe'en in A Suburb," included in his anthology, *The Ancient Track: The Complete Poetical Works of H. P. Lovecraft;* to Stephen Davies at Mt. Royal College's Gaslight website for his help locating publication information; and to The Society of Authors for permission to reprint an excerpt from James Stephens' "The Feast of Samhain." My warmest thanks go to Tina Reuwsaat for all her help, and to Patricia Busacker, Jim Cooke, Kaye Denny, and Tim Reuwsaat for offering opinions on which stories to choose.

Most of all, my thanks go to my husband, Gary, for picking up the slack I left lying around the house, and for his superhuman editing.

INTRODUCTION

This is not a horror anthology, though horror can be found here. Nor is it a collection of ghost stories, though there are ghosts. It's not meant to make you quake in your chair, but rather to have you feel the ground sink quietly, slowly under your feet, so you don't notice the shift.

Older Halloween literature serves up a holiday you might not recognize at first. There's a soulfulness we're not used to anymore. By virtue of the way lives were lived in the sixteenth, seventeenth, and eighteenth centuries, there's a stronger bond between the living and the dead. Because of more primitive science and medicine, there's an acceptance of fate we may find foreign, a reliance on charms we have trouble imagining. Due to social notions popular in the nineteenth and early twentieth centuries, Halloween has a romantic cast that may strike us as just plain odd.

Here the reader can find the bones of Halloween. Its literature over the past four hundred years exposes a time tied to the quickening dark, to seasonal change, to death, to the movement of beings—fairies, witches, dead souls—through the night. Halloween was once imagined as a rift in reality where time slipped by without the traveler knowing he'd gone missing. As a night to return home, dead or alive. There was fear, yes, but it was fear of loss—of children and family, of land, crops, and place. This night wasn't about murder or violence, but rather about the unquiet of guilt, anticipation of the unknown, of facing the consequences of meddling with things you couldn't—or shouldn't—control. These Halloweens meant something; they held a place in the year for magic, for mourning, for first love. For fear. In Halloween literature, the otherworld is always and uniquely present. On this night, it can be broached, or we, if we're willing, can open our eyes wide enough to see it.

A Halloween Reader is made up of poems, stories, and plays written by those with credentials neither you nor I can claim—they're dead. The anthology contains a Halloween summoned by writers from the sixteenth through the early twentieth centuries who conjure the night to set a scene, twist a plot, or explain the seemingly inexplicable, like madness or time travel. Here is Halloween as it was *imagined*: a time for games and storytelling; a portentous time to make amends and wishes; a solemn time to remember the dead. It was a time to come home and a time for adventure; a time of mourning, of dead souls, of rotting corpses that, like sin, won't release their grip. *A Halloween Reader* ends with selections from the early twentieth century, when the holiday is well on its way to becoming a big and boisterous fixture on the American calendar. It ends before much of Halloween literature becomes synonymous with horror; before it is folded into the literature of children.

Death and Plenty

> The wings of the birds
> Are clotted with ice.
> I have but one story—
> Summer is gone.
>
> —ninth century Irish lyric, trans. Sean O'Faolain

Halloween originally emerged in the British Isles, where late autumn was gray and ominous, the beginning of the dead season. Poets from this part of the world filled their lines with funeral imagery: "And the year / On the earth, her deathbed, in shroud of leaves dead, / is lying (Shelley, "Autumn. A Dirge"). Halloween led off the season of loss—of birds, flowers, the warmth of the sun. It was also, poetically, a season of truth, for bare branches revealed the clearest view. The early dark of late October, too, was unsettling. It was a time of change: "there is a fearful spirit busy now" (Procter, "Autumn"). Earth clutched at dull gray covers, knowing full well that come November she would freeze to death.

But Halloween was also a time of plenty. All Hallows, or All Saints—a feast day in the Catholic Church placed on November 1 in the ninth century— marked the end of the farmer's year. Larders were full, flocks sheltered, and for the foreseeable future there was time enough for pleasure and, importantly, food enough to share. Throughout the old winter holidays, masking, tricks, performances, and processions were enacted in exchange for treats or money. All Hallows began the season.

The literature of Halloween reflects both death and plenty. The groaning board is full, but the night is windy, cold, and dark. People huddle congenially around a hearth fire, but, outside, skeletal knuckles tap incessantly. There are two at this table, sitting opposite each other, sharing a bottle of wine. One is in full view, curiously probing the future. The other is in shadow, all-knowing, only occasionally letting out a shriek or a shred of information. Imagining Halloween begins with picturing what is just beyond the edge of light, outside the warm hut, just beyond the castle walls at night; what happens when you close your eyes to sleep; what goes on beneath fertile ground, under the mounds.

Like the folk history of Halloween, its literary history also tells a story.

Poets and Peat Fires

Scots poet Alexander Montgomerie's "The Flyting of Montgomerie and Polwart" etches a Halloween picture from 400 years ago. Already it is a creepy night when fairies and "elrich [weird, inhuman] Incubus" ride, and on this night is born the villainous Polwart, so stinking and foul that witches curse the devil for giving them such an odious baby.

Over two centuries later, Montgomerie's countryman Allan Cunningham published "The Maid of Elvar" (1832), in which all the elements we think of as belonging to modern Halloween are lined up in a row. There's a dramatic setting:

> The stars are sunk in heaven, a darksome cloud
> Conceals the moon, and mist conceals the brook:
> The mountain's swathed up in a snowy shroud . . .

Witches and jack-o-lantern lights:

> Hags on their ragwort chariots come abroad,
> Wild Will his treacherous lamp hangs o'er the pool . . .

Mischief:

> It's not for pious folks abiding
> The misrule in the air, and witches rudely riding.

And demonic creatures:

> While loosed from pangs in hell's hot penal clime,
> As a dark exhalation from the ground,
> Satan will rise and rule his grim conclave around.

What the old Scots literature left behind, aside from a list of Halloween charms and a taste of Scots country life, reeks of sulfur.

Yet just across the Irish sea, in the ballad "A Halloween Chant—The Midnight Flitting of the Corpse and Tomás MacGahan" (written down sometime between 200 and 350 years ago), Halloween has less to do with spirits of evil and more with finding a resting ground. Having and protecting a home, and homecoming, are themes that recur in Irish Halloween literature. Samhain ("summer's end," November 1) was the time herds migrated to their winter pastures; in Celtic mythology the fairies, likewise, were on the move. Starting no later than the eighteenth century, many Irishmen worked abroad in the summer and returned home at Samhain (some scholars propose "Sam" in the word Samhain refers to "together"). Mythological history also describes important gatherings at the central seats of Ireland: at Tara, warriors convened to fend off annual attacks from the otherworld. If an Ulsterman did not come to Emain at Samhain, he was believed to be mad, and his gravestone placed.

Unlike residents of Great Britain, most of whom converted to Protestantism during the Reformation, many Irish remained Roman Catholic. While Protestants rejected purgatory and diabolicized ghosts, Catholics kept up annual remembrance of the dead on All Souls' Day, November 2. The intersection of All Souls' and Halloween is well-traveled: disembodied souls and the imperative to provide for the dead are embedded in Irish Halloween literature. In Dora Sigerson Shorter's "The One Forgotten," a man forgets to put out a chair for his wife to visit on that night. When her spirit comes, he is asleep, and she leaves heartbroken. His granddaughters laugh at the old man's sudden remorse upon waking: "How he goes groaning, wrinkle-faced and hoar, / He is so old, and angry with his age— / Hush! hear the banshee sobbing past the door."

Celts reputedly believed death is at the center of a long life, and indeed, much of the literature of Halloween, especially Irish, concerns itself with who's dead and who's alive, who's both at once, and who's dead and doesn't know it.

But one island's literature can't be wholly separated from the other's. The original word for an inhabitant of Ireland was "Scot." Many Irish immigrated to the Scottish Highlands and Isles in the early Middle Ages, Scottish and English settlers were "planted" in northern Ireland in the seventeenth century, and workers often traveled between the countries. Writers from the British Isles—from all of its lands—have handed us a Halloween full of spunk, laced with the danger of last chances. If Janet can't pull Tam Lin from his horse on Halloween, she'll lose him. If you don't watch over your children at sunset in late October, the fairies will steal them. On Halloween night, keep one eye on your loved ones, and the other on the door bolt. It is a literature of loss and warning: don't stay too long in the world of fairy.

Never forget those who have gone before. Travel if you must, but always, always, come home.

The Bard of Ayrshire

In 1799 Englishman John Cross produced a play in the New Royal Circus in St. George's Fields called *Halloween; or, the Castles of Athlin and Dunbayne.* The play's plot was drawn from a similarly titled novel, *The Castles of Athlin and Dunbayne. A Highland Story* (1789) by Gothic writer Ann Radcliffe, but Cross bookended his "Scotch Spectacle" with Halloween themes to add atmosphere and otherworldliness. He was likely capitalizing on the popularity of a Scots poet, and a Scots poem, recently published: Robert Burns' "Halloween."

Scottish independence had been defeated in 1707 with the Act of Union (uniting Scotland and England under British rule), and many Scots feared a loss of cultural integrity. Burns was one of a group of writers who mined his country's folklife for poetic material, both to preserve it and to bolster Scottish pride. His "Halloween" (1786) gives a detailed description of the night of October 31 in a cottage in southwestern Scotland.

Burns' poem included Halloween charms he said he learned from his mother's highlander maid: burning nuts, pulling cabbage stalks, eating apples in front of a mirror, and many more. What people were really doing on Halloween in the late 1700s and what Burns depicted them as doing are probably similar, but Burns' work was poetry, not history. Regardless, by the late nineteenth century Burns' "Halloween" had become a blueprint for both fictional and actual Halloween celebrations, attesting to how popular perception can be shaped by a single imaginative work. The charms Burns helped immortalize lasted, in popular literature at least, well into the twentieth century.

"Halloween" was included in the very first edition of *Poems, chiefly in the Scottish Dialect.* By 1787 there were editions published in Edinburgh and London, and by 1788 American booksellers had the book. Although Burns' work was widely enjoyed, it was read especially passionately by ex-patriot Scots in the United States and Canada, where his poetry came to stand for Scotland before the Act of Union. The Scottishness of "Halloween"—which includes more dialect than other Burns poem—may have made it more popular than it would have been otherwise.

On both sides of the Atlantic, "Halloween" inspired countless poems with and without credit to Burns. The poem dovetailed perfectly with Victorian interest in all things eerie, rustic, celebratory, and ancient, and the poem's images and sense of sport were imported full-bore into romantic stories and light verse. Annotated calendars consistently drew Halloween content from sources such as John Brand's *Observations on Popular Antiquities;* Brand footnotes Burns' "Halloween" as his main source. By the end of the nineteenth century, the eve of October 31 had a public face, and, more often than not, it was the face Burns had given it.

This Night of All Nights in the Year

"Said we, then—the two then—"Ah can it
Have been that the woodlandish ghouls—
The pitiful, the merciful ghouls—
To bar up our way and to ban it
From the secret that lies in these wolds—
Had drawn up the spectre of a planet
From the limbo of lunary souls—

—Edgar Allan Poe,
To_____. Ulalume: A Ballad (1847)

In what's considered America's first opera, *The Disappointment* (1767), a conjurer fools four Pennsylvania colony folks by convincing them he's got a magic divining rod "cut on All-Hallow's Eve, at twelve o'clock at night, with my back to the moon" that will lead them to pirate's treasure. Playwright Andrew Barton uses the Halloween reference, among many others, to clue in the audience: these folks are so gullible they'll believe anything. In "Fiend's Field" (1832, published in Philadelphia but set in Britain), we meet Tony Ryecroft, who practices Rosicrucian-style alchemy, spouts fake Latin, and conducts fiery Halloween rituals, all to hoodwink a land-rich neighbor. Here in very young America, Halloween is a code word for hoax, a night to prey on the naive with a wink to the wise. This is not the first time, or the last, that Halloween has been pressed into the service of satire and humor.

Sixteenth-century poet Montgomerie uses Halloween to yank on Polwart's grotesqueries by naming it his birthday. Burns pits encyclopedic divination notes to "Halloween" against the slapstick—and largely futile—antics of his country folk as they actually try the charms. In *A Hallowe'en Party* (Caroline Ticknor, 1896), the narrator, Dodge, is subjected to every torture a Victorian party can deal: the guests dunk for apples and Dodge nearly drowns; they share a cake filled with tokens and Dodge swallows a button; the men dash around the outside of the house and our hero nearly decapitates himself on a clothesline. Halloween was a country phenomenon—with all its attendant stereotypes—and remained so in literature even after cities began to crowd in on ports and pasture land. Dodge lives in New York, but his party is outside the city, an "old fashioned" Halloween.

By the end of the nineteenth century, the world had been turned on its head. Darwin had published *The Origin of the Species* (1859), Freud had begun peeling back the brain to reveal an unconscious, and archeology, spurred by excavations in Egypt and Greece, excited the public imagination. Victorians began to see history as a series of layers, and set about finding old stories, ballads, and poems as if they were fossils that could tell what life was really like in the past. Surrounded by factories and machinery, the world's first industrial societies came to hunger for the country, for a simpler time they saw as more connected to nature and a deeper truth. Halloween, as imagined by Victorians—rural, rudimentary, and demanding a certain amount of innocence—was entrancing. In this culture, and in its literature, there was comfort in ancient traditions, in things that did not change. Halloween, as portrayed in much of the era's popular literature, reversed itself. Instead of a naïve fool being the butt of Halloween trickery, it was now the foolish sophisticate who refused to believe in the power of Halloween and received his or her comeuppance. Over and over again, Halloween's charms proved true, and only the arrogant and disillusioned refused to put faith in them.

Take, for example, "The Face in the Glass" (1891), in which a stodgy, absentminded writer spends a wakeful night convinced he sees the semi-opaque silhouette of a woman standing outside his bedroom on Halloween. Like a face-in-the-mirror charm that predicted a spouse, this silhouette—"like a creature turned to stone by some sudden bolt hurled from the hand of a swift fate"—prophesied the writer's future. Halloween trumps the disbeliever. Ethel Barton, the protagonist in "By Cupid's Trick" (1885), suffers from a common modern disease: she's all too practical, especially when it comes to Halloween. "Then what's the use of trying all these silly tricks?" she asks. But while eating an apple at midnight and looking into a mirror, Ethel's true love does, in fact, walk through the door. Ethel, not only reunited with her man, has now been initiated: she believes in Halloween.

In the late nineteenth-century—an age of reading dominated by the periodical press—how Halloween was described in print became as important as how it was actually practiced. While some people certainly celebrated the holiday, a much larger number read Halloween stories and poems, and studied illustrations published in magazines and newspapers. Halloween fell into the public domain, and as with the adoption of Christmas trees, people became enamored of the holiday simply by reading about it. And while the popular press continued to mine Halloween for its fortunetelling details, another sort of writing had begun percolating, a literature of supernatural fiction and horror.

Halloween was enough of a presence in the nineteenth century that some writers—J.S. Le Fanu in the British Isles and Edgar Allan Poe in America—could submerge it in their work, hold it just under the surface to sharpen tension or etch atmosphere. In Le Fanu's "The Child That Went With The Fairies" (1870), All Hallows Eve is implied, but never mentioned. It's late autumn, leaves have fallen, it's getting dark, and the little ones are playing on the road. A carriage appears from a mountain well-known to harbor the supernatural. The reader knows what night it is, and knows this is not going to end well. It's all he can do to not shout, "Run!" In Poe's poem "Ulalume," the reader fills in the blanks of "this night of all nights of the year." A ghoul-haunted wood, a tomb, a man and his soul, a loss? By the time Le Fanu and Poe wrote their deliciously unnerving stories and poems, only a few creepy elements were needed to conjure Halloween.

Nocturne

So fancy takes the mind, and paints
The darkness with eidolon light,
And writes the dead's romance in night
On the dim Evening of All Saints.

—Madison J. Cawein, *Intimations of the Beautiful* (1911)

Dead souls, fairies, spirit creatures—it's no wonder they have secrets, they've been to places we can't imagine. To dark places. Vision, and lack of it, are intrinsic to Halloween literature: the dead can see the future; we can't. The dead live in darkness; we're afraid of darkness. Halloween is one time of the year when it can all come together, when the spirit world can be solicited, invaded, envisioned. What you need to be able to see, of course, is a pitch-black night.

James Stephens dissects the dark in his "The Feast of Samhain" (1924): "Here the light was golden, and here it became grey, and here, a step farther, it became blue or purple, and here, but two paces beyond, it was no longer a colour; it was a blackness, an invisibility." It's as if the darkness of Halloween is so dense that only on this blackest of nights can we see things that are normally dim—the ghostly shapes that surround us. It is as if we have to lose our sense of sight, our grasp of the familiar, and be lost—as so many characters are in Halloween literature—to be able to see the otherworld. Keningale, in "Ken's Mystery" (1883), gets lost in the darkness outside an Irish barracks on his way home from a Halloween celebration; only then does he run into the sphinx-like Elsie, his guide to the other side. The protagonist of Yeats' "Red Hanrahan" (1904) follows a hare conjured by an old stranger on Samhain night, and finds himself outside in the dark, lost and exhausted. Only then does he notice the dim light on the hillside that leads him into the otherworld. Young and beautiful Nann (Le Braz, "All Souls' Eve in Lower Brittany," 1897), determined to search purgatory for her dead husband, goes missing for a year. When she returns, she's ancient and reeks of burnt flesh.

There is a sense of free-fall in this getting lost in the dark. Time is suspended; place is unrecognizable; characters must open themselves to new experience and let go of the ordinary. The protagonist in "Ken's Mystery" returns from the darkness haunted and drained, having lived through over 200 years in but one night. The narrator, upon hearing Ken's story, muses: "What is time? What is life? I felt myself begin to doubt the reality of all things." This journey into the dark—that is sometimes consciousness, sometimes the blackness of evil, sometimes death—is not easy. But the desire to know more drives the plots and poetic arcs of much of Halloween literature. Red Hanrahan comes back from the fairy world empty-handed, aged and starving, maddened. Most of us aren't meant to go there. Those who do return have changed, and they don't like to talk about it.

The 20th Century:
When the Dead Can Yearn
and the Dead Can Smite

> For the year's on the turn and it's All Souls' night,
> When the dead can burn and the dead can smite.

> —Edith Wharton, *All Souls* (1909)

The dead can be terrifying, but useful. Nineteenth-century writers fondly name them, or call them "my dear." They embrace and are embraced by the dead:

> That the night of all nights is this,
> When elm shall crack and lead shall part,
> When moulds shall sunder and shot bolts start
> To let you through to my kiss."

> —Edith Nesbit, *The Vain Spell* (1898)

The dead teach, they predict, they warn. James Russell Lowell's Reverend Dr. Death ("The Black Preacher," 1864) gives a sermon to the damned each year on All Souls' Eve, but it's meant for us: don't do as these wretched souls did, because if you wait for tomorrow to pray or love, you just might find yourself sitting in an abandoned church with a bunch of jittery bone-bags enduring the same sermon every year.

Then, early in the twentieth century, this familiarity began to erode. More and more in Halloween literature, the dead are adrift. They become separate, like Maria in James Joyce's "Clay" (1916). She's homeless, without family, making her way through a sea of souls to return to what passes for her family on Halloween night. Alive, but spiritually gutted, Maria is one of the walking dead of early twentieth century Dublin. And Halloween is the night she can, like a lonely spirit, return home. Alive, but not fully; dead, but not buried.

In this new century of burgeoning cities, crowds, and industry, the dead can become disconnected and terrifying, as if humans cut loose from their ancestors begin to fear them. More and more, writers use Halloween to evoke a sickening sense of evil under the surface, a subconscious dread:

> Something that lies there, under weed and ooze,
>   with wide and awful eyes
> And matted hair, and limbs the waters bruise,
>   That strives, yet can not rise."

> —Madison J. Cawein, *The Wood Water* (1905)

H.P. Lovecraft's dead are not instructive, they're aggressive. They spring from tombs: "And the dead leap gay in the pallid ray, / Sprung out of the tomb's black maw / To shake the world with awe." ("Hallowe'en In A Suburb," 1926)

In early twentieth-century Halloween literature, the dead are on the move again, riding from the realm of personal loss toward that of random horror. You can sense, as the new century grows, there are bodies stirring underground. Halloween's games and charms fade as the unquiet of real evil, real madness, dawns. This is a faceless evil, but not supernatural. It's human. Gas warfare was man-made, its victims powerless, and the world was aghast at its physical horror. By the end of World War I there were too many dead. Maybe they knew too much.

We are all dying, always. The boundary between the vibrant world we live in and the underground world of worms is thin and brittle; it's only a matter of time. What makes the older Halloween literature so enthralling is that it lets us travel back and forth to the land of the dead without consequence. No coin under the tongue is necessary, no smell of sulfur to beat out of our clothes when we return.

Come closer to the fire, everyone, it's cold tonight. Everything I'm about to tell you is true.

It just might not have happened.

A Note on the Texts

All texts are reproduced as they were printed, with arcane punctuation and original spellings left intact. There are two exceptions: spellings that are clearly typographical errors have been corrected, and arcane characters such as the long "s" have been modernized.

Dates included are the publication dates of the editions whose text is reprinted here; additional information is sometimes included to place the pieces in chronological order.

The works are in chronological order within each section and subsection.

The selections were chosen for many reasons, including length and how representative a piece is, and some can't help but be chosen by personal taste. For each Halloween poem, story, or play you find here, there are many more. Sources listed in the bibliography may help direct the reader to additional reading.

PART I.

Poems

THE CELTIC IMAGINATION

Montgomeries Answere to Polwart
(1887; written circa 1580)

Alexander Montgomerie
[Excerpt from *The Flyting Betwixt Montgomerie and Polwart* in which Montgomerie describes the birth of his rival, Polwart]

I can tell thee, how, when, where and
    wha gat thee;
The quhilk was neither man nor wife,   [Which]
Nor humane creature on life:
Thou stinkand steirer vp of strife,
False howlat, have at thee!   [cowering owlet]

In the hinder end of haruest on
    Alhallow euen,
When our *good nighbours* doe ryd,   [fairies]
    gif I read right,   [if]
Some *buckled* on a *bunwand,* and   [mounted; ragweed]
    some on a been,
Ay trottand in trupes from the twilight;
Some *sadleand* a *shoe aip* all   [riding; she-ape]
    graithed into green,   [arrayed in green]
Some *hobland* on ane hempstalke,   [rising]
    hoveand to the hight.   [rising on high]
The King of Pharie, and his court,
    with the Elfe Queen,

With many *elrich* Incubus, was rydand   [weird]
   that night.
There ane elf, on ane aipe, ane *vnsell* begat,   [wretch]
Into ane *pot,* by Pomathorne;   [pothole in a peat bog]
That *bratchart* in ane *busse* was borne;   [brat; bush]
They fand ane monster, on the morne,
War faced nor a cat.   [uglier than a lump of manure]

The Weird Sisters wandring, as they
   were wont then,
Saw *reavens rugand* at that *ratton*   [ravens; tugging; rat]
   be a *ron ruit.*   [rowan root]
They mused at the mandrake*
   vnmade like a man;
A beast *bund* with a *bonevand*   [bound; piece of straw]
   in ane *old buit.*   [boot]
How that *gaist* had been gotten,   [ghost]
   to gesse they began,
Weil swyld in a swynes skin and   [grudgingly wrapped]
   smerit ouer with *suit;*   [smeared over; soot]
The bellie that it first *bair*   [bore]
   full bitterly they *ban.*   [curse]
Of this mismade *mowdewart,*   [mole]
   mischief they *muit.*   [mutter]
That cruiked, *camschoche* croyll,   [crooked one, i.e. the devil]
   vnchistned, they curse;
They bade that *baiche* sould not be but   [child—slang]
The *glengore, gravell,* and the *gut,*   [syphilis; gallstones; gout]
And all the plagues that first were put
Into Pandoraes purse.

*mandrake root was said to be used by sorcerers; that it has a human heart; that it screams when pulled out of the earth, and that whoever hears the screams dies or goes mad.

A Halloween Chant—The Midnight Flitting of the Corpse and Tomás MacGahan (old Irish ballad)

Translated by Joan Keefe, 1977

"My walking through the night, MacGlynn,
Was a cause of mirth, of spiteful mirth,
With the damned corpse with no chance of burial
Amongst the deadmen, amongst the dead."

"Raise up my body without rejoicing
And I'll give you a bullock, a fattened cow"
"If I agree to make this bargain
Where is the bullock, the fattened cow?"

"Small John Bingham, tall John Bingham,
They are my surety, they are my pledge,
I wrote an agreement in twisted scripture
To Bealan Assan, to Bealan Assan,

You will find a pot in the heap of lime,
Gray and ashy, ashy and gray,
Bring it with you under your arm
For food on the journey, food on the way."

The corpse was taken on Tomás's back
along the byeways, along the byeways,
by narrowing lanes, stony and gloomy
by the pale moonlight, by the pale moonlight.

A lengthy journey, sadly, crossways,
through drenching bogs, drenching moors,
west to Louth, great and holy,
of the grassy tombs, the grass-grown tombs.

"You will find a spade at your right hand
Behind the door, at the back of the door,
Strike a strong cut, a cut not faltering
Into the ground, down in the ground."

"I struck a strong cut, bold and deep
Into the ground, down in the ground,
Till I broke the shinbone of a foreign clown
Who was asleep there, who was asleep."

"Blast your guts" said the foreign trooper
"Where's my gun, is my pistol there?"
Said Mary Reilly, wife of Lord Guido
"Clear out of here, clear out of here."

"Oro, Tomás, oh, oh, oh,
Do not leave me, don't leave me here,
There's the son of my mother's cousin in Creggan,
Where I should be buried, I should be buried."

The corpse was taken on Tomás's back
on its lonely tour, its lonely tour
by roads that were narrow, stony and twisted
by the light of the moon, light of the moon.

"Sad, unhappy, I hurried down
On to Creggan, to Creggan More,
I found a spade at my right hand
Behind the door, behind the door.

Then I broke the jawbone of Watson Harford
Who was in the ground, down in the ground."
"Hububoo!" the blacksmith stammered
"Where's my hammer, where's my hammer?"

"Oro, Tomás, oh, oh, oh,
Don't leave me here, don't leave me here,
Since I have an uncle's son in Derry
There I'll be buried, there I'll be buried."

The corpse was taken on Tomás's back
just as before, just as before,
going weakly, worn-out, weary
down to Derry, down to Derry.

"When I got to the place I was bedraggled
With no courage left, no courage left,
The gates were strongly locked against me
And I pushed them hard, I pushed them hard."

"Defend your walls" Sir Walker calls,
"Or they'll be taken or they'll be taken,
Who knocks so hard? Each to his part
Come dead awaken, come dead awaken!"

Bones and coffins rose up straight
out of the clay, out of the clay,
and sat with no gap in an awful rage
on top of the walls, on top of the walls.

"A hundred damned curses" chorused the crowd
"What's the matter, what's the matter?"
"It's one of yourselves that's recently dead
Seeking burial, seeking burial,

"His cousin is here and that's the reason
Here you have him, here you have him."
"Who of his people is buried here
To claim admittance, to claim admittance?"

"I don't know the name or tribe of the madman
At the end of his life, the end of his life,
There's a shake and complaint left in him yet
So ask himself, ask himself."

Halloween[1] (1900; 1st pub. 1786)

Robert Burns
[The introduction, epigraph and footnotes are Burns'; footnotes can be found in their entirety in Notes.]

The following Poem will by many readers be well enough understood; but for the sake of those who are unacquainted with the manners and traditions of the country where the scene is cast, notes are added to give some account of the principal charms and spells of that night, so big with prophecy to the peasantry in the west of Scotland. The passion of prying into futurity makes a striking part of the history of human nature, in its rude state, in all ages and nations; and it may be some entertainment to a philosophic mind if any such should honour the author with a perusal, to see the remains of it, among the more unenlightened in our own.—R.B.

Yes! let the rich deride, the proud disdain,
The simple pleasures of the lowly train;
To me more dear, congenial to my heart,
One native charm, than all the gloss of art.

—Goldsmith

I.

Upon that night, when Fairies light
On Cassilis Downans[2] dance,
Or owre the *lays,* in splendid blaze,   [fields]
On sprightly coursers prance;
Or for Colean the rout is ta'en,
Beneath the moon's pale beams;
There, up the Cove,[3] to stray an' rove,
Amang the rocks and streams
To sport that night:

II.

Amang the bonie winding banks,
Where Doon rins, *wimplin,* clear,   [meandering]
Where Bruce[4] ance ruled the martial ranks,
An' shook his Carrick spear;
Some merry, friendly, country-folks
Together did convene,

To burn their *nits,* an' *pou their stocks,*   [nuts; pull their stalks]
An' *haud* their Halloween   [hold]
Fu' *blythe* that night.   [merrily]

III.

The lasses *feat,* an' cleanly neat,   [trim]
Mair *braw* than when they're fine;   [gaily appareled]
Their faces blythe fu' sweetly *kythe*   [appearing]
Hearts *leal,* an' warm, an' *kin':*   [loyal; kind]
The lads *sae trig,* wi' *wooer-babs*   [spruced up; love knots]
Weel-knotted on their garten;
Some unco *blate,* an' some *wi' gabs*   [bashful; gossipy]
Gar lasses' hearts gang startin   [Compel]
Whyles fast at night.

IV.

Then, first an' foremost, thro' the *kail,*   [cabbage plot]
Their stocks[5] *maun* a' be sought *ance;*   [must; once]
They *steek their een,* an' *grape an' wale*   [shut their eyes; grope and choose]
For *muckle* anes, an' *straught* anes.   [large; straight]
Poor *hav'rel* Will fell aff the drift,   [half-witted]
An' wandered thro' the bow-kail,
An' *pow't* for want o' better shift,   [pulled]
A runt, was like a sow-tail,
Sae bow't that night.   [So bent]

V.

Then, straught or crooked, *yird* or *nane,*   [full of earth; none]
They roar an' cry *a' throu'ther;*   [pell mell]
The *vera* wee-things, toddlin, *rin*   [very; run]
Wi' stocks out-*owre their shouther:*   [over their shoulder]
An' gif the *custock's* sweet or sour,   [center of the cabbage stalk]
Wi' *joctelegs* they taste them;   [a folding knife]
Syne coziely, aboon the door,   [And then comfortably, above]
Wi' *cannie* care, they've plac'd them   [gentle]
To lie that night.

VI.

The lasses *staw frae* 'mang them *a',*   [stole away from; all]
To pou their stalks o' *corn,*[6]   [wheat: corn, in Burns' time, means any grain]

But Rab slips out, an' jinks about,
Behint the muckle thorn:
He grippit Nelly hard an' fast;
Loud *skirl'd* a' the lasses;   [shrieked]
But her *tap-pickle maist* was lost,   [top of the wheat stalk; almost]
Whan *kiutlin* in the *fause-house*[7]   [cuddling; opening in a grain stack]
Wi' him that night.

VII.

The auld Guidwife's *weel-hoordet* nits[8]   [well-hoarded]
Are round an' round divided,
An' monie lads' an' lasses' fates
Are there that night decided:
Some kindle *couthie,* side by side,   [lovingly]
An' burn *thegither* trimly: [together]
Some start awa wi' saucy pride,
An' jump out-owre the *chimlie*   [fireplace]
Fu' high that night.

VIII.

Jean slips in *twa,* wi' *tentie e'e;*   [two; careful eye]
Wha 'twas, she wadna tell;
But this is *Jock,* an' this is *me,*
She says in to herself:
He *bleez'd* owre her, an' she owre him,   [blazed]
As they wad never *mair* part;   [more]
Till fuff! he started up the *lum,*   [chimney]
And Jean had e'en a *sair* heart   [sore]
To see't that night.

IX.

Poor Willie, wi' his bow-kail runt,
Was *brunt* wi' *primsie* Mallie;   [burned; prudish]
An' Mary, nae doubt, *took the drunt,*   [sulked]
To be compar'd to Willie:
Mall's nit lap out, wi' pridefu' fling,
An' her *ain fit,* it brunt it;   [own foot]
While Willie *lap,* an' swoor by jing,   [leapt]
'Twas just the way he wanted
To be that night.

X.

Nell had the fause-house in her min',
She *pits* hersel an' Rob in;   [puts]
In loving *bleeze* they sweetly join,   [blaze]
Till white in *ase* they're *sobbin:*   [ash; hissing]
Nell's heart was dancing at the view;
She whisper'd Rob to *leuk* for't: [look]
Rob, *stownlins, prie'd* her bonie *mou,*   [stealthily; kissed; mouth]
Fu' *cozie* in the *neuk* for't,   [snuggly; nook]
Unseen that night.

XI.

But Merran sat behint their backs,
Her thoughts on Andrew Bell;
She lea'es them *gashin at their cracks,*   [talking and joking]
An' slips out by hersel:
She thro' the yard the nearest taks,
An' to the kiln she goes then,
An' *darklins grapit for the bauks,*   [gropes in the dark for the crossbeams]
And in the blue-clue⁹ throws then,
Right fear't that night.

XII.

An' ay she *win't,* an' ay she *swat*   [wound; did sweat]
I wat she *made nae jaukin;*   [didn't dally]
Till something held within the *pat,*   [kiln]
Guid Lord! but she was *quakin!*   [quaking]
But whether 'twas the *Deil* himsel,   [Devil]
Or whether 'twas a *bauk-en',*   [beam-end]
Or whether it was Andrew Bell,
She did na wait on talkin
To *spier* that night.   [inquire]

XIII.

Wee Jenny to her *graunie* says,   [grannie]
'Will ye go wi' me, graunie?
I'll eat the apple at the glass,¹⁰
I *gat frae* uncle Johnie.'   [got from]
She fuff't her pipe wi' *sic a lunt,*   [such a puff of smoke]
In wrath she was *sae vap'rin,*   [so agitated]

She notic't na, an *aizle* brunt   [hot cinder]
Her *braw,* new, *worset* apron   [brand; worsted]
Out thro' that night.

XIV.

'Ye little *skelpie-limmer's* face!   [slang term for a girl]
I *daur* you try sic sportin,   [dare]
As *seek the Foul Thief onie* place,   [seek the Devil; any]
For him to *spae* your fortune: [prophesy]
Nae doubt but ye may get a sight!
Great cause ye hae to fear it;
For *monie a ane* has gotten a fright,   [many a one]
An' liv'd an' died *deleeret,*   [insane]
On sic a night.

XV.

"Ae hairst afore the *Sherra-moor,*   [One harvest; battle of Sheriffmuir, 1715]

I mind't as *weel's yestreen*—   [well been yesterday]
I was a *gilpey* then, I'm sure   [young girl]
I was na past fyfteen:
The *simmer* had been *cauld an' wat,*   [summer; cold and wet]
An' *stuff* was *unco green;*   [corn or grain; too wet]
An' ay a *rantin kirn* we gat,   [jovial harvest home]
An' just on Halloween
It fell that night.

XVI.

'Our *stibble-rig* was Rab M'Graen,   [reaper who takes the lead]
A clever, sturdy fallow;
His sin gat Eppie Sim *wi' wean,*   [with child]
That lived in Achmacalla:
He gat hemp-seed,[11] I mind it *weel,*   [well]
An' he made unco light o 't;
But monie a day was by himsel,
He was sae *sairly* frighted   [sorely]
That vera night.'

XVII.

Then up gat *fechtin* Jamie Fleck,   [fighting]

An' he swoor by his conscience,
That he could *saw* hemp-seed a peck;   [sow]
For it was a' but nonsense:
The auld *guidman raught* down the *pock,*   [goodman; reached; bag]
An' out a handfu' *gied* him;   [gave]
Syne bad him slip frae 'mang the folk,   [Then told him slip from]
Sometime when *nae ane* see'd him,   [no one]
An' try't that night.

XVIII.

He marches thro' amang the stacks,
Tho' he was something *sturtin;*   [timorous]
The *graip* he for a harrow taks,   [dung fork]
An' *haurls at his curpin:*   [drags his horse crupper behind
                                                            him]

And ev'ry now an' then, he says,
'Hemp-seed I saw thee,
An' her that is to be my lass,
Come after me, an' draw thee
As fast this night.'

XIX.

He wistl'd up *Lord Lennox' March,*
To keep his courage cheery;
Altho' his hair began to arch,
He was sae *fley'd* an' eerie: [frightened]
Till presently he hears a squeak,
An' then a *grane an' gruntle;*   [groan and grunt]
He by his *shouther* gae a *keek,*   [shoulder; peep]
An' *tumbled wi' a wintle*   [somersaulted]
Out-owre that night.

XX.

He roar'd a horrid murder-shout,
In dreadfu' desperation!
An' young an' auld come rinnin out,
An' hear the sad narration:
He swoor 'twas *hilchin* Jean M'Craw,   [hobbling]
Or *crouchie* Merran Humphie—   [hunchbacked]

Till stop! she trotted thro' them a'
An' wha was it but *Grumphie*   [the sow]
Asteer that night?   [Astir]

XXI.

Meg *fain wad* to the barn *gaen,*   [would have; gone]
To *winn* three *wechts* o' naething;[12]   [winnow; a hoop used for winnowing]
But for to meet the Deil *her lane,*   [alone]
She pat but little faith in:
She gies the herd a *pickle* nits,   [few]
An' twa red-cheekit apples,
To watch, while for the barn she sets
In hopes to see Tam Kipples
That vera night.

XXII.

She turns the key wi' *cannie thraw,*   [gentle twist]
An' owre the threshold ventures;
But first on *Sawnie gies a ca',*   [calls out the name of Satan]
Syne baudly in she enters: [Then boldly]
A *ratton* rattl'd up the wa',   [rat]
An' she cry'd, L__d preserve her!
An' ran thro' *midden-hole* an' a',   [a gutter at the bottom of a dung hill]
An' pray'd wi' zeal and fervour
Fu' fast that night.

XXIII.

They *hoy't* out Will, wi' *sair* advice;   [urged; strong]
They *hecht* him some fine *braw ane;*   [promised; handsome one]
It chanc'd the stack he *faddom't* thrice,[13]   [fathomed]
Was *timmer-propt for thrawin:*   [propped with timber against the wind]
He taks a *swirlie,* auld moss-oak   [timber full of knots]
For some black gruesome *carlin;*   [old woman]
An' *loot a winze,* an' drew a stroke,   [let fly an oath]
Till skin in *blypes* cam haurlin   [shreds came peeling]
Aff's nieves that night.   [Off his fists]

XXIV.

A wanton widow Leezie was,
As *cantie* as a kittling;   [lively]

But och! that night, amang the *shaws,*   [small woods]
She gat a fearfu' settlin!
She thro' the *whins,* an' by the *cairn,*   [prickly evergreen bushes; gorse]
An' owre the hill gaed *scrievin;*   [swiftly]
Whare three *lairds'* lands met at a *burn,*[14]   [lords'; stream]
To dip her left *sark*-sleeve in   [shirt]
Was bent that night.

XXV.

Whyles owre a *linn* the *burnie* plays,   [waterfall; rivulet]
As thro' the glen it wimpl't;
Whyles round a rocky *scaur* it strays,   [bank]
Whyles in a *wiel* it dimpl't;   [eddy]
Whyles glitter'd to the nightly rays,
Wi' bickerin', dancin' dazzle;
Whyles *cookit* underneath the *braes,*   [disappeared; hillsides]
Below the spreading hazel,
Unseen that night.

XXVI.

Amang the *brachens,* on the brae,   [ferns]
Between her an' the moon,
The Deil, or else an *outler quey,*   [stray young cow]
Gat up an' gae a croon:
Poor Leezie's heart *maist lap the hool;* [almost leapt out of her chest]
Near *lav'rock*-height she jumpit,   [lark's]
But *mist a fit,* an' in the pool   [lost her footing]
Out-owre the lugs she plumpit,   [over her ears she fell]
Wi' a plunge that night.

XXVII.

In order, on the clean hearth-stane,
The luggies three[15] are ranged;
And ev'ry time great care is taen
To see them duly changed:
Auld uncle John, wha wedlock's joys
Sin' Mar's-year did desire,   [Since Earl of Mar's rebellion in 1715]
Because he gat the *toom* dish thrice,   [empty]
He heav'd them on the fire
In wrath that night.

XXVIII.

Wi' merry sangs, an' friendly cracks,
I *wat* they did na weary;   [know]
And unco tales, an' funnie jokes—
Their sports were cheap an' cheery;
Till butter'd *sow'ns,*[16] wi' fragrant *lunt,*   [cooked oats; steam]
Set a' their *gabs a-steerin;*   [mouths watering]
Syne, wi' a social glass o' *strunt,*   [whiskey]
They parted aff careerin
Fu' blythe that night.

Tam Lin (1904, 1st pub. 1792)

Popular ballad

O I forbid you, maidens a',
That wear gowd on your hair,
To come or gae by Carterhaugh,
For young Tam Lin is there.

There's nane that gaes by Carterhaugh
But they leave him a *wad,*   [promise]
Either their rings, or green mantles,
Or else their maidenhead.

Janet has *kilted* her green kirtle   [tucked]
A little *aboon* her knee,   [above]
And she has broded her yellow hair
A little aboon her *bree,*   [brow]
And she's awa to Carterhaugh,
As fast as she can hie.

When she came to Carterhaugh
Tam Lin was at the well,
And there she fand his steed standing,
But away was himsel.

She had na *pu'd* a double rose,   [picked]
A rose but only *twa,*   [two]
Till up then started young Tam Lin,
Says, Lady, thou's *pu nae mae.*   [pull no more]

Why pu's thou the rose, Janet,
And why breaks thou the *wand?*   [stem]
Or why comes thou to Carterhaugh
Withoutten my command?

'Carterhaugh, it is my ain,
My daddie gave it me;
I'll come and gang by Carterhaugh,
And ask nae leave at thee.'

Janet has kilted her green kirtle
A little aboon her knee,
And she has *snooded* her yellow hair   [bound up]
A little aboon her bree,
And she is to her father's *ha,*   [hall]
As fast as she can hie.

Four and twenty ladies fair
Were playing at the *ba,*   [ball]
And out then cam the fair Janet,
Ance the flower amang them a'.

Four and twenty ladies fair
Were playing at the chess,
And out then cam the fair Janet,
As green as onie glass.

Out then spak an auld grey knight,
Lay oer the castle *wa,*   [wall]
And says, Alas, fair Janet, for thee
But we'll be blamed a'.

'Haud your tongue, ye auld fac'd knight,
Some ill death may ye die!
Father my *bairn* on whom I will,   [baby]
I'll father nane on thee.'

Out then spak her father dear,
And he spak meek and mild;
'And ever alas, sweet Janet,' he says,
'I think thou gaes wi child.'

'If that I gae wi child, father,
Mysel maun bear the blame;
There's neer a *laird about your ha*   [lord about your hall]
Shall get the *bairn's* name.

'If my love were an earthly knight,
As he's an elfin grey,
I wad na gie my ain true-love
For nae lord that ye hae.

'The steed that my true-love rides on
Is lighter than the wind;
Wi *siller* he is shod before   [silver]
Wi burning *gowd* behind.'   [gold]

Janet has kilted her green kirtle
A little aboon her knee,
And she has snooded her yellow hair
A little aboon her bree,
Aud she's awa to Carterhaugh,
As fast as she can hie.

When she cam to Carterhaugh,
Tam Lin was at the well,
And there she fand his steed standing,
But away was himsel.

She had na pu'd a double rose,
A rose but only twa,
Till up then started young Tam Lin,
Says, Lady, thou pu's nae mae.

Why pu's thou the rose, Janet,
Amang the groves sae green,
And a' to kill the bonie babe
That we gat us between?

'O tell me, tell me, Tam Lin,' she says,
'For's sake that died on tree,
If eer ye was in holy chapel,
Or christendom did see?'

'Roxbrugh he was my grandfather,
Took me with him to bide,
And ance it fell upon a day
That *wae* did me betide.   [woe]

'And ance it fell upon a day,
A cauld day and *a snell,*   [bitter]
When we were *frae* the hunting come,   [from]
That frae my horse I fell;

The Queen o Fairies she caught me,
In yon green hill to dwell.

'And pleasant is the fairy land,
But, an eerie tale to tell,
Ay at the end of seven years   [Always]
We pay a *tiend* to hell;   [tithe]
I am sae fair and *fu* o flesh,   [full]
I'm feard it be mysel.

'But the night is Halloween, lady,
The morn is Hallowday;
Then win me, win me, an ye will,
For *weel I wat* ye may.   [well I know]

'Just at the mirk and midnight hour
The fairy folk will ride,
And they that *wad* their true-love win,   [promise]
At Miles Cross they *maun bide.'*   [must wait]

'But how shall I thee ken, Tam Lin,
Or how my true-love know,
Amang sae mony *unco* knights   [strange]
The like I never saw?'

'O first let pass the black, lady,
And *syne* let pass the brown,   [then]
But quickly run to the milk-white steed,
Pu ye his rider down.

'For I'll ride on the milk-white steed,
And ay nearest the town;
Because I was an earthly knight
They gie me that renown.

'My right hand will be glovd, lady,
My left hand will be bare,
Cockt up shall my bonnet be,
And kaimd down shall my hair,
And thae's the *takens* I gie thee,   [tokens]
Nae doubt I will be there.

'They'll turn me in your arms, lady,
Into an esk and adder;
But hold me fast, and fear me not,
I am your bairn's father.

'They'll turn me to a bear sae grim,
And then a lion bold;
But hold me fast, and fear me not,
As ye shall love your child.

'Again they'll turn me in your arms
To a *red het gaud of airn;*   [red-hot bar of gold]
But hold me fast, and fear me not,
I'll do to you nae harm.

'And last they'll turn me in your arms
Into the burning *gleed;*   [coal]
Then throw me into well water,
O throw me in wi speed.

'And then I'll be your ain true-love,
I'll turn a naked knight;
Then cover me wi your green mantle,
And cover me out o sight.'

Gloomy, gloomy was the night,
And eerie was the way,
As fair Jenny in her green mantle
To Miles Cross she did gae.

About the middle o the night
She heard the bridles ring;
This lady was as glad at that
As any earthly thing.

First she let the black pass by,
And syne she let the brown;
But quickly she ran to the milk-white steed,
And pu'd the rider down.

Sae weel she minded whae he did say,

And young Tam Lin did win;
Syne coverd him wi her green mantle,
As blythe's a bird in spring.

Out then spak the Queen o Fairies,
Out of a bush o broom:
'Them that has gotten young Tam Lin
Has gotten a stately groom.'

Out then spak the Queen o Fairies,
And an angry woman was she:
'Shame betide her *ill-far'd* face,   [ill favored]
And an ill death may she die,
For she's *taen awa* the boniest knight   [taken away]
In a' my companie.

'But had I *kend,* Tam Lin,' she says,   [known]
'What now this night I see,
I wad hae *taen out thy twa grey een,*   [taken out thy two grey eyes]
And put in *twa een o tree.'*   [two of wood]

St. Swithin's Chair (1855; 1st. pub. 1829)

Sir Walter Scott
[Excerpt from *Waverley*]

On Hallow-Mass Eve, ere ye boune ye to rest,
Ever beware that your couch be blessed;
Sign it with cross, and sain it with bead,
Sing the Ave, and say the Creed.

For on Hallow-Mass Eve the Night-Hag will ride,
And all her nine-fold sweeping on by her side,
Whether the wind sing lowly or loud,
Sailing through moonshine or swath'd in the cloud.

The Lady she sat in St. Swithin's Chair,
The dew of the night has damp'd her hair:
Her cheek was pale—but resolved and high
Was the word of her lip and the glance of her eye.

She mutter'd the spell of Swithin bold,
When his naked foot traced the midnight wold,
When he stopp'd the Hag as she rode the night,
And bade her descend, and her promise plight.

He that dare sit on Saint Swithin's Chair,
When the Night-Hag wings the troubled air,
Questions three, when he speaks the spell,
He may ask, and she must tell.

The Baron has been with King Robert his liege,
These three long years in battle and siege;
News are there none of his weal or his woe,
And fain the Lady his fate would know.

She shudders and stops as the charm she speaks;—
Is it the moody owl that shrieks?
Or is that sound, betwixt laughter and scream,
The voice of the Demon who haunts the stream?

The moan of the wind sunk silent and low,
And the roaring torrent had ceased to flow;
The calm was more dreadful than raging storm,
When the cold grey mist brought the ghastly form!

The Maid of Elvar (1832)

Allan Cunningham
[In this excerpt, a group has gathered to tell stories of weird Halloween; stern warnings fall on those who take the tales lightly.]

XXXVI.

But he who tries a more adventurous spell—
A spell men say will either kill or cure—
Steals out unnoted o'er the haunted fell,
What time the moon reigns in the witching hour,
And dips his shirt-sleeve where two rivulets pour
Their mingling waters south; then home he hies,
Hangs it before the fire, and asks the power
Of this night to make his true love's form arise,
And turn the fated sleeve, as slow it reeking dries.

XXXVII.

To some have come no sweet and smiling maid,
But a cold hand held shivering from a shroud;
And some have seen a gliding spectral shade,
Descend, as comes a star-beam from a cloud,
And turn the sleeve, look upward and seem proud;
Then beckon them to take the immortal road.—
And some have heard a summons dread and loud,
Enough to make the soul quit its clay load,
Saying, "Rise, ye guilty spirit—come and be judged of God!"

XXXVIII.

And *meikle* warning had the adventurous wight,   [strong]
Lest on his errand he might stay to mark
By a lone fire of hemlock glimmering bright,
A hoary hag at her unhallowed wark,
A beverage brewing fit to wile the lark
From his sweet morning carol, and compel
The hind of mind and body *steeve* and stark;   [staunch]
Forsake the powers of heaven for shapes of hell,
And wile him amorouslie with wrinkled hags to *mell*.   [meld]

XXXIX.

"And oh my child, put ye God's holy book

Into your bosom: even with that beware;"
A matron said: "A fiend deceitful took
A fair maid's form once, with dishevelled hair,
An azure eye, a snowy bosom bare,
And godless tongue; into Cumlongan brake
She wiled Mark Snedden to her treacherous lair,
And when his amorous thirst he sought to slake
She gave him *gibbeted* bones in his embrace to take.   [executed by hanging]

XL.

"And chief beware when comes the gloaming gray
Of Hallow-eve: hell keeps an open road,
For those who go from gospel paths astray,
Hags then to seek their *palfreys* come abroad,   [horses]
They'll soon transform ye to a steed, and goad
Ye with the infernal spur and magic rein.
I knew a lad—he dwelt in Quarrelwood,
Was handled so, he shook the shuddering plain,
With brazen hoofs, neighed loud, and tossed a fiery mane.

XLI.

"And oh, my son, shun ye the Solway sand,
Where wizards visionary vessels ride,
And moor their golden halsers to the strand;
Their silk sails spread with all a sailor's pride,
And long-haired mermaids carolling on their side
Enchanting songs of such a powerful strain,
That mortals may not choose but climb and bide,
To hear their melody. Flash o'er the main,
Fast flies the fairy bark:—home sees them ne'er again."

The Fire That Burned So Brightly (1872)

Robert Dwyer Joyce

I.

There was a light in the windowpane,
Still burning, brightly burning,
And it gleamed afar over Cleena's main,
On Donall's bark returning;
And he looked up, the cliffs between
Where the hamlet glimmered nightly,
And thought he saw his own Kathleen
By the flame that burned so brightly.

II.

It was upon All Hallow's night,
When the candles bright were burning,
That the beams fell from that constant light,
On Donall's bark returning;
It lit like a star the darkening scene,
And made his heart beat lightly,
For he thought he saw his own Kathleen
By the flame that burned so brightly.

III.

He moored his bark the hamlet near,
Where the candles bright were burning,
But a mournful wail met his startled ear,
All-Hallow's night returning;
And he heard a name in that piercing keen,
And saw a shroud gleam whitely—
'Twas the waking light of his own Kathleen,
The flame that burned so brightly!

The Spalpeen* (Ballad, 1872)

Robert Dwyer Joyce

When comes across the mountains the winters of the year,
With merry jokes and laughter the spalpeens gay are here;
I love the first of autumn, but more sweet Hallowe'en,
For it brings back my Johnnie, my rattling, gay Spalpeen!

His hair is like the raven that flies about Knockrue,
And stately is his form; his heart is kind and true,—
O, he's kindest, best, and bravest of all I've ever seen,
And until death I'll love him, my rattling, gay Spalpeen!

There's something in my Johnnie that pains my secret mind;
He's statelier than his comrades, his manners more refined;
I fear he's some rich rover, fit husband for a queen;
And yet I can't but love him, my rattling, gay Spalpeen!

The first night that I met him, I found him fond and *leal;* [loyal]
I took him for my partner, and tripped a *mazy* reel,— [dizzy]
It was the "New-Mown Meadows" and then the light Moneen**
We danced—until I loved him, my rattling, gay Spalpeen!

The leaves of dying autumn by chilling winds were lost,
The corn was stacked securely, the hills were gray with frost,
When by the turf-fire blazing, were met at Hallowe'en
The farmers' sons and daughters, and many a gay Spalpeen.

The old man in the corner sat in his elbow-chair,
At all his jokes the laughter rose free from grief or care;
The *Bean-a-thee* sat smiling, and said she ne'er had seen [woman of the house]

A dancer like young Johnnie, the rattling, gay Spalpeen.

They've laughed round many an apple, they've burned the nuts in glee,
"And some will soon get married, and some will sail the sea!"
They've danced for th' ancient piper, they've joked and sung between,
And told their wondrous legends, each rattling, gay Spalpeen!

Then Johnnie took the daughter, the eldest, by the hand,—
It was his own Bawn Ellen, the fairest in the land;
He led her towards her parents, with fond and manly mien,
While all stood hushed around him, the rattling, gay Spalpeen!

"I've come across the mountains far, far from home, to find
A wife above all others, both simple, fair and kind;
She's standing now beside me, the loveliest I have seen!"
Upspoke, with manly bearing, the rattling, gay Spalpeen.

"I know she's good and constant—for me would lose her life;
I have a home to give her, and ask her for my wife!"
He's doffed the old gray garment—before them all is seen
The lord of many a town-land, that rattling, gay Spalpeen!

Old Father James came early, and blessed the loving pair;
She's off with her dear bridegroom toward Kerry's hills so fair;
O'er many a fertile valley she reigns just like a queen,
Loving, and loved by, Johnnie, her rattling, gay Spalpeen!

* Spalpeen: A wandering laboring man. The circumstance related in the ballad happened in county Limerick. It was not at all an uncommon thing for wild young sons of the higher class of farmers to go off on their adventures, in the palmy days of potato-digging, with the spalpeens; and many a wild prank they played in their peregrinations. [RDJ]

**Moneen: a kind of jig—the wildest, most athletic, and spirited of all the Irish dances. [RDJ]

All Souls' Night* (1907)

Dora Sigerson Shorter

O mother, mother, I swept the hearth, I set his chair and the white board spread,
I prayed for his coming to our kind Lady when Death's sad doors would let out the dead;
A strange wind rattled the window-pane, and down the lane a dog howled on.
I called his name and the candle flame burnt dim, pressed a hand the door-latch upon.
Deelish! Deelish! my woe forever that I could not sever coward flesh from fear.
I called his name and the pale Ghost came; but I was afraid to meet my dear.

O mother, mother, in tears I checked the sad hours past of the year that's o'er,
Till by God's grace I might see his face and hear the sound of his voice once more;
The chair I set from the cold and wet, he took when he came from unknown skies
Of the Land of the Dead, on my bent brown head I felt the reproach of his saddened eyes;
I closed my lids on my heart's desire, crouched by the fire, my voice was dumb.
At my clean-swept hearth he had no mirth, and at my table he broke no crumb.
Deelish! Deelish! my woe forever that I could not sever coward flesh from fear.
His chair put aside when the young cock cried, and I was afraid to meet my dear.

*There is a superstition in some parts of Ireland that the dead are allowed to return to earth on the 2nd of November (All Souls' Night), and the peasantry leave food and fire for their comfort, and set a chair by the hearth for their resting before they themselves retire to bed. [DSS]

GHOST LOVERS AND THE DYING SEASON

Halloween. A Romaunt. (1846, written 1838)

Arthur Cleveland Coxe
[Excerpt]

III.

I have been near the gates of death,
And know 'tis hard to die;
That the mortal flesh it shuddereth
In the spell of death to lie:
That fearful it is—the ebbing breath;
And awful—the closing eye,
When powerless all, it curtaineth
The soul, from the loved ones by;
When it closeth slow o'er the leaden gaze,
That wraps, like the mariner's home, in a haze,
The dear ones that comfort us nigh.

IV.

'Tis awful,—the hour when death comes on,
When the voice of cheer or wail is gone;
To feel the lip o'er the dry tooth ope,
To catch half a ray through the eyelid's scope,
Then shudder, though powerless all, to feel
The frost o'er the glazing orbs congeal,
When the breath grows low, and the heart is chill,
Though the blood creeps ghostlike around it still,
And to gasp a moment, and struggle, and try
To yield the starved spirit,—and groan,—and die,
And still to flicker a dying hour,
When life still hovers, and seems to lower,
Though voice hath no spell, and the pulse no power.

To _____. Ulalume: A Ballad (1847)

Edgar Allan Poe

The skies they were ashen and sober;
The leaves they were crispèd and sere—
The leaves they were withering and sere;
It was night in the lonesome October
Of my most immemorial year;
It was hard by the dim lake of Auber,
In the misty mid region of Weir—
It was down by the dank tarn of Auber,
In the ghoul-haunted woodland of Weir.

Here once, through an alley Titanic,
Of cypress, I roamed with my Soul—
Of cypress, with Psyche, my Soul.
There were days when my heart was volcanic
As the scoriac rivers that roll—
As the lavas that restlessly roll
Their sulphurous currents down Yaanek
In the ultimate climes of the pole—
That groan as they roll down Mount Yaanek
In the realms of the boreal pole.

Our talk had been serious and sober,
But our thoughts they were palsied and sere—
Our memories were treacherous and sere—
For we knew not the month was October,
And we marked not the night of the year—
(Ah, night of all nights in the year!)
We noted not the dim lake of Auber—
(Though once we had journeyed down here)—
We remembered not the dank tarn of Auber
Nor the ghoul-haunted woodland of Weir.

And now, as the night was senescent,
And star-dials pointed to morn—
As the star-dials hinted of morn—
At the end of our path a liquescent

And nebulous lustre was born,
Out of which a miraculous crescent
Arose with a duplicate horn—
Astarte's bediamonded crescent
Distinct with its duplicate horn.

And I said—"She is warmer than Dian:
She rolls through an ether of sighs—
She revels in a region of sighs:
She has seen that the tears are not dry on
These cheeks, where the worm never dies,
And has come past the stars of the Lion
To point us the path to the skies—
To the Lethean peace of the skies—
Come up, in despite of the Lion,
To shine on us with her bright eyes—
Come up through the lair of the Lion,
With Love in her luminous eyes."

But Psyche, uplifting her finger,
Said—"Sadly this star I mistrust—
Her pallor I strangely mistrust:—
Oh, hasten!—oh, let us not linger!
Oh, fly!—let us fly!—for we must."
In terror she spoke, letting sink her
Wings till they trailed in the dust—
In agony sobbed, letting sink her
Plumes till they trailed in the dust—
Till they sorrowfully trailed in the dust.

I replied—"This is nothing but dreaming:
Let us on by this tremulous light!
Let us bathe in this crystalline light!
Its Sybillic splendor is beaming
With Hope and in Beauty to-night:—
See!— it flickers up the sky through the night!
Ah, we safely may trust to its gleaming,
And be sure it will lead us aright—
We safely may trust to a gleaming
That cannot but guide us aright,

Since it flickers up to Heaven through the night."

Thus I pacified Psyche and kissed her,
And tempted her out of her gloom—
And conquered her scruples and gloom:
And we passed to the end of the vista,
And were stopped by the door of a tomb—
By the door of a legended tomb;
And I said—"What is written, sweet sister,
On the door of this legended tomb?"
She replied—"Ulalume—Ulalume—
'Tis the vault of thy lost Ulalume!"

Then my heart it grew ashen and sober
As the leaves that were crispèd and sere—
As the leaves that were withering and sere,
And I cried—"It was surely October
On *this* very night of last year
That I journeyed—I journeyed down here—
That I brought a dread burden down here—
On this night of all nights in the year,
Ah, what demon has tempted me here?
Well I know, now, this dim lake of Auber—
This misty mid region of Weir—
Well I know, now, this dank tarn of Auber,
This ghoul-haunted woodland of Weir."

Said we, then—the two, then—"Ah can it
Have been that the woodlandish ghouls—
The pitiful, the merciful ghouls—
To bar up our way and to ban it
From the secret that lies in these wolds—
From the thing that lies hidden in these wolds—
Had drawn up the spectre of a planet
From the limbo of lunary souls—
This sinfully scintillant planet
From Hell of the planetary souls?"

The Vain Spell (1898)

Edith Nesbit

The house sleeps dark and the moon wakes white,
The fields are alight with dew;
Oh, will you not come to me, Love, to-night?
I have waited the whole night through,
For I knew,
O Heart of my heart, I knew by my heart,
That the night of all nights is this,
When elm shall crack and lead shall part,
When moulds shall sunder and shot bolts start
To let you through to my kiss."

So spake she alone in the lonely house.
She had wrapped her round with the spell,
She called the call, she vowed the vow,
And the heart she had pledged knew well
That this was the night, the only night,
When the moulds might be wrenched apart,
When the living and dead, in the dead of the night,
Might clasp once more, in the grave's despite,
For the price of a living heart.

But out in the grave the corpse lay white
And the grave clothes were wet with dew;
"Oh, will you not come to me, Love, to-night,
I have waited the whole night through,
For I knew
That I dared not leave my grave for an hour
Since the hour of all hours is near,
When you shall come to the hollow bower,
In a cast of the wind, in a waft of the Power,
To the heart that to-night beats here!"

The moon grows pale and the house sleeps still;
Ah, God! do the dead forget?
The grave is white and the bed is chill,
But a guest may be coming yet.

But the hour has come and the hour has gone
That never will come again;
Love's only chance is over and done,
And the quick and the dead are twain, not one
And the price has been paid in vain.

A Ballad of Halloween (1900)

Theodosia Garrison

All night the wild wind on the heath
Whistled its song of vague alarms;
The poplars tossed their naked arms
All night in some mad dance of death.

Mignon Isá hath left her bed
And bared her shoulders to the blast;
The long procession of the dead
Stared at her as it passed.

"Oh, there, methinks, my mother smiled,
And there my father walks forlorn,
And there was the little nameless child
That was the parish scorn.

And there my olden comrades move,
And there my sister smiles apart,
But nowhere is the fair, false love
That broke my loving heart.

"Oh, false in life, oh, false in death,
Wherever thy mad spirit be,
Could it not come this night," she saith,
"To keep a tryst with me?"

Mignon Isá hath turned alone;
Bitter the pain and long the years;
The moonlight on the cold gravestone
Was warmer than her tears.

All night the wild wind on the heath
Whistled its song of vague alarms;
The poplars tossed their naked arms
All night in some mad dance of death.

Superstition (1902)

Madison J. Cawein

In the waste places, in the dreadful night,
When the wood whispers like a wondering mind,
And silence sits and listens to the wind,
Or, midst the rocks, to some wild torrent's flight;
Bat-browed thou wadest with thy wisp of light*
Among black pools the moon can never find;
Or, owlet-eyed, thou hootest to the blind
Deep darkness from some cave or haunted height.
He who beholds but once thy fearsome face,
Never again shall walk alone! but wan
And terrible attendants shall be his—
Unutterable things that have no place
In God or Beauty—that compel him on,
Against all hope, where endless horror is.

*A will-o-the-wisp is another name for jack-o'-lantern, and refers to the meandering light of combustible gasses created by decomposing matter, often found near swamps or churchyards. In folklore it was believed to purposely lead people to their deaths, to signal a dead body, or to be the soul of a dead man.

The Wood Water (1905)

Madison J. Cawein

An evil, stealthy water, dark as hate,
Sunk from the light of day,
'Thwart which is hung a ruined water-gate,
Creeps on its stagnant way.

Moss and the spawny duckweed, dim as air,
And green as copperas,
Choke its dull current; and, like hideous hair,
Tangles of twisted grass.

Above it sinister trees,—as crouched and gaunt
As huddled Terror,—lean;
Guarding some secret in that nightmare haunt,
Some horror they have seen.

Something the sunset points at from afar,
Spearing the sullen wood
And hag-gray water with a single bar
Of flame as red as blood.

Something the stars, conspiring with the moon,
Shall look on, and remain
Frozen with fear; staring as in a swoon,
Striving to flee in vain.

Something the wisp that, wandering in the night,
Above the ghastly stream,
Haply shall find; and, filled with frantic fright,
Light with its ghostly gleam.

Something that lies there, under weed and ooze,
With wide and awful eyes
And matted hair, and limbs the waters bruise,
That strives, yet can not rise.

The One Forgotten (1907)

Dora Sigerson Shorter

A spirit speeding down on All Souls' Eve
From the wide gates of that mysterious shore
Where sleep the dead, sung softly and yet sweet.
"So gay a wind was never heard before,"
The old man said, and listened by the fire;
And, "'Tis the souls that pass us on their way,"
The young maids whispered, clinging side by side,
So left their glowing nuts awhile to pray.

Still the pale spirit, singing through the night,
Came to this window, looking from the dark
Into the room; then passing to the door,
Where crouched the whining dog, afraid to bark,
Tapped gently without answer, pressed the latch,
Pushed softly open, and then tapped once more.
The maidens cried, when seeking for the ring,
"How strange a wind is blowing on the door!"

And said the old man, crouching to the fire:
"Draw close your chairs, for colder falls the night;
Push fast the door, and pull the curtains to,
For it is dreary in the moon's pale light."
And then his daughter's daughter with her hand
Passed over salt and clay to touch the ring,
Said low, "The old need fire, but ah! the young
Have that within their heart to flame and sting."

And then the spirit, moving from her place,
Touched there a shoulder, whispered in each ear,
Bent by the old man, nodding in his chair,
But no one heeded her, or seemed to hear.
Then crew the black cock, and so weeping sore
She went alone into the night again,
And said the greybeard, reaching for his glass,
"How sad a wind blows on the window-pane!"

And then from dreaming the long dreams of age
He woke, remembering, and let fall a tear:
"Alas! I have forgot—and have you gone?—
I set no chair to welcome you, my dear."
And said the maidens, laughing in their play,
"How he goes groaning, wrinkled-faced and hoar,
He is so old, and angry with his age—
Hush! hear the banshee sobbing past the door."

Hallowe'en (1908)

Madison J. Cawein

It was down in the woodland on last Hallowe'en,
Where silence and darkness had built them a lair,
That I felt the dim presence of her, the unseen,
And heard her step on the hush-haunted air.

It was last Hallowe'en in the glimmer and swoon
Of mist and of moonlight, where once we had sinned,
That I saw the gray gleam of her eyes in the moon,
And hair, like a raven, blown wild on the wind.

It was last Hallowe'en where starlight and dew
Made mystical marriage on flower and leaf,
That she led me with looks of a love, that I knew
Was dead, and the voice of a passion too brief.

It was last Hallowe'en in the forest of dreams,
Where trees are eidolons and flowers have eyes,
That I saw her pale face like the foam of far streams,
And heard, like the night-wind, her tears and her sighs.

It was last Hallowe'en, the haunted, the dread,
In the wind-tattered wood, by the storm-twisted pine,
That I, who am living, kept tryst with the dead,
And clasped her a moment who once had been mine.

All Souls (1909)

Edith Wharton

I.

A thin moon faints in the sky o'erhead,
And dumb in the churchyard lie the dead.
Walk we not, Sweet, by garden ways,
Where the late rose hangs and the phlox delays,
But forth of the gate and down the road,
Past the church and the yews, to their dim abode.
For it's turn of the year and All Souls' night,
When the dead can hear and the dead have sight.

II.

Fear not that sound like wind in the trees:
It is only their call that comes on the breeze;
Fear not the shudder that seems to pass:
It is only the tread of their feet on the grass;
Fear not the drip of the bough as you stoop:
It is only the touch of their hands that grope—
For the year's on the turn and it's All Souls' night,
When the dead can yearn and the dead can smite.

III.

And where should a man bring his sweet to woo
But here, where such hundreds were lovers too?
Where lie the dead lips that thirst to kiss,
The empty hands that their fellows miss,
Where the maid and her lover, from sere to green,
Sleep bed by bed, with the worm between?
For it's turn of the year and All Souls' night,
When the dead can hear and the dead have sight.

IV.

And now they rise and walk in the cold,
Let us warm their blood and give youth to the old.
Let them see us and hear us, and say: "Ah, thus
In the prime of the year it went with us!"
Till their lips drawn close, and so long unkist,

Forget they are mist that mingles with mist!
For the year's on the turn, and it's All Souls' night,
When the dead can burn and the dead can smite.

V.

Till they say, as they hear us—poor dead, poor dead!—
"Just an hour of this, and our age-long bed—
Just a thrill of the old remembered pains
To kindle a flame in our frozen veins,
A touch, and a sight, and a floating apart,
As the chill of dawn strikes each phantom heart—
For it's turn of the year and All Souls' night,
When the dead can hear and the dead have sight."

VI.

And where should the living feel alive
But here in this wan white humming hive,
As the moon wastes down, and the dawn turns cold,
And one by one they creep back to the fold?
And where should a man hold his mate and say:
"One more, one more, ere we go their way"?
For the year's on the turn, and it's All Souls' night,
When the living can learn by the churchyard light.

VII.

And how should we break faith who have seen
Those dead lips plight with the mist between,
And how forget, who have seen how soon
They lie thus chambered and cold to the moon?
How scorn, how hate, how strive, we too,
Who must do so soon as those others do?
For it's All Souls' night, and break of the day,
And behold, with the light the dead are away . . .

Hallowe-e'en, 1914 (1918)

W.M. Letts

"Why do you wait at your door, woman,
Alone in the night?"
"I am waiting for one who will come, stranger,
To show him a light.
He will see me afar on the road
And be glad at the sight."

"Have you no fear in your heart, woman,
To stand there alone?
There is comfort for you and kindly content
Beside the hearthstone."
But she answered, "No rest can I have
Till I welcome my own."

"Is it far he must travel to-night,
This man of your heart?"
"Strange lands that I know not and pitiless seas
Have kept us apart,
And he travels this night to his home
Without guide, without chart."

"And has he companions to cheer him?"
"Aye, many," she said.
"The candles are lighted, the hearthstones are swept,
The fires glow red.
We shall welcome them out of the night—
Our home-coming dead."

All Souls' Eve (1920)

Darl Macleod Boyle

The evening is dark, and the sky is misty, and the wind blows low;
O wind, cease swaying the bare, bare branches, bending them
    to and fro,
They look too like ghosts in the pale moonlight,
Ah, too like ghosts in the dusky night,
When ghosts glide to and fro!

O ghosts not laid, and ghosts forgotten, and ghosts of the
    evil dead,
Why will ye come to sear my heart, when I thought ye had
    gone, and fled,
Why do ye come on this night of the year,
Does it ease your pain to behold my fear,
Since all is done and said?

Hallowe'en in a Suburb (2001; 1st pub. 1926)

H.P. Lovecraft

The steeples are white in the wild moonlight,
And the trees have a silver glare;
Past the chimneys high see the vampires fly,
And the harpies of upper air,
That flutter and laugh and stare.

For the village dead to the moon outspread
Never shone in the sunset's gleam,
But grew out of the deep that the dead years keep
Where the rivers of madness stream
Down the gulfs to a pit of dream.

A chill wind blows thro' the rows of sheaves
In the meadows that shimmer pale,
And comes to twine where the headstones shine
And the ghouls of the churchyard wail
For harvests that fly and fail.

Not a breath of the strange grey gods of change
That tore from the past its own
Can quicken this hour, when a spectral pow'r
Spreads deep o'er the cosmic throne
And looses the vast unknown.

So here again stretch the vale and plain
That moons long-forgotten saw,
And the dead leap gay in the pallid ray,
Sprung out of the tomb's black maw
To shake all the world with awe.

And all that the morn shall greet forlorn,
The ugliness and the pest
Of rows where thick rise the stones and brick,
Shall some day be with the rest,
And brood with the shades unblest.

Then wild in the dark let the lemurs bark,
And the leprous spires ascend;
For new and old alike in the fold
Of horror and death are penn'd,
For the hounds of Time to rend.

It Happened One Halloween . . .

The Ferry House. A Scottish Tale of Halloween. (1834)

John Galt

The day was come, the trysted day,	
That drew me from the moors away,	
In wynd, or close, or stair, to *speer*	[ask]
If *wins blithe* luckie Fortune here.	[gladly finds her way]
With heavy step one afternoon,	
Bearing my gun, my song a croone,	
I thought with scad of day to reach	
The Ferry publick on the beach;	
And long ere night had closed her *brods,*	[shutters]
To cross the loch, and sleep where cods	
And *weel* made beds, with sheets, I wot,	[well]
Show inns may be where clans are not.	
But all the road I had to travel,	
Was just a clay eclipse of gravel,	
And every step I forward *ettled,*	[tried]
A *backward slidder whelp'd or kittled.*	[slid/stumbled backwards]
The day was sober, gray, and still,	
With plaid o' mist was wrapp'd the hill.	
The *burn* ran brown; the heather bell	[brook]
Shed tears, for what—it couldna tell.	
The crows held synod, and discoursed	
Of *dules* ordained, and dooms the worst;	[sorrows]

An owl flew past—her zealous passage
Show'd she was earnest on a message.

Star of the glen, the primrose pale
Gleams meekly in the shaggy vale;
The witch-forbidding row'ns display
Their cluster'd sparks of heatless ray;
The sloes with sullen ripeness glow,
As maids unsought, stale virgins grow;
And nuts—the crop is poor, I ween—
Ha! I forget 'tis Halloween.
But I must hasten while 'tis light—
The *Deil,* they say, has rope this night.   [Devil]
A something in forgotten time,
Still makes this haunted night sublime;
A shadowy shape, a mystery past,
Vast, black, and strange, behind is cast!

Dreigh was the way, but by and by   [Tedious]
I saw a star, no in the sky,
But in the publick's window near,
The eye of shelter beaming clear;
The wick so short, the candle tall,
Denoted James was within call;
But from its *houff* the *cobble* flown,   [shelter; boat]
Show'd he was o'er the Ferry gone.

There was no help—I could but bide
For his return, let what betide;
So at the door I tirl'd the pin—
It opened, and I slippet in;
For I had heard his *marrow* lay   [mate/wife]
At death's door sick, but she was clay.

Stretch'd on the bed, in *deadals* drest,   [death's clothes]
A plate of salt* lay on her breast;
Quaite was the house, for death was in it—   [Quiet]
There lay the corpse—alas! auld Janet!

No doubt the sight was very *fleein,*   [frightening]
But well I knew she had been *deein,*   [dying]
And heard it said, a day or two
Were all that she might *warsle* thro'.   [struggle]
It *gied,* tho', to my heart a stang,   [gave]
To see her *yird* I knew sae lang;   [buried]
So down afore the corpse I sat,
And *lainly* eerie all but *grat.*   [lonely; wept]

I thought of life—a shuttle flying—
Of *bairns* and bears—all flesh that's dying,   [babies]
And life, that's like the blooming rose,—
In morning sunshine blithe it blows.
The flower is pluck'd—its soul, the smell,
Where is it now? in heaven or hell?

Oh, mortal man! within the glass
Thy ebbing sand is growing less,
And at thy elbow, dart in hand,
Ready to strike, grim Death doth stand,
With orbless holes where eyes have been;
A skull he wears—it's Halloween!

I felt I was almost asleep,
My limbs were tired, the way was deep,
But to behold again *that* sight,
Put soon irreverent sleep to flight,
While sad to my remembrance came
The lambent glory of a name.

Ah! what avails it now, I said,
To her that lies in yon still bed,
What *gauds* of pride, or gems of grace,   [golds]
Adorn the living female race?
What shouts of jeopardy or joy,
The *carlin's* slumber can destroy?   [old woman's]
What flattery soothe the calm cold heart,
When dust from dust no more shall part,
And all to life and fancy dear,
Lie hush'd—hush'd—hush'd upon the bier?
There sleep the tuneful and the brave;
The master there, and there the slave,
Afar from boiling-house or pen—
Gods! I forget—I dream again!

Vex'd with myself, I leave my chair—
Go to the door, breathe caller air,
But soon resume my doleful seat,
And morals strange I soon repeat;
For there, before me, lay the dead,
A thing to shake the soul with dread,
Nor is it wise, full well I ween,
To wake a corpse on Halloween.

Then, in an awed and solemn strain,
I ruminated thus again—
What was this world before e'er life,
Death's parent, felt th' unfilial knife—
What was ere space was fill'd with rings,
Orbits of stars, and starry things?

While yet I spoke, I saw the door
Flung gently wide, and sad and sour,
Of mean attire, two labourous men
Come softly with a coffin *ben.*   [in]
They lay it down forenent the bed,
And from a shelf across the head,
Take, all in silence, from its place,
A *gardevine,* and syne a glass;   [whiskey jar]
They spoke not, but one held it out,
The other fill'd it—full, no doubt.

Being refresh'd they rise, and lay
The shapen lump of kirkyard clay
Within the coffin's dismal womb,
Dread prologue to the grave and tomb.
When all was done, with stealthy feet,
I saw them from the house retreat.

But long the silent room of death
Was not serene—I saw a wraith—
Auld Janet's—as I live I saw her
Come out from hiding in a drawer,
And lift the coffin lid and raise
The dead as drest in its last *claes*.   [clothes]

While mute I gaz'd, she tore the shroud,
Death's vestment, off, and cried aloud—
"My true gudeman, awake, prepare,
With you this night I'll mak my lair;
Joe of my youth, shake off this trance,
With us the jointless dead shall dance;
A minstrel *spring,* at tryst or fair,   [lively tune]
Is gay to hear, but we'll compare
The dead man's reel, the grave's *strathspey,*   [a Highlands dance]
That the blind worms and maggots play,
With rubs of *thairm,* that mortal men   [fiddle strings]
Make when long parted meet again."

Then up full brisk the mort arose,
Awak'ning from its dumb repose,
But, oh! he was a sight to see,
As one that died in poverty;
For he was gaunt, the flesh was gone,
Without was skin, within was bone;
His *een* did shine like blobs of dew;   [eyes]
But, oh! his mouth! it *gart me grue!*   [made my flesh creep]
His neck was long, his legs and arms
Were things but seen at witching charms;
He was as Hunger's eager gnaw
Had *toom'd* his inside, *kite* and a'!   [emptied; stomach]
He seem'd well pleas'd, his een did show it,

Heavens hide thae teeth! for I'm no poet;
To look on sights forbid life's forfeit,
Sights! necromancies of a surfeit.

But ere I wist, like lightning shed,
A change came o'er the living dead;
He seem'd of glass—of shapen air,
An outline thing, a lightless glare,
And all the house appear'd to be
Fill'd with a countless companie,
Since the first dawn of ages born,
Those that had been their pride and scorn—
The dead were there, for wondrous then,
A mystery met my sharpen'd ken.

Between all edges, forms, and things,**
That corporal sense to vision brings,
I saw departed spirits shine,
Souls that had liv'd, a dim outline,
Theirs who had earn'd the world's applause,
And theirs who perish'd by the laws—
All, all appear'd, as if I sat
For trial in Jehosaphat.

Again the door was open thrown,
And one by one, to me all known,
Successive enter'd, old and young;
The shadowy bridegroom then had tongue,
And welcom'd them with courtesy,
Beckon'd them in, *syne* said to me,   [then]
"Rise, stranger, rise, sir, ye *maun* come,—   [must]
But, oh! this night to take ye home!"

'Twas James that spoke—a moment's gleam
Show'd I had dreamt a prophet's dream;
For those I saw, the guests were they,
Since ta'en by Death: this *gars* me say,   [makes]
While heaven is blue and earth is green,
Wake not a corpse on Halloween.

* A plate of salt placed on a corpse was thought to prevent the body from swelling. It was also part of sin-eating, where a designated person—the sin eater, who was paid for his services—ate a piece of bread left on the salt dish, and, by proxy, the sins of the departed.

** This thought is derived from those kind of mystical engravings in which the French excel, where the picture presents at the first glance one subject, and upon examination shows in the outlines another. [JG]

The Black Preacher. A Breton Legend (1864)

James Russell Lowell

At Carnac in Brittany, close on the bay,
They show you a church, or rather the gray
Ribs of a dead one, left there to bleach
With the wreck lying near on the crest of the beach;
Roofless and splintered with thunder-stone,
'Mid lichen-blurred gravestones all alone,
'Tis the kind of ruin strange sights to see
That may have their teaching for you and me.

Something like this, then, my guide had to tell,
Perched on a saint cracked across when he fell.
But since I might chance give his meaning a wrench,
He talking his *patois* and I English-French,
I'll put what he told me, preserving the tone,
In a rhymed prose that makes it half his, half my own.

An abbey-church stood here, once on a time,
Built as a death-bed atonement for crime:
'Twas for somebody's sins, I know not whose;
But sinners are plenty, and you can choose.
Though a cloister now of the dusk-winged bat,
'Twas rich enough once, and the brothers grew fat,
Looser in girdle and purpler in jowl,
Singing good rest to the founder's lost soul.
But one day came Northmen, and lithe tongues of fire
Lapped up the chapter-house, licked off the spire,
And left all a rubbish-heap, black and dreary,
Where only the wind sings *miserere*.
Of what the monks came by no legend runs,
At least they were lucky in not being nuns.

No priest has kneeled since at the altar's foot,
Whose crannies are searched by the nightshade's root,
Nor sound of service is ever heard,
Except from throat of the unclean bird,
Hooting to unassoiled shapes as they pass

In midnights unholy his witches' mass,
Or shouting "Ho! ho!" from the belfry high
As the Devil's sabbath-train whirls by;
But once a year, on the eve of All-Souls,
Through these arches dishallowed the organ rolls,
Fingers long fleshless the bell-ropes work,
The chimes peal muffled with sea-mists mirk,
The skeleton windows are traced anew
On the baleful flicker of corpse-lights blue,
And the ghosts must come, so the legend saith,
To a preaching of Reverend Doctor Death.

Abbots, monks, barons, and ladies fair
Hear the dull summons and gather there:
No rustle of silk now, no clink of mail,
Nor ever a one greets his church-mate pale;
No knight whispers love in the *châtelaine's* ear,
His next-door neighbor this five-hundred year;
No monk has a sleek *benedicite*
For the great lord shadowy now as he;
Nor needeth any to hold his breath,
Lest he lose the least word of Doctor Death.

He chooses his text in the Book Divine,
Tenth verse of the Preacher in chapter nine:—
"'Whatsoever thy hand shall find thee to do,
That do with thy whole might, or thou shalt rue;
For no man is wealthy, or wise, or brave
In that quencher of might-be's and would-be's, the grave.'
Bid by the Bridegroom, 'to-morrow,' ye said,
And To-morrow was digging a trench for your bed;
Ye said, 'God can wait; let us finish our wine';
Ye had wearied Him, fools, and that last knock was mine!"

But I can't pretend to give you the sermon,
Or say if the tongue were French, Latin, or German;
Whatever he preached in, I give you my word
The meaning was easy to all that heard;
Famous preachers there have been and be,
But never was one so convincing as he;

So blunt was never a begging friar,
No Jesuit's tongue so barbed with fire,
Cameronian never, nor Methodist,
Wrung gall out of Scripture with such a twist.

And would you know who his hearers must be?
I tell you just what my guide told me:
Excellent teaching men have, day and night,
From two earnest friars, a black and a white,
The Dominican Death and the Carmelite Life;
And between these two there is never strife,
For each has his separate office and station,
And each his own work in the congregation;
Whoso to the white brother deafens his ears,
And cannot be wrought on by blessings or tears,
Awake in his coffin must wait and wait,
In that blackness of darkness that means *too late,*
And come once a year, when the ghost-bell tolls,
As till Doomsday it shall on the eve of All-Souls,
To hear Doctor Death, whose words smart with the brine
Of the Preacher, the tenth verse of chapter nine.

The Eve of All-Saints (1908)

Madison J. Cawein

I.

This is the tale they tell
Of an Hallowe'en;
This is the thing that befell
Me and the village belle,
Beautiful Amy Dean.

II.

Did I love her? God and she,
They know and I!
Ah, she was the life of me—
Whatever else may be
Would God that I could die!

III.

That Hallowe'en was dim;
The frost lay white
Under strange stars and a slim
Moon in the graveyard grim,
Pale with its slender light.

IV.

They told her: "Go alone,
With never a word,
To the burial-plot's unknown
Grave with the oldest stone,
When the clock on twelve is heard.

V.

"Three times around it pass,
With never a sound;
Each time a wisp of grass
And myrtle pluck; then pass
Out of the ghostly ground.

VI.

"And the bridegroom that's to be,

At smiling wait,
With a face like mist to see,
With graceful gallantry
Will bow you to the gate."

VII.

She laughed at this and so
Bespoke us how
To the burial-place she'd go.—
And I was glad to know,
For I'd be there to bow.

VIII.

An acre from the farm
The village dead
Lay walled from sun and storm;
Old cedars, of priestly form,
Waved darkly overhead.

IX.

I loved; but never could say
The words to her;
And waited, day by day,
Nursing the hope that lay
Under the doubts that were.—

X.

She passed 'neath the iron arch
Of the legended ground;—
And the moon, like a twisted torch,
Burned over one lonesome larch;—
She passed with never a sound.

XI.

Three times the circle traced;
Three times she bent
To the grave that the myrtle graced;
Three times—then softly faced
Homeward and slowly went.

XII.

Had the moonlight changed me so?
Or fear undone
Her stepping soft and slow?
Did she see and did not know?
Or loved she another one?

XIII.

Who knows?—She turned to flee
With a face so white
It haunts and will haunt me:—
The wind blew gustily:
The graveyard gate clanged tight.

XIV.

Did she think it I or—what,
Clutching her dress?
Her face so wild that not
A star in a stormy spot
Shows half so much distress.

XV.

I spoke; but she answered naught.
"Amy," I said,
"'Tis I!"—as her form I caught . . .
Then laughed like one distraught,
For the beautiful girl was dead! . . .

XVI.

This is the tale they tell
Of that Hallowe'en;
This is the thing that befell
Me and the village belle,
Beautiful Amy Dean.

The Jack-o'-Lantern (1909)

Madison J. Cawein

Last night it was Hallowe'en.
Darkest night I've ever seen.
And the boy next door, I thought,
Would be glad to know of this
Jack-o'-lantern father brought
Home from Indianapolis.

And he *was* glad. Borrowed it.
Put a candle in and lit;
Hid among the weeds out there
In the side lot near the street.
I could see it, eyes aglare,
Mouth and nose red slits of heat.

My! but it looked scary! He
Perched an old hat on it, see?
Like some hat a scarecrow has,
Battered, tattered all around;
And he fanned long arms of grass
Up and down above the ground.

First an Irish woman, shawled,
With a basket, saw it; bawled
For her Saints and wept and cried,
"Is it you, Pat? Och! I knew
He would git you whin you died!
Faith! there's little change in you!"

Then the candle sputtered, flared,
And went out; and on she fared,
Muttering to herself. When lit,
No one came for longest while.
Then a man passed; looked at it;
On his face a knowing smile.

Then it scared a colored girl
Into fits. She gave a whirl
And a scream and ran and ran—
Thought Old Nick had hold her skin;
And she ran into a man,
P'liceman, and *he* run her in.

But what pleased me most was that
It made one boy lose his hat;
A big fool who thinks he's smart,
Brags about the boys he beat:
Knew he'd run right from the start:
Biggest coward on the street.

Then a crowd of girls and boys
Gathered with a lot of noise.
When they saw the lantern, well!
They just took a hand: they thought
That they had *him* when he fell;
But he turned on them and fought.

He just took that lantern's stick,
Laid about him hard and quick,
And they yelled and ran away.
Then he brought me all he had
Of my lantern. And, I say,
Could have *cried* I was so mad.

FUN AND GAMES: LIGHT VERSE

The Ghost (1914, written circa 1780)

Vicomte de Parny, translated by John Payne

I know not what they do down there.
If from the womb of the deep Night
One may come back unto the light,
I shall return, misdoubt it ne'er.
But I shall not the fashions ape
Of yonder phantoms indiscreet,
That come in shroud and winding-sheet
And with a grim and haggard shape,
That terror in the bosom stir,
Add foulness to the favour foul
One gathers in the sepulchre.
To please you jealous even in death,
Myself invisible I'll make.
Oft, of the zephyr's softest breath
The waft insensible I'll take.
Nay, all my sighs for you shall be:
They shall a-tremble set the plumes
Upon your tresses, carelessly
Upbound and knotted, and set free
The faint scent that your locks perfumes.
Nay, if the rose you cherish so
Relive within its vase of white,
If your rekindling tapers glow
More clear and give a livelier light,
If a new carmine, as of dawn,
Across your features sudden run,
If the knot over-straightly drawn
Of your sweet breast come oft undone,
And if the sofa under you
More softly yield to your idlesse,
Vouchsafe a smile of thanks unto
These cares all of my tenderness.
Nay, when the charms I see again,
With which my hand toyed heretofore,

My amorous voice regrets will fain
To murmur be for days of yore;
And you will think that harp to hear,
Which, whiles, beneath my fingers prest,
Availed t'express unto your ear
What my heart did to me suggest.
Unto the sweetness of your sleep
A charm of fiction fair I'll add
And with a dream, from slumber deep
I'll cause your wakening to be glad.
Your beauties naked shall I see,
Perfect contours, charms ripe and rife,
All shall I witness.—But, ah me!
The dead do not return to life.

Hallowe'en (1895)

Joel Benton

Now, when the owl makes wild ado
With his sad *tu-whit tu-who,*
'Tis the night for erie things,
When shadows from unearthly wings
Born in umbrageous' solitude
Gloom the meadow and the wood.

But still around the rustic fire,
In spite of spirits dark and dire,
Is heard a joyful, frolic noise
Of half a score of girls and boys
Over the nut and apple games
Commingled with their mated names.

Others—although the chimney roars
Its ancient welcome—out-of-doors
Run to the oat-stack or the barn;
Untwisting, some, a ball of yarn,
Or seeking in the spectral brook
Some telltale apparition's look.

No end of schemes were there of old
By which love's tender charms were told;
And still may fairies intervene
To bless the fates of Halloween.

The Charms (1903)

Emma A. Opper

Last night 'twas witching Hallowe'en,
Dearest; an apple russet-brown
I pared, and thrice above my crown
Whirled the long skin; they watched it keen;
I flung it far; they laughed and cried me shame—
Dearest, there lay the letter of your name!

Took I the mirror then, and crept
Down, down the creaking narrow stair;
The milk-pans caught my candle's flare,
And mice walked soft and spiders slept;
I spoke the spell, and stood the magic space,
Dearest—and in the glass I saw your face!

And then I stole out in the night
Alone; the frogs piped sweet and loud,
The moon looked through a ragged cloud;
Thrice round the house I sped me light,
Dearest; and there, methought—charm of my charms!—
You met me, kissed me, took me to your arms!

Hallowe'en (1910)

John Kendrick Bangs

Bring forth the raisins and the nuts—
To-night All Hallows' Spectre struts
Along the moonlit way.
No time is this for tear or sob,
Or other woes our joys to rob,
But time for Pippin and for Bob,
And Jack o' lantern gay.

Come forth, ye lass and trousered kid,
From prisoned mischief raise the lid,
And lift it good and high.
Leave grave old Wisdom in the lurch,
Set Folly on a lofty perch,
Nor fear the awesome rod of birch
When dawn illumes the sky.

'Tis night for revel, set apart
To reillume the darkened heart,
And rout the hosts of Dole.
'Tis night when Goblin, Elf, and Fay,
Come dancing in their best array
To prank and royster on the way,
And ease the troubled soul.

The ghosts of all things, past parade,
Emerging from the mist and shade
That hid them from our gaze,
And full of song and ringing mirth,
In one glad moment of rebirth,
Again they walk the ways of earth,
As in the ancient days.

The beacon light shines on the hill
The will-o'-wisps the forests fill
With flashes filched from noon;
And witches on their broomsticks spry

Speed here and yonder in the sky,
And lift their strident voices high
Unto the Hunter's moon.

The air resounds with tuneful notes
From myriads of straining throats,
All hailing Folly Queen;
So join the swelling choral throng,
Forget your sorrow and your wrong,
In one glad hour of joyous song
To honor Hallowe'en.

The Owlet (1911)

Madison J. Cawein

I.

When dusk is drowned in drowsy dreams,
And slow the hues of sunset die;
When firefly and moth go by,
And in still streams the new moon seems
Another moon and sky:
Then from the hills there comes a cry,
The owlet's cry:
A shivering voice that sobs and screams,
With terror screams:—
"Who is it, who is it, who-o-o?
Who rides through the dusk and dew,
With a pair of horns,
As thin as thorns,
And face a bubble-blue? -
Who, who, who!
Who is it, who is it, who-o-o?"

II.

When night has dulled the lily's white,
And opened wide the moonflower's eyes;
When pale mists rise and veil the skies,
And round the height in whispering flight
The night-wind sounds and sighs:
Then in the wood again it cries,
The owlet cries:
A shivering voice that calls in fright,
In maundering fright:—
"Who is it, who is it, who-o-o?
Who walks with a shuffling shoe
'Mid the gusty trees,
With a face none sees,
And a form as ghostly, too?—
Who, who, who!
Who is it, who is it, who-o-o?"

III.

When midnight leans a listening ear
And tinkles on her insect lutes;
When 'mid the roots the cricket flutes,
And marsh and mere, now far, now near,
A jack-o'-lantern foots:
Then o'er the pool again it hoots,
The owlet hoots:
A voice that shivers as with fear,
That cries with fear:—
"Who is it, who is it, who-o-o?
Who creeps with his glowworm crew
Above the mire
With a corpse-light fire,
As only dead men do?—
Who, who, who!
Who is it, who is it, who-o-o?"

De Ole Moon Knows (1921)

Lettie C. VanDerveer

Mighty queer doin's eroun' to-night;
Yo' caint be shuah dat yo' haid's on right.
How did de bucket git outen de well?
De ole moon knows, but he won' tell.

Who paint de hen-house red, white an' blue,
An' nail up de do' so yo' cain't git froo?
Who put de rain barrel onto de stoop,
An' shet de ole cat in de chicken-coop?

Who tied a great big sign "For Sail"
Onto de end of de red cow's tail?
Who pulled de rope on de ole church bell?
De ole moon knows, but he won' tell.

How did de front gate happen to be
Settin' up high in de apple tree?
Who put a big green cabbage haid
Right in de middle de flowah bed?

How come dat scare-crow settin' there
On de front po'ch in de rockin' chair?
De ole moon laugh, an' he blink he eye,
Chucklin' away up in de sky.

Mebbe it's spooks,—yes, mebbe so;—
They's up to such doin's, spooks is, yo' know.
Sompins bewitched things; who cast de spell?
De ole moon know, but he won' tell.

When the Woodchuck Chuckles (1921)

Lettie C. VanDerveer

When the screech-owl screeches,
And the hoot owl hoots,
And the bat goes batting around;
Then the woodchuck chuckles
At the sights he sees,
Peeking out of a hole in the ground

For the spooks are spooking,
And the fairies fare
Forth to a phantom tune;
And dance all over
The pumpkin's pumps,
By the light of the moony old moon.

And the nuts go nutty,
And the squashes squash
The cabbage's cab to bits;
And the imps impatient
Not to be outdone
Throw the cats into cat-fits.

Then the woodchuck chuckles
Just a chuck too loud!
And there's never a one to be seen.
At the cucumber's cue
They all skidoo,
On the night of Hallowe'en.

PART II.

Stories

THE STORYTELLER'S ART

"The pagan magicians handed it [magic] to their quasi-Christian successors, and when these worthies departed to some world more worthy of them, their system exploded in fragments, and fell under the wise control of our storytellers."

—Patrick Kennedy

Black Stairs on Fire (1891; 1st edition 1866)

Patrick Kennedy

On the top of the hill of *Cnoc-na-Cro'* (Gallows Hill) in Bantry, just in full view of the White Mountain, Cahir Rua's Den, and Black Stairs, there lived a poor widow, with a grandchild, about fifteen years old. It was All-Holland Eve,* and the two were about going to bed when they heard four taps at the door, and a screaming voice crying out. "Where are you, feet-water?" and the feet-water answered, "Here in the tub." "Where are you, band of the spinning wheel?" and it answered, "Here, fast round the rim, as if it was spinning." "Besom, [broom] where are you?" "Here, with my handle in the ash-pit." "Turf-coal, where are you?" "Here, blazing over the ashes." Then the voice screamed louder, "Feet-water, wheel-band, besom, and turf-coal, let us in, let us in!" and they all made to the door.

Open it flew, and in rushed frightful old hags, wicked, shameless young ones, and the *old boy* himself, with red horns and a green tail. They began to tear and tatter round the house, and to curse and swear, and roar and bawl, and say such things as almost made the poor women sink through the hearth-stone. They had strength enough however, to make the sign of the cross, and call on the Holy Trinity, and then all the witches and their master yowled with pain. After a little the girl strove to creep over to the holy water croft that was hanging at the bed's head, but the whole bilin' of the wicked creatures kep' in a crowd between her and it. The poor grandmother fell in a faint, but the little girl kep' her senses.

The old fellow made frightful music for the rest, stretching out his nose and playing the horriblest noise on it you ever heard, just as if it was a German

103

flute. "Oh!" says the poor child, "if Granny should die or lose her senses what'll I do? and if they can stay till cockcrow, she'll never see another day." So after about half an hour, when the hullabullo was worse than ever, she stole out without being noticed or stopped, and then she gave a great scream, and ran in, and shouted, "Granny, granny! come out, come out, Black Stairs is a-fire!" Out pelted both the devil and the witches, some by the windows, some by the door; and the moment the last of them was out, she clapped the handle of the besom where the door-bolt ought to be, turned the button in the window, spilled the feet-water into the channel under the door, loosed the band of the spinning-wheel, and raked up the blazing coal under the ashes.

Well, the poor woman was now come to herself, and both heard the most frightful roar out in the bawn, where all the company were standing very lewd** of themselves for being so easily taken in. The noise fell immediately, and the same voice was heard. "Feet-water, let me in." "I can't," says feet-water; "I am here under your feet." "Wheel-band, let me in." "I can't—I am lying loose on the wheel-seat." "Besom let me in." "I can't—I am put here to bolt the door." "Turf-coal, let me in." "I can't—my head is under the gree-shach." "Then let yourselves and them that owns you have our curse for ever and a day." The poor women were now on their knees, and cared little for their curses. But every Holy Eve during their lives they threw the water out as soon as their feet were washed, unbanded the wheel, swept up the house, and covered the big coal to have the seed of the fire next morning.

*All Holland Eve, Hall'eve, Holy Eve, Hallowtide, November Eve, and Samhain Eve or Night are other names for Halloween.

**"Regretful, ashamed," the root being "leiden," to suffer. Many words and expressions among our folk of the Pale are looked on as abuses or perversions, when they are in truth but old forms still carefully preserved. [PK]

The Child That Went With the Fairies (1870)

Joseph Sheridan le Fanu

Eastward of the old city of Limerick, about ten Irish miles, under the range of mountains known as the Slieveelim hills, famous as having afforded Sarsfield a shelter among their rocks and hollows, when he crossed them in his gallant descent upon the cannon and ammunition of King William, on its way to the beleaguering army, there runs a very old and narrow road. It connects the Limerick road to Tipperary with the old road from Limerick to Dublin, and runs by bog and pasture, hill and hollow, straw-thatched village, and roofless castle, not far from twenty miles.

Skirting the heathy mountains of which I have spoken, at one part it becomes singularly lonely. For more than three Irish miles it traverses a deserted country. A wide, black bog, level as a lake, skirted with copse, spreads at the left, as you journey northward, and the long and irregular line of mountain rises at the right, clothed in heath, broken with lines of grey rock that resemble the bold and irregular outlines of fortifications, and riven with many a gully, expanding here and there into rocky and wooded glens, which open as they approach the road.

A scanty pasturage, on which browsed a few scattered sheep or kine, skirts this solitary road for some miles, and under shelter of a hillock, and of two or three great ash-trees, stood, not many years ago, the little thatched cabin of a widow named Mary Ryan.

Poor was this widow in a land of poverty. The thatch had acquired the grey tint and sunken outlines, that show how the alternations of rain and sun have told upon that perishable shelter.

But whatever other dangers threatened, there was one well provided against by the care of other times. Round the cabin stood half a dozen mountain ashes, as the rowans, inimical to witches, are there called. On the worn planks of the door were nailed two horse-shoes, and over the lintel and spreading along the thatch, grew, luxuriant, patches of that ancient cure for many maladies, and prophylactic against the machinations of the evil one, the house-leek. Descending into the doorway, in the chiar' oscuro of the interior, when your eye grew sufficiently accustomed to that dim light, you might discover, hanging at the head of the widow's wooden-roofed bed, her beads and a phial of holy water.

Here certainly were defences and bulwarks against the intrusion of that unearthly and evil power, of whose vicinity this solitary family were constantly reminded by the outline of Lisnavoura, that lonely hill-haunt of the "Good people," as the fairies are called euphemistically, whose strangely dome-like summit rose not half a mile away, looking like an outwork of the long line of mountain that sweeps by it.

It was at the fall of the leaf, and an autumnal sunset threw the lengthening shadow of haunted Lisnavoura, close in front of the solitary little cabin, over the undulating slopes and sides of Slieveelim. The birds were singing among the branches in the thinning leaves of the melancholy ash-trees that grew at the roadside in front of the door. The widow's three younger children were playing on the road, and their voices mingled with the evening song of the birds. Their elder sister, Nell, was "within in the house," as their phrase is, seeing after the boiling of the potatoes for supper.

Their mother had gone down to the bog, to carry up a hamper of turf on her back. It is, or was at least, a charitable custom—and if not disused, long may it continue—for the wealthier people when cutting their turf and stacking it in the bog, to make a smaller stack for the behoof of the poor, who were welcome to take from it so long as it lasted, and thus the potato pot was kept boiling, and the hearth warm that would have been cold enough but for that good-natured bounty, through wintry months.

Moll Ryan trudged up the steep "bohereen" whose banks were overgrown with thorn and brambles, and stooping under her burden, re-entered her door, where her dark-haired daughter Nell met her with a welcome, and relieved her of her hamper.

Moll Ryan looked round with a sigh of relief, and drying her forehead, uttered the Munster ejaculation:

"Eiah wisha! It's tired I am with it, God bless it. And where's the craythurs, Nell?"

"Playin' out on the road, mother; didn't ye see them and you comin' up?"

"No; there was no one before me on the road," she said, uneasily; "not a soul, Nell; and why didn't ye keep an eye on them?"

"Well, they're in the haggard, playin' there, or round by the back o' the house. Will I call them in?"

"Do so, good girl, in the name o' God. The hens is comin' home, see, and the sun was just down over Knockdoulah, an' I comin' up."

So out ran tall, dark-haired Nell, and standing on the road, looked up and down it; but not a sign of her two little brothers, Con and Bill, or her little sister, Peg, could she see. She called them; but no answer came from the little haggard, fenced with straggling bushes. She listened, but the sound of their voices was missing. Over the stile, and behind the house she ran—but there all was silent and deserted.

She looked down toward the bog, as far as she could see; but they did not appear. Again she listened—but in vain. At first she had felt angry, but now a different feeling overcame her, and she grew pale. With an undefined boding she looked toward the heathy boss of Lisnavoura, now darkening into the deepest purple against the flaming sky of sunset.

Again she listened with a sinking heart, and heard nothing but the farewell twitter and whistle of the birds in the bushes around. How many stories had she listened to by the winter hearth, of children stolen by the fairies, at night-fall, in lonely places! With this fear she knew her mother was haunted.

No one in the country round gathered her little flock about her so early as this frightened widow, and no door "in the seven parishes" was barred so early.

Sufficiently fearful, as all young people in that part of the world are of such dreaded and subtle agents, Nell was even more than usually afraid of them, for her terrors were infected and redoubled by her mother's. She was looking towards Lisnavoura in a trance of fear, and crossed herself again and again, and whispered prayer after prayer. She was interrupted by her mother's voice on the road calling her loudly. She answered, and ran round to the front of the cabin, where she found her standing.

"And where in the world's the craythurs—did ye see sight o' them any-where?" cried Mrs. Ryan, as the girl came over the stile.

"Arrah! mother, 'tis only that they're run down the road a bit. We'll see them this minute coming back. It's like goats they are, climbin' here and run-nin' there; an' if I had them here, in my hand, maybe I wouldn't give them a hiding all round."

"May the Lord forgive you, Nell! the childhers gone. They're took, and not a soul near us, and Father Tom three miles away! And what'll I do, or who's to help us this night? Oh, wirristhru, wirristhru! The craythurs is gone!"

"Whisht, mother, be aisy: don't ye see them comin' up."

And then she shouted in menacing accents, waving her arm, and beckon-ing the children, who were seen approaching on the road, which some little way off made a slight dip, which had concealed them. They were approaching from the westward, and from the direction of the dreaded hill of Lisnavoura.

But there were only two of the children, and one of them, the little girl, was crying. Their mother and sister hurried forward to meet them, more alarmed than ever.

"Where is Billy—where is he?" cried the mother, nearly breathless, so soon as she was within hearing.

"He's gone—they took him away; but they said he'll come back again," answered little Con, with the dark brown hair.

"He's gone away with the grand ladies," blubbered the little girl.

"What ladies—where? Oh, Leum, asthora! My darlin', are you gone away at last? Where is he? Who took him? What ladies are you talkin' about? What way did he go?" she cried in distraction.

"I couldn't see where he went, mother; 'twas like as if he was going to Lisnavoura."

With a wild exclamation the distracted woman ran on towards the hill alone, clapping her hands, and crying aloud the name of her lost child.

Scared and horrified, Nell, not daring to follow, gazed after her, and burst into tears; and the other children raised high their lamentations in shrilly rivalry.

Twilight was deepening. It was long past the time when they were usually barred securely within their habitation. Nell led the younger children into the cabin, and made them sit down by the turf fire, while she stood in the open door, watching in great fear for the return of her mother.

After a long while they did see their mother return. She came in and sat down by the fire, and cried as if her heart would break.

"Will I bar the doore, mother?" asked Nell.

"Ay, do—didn't I lose enough, this night, without lavin' the doore open, for more o' yez to go; but first take an' sprinkle a dust o' the holy waters over ye, acuishla, and bring it here till I throw a taste iv it over myself and the craythurs; an' I wondher, Nell, you'd forget to do the like yourself, lettin' the craythurs out so near nightfall. Come here and sit on my knees, asthora, come to me, mavourneen, and hould me fast, in the name o' God, and I'll hould you fast that none can take yez from me, and tell me all about it, and what it was—the Lord between us and harm—an' how it happened, and who was in it."

And the door being barred, the two children, sometimes speaking together, often interrupting one another, often interrupted by their mother, managed to tell this strange story, which I had better relate connectedly and in my own language.

The Widow Ryan's three children were playing, as I have said, upon the narrow old road in front of her door. Little Bill or Leum, about five years old, with golden hair and large blue eyes, was a very pretty boy, with all the clear tints of healthy childhood, and that gaze of earnest simplicity which belongs not to town children of the same age. His little sister Peg, about a year elder, and his brother Con, a little more than a year elder than she, made up the little group.

Under the great old ash-trees, whose last leaves were falling at their feet, in the light of an October sunset, they were playing with the hilarity and eagerness of rustic children, clamouring together, and their faces were turned toward the west and the storied hill of Lisnavoura.

Suddenly a startling voice with a screech called to them from behind, ordering them to get out of the way, and turning, they saw a sight, such as they never beheld before. It was a carriage drawn by four horses that were pawing and snorting, in impatience, as if just pulled up. The children were almost under their feet, and scrambled to the side of the road next their own door.

This carriage and all its appointments were old-fashioned and gorgeous, and presented to the children, who had never seen anything finer than a turf car, and once, an old chaise that passed that way from Killaloe, a spectacle perfectly dazzling.

Here was antique splendour. The harness and trappings were scarlet, and blazing with gold. The horses were huge, and snow white, with great manes, that as they tossed and shook them in the air, seemed to stream and float sometimes longer and sometimes shorter, like so much smoke—their tails were long, and tied up in bows of broad scarlet and gold ribbon. The coach itself was glowing with colours, gilded and emblazoned. There were footmen behind in gay liveries, and three-cocked hats, like the coachman's; but he had a great wig, like a judge's, and their hair was frizzed out and powdered, and a long thick "pigtail," with a bow to it, hung down the back of each.

All these servants were diminutive, and ludicrously out of proportion with the enormous horses of the equipage, and had sharp, sallow features, and small, restless fiery eyes, and faces of cunning and malice that chilled the children. The little coachman was scowling and showing his white fangs under his cocked hat, and his little blazing beads of eyes were quivering with fury in their sockets as he whirled his whip round and round over their heads, till the lash of it looked like a streak of fire in the evening sun, and sounded like the cry of a legion of "fillapoueeks" in the air.

"Stop the princess on the highway!" cried the coachman, in a piercing treble.

"Stop the princess on the highway!" piped each footman in turn, scowling over his shoulder down on the children, and grinding his keen teeth.

The children were so frightened they could only gape and turn white in their panic. But a very sweet voice from the open window of the carriage reassured them, and arrested the attack of the lackeys.

A beautiful and "very grand-looking" lady was smiling from it on them, and they all felt pleased in the strange light of that smile.

"The boy with the golden hair, I think," said the lady, bending her large and wonderfully clear eyes on little Leum.

The upper sides of the carriage were chiefly of glass, so that the children could see another woman inside, whom they did not like so well.

This was a black woman, with a wonderfully long neck, hung round with many strings of large variously-coloured beads, and on her head was a sort of turban of silk, striped with all the colours of the rainbow, and fixed in it was a golden star.

This black woman had a face as thin almost as a death's-head, with high cheek-bones, and great goggle eyes, the whites of which, as well as her wide range of teeth, showed in brilliant contrast with her skin, as she looked over the beautiful lady's shoulder, and whispered something in her ear.

"Yes; the boy with the golden hair, I think," repeated the lady.

And her voice sounded sweet as a silver bell in the children's ears, and her smile beguiled them like the light of an enchanted lamp, as she leaned from the window, with a look of ineffable fondness on the golden-haired boy, with the large blue eyes; insomuch that little Billy, looking up, smiled in return with a wondering fondness, and when she stooped down, and stretched her jewelled arms towards him, he stretched his little hands up, and how they touched the other children did not know; but, saying, "Come and give me a kiss, my darling," she raised him, and he seemed to ascend in her small fingers as lightly as a feather, and she held him in her lap and covered him with kisses.

Nothing daunted, the other children would have been only too happy to change places with their favoured little brother. There was only one thing that was unpleasant, and a little frightened them, and that was the black woman, who stood and stretched forward, in the carriage as before. She gathered a rich silk and gold handkerchief that was in her fingers up to her lips, and seemed to thrust ever so much of it, fold after fold, into her capacious mouth, as they thought to smother her laughter, with which she seemed convulsed, for she was shaking and quivering, as it seemed, with suppressed merriment; but her eyes, which remained uncovered, looked angrier than they had ever seen eyes look before.

But the lady was so beautiful they looked on her instead, and she continued to caress and kiss the little boy on her knee; and smiling at the other children she held up a large russet apple in her fingers, and the carriage began to move slowly on, and with a nod inviting them to take the fruit, she dropped it on the road from the window; it rolled some way beside the wheels, they following, and then she dropped another, and then another, and so on. And the same thing happened to all; for just as either of the children who ran beside had caught the rolling apple, somehow it slipt into a hole or ran into a ditch, and looking up they saw the lady drop another from the window, and so the chase was taken up and continued till they got, hardly knowing how far they had gone, to the old cross-road that leads to Owney. It seemed that there the horses' hoofs and carriage wheels rolled up a wonderful dust, which being caught in one of those eddies that whirl the dust up into a column, on the calmest day, enveloped the children for a moment, and passed whirling on towards Lisnavoura, the carriage, as they fancied, driving in the centre of it; but suddenly it subsided, the straws and leaves floated to the ground, the dust dissipated itself, but the white horses and the lackeys, the gilded carriage, the lady and their little goldenhaired brother were gone.

At the same moment suddenly the upper rim of the clear setting sun disappeared behind the hill of Knockdoula, and it was twilight. Each child felt the transition like a shock—and the sight of the rounded summit of Lisnavoura, now closely overhanging them, struck them with a new fear.

They screamed their brother's name after him, but their cries were lost in the vacant air. At the same time they thought they heard a hollow voice say, close to them, "Go home."

Looking round and seeing no one, they were scared, and hand in hand—the little girl crying wildly, and the boy white as ashes, from fear—they trotted homeward, at their best speed, to tell, as we have seen, their strange story.

Molly Ryan never more saw her darling. But something of the lost little boy was seen by his former playmates.

Sometimes when their mother was away earning a trifle at hay-making, and Nelly washing the potatoes for their dinner, or "beatling" clothes in the little stream that flows in the hollow close by, they saw the pretty face of little Billy peeping in archly at the door, and smiling silently at them, and as they ran to embrace him, with cries of delight, he drew back, still smiling archly, and when they got out into the open day, he was gone, and they could see no trace of him anywhere.

This happened often, with slight variations in the circumstances of the visit. Sometimes he would peep for a longer time, sometimes for a shorter time, sometimes his little hand would come in, and, with bended finger, beckon them to follow; but always he was smiling with the same arch look and wary silence—and always he was gone when they reached the door. Gradually these visits grew less and less frequent, and in about eight months they ceased altogether, and little Billy, irretrievably lost, took rank in their memories with the dead.

One wintry morning, nearly a year and a half after his disappearance, their mother having set out for Limerick soon after cock-crow, to sell some fowls at the market, the little girl, lying by the side of her elder sister, who was fast asleep, just at the grey of the morning heard the latch lifted softly, and saw little Billy enter and close the door gently after him. There was light enough to see that he was barefoot and ragged, and looked pale and famished. He went straight to the fire, and cowered over the turf embers, and rubbed his hands slowly, and seemed to shiver as he gathered the smouldering turf together.

The little girl clutched her sister in terror and whispered, "Waken, Nelly, waken; here's Billy come back!"

Nelly slept soundly on, but the little boy, whose hands were extended close over the coals, turned and looked toward the bed, it seemed to her, in fear, and she saw the glare of the embers reflected on his thin cheek as he turned toward her. He rose and went, on tiptoe, quickly to the door, in silence, and let himself out as softly as he had come in.

After that, the little boy was never seen any more by any one of his kindred.

"Fairy doctors," as the dealers in the preternatural, who in such cases were called in, are termed, did all that in them lay—but in vain. Father Tom came down, and tried what holier rites could do, but equally without result. So little Billy was dead to mother, brother, and sisters; but no grave received him. Others whom affection cherished, lay in holy ground, in the old church-yard of Abington, with headstone to mark the spot over which the survivor might kneel and say a kind prayer for the peace of the departed soul. But there was no landmark to show where little Billy was hidden from their loving eyes, unless it was in the old hill of Lisnavoura, that cast its long shadow at sunset before the cabin-door; or that, white and filmy in the moonlight, in later years, would occupy his brother's gaze as he returned from fair or market, and draw from him a sigh and a prayer for the little brother he had lost so long ago, and was never to see again.

All Souls' Eve in Lower Brittany (1897)

Anatole le Braz
[Excerpts]

The Brêtons have a striking name for November. They call it the black month. The delicate blue tints which bathed the horizon in the bright days of early autumn begin to fade and darken; and as the fogs grow more dense, a melancholy greyness, vague at first but soon becoming fixed and permanent, silently envelops the entire landscape. I know few things more impressive than the road from Quimper to Spézet over the Montagne-Noire in the black month. A keen wind smites you in the face, the moment you are outside the suburbs of the town; still, so long as you are skirting the red hills, and the valleys with their lingering tints of yellowish green, something of the gaiety of prosperous Cornouailles stays with you. Then, suddenly, you begin the climb into a very different sort of country; you seem to be ascending, step by step, a vast and sombre staircase. On either side of you, the land lies waste, a stern, colorless funereal desert. Few trees or none—a sickly dwarf oak or two, twisted and deformed—an occasional group of pines, moaning audibly, as it would seem, over the surrounding desolation. In all the pass, there is not one of those rural inns, those licensed victuallers with a bunch of mistletoe or a bough of laurel hung out by way of sign, which you find scattered along the waysides everywhere else in Brittany. The carriers fight shy of these solitudes, yet the road is wide, and here and there it recalls the forlorn majesty of certain avenues in the neighborhood of Versailles. It might be made out of the ill-joined sections of some ancient Roman way. After passing Briec,—the capital of the canton, a town whose administrative importance is emphasized to the passer-by, chiefly by the zinc flag over the police-station, squeaking in the wind like a rusty vane, you plunge at once into the true Ménez—or wild mountain country.

It is an inhospitable region, haunted by legends which are little calculated to reassure the mind. The famous woman-bandit, Marion du Faouët, whose name is never mentioned without a shudder even now, practiced her abominations here in the eighteenth century. In the cry of the osprey, the mountaineers think they hear the shriek of her whistle, "which was so sharp that it pierced the traveller's soul, and so loud that it brought the leaves off the trees." Her ghost continues to pervade the region, riding on stormy nights a beast of darkness whose hoofs make no noise, but only leave streaks of blood along the ground. The very names of the places call up sinister images, and the only hamlet in all this desert—such a pitiful one!—is named *Laz*, which means murder.

A local proverb offers the following advice to travellers in the mountains:

"When you leave Briec cross yourself. When you turn off toward Laz invoke your guardian angel." For if brigands are no longer to be feared one is still exposed to the ill-offices of those spirits inimical to man, who hold undisputed sway over these inviolate altitudes. The popular memory is inexhaustible, as regards the nasty tricks which have been played by the uncanny folk upon inoffensive wayfarers. They shut you up in enchanted rings. They unroll before you magic footpaths, where you may go on and on forever—walking as it were, in our sleep and never waking.

It is evident therefore that, in spite of its apparent loneliness, the Ménez is only too densely inhabited. And I have not said a word about the genuine ghosts, who are as thick there as heather and rushes. It is, in fact, a sort of terrestrial annex to purgatory, a place of probation and penitence for disembodied souls. The rather monumental aspect of the crests of black schist which bristle along the hilltops, may have had its part, I fancy, in inducing this belief. The eye is caught on every side, by rocky ridges, and pyramidal piles of stones, which remind one strongly of the burial-places of barbaric times. Here and there, as far as the eye can reach, huge mysterious cairns may be discerned set in rows along the horizon, and the whole country does in face present the aspect of an immense pre-historic cemetery.

Communication with Spézet is rare and not easy. On the advice of my friend the rag-man whose name is Ronan Le Braz, I had availed myself of a carrier's wagon which had gone down the night before, to the market at Quimper, and was returning to the mountains laden with all sorts of merchandise. I had perched myself upon the top of this miscellaneous mass, and my position if not precisely comfortable was a good one for observation. My conductress, for the carrier was a woman, sat on one of the shafts, with her legs hanging, and exchanged a few words from time to time, now with the sorry nag who composed her entire team, and now with myself. She was a great wild-looking creature, almost a giantess. On her head, which was too small for her body, she wore a little flat cap, and her rough speech was decidedly masculine. . . .

All at once in obedience to some mysterious impulse, the woman began to hum disconnected fragments of some rustic lament. Her voice, muffled at first, rose, little by little, to a powerful and piercing pitch; and I shall never forget the strange impression I received as I heard soaring into the twilight and re-echoed from afar, across the vast sepulchral country—that strong, hoarse monody—that wild incantation fraught with a sort of tragic grandeur. The stony shapes of the Ménez seemed bending their ears to listen, and shudderings of awe and mystery passed over the landscape below. A solitary voice at night always makes the general silence more impressive.

"Are you afraid, that you sing so loud?" I asked the woman.

"Afraid? No. These places know me well enough! But haven't you heard lit-tle rustling noises, when there was nobody in sight? It's the saying among us that, on the eve of their anniversary, the dead are hurrying along all the roads, to the places where they used to live. And you, know, of course, that they don't like to meet living people. So I sing, just to let them know that I am here."

Night had now fallen, and the woman lighted a tin lamp, or lantern with a conical top, and fastened it to one of the steps of the cart. It added not a lit-tle to the weirdness of our progress to see the shadow of the horse assuming by that fitful light, the proportions of a beast of the Apocalypse. All at once, from somewhere on our right a church-bell began ringing, with a tinkling, timorous tone. We had arrived at Spézet. . . .

I inquired my way to the inn of Ronan Le Braz, but he had heard the noise of the cart, and was on the watch for me, standing on the threshold of his cot-tage and holding a lighted candle.

"Here you are at last, cousin!" he exclaimed with an air of mischievous good-fellowship, peculiar to himself; and drew me toward the fireplace where the evening meal was cooking over a fire of blazing furze, while his wife kept up the conflagration by incessantly pushing in more of the thorny branches with a small iron fork. He proceeded formally to introduce us:—

"Gäida, this is the gentleman I told you about: the one who makes people tell him the country legends; and then he repeats them to the folks in France."

"Good," said Gäida, lifting up a beaming face, "You have come at the right minute for we have old Nann here to-night. She has not lived in the parish for thirty years, but all her dead are buried here, and she is back, just now of course, on their account. She is at vespers at this moment, but—"

"By the way," said Ronan, "wouldn't you like to go yourself to the 'black vespers?'"

"By all means!" and we started forthwith for the church, which we could see dimly lighted, and looming in the midst of the burying-ground on the other side of the square. A flight of broken stone steps led to the porch, and I was struck the instant I entered, by that humid chill which pervades all the old Armorican sanctuaries, with their walls bespotted with saltpetre and stained with green moss, they look as though they might be submarine chapels, long drowned, and only just brought to light. In the middle of the nave stood the catafalque, or, as they call it in Brittany the *funeral-stool,* bear-ing upon one side a translation into the local dialect of the Latin motto *Hodie mihi cras tibi* [Today for me, tomorrow for you]. It was surrounded by women, crouching rather than kneeling, while the men gathered in the side-aisles, barely distinguishable by the dim light of the tallow candles fastened at intervals to the pillars. When the priest had pronounced the absolution the men and women began to intone together a Brêton canticle of infinite sadness, breathing a pessimism at once unaffected and poignant. It was all about the brevity of human existence, its rare joys and manifold woes; how small a thing it is to live; how happy to die. It praised the dead for having done with all this, and paid their debt to destiny.

To this chant succeeded the prayer of the whole congregation, after which they dispersed, to prostrate themselves in the cemetery on the graves of their own people. Poor miserable monuments they were, in most cases a mere slab of slate-stone rudely squared but invariably furnished with the little stone cup for holy-water, where friends and kindred piously dip their fingers every Sunday when they come out from mass.

"And now," whispered Ronan, "we'll go to the charnel-house."

A large part of the crowd had already preceded us. Through the door, which was opened for the occasion, and beyond the iron bars of the unglazed window-spaces the eye discerned a confused heap of decaying skulls, and white, phosphorescent bones. Two of the skulls were set up on the window-ledge, and seemed to regard the intruders fixedly out of their vacant eyes. We knelt down in the grass, like the others, while an aged crone, almost as colorless under her hooded mourning-cloak as the human débris which encumbered the ossuary, recited aloud in a broken voice one of the most thrilling hymns of the Brêton liturgy, the charnel-house hymn.

"Come Christians and look upon all that is left of our fathers and mothers, our brothers and sisters, our neighbors and our dearest friends. How pitiful the state to which they have fallen!"

"They are in fragments, they are in morsels; of some there is naught left but dust. This is what death and burial have brought them to. They are alike one to another. They are like themselves no more."

It is Villon's ballad minus the irony, and with a deeply religious accent. After each strophe the old woman paused, and there arose from the people present a confused murmur of: "God pardon the *Anaon*," that is the *departed souls*. Most of the women were telling their beads with one hand, while they held, with the other, on a level with their faces, tiny wax tapers which lit up the fog in that corner of the cemetery, with a pensive illumination, like that of misty moonshine.

"The woman who led the prayer," said Ronan in my ear, "was Nann—Nann Coadélez; the one who knows so many stories and is lodging with us to-night.". . .

I found her at the inn sitting in the chimney-corner, in one of the high-backed oaken chairs carved with barbaric hieroglyphics, which are peculiar to the country. The firelight threw into high relief her stern, sibylline features. She had flung aside her mourning-cloak, but her head was still muffled in a black woollen hood, the flaps of which fluttered over her shoulders with every breath of wind let in by the opening door, like the wings of some ill-omened crow, just poised for flight. With her hooked nose and burning eyes, her dry and sunken mouth and the bitter curve of her lips, she had an almost Dantesque expression, nor did it surprise me in the least when our hostess said to her, quite simply, and without a touch of mockery:—

"It's true, old Nanna, is it not? that you went once to purgatory, and that there has been a burning smell about you ever since?"

"Pray God," replied the crone haughtily, "that you may one day be admitted there yourself, in spite of your sins!" and drawing from the pocket of her apron a small clay pipe, she packed it slowly and then began smoking with short, regular puffs.

The inn now filled with people, mostly men with rude, clean-shaven faces, and frank, child-like eyes. They drew up in a line before the desk as they came in, or stood in scattered groups around the vast room with folded arms, and speaking little to one another. Presently Ronan said: "You are served," and then they all stretched out their hands, each took the glass which was offered him, drained it at a draught and handed it back, after letting the last few drops of liquor fall upon the ground, with all the solemnity of ancient priests performing a libation. . . .

The door had opened to admit the entrance of a singular personage with a long body which looked as though it had been broken in two, and swinging arms terminating in immense hands, which almost dragged upon the ground. He greeted us all round in a small, soft, quavering voice; all heads were turned at once, and there fell upon the features a sudden silence. They drew back with a sort of timorous respect, in order to permit the newcomer to approach the desk.

"Is it you, Michael Quizan?" asked the inn-keeper, smiling rather constrainedly, "You are not dead yet then, in spite of the rumor?"

I got up and came nearer.

"It's a queer fish," said one of the peasants to me, in confidence. "He has been for forty years the regular grave-digger of the parish. But he had an accident awhile ago which affected his mind a little, and he has not worked since then. He is always roaming about the hills and valleys, telling absurd tales wherever he goes. Men shun him like sin, but they always treat him with a certain deference, on account of his great age and his infirmity. And then, you know, there are some folks here, who think that mad people are in constant communication with the other world."

The strange old man, however, instead of answering Ronan le Braz' inquiry, scanned the countenances about him with a searching gaze.

"Whom are you looking for?" demanded Ronan.

"Nobody," the old man this time condescended to articulate. "You mind your business, and I'll mind mine."

His inspection concluded he began to count upon his fingers, *mezza voce:* "One, two, three, four. Yes, that's it! Four."

He lifted his head, which had drooped while he made his mysterious calculation, and said, in the tone of a judge pronouncing sentence: "There are four living men here who will be four dead men before the end of a month. Two of them are over fifty, and the other two between twenty-six and thirty. If you wish me to name them, I will."

"Thank you, Michael," the inn-keeper made haste to reply. "We don't in the least doubt your knowledge of hidden things, but we much prefer that you should keep it to yourself."

"Just as you please!" murmured the insane man; and he made his way back to the door, bent nearly double, and sweeping the floor with his big hands.

"There's an old sorcerer for you!" said Ronan, when the steps of the ex-grave-digger had died away in the distance.

He laughed but without conviction. The others remained silent and disturbed. The old man's words had sent a strong chill through the assembly. The atmosphere of the big room seemed charged with an odor from the grave, and every brow was visibly darkened by the same anxious thought, "What if I were one of the *four.*" The inn-keeper proposed a dram. "Let us drink to the memory of our dead," said he. Then, turning to me, "Michael Quizan," he explained, "is considered rather a bird of ill omen among us here. He is sometimes called the *death-bird.* He lives in the mountains all the year, like a wolf. They say he spends days and nights talking with the *Souls,* who are working out their expiation up there among the brakes and underbrush. The *Ankou* [Death] treats him like a comrade; chats with him quite familiarly as they travel along, and tells him all his secrets. Belated shepherds have often surprised them colloguing together." "That is quite true," put in a mountaineer. "Only last week the little shepherd at Cäerléon came rushing down to the farm, all out of breath, blood on his feet, face whiter than a shroud. 'Good Heavens, what's the matter?' cried out old Lena in a panic. 'The matter is,' said the shepherd-boy, 'that I heard the *Ankou* telling Michael Quizan that he'd have a harvest to-night down here in Cäerléon.' And sure enough, we buried the lord of the manor the next day. It was Jean Rozvilien, and his men found him dead at the end of a furrow he had just been tracing, with his hands still on the plow-handle." The peasants bowed in sign of assent and Ronan resumed his narrative: "As many as fifteen or twenty times a year, you'll hear it said that old Michael, the grave-digger, has given up the ghost at last. Sometimes he's been eaten alive by foxes and badgers; sometimes he has fractured his skull by falling off a precipice. Not a bit of it! Sure as ever All-Souls' eve comes round, the uncanny old chap turns up again. Public report has killed him so many times that one doesn't feel quite sure whether he comes from the mountains or the tomb, whether he's alive, or one of the dead himself! Well, my dear gentleman, you've seen him for yourself! Now he will go the round of the village and tell the same string of lies, or nearly the same, in every house." "Are you quite sure," asked some one, "that they are lies?"

"Oh well, call them what you like," answered Ronan; then added in a graver tone, "After all, we are never sure of anything in this world of mystery! The cleverest of us have to feel our way."

Just then the ranks of the revellers opened and Gäida came forward, slim and brown, and bearing in her outstretched hands a huge bowl of lard soup, the steam of which enveloped her like a white cloud. . . .

After setting out upon the table the items of a frugal but appetizing meal, the hostess was about leaving me to the society of the works of arts upon the walls, when a sudden recollection caused her to return briskly. "By the way," she began, "did you notice how sullen old Nann was when I alluded to her trip into the other world? Perhaps you thought I had been jesting, but if you will please to remember, she did not dare contradict me. The circumstances are perfectly well known all about here. Just as true as I am an honest woman Nanna Coadélez went alive into Purgatory and came back again!"

"Did she tell of it herself?"

"Oh no! She never denies it, however, but she looks vexed when it is mentioned, and cuts the conversation short, just as she did to-night. Very likely nothing would ever have been known of her adventure, but for that dreadful creature Michael."

"What, Michael the madman?"

"Yes, or Michael the seer, just as you please! At all events, the story is this. It was about thirty-six years ago. Nanna was just rising forty years old. I did not know her then, because I wasn't born, but the people of her age will tell you that there wasn't her equal in all Cornouailles, for a handsome face and a keen wit. She and her husband were cultivating the estate of Kerzonn, which gets both the morning and the afternoon sun, and goes all the way from St. Bridget's Chapel to the river Aulme. You never knew a happier or more united household, but, ah, me! They say the *Ankou* always likes best to stop at the merriest thresholds. *The man with the scythe* went to Kerzonn without an invitation and Nanna Coadélez put on widow's weeds. She could not be resigned to the blow which had fallen on her. Day and night she sat by the hearthstone obstinately refusing all nourishment. Her tears were her meat.

"Well, one afternoon Michael Quizan who was already grave-digger at that time, came and sat down beside her, and he said:—

"'Poor, dear Nanna! Don't you know that the country of the dead is just like this of ours which is farmed by the living? Just as too much rain-fall spoils our crops, if you shed too many tears over the dead, it is bad for their eternal salvation. You may believe what I say, Nanna Coadélez! Men of my trade have a special sense. There is a secret voice which tells them what is going on in the hollows they have scooped out. Every night of my life I can hear your husband's body turning and re-turning in his coffin, as if he were very weary indeed and couldn't sleep for the insects. Now that's a sign that his soul isn't happy in Purgatory, and I think it is because of the wildness of your grief.'

"When he said this, it seems that Nann screamed out, 'Not happy, did you say? Not happy? Well, if it costs me my life, and more, I'll know, Michael Quizan, whether you've spoken the truth!'

"The next day, she made off, unbeknown to any of her people. Where did she go? Nobody knows. She was away almost a year, and one of her brothers was put in to manage matters at the farm. Finally, near Christmas-time she reappeared, but, poor dear, in what a state, and how changed from what she had been! Her very brother hardly knew her. Her fresh complexion was all dried up, her hair was a white as snow, and her eyes which used to be so pleasant, had a sort of sullen fire in them. More than all this, there was a strange smell about her. *A smell like roasted flesh.* They tried to make her talk, but all she would say was, 'Mind your business.' Of course, the tongues wagged all the same, and the most contradictory stories got about. But when Michael Quizan heard that Nann had come back, he went, one day, to Kerzonn and he found her milking the cows. 'Ah ha!' says he, 'I'm glad to see that you have got back to work again. And how about your journey, Nanna? Was it successful? Did you get good news of your husband, Pêr Coadélez?' 'You,' she said, without lifting her eyes, 'be pleased to go your ways!' But he persisted, and then, all at once, she sprang up and shrieked out,—

"'Off with you, you churchyard polecat! Out of my sight this instant, or I'll have you torn in pieces by the watch-dog!' And she lightened at him with her angry eyes.

"But all he said was, 'Now I know what it is you've been hiding from us all! Your eyes are flame-color. They have seen the *place of fire!*'

"From that time on, the mistress of Kerzonn was just an object of awe and curiosity in the parish. Not only was it considered certain that she had visited Purgatory but they used to give all the particulars of the means she employed to compass her end, and all the obstacles she encountered on the dark ways she had to travel. There couldn't be so much talk, of course, without its coming to Nann's ear; all the farm-servants were gossiping about it. For a long time she pretended not to hear, as also not to see that at church on Sundays, her neighbors pulled their chairs away from her's *[sic]* superstitiously, and that the children in the street pointed at her and said: 'that's the woman who has been in the land of the Souls.' But it troubled her all the same, and the proof is, that she got rid of her fine place at Kerzonn at the first opportunity and rented, at the halves, a miserable little holding, down Lannédern way, some six leagues from here.

"Well, that is all. Do you think, or don't you? that it is Nanna Coadélez' true story? They don't say so much about it now, but when I was a young girl, she used still to go out watching; and, for my part, I always think of it at this season, when the tall, dry figure of old Nann rises up in the doorway and she asks for a lodging. If you could only take the padlock off the lips of that woman, who might learn a good deal about those who are gone."

Gäida paused dreamily, letting her long, brown eyelashes sweep her rosy cheeks, and still clasping the chair back with her hands, as she had done during our entire interview.

"What did the old woman say last night?" I asked her, "when Michael Quizan came in?"

"Nothing, sire. They always pretend not to know one another, those two, but that's another story, more mysterious than the first. The tale goes that when Nanna crossed the bounds of this parish, she invoked her ancestors, and called for vengeance on the grave-digger, and cursed him in his limbs and his faculties. And so, not long after, Michael was found one morning in his bed, quite motionless, with his back broken, and his eyes wild, and his reason gone. The dead of Kerzonn had come down the graveyard steps, to accomplish Nann's malediction."

Red Hanrahan (1914; 1st pub. 1904)

W. B. Yeats

Hanrahan, the hedge schoolmaster, a tall, strong, red-haired young man, came into the barn where some of the men of the village were sitting on Samhain Eve. It had been a dwelling-house, and when the man that owned it had built a better one, he had put the two rooms together, and kept it for a place to store one thing or another. There was a fire on the old hearth, and there were dip candles stuck in bottles, and there was a black quart bottle upon some boards that had been put across two barrels to make a table. Most of the men were sitting beside the fire, and one of them was singing a long wandering song, about a Munster man and a Connaught man that were quarelling about their two provinces.

Hanrahan went to the man of the house and said that, "I got your message"; but when he had said that, he stopped, for an old mountainy man that had a shirt and trousers of unbleached flannel, and that was sitting by himself near the door, was looking at him, and moving an old pack of cards about in his hands and muttering. "Don't mind him," said the man of the house; "he is only some stranger came in awhile ago, and we bade him welcome, it being Samhain night, but I think he is not in his right wits. Listen to him now and you will hear what he is saying."

They listened then, and they could hear the old man muttering to himself as he turned the cards, "Spades and Diamonds, Courage and Power; Clubs and Hearts, Knowledge and Pleasure."

"That is the kind of talk he has been going on with for the last hour," said the man of the house, and Hanrahan turned his eyes from the old man as if he did not like to be looking at him.

"I got your message," Hanrahan said then; "'He is in the barn with his three first cousins from Gilchreist,' the messenger said, 'and there are some of the neighbours with them.'"

"It is my cousin over there is wanting to see you," said the man of the house, and he called over a young frieze-coated man, who was listening to the song, and said, "This is Red Hanrahan you have the message for."

"It is a kind message, indeed," said the young man, "for it comes from your sweetheart, Mary Lavelle."

"How would you get a message from her, and what do you know of her?"

"I don't know her, indeed, but I was in Loughrea yesterday, and a neighbour of hers that had some dealings with me was saying that she bade him send you word, if he met any one from this side in the market, that her mother has died from her, and if you have a mind yet to join with herself, she is willing to keep her word to you."

"I will go to her indeed," said Hanrahan.

"And she bade you make no delay, for if she has not a man in the house before the month is out, it is likely the little bit of land will be given to another."

When Hanrahan heard that, he rose up from the bench he had sat down on. "I will make no delay indeed," he said; "there is a full moon, and if I get as far as Gilchreist to-night, I will reach to her before the setting of the sun to-morrow."

When the others heard that, they began to laugh at him for being in such haste to go to his sweetheart, and one asked him if he would leave his school in the old limekiln, where he was giving the children such good learning. But he said the children would be glad enough in the morning to find the place empty, and no one to keep them at their task; and as for his school he could set it up again in any place, having as he had his little inkpot hanging from his neck by a chain, and his big Virgil and his primer in the skirt of his coat.

Some of them asked him to drink a glass before he went, and a young man caught hold of his coat, and said he must not leave them without singing the song he had made in praise of Venus and of Mary Lavelle. He drank a glass of whisky, but he said he would not stop but would set out on his journey.

"There's time enough, Red Hanrahan," said the man of the house. "It will be time enough for you to give up sport when you are after your marriage, and it might be a long time before we will see you again."

I will not stop," said Hanrahan; "my mind would be on the roads all the time, bringing me to the woman that sent for me, and she lonesome and watching till I come."

Some of the others came about him, pressing him that had been such a pleasant comrade, so full of songs and every kind of trick and fun, not to leave them till the night would be over, but he refused them all, and shook them off, and went to the door. But as he put his foot over the threshold, the strange old man stood up and put his hand that was thin and withered like a bird's claw on Hanrahan's hand, and said: "It is not Hanrahan, the learned man and the great songmaker, that should go out from a gathering like this, on a Samhain night. And stop here, now," he said, "and play a hand with me; and here is an old pack of cards has done its work many a night before this, and old as it is, there has been much of the riches of the world lost and won over it."

One of the young men said, "It isn't much of the riches of the world has stopped with yourself, old man," and he looked at the old man's bare feet, and they all laughed. But Hanrahan did not laugh, but he sat down very quietly, without a word. Then one of them said, "So you will stop with us after all,

Hanrahan"; and the old man said: "He will stop indeed, did you not hear me asking him?"

They all looked at the old man then as if wondering where he came from. "It is far I am come," he said, "through France I have come, and through Spain, and by Lough Greine of the hidden mouth and none has refused me anything." And then he was silent and nobody liked to question him, and they began to play. There were six men at the boards playing, and the others were looking on behind. They played two or three games for nothing, and then the old man took a fourpenny bit, worn very thin and smooth, out from his pocket, and he called to the rest to put something on the game. Then they all put down something on the boards, and little as it was it looked much, from the way it was shoved from one to another, first one man winning it and then his neighbour. And sometimes the luck would go against a man and he would have nothing left, and then one or another would lend him something, and he would pay it again out of his winnings, for neither good nor bad luck stopped long with any one.

And once Hanrahan said as a man would say in a dream, "It is time for me to be going the road"; but just then a good card came to him, and he played it out, and all the money began to come to him. And once he thought of Mary Lavelle, and he sighed; and that time his luck went from him, and he forgot her again.

But at last the luck went to the old man and it stayed with him, and they had flowed into him, and he began to laugh little laughs to himself, and to sing over and over to himself, "Spades and Diamonds, Courage and Power," and so on, as if it was a verse of a song.

And after a while any one looking at the men, and seeing the way their bodies were rocking to and fro, and the way they kept their eyes on the old man's hands, would think they had drink taken, or that the whole store they had in the world was put on the cards; but that was not so, for the quart bottle had not been disturbed since the game began, and was nearly full yet, and all that was on the game was a few sixpenny bits and shillings, and maybe a handful of coppers.

"You are good men to win and good men to lose," said the old man, "you have play in your hearts." He began then to shuffle the cards and to mix them, very quick and fast, till at last they could not see them to be cards at all, but you would think him to be making rings of fire in the air, as little lads would make them with whirling a lighted stick; and after that it seemed to them that all the room was dark, and they could see nothing but his hands and the cards.

And all in a minute a hare made a leap out from between his hands, and whether it was one of the cards that took that shape, or whether it was made out of nothing in the palms of his hands, nobody knew, but there it was running on the floor of the barn, as quick as any hare that ever lived.

Some looked at the hare, but more kept their eyes on the old man, and while they were looking at him a hound made a leap out between his hands, the same way as the hare did, and after that another hound and another, till there was a whole pack of them following the hare round and round the barn.

The players were all standing up now, with their backs to the boards, shrinking from the hounds, and nearly deafened with the noise of their yelping, but as quick as the hounds were they could not overtake the hare, but it went round, till at the last it seemed as if a blast of wind burst open the barn door, and the hare doubled and made a leap over the boards where the men had been playing, and out of the door and away through the night, and the hounds over the boards and through the door after it.

Then the old man called out, "Follow the hounds, follow the hounds, and it is a great hunt you will see to-night," and he went out after them. But used as the men were to go hunting after hares, and ready as they were for any sport, they were in dread to go out into the night, and it was only Hanrahan that rose up and that said, "I will follow. I will follow on."

"You had best stop here, Hanrahan," the young man that was nearest him said, "for you might be going into some great danger." But Hanrahan said, "I will see fair play, I will see fair play," and went stumbling out of the door like a man in a dream, and the door shut after him as he went.

He thought he saw the old man in front of him, but it was only his own shadow that the full moon cast on the road before him, but he could hear the hounds crying after the hare over the wide green fields of Granagh, and he followed them very fast for there was nothing to stop him; and after a while he came to smaller fields that had little walls of loose stones around them, and he threw the stones down as he crossed them, and did not wait to put them up again; and he passed by the place where the river goes underground at Ballylee, and he could hear the hounds going before him up towards the head of the river. Soon he found it harder to run, for it was uphill he was going, and clouds came over the moon, and it was hard for him to see his way, and once he left the path to take a short cut, but his foot slipped into a bog-hole and he had to come back to it. And how long he was going he did not know, or what way he went, but at last he was up on the bare mountain, with nothing but the rough heather about him, and he could neither hear the hounds nor any other thing. But their cry began to come to him again, at first far off and then very near, and when it came quite close to him, it went up all of a sudden into the air, and there was the sound of hunting over his head; then it went away northward till he could hear nothing at all. "That's not fair," he said, "that's not fair." And he could walk no longer, but sat down on the heather where he was, in the heart of Slieve Echtge, for all the strength had gone from him, with the dint of the long journey he had made.

And after a while he took notice that there was a door close to him, and a light coming from it, and he wondered that being so close to him he had not seen it before. And he rose up, and tired as he was he went in at the door, and although it was night time outside, it was daylight he found within. And presently he met with an old man that had been gathering summer thyme and yellow flag-flowers, and it seemed as if all the sweet smells of the summer were with them. And the old man said: "It is a long time you have been coming to us, Hanrahan the learned man and the great songmaker."

And with that he brought him into a very big shining house, and every grand thing Hanrahan had ever heard of, and every colour he had ever seen, were in it. There was a high place at the end of the house, and on it there was sitting in a high chair a woman, the most beautiful the world ever saw, having a long pale face and flowers about it, but she had the tired look of one that had been long waiting. And there were sitting on the step below her chair four grey old women, and the one of them was holding a great cauldron in her lap; and another a great stone on her knees, and heavy as it was it seemed light to her; and another of them had a very long spear that was made of pointed wood; and the last of them had a sword that was without a scabbard.

Hanrahan stood looking at them for a long time, but none of them spoke any word to him or looked at him at all. And he had it in his mind to ask who that woman in the chair was, that was like a queen, and what she was waiting for; but ready as he was with his tongue and afraid of no person, he was in dread now to speak to so beautiful a woman, and in so grand a place. And then he thought to ask what were the four things the four grey old women were holding like great treasures, but he could not think of the right words to bring out.

Then the first of the old women rose up, holding the cauldron between her two hands, and she said "Pleasure," and Hanrahan said no word. Then the second old woman rose up with the stone in her hands, and she said "Power"; and the third old woman rose up with a spear in her hand, and she said "Courage"; and the last of the old women rose up having the sword in her hands, and she said "Knowledge." And every one, after she had spoken, waited as if for Hanrahan to question her, but he said nothing at all. And then the four old women went out of the door, bringing their four treasures with them, and as they went out one of them said, "He has no wish for us"; and another said, "He is weak, he is weak"; and another said, "He is afraid"; and the last said, "His wits are gone from him." And then they all said, "Echtge, daughter of the Silver Hand, must stay in her sleep. It is a pity, it is a great pity."

And then the woman that was like a queen gave a very sad sigh, and it seemed to Hanrahan as if the sigh had the sound in it of hidden streams; and if the place he was in had been ten times grander and more shining than it was, he could not have hindered sleep from coming on him; and he staggered like a drunken man and lay down there and then.

When Hanrahan awoke, the sun was shining on his face, but there was white frost on the grass around him, and there was ice on the edge of the stream he was lying by, and that goes running on through Daire-caol and Druim-da-rod. He knew by the shape of the hills and by the shining of Lough Greine in the distance that he was upon me of the hills of Slieve Echtge, but he was not sure how he came there; for all that had happened in the barn had gone from him, and all of his journey but the soreness of his feet and the stiffness in his bones. . . .

It was a year after that, there were men of the village of Cappaghtagle sitting by the fire in a house on the roadside, and Red Hanrahan that was now very thin and worn and his hair very long and wild, came to the half-door and asked leave to come in and rest himself; and they bid him welcome because it was Samhain night. He sat down with them, and they gave him a glass of whisky out of a quart bottle; and they saw the little inkpot hanging about his neck, and knew he was a scholar, and asked for stories about the Greeks.

He took the Virgil out of the big pocket of his coat, but the cover was very black and swollen with the wet, and the page when he opened it was very yellow, but that was no great matter, for he looked at it like a man that had never learned to read. Some young man that was there began to laugh at him then, and to ask why did he carry so heavy a book with him when he was not able to read it.

It vexed Hanrahan to hear that, and he put the Virgil back in his pocket and asked if they had a pack of cards among them, for cards were better than books. When they brought out the cards he took them and began to shuffle them, and while he was shuffling them something seemed to come into his mind, and he put his hand to his face like one that is trying to remember, and he said: "Was I ever here before, or where was I on a night like this?" and then of a sudden he stood up and let the cards fall to the floor, and he said, "Who was it brought me a message from Mary Lavelle?"

"We never saw you before now, and we never heard of Mary Lavelle," said the man of the house. "And who is she," he said, "and what is it you are talking about?"

"It was this night a year ago, I was in a barn, and there were men playing cards, and there was money on the table, they were pushing it from one to another here and there—and I got a message, and I was going out of the door to look for my sweetheart that wanted me, Mary Lavelle." And then

Hanrahan called out very loud: "Where have I been since then? Where was I for the whole year?"

"It is hard to say where you might have been in that time," said the oldest of the men, "or what part of the world you may have travelled; and it is like enough you have the dust of many roads on your feet; for there are many go wandering and forgetting like that," he said, "when once they have been given the touch."

"That is true," said another of the men. "I knew a woman went wandering like that through the length of seven years; she came back after, and she told her friends she had often been glad enough to eat the food that was put in the pig's trough. And it is best for you to go to the priest now," he said, "and let him take off you whatever may have been put upon you."

"It is to my sweetheart I will go, to Mary Lavelle," said Hanrahan; "it is too long I have delayed, how do I know what might have happened to her in the length of a year?"

He was going out of the door then, but they all told him it was best for him to stop the night, and get strength for the journey; and indeed he wanted that, for he was very weak, and when they gave him food he ate it like a man that had never seen food before, and one of them said, "He is eating as if he had trodden on the hungry grass." It was in the white light of the morning he set out, and the time seemed long to him till he could get to Mary Lavelle's house. But when he came to it, he found the door broken, and the thatch dropping from the roof, and no living person to be seen. And when he asked the neighbours what had happened her, all they could say was that she had been put out of the house, and had married some labouring man, and they had gone looking for work to London or Liverpool or some big place. And whether she found a worse place or a better he never knew, but anyway he never met with her or with news of her again.

The Feast of Samhain (1924)

James Stephens
[Excerpt]

Chapter I.

It was decided that the evening meal should be eaten on the lawn before the palace. A tent had been set under a tree and a fire was built in front of it. Torches were tied to the branches of the tree, and others were fixed to stakes driven into the ground; so there was plenty of light; and in the ring cast by these flares there was great animation.

But beyond this circle, where the smoke went drifting in grey billows, night was already brooding, and minute by minute the darkness became deep and deeper.

No stars were visible. There was no sky to be seen. There was nothing for the eye to rest on. And if a man had placed his hand before his face he would not have been able to see his hand.

Little by little the last loitering couples were driven from dusk vistas to the centre of the lawn; and little by little the merry talk became grave, and the loud voices were hushed. Soon there was no one moving outside the circle of light except servants who had to draw water from the well, or perform other outdoor duties.

Even these did not move abroad, for this was the month of Samhain, and the one night of the year in which whoever has the will and the courage may go to Faery.

The servants even did not stir without. They had accumulated all the water which could possibly be used that night. The storehouses, the piggeries, the sheep-cotes and hen-roosts had been closed for the night; and around each of these, and all around Cruachan Ai, and all about every hamlet in Ireland, incantations had been uttered, and magical circles drawn against the Masters of Magic.

While waiting for the meats to he brought, Ailill lay in the opening of the tent staring beyond the fire at that great blackness. Maeve was at the back of the tent sharing nuts that had been stewed in honey between three royally clamorous children, and exchanging apples with Fergus mac Roy, and glances also which were meant for no other eye than his. Other people also were stretched about the tent, chattering aimlessly and all impatient for their supper.

"The meal will be ready soon," said Maeve. "It is late because of the games, but it will be ready very soon now."

Or she would detail his future to an impatient champion:

"There is roast meat and boiled, my dear. There is fish stewed in milk, and birds boiled with spices. There are puddings of minced flesh and sweet bread. There is white thin milk, and thick yellow milk. There are many different kinds of broth. There is wine from far countries, and mead, my love, made by myself from the honey gathered by my own bees in the flowers that grow about Cruachan. And after that there is ale, and red-cheeked apples.

"It will be ready very soon, my darlings."

Chapter II.

"I wonder would any man dare go abroad to-night, said Ailill, as he stared against the darkness. "I seem to hear already the brisk tread of the people of Dana moving out there beyond the light."

"I hear something," a companion averred.

"You hear the wind stirring in lazy branches," said a third.

"Was *that* the wind?"

"It was a ferret."

"Was it so?" Ailill queried. "If you will go to the hill where the outlaws were hanged yesterday, and if you will tie a withy round the foot of one of the hanging men, I will give you a present."

"I'll do that."

But in two minutes the man returned, saying that he heard things moving and did not care to go farther.

"I thought you would come back, my pulse," said Ailill.

Two others ventured, and returned terrified.

"The night is dark, and there are demons about," said Maeve, "no man would go out on the eve of Samhain, even for a prize."

Then Nera stepped forward.

"What prize are you offering, Majesty?"

"This gold-hilted sword," the King replied, looking at him mockingly.

"I will go," said Nera.

"Go, with my love," said the King, "but," as Nera stepped from the tent, "I shall expect you back in a minute, dear heart."

"I will come for my prize," said Nera.

He walked through the flare of the torches, and the company watched him go.

He came to the end of the lawn where the light began to fail, and, as he walked, he looked closely at what light was left.

Here the light was golden, and here it became grey, and here, a step farther, it became blue or purple, and here, but two paces beyond, it was no longer a colour; it was a blackness, an invisibility.

It would be wrong to say that the young man was not afraid. Given the night and the deed that he had undertaken, any man might have shown the fear which he kept hidden. But his will was set, and he knew that, even if he could not go on, he would not turn back; so he bent his mind inflexibly on the hill before him, and on the swinging figures which he had to meet.

The man whose mind is thus set is conscious of himself to that extent, but in other and curious ways he has ceased to be quite his own master, for while the mind is concentrated and engaged on one sole matter we are blind and deaf to all others, and we may be interfered with beyond our knowledge.

Nera turned to look over his shoulder, and, when he saw the tent, now curiously distant and precise, and the figures that moved unhurriedly about it, it was as though he were peeping into or at another world.

Then he set out with long, strong paces in the direction of the hill. But he kept his sword in his hand and his buckler on his arm.

Chapter III.

He knew his way to the hill. Indeed, he had been there on the previous day when these malefactors were swung, and he remembered that they had been a troublesome couple.

One of them had said:

"It is not often that notable miscreants are ended, and everybody has a right to look on wonders. There are not enough women present," he complained.

The other outlaw contented himself with a criticism of all that was done for him, and of the looks and qualities of his guard. When the rope had been fixed on his neck he yawned so widely that it was disarranged, and had to be settled again.

"Keep your yawns to yourself," said the captain of the guard, "and please to let my men do their duty."

"I'm sleepy," the outlaw objected.

"Even if you are," said the captain of the guard, "you need not hinder my men."

"One must be polite in company," said the outlaw, "so I'll do my best not to yawn until you have finished with me."

He did his best.

The other rogue remarked that he had become thirsty standing all that time.

"There is nothing here to drink," the captain returned.

"It doesn't matter," the rogue answered. "It just struck me, and I mentioned it."

Nera remembered these men, and he remembered in especial the face of the thirsty man—a long, hatchet-face, with a great nose on it, and a close-curling beard on the chin. He had seemed to be thinking deeply and discontentedly at the last moment, and had obviously dismissed what was happening about him for more private imaginings.

As he walked the face of this man appeared before him with such suddenness that he almost drove at it with his sword; but, recognising at the same instant that it was merely his imagination at play, he banished the phantom and went on.

Although he knew the way so well it was nevertheless not easy to keep to it in that darkness, and he paused a few times to reconstruct the path he had already come, and to calculate from it the direction in which he should continue.

He had not far to go.

Barely five minutes' march lay between the lawn of Royal Cruachan and the place towards which he was bent, and, given only a general direction, he could not miss the hill.

He passed through a bushy place which swished and crackled about his ears; came out on turf that sank and rose with its clear elastic noise; and then he came on the rising ground which told that the hill had begun.

He held the sword thrust in front of him as he trod upwards, not to ward off goblins, but so that he might feel if a tree was in his path or a boulder.

There were not many trees to he sure, but there were huge outcropping rocks carved to every kind of edge and knob and projection that one could think of, and if a man stumbled against one of these his skull could be broken, or his shin bone might get a crack that would leave him hopping for a month.

Chapter IV.

He came to the top of the hill, and found that, careful as he had been, he had yet moved somewhat from the direct path, and was some score of yards east of the point he aimed for.

Up here it was not so dark as it had been among the trees and boulders below. Or perhaps the fact that he was on an eminence tended to make him look upwards and catch such rays of light as there might be.

While walking below he had kept his eyes to the ground, following, although not seeing, his feet; and adding, thus, to the darkness that descended from the atmosphere the deeper blackness which arose from the ground. Or it might be that his eyes had become more accustomed to darkness, and, although he could not exactly see, he could, as it were, surmise; for he began to distinguish between the various darknesses that lay about him, and was aware of gradations among these dusks.

Here there was the black of ebony—it was a boulder.

Here was a sketchy incomplete blackness—it was a bush.

Beyond was not a blackness but a darkness, and that was space.

Beneath him there was a velvet gloom, and that was the ground.

And above there was a darkness, not to be described, but to be thought of, as a movement, and that was the sky.

He moved to the right searching for the one tree which grew on the hill, and, after a cautious exploration, he found it, and stood listening to the slow creakings which told that this was indeed his tree.

As he moved forward a foot tapped him gently on the mouth, and he leaped back with his sword uplifted, staring blindly, and listening with all his blood.

Then he smiled to himself, rattled the sword into its scabbard, and, putting his hand resolutely forward, he laid hold of that foot.

Chapter V.

He took the withy he had prepared out of his belt and began to fix it on the foot, but the thing was too elastic, and each time that he thought he had it right it sprang open.

From above his head, out of and into darkness, there came a hoarse and bubbling whisper, a rusty stammering that thudded his heart most out of his breast and his soul all but out of his body.

"You'll never tie it that way," said the voice. "Put a peg into it, decent man, or stick your brooch through it if you have no peg."

Nera almost let go the foot, but a savage obstinacy came on him, and he hit with his upper teeth on his lower lip until he nigh bit it in two.

"Very well," said he to the voice, "I'll stick my brooch in."

He did so, and the withy held.

"You are not dead?" said he to the man above him.

"Not out and out," the man replied.

"How does it happen that you are still alive?"

"It happened this way," replied that creaky and rusty tone; "when they were hanging me I was very thirsty, and ever since I have been too thirsty to die."

"It is a hard case," said Nera.

"Well," said he then, "I'll be moving, for I'm going to get a prize for what I did tonight to your foot."

"It was a good manly job," said the voice.

"It was," Nera admitted, "considering the kind of thing I had to do, and the sort of night in which I had to do it."

"But," said the voice above, "prove to me that you are really a courageous man."

"How would I prove that?" Nera asked.

"Take me down off this tree and carry me to some place where I can get a drink."

"You've been sentenced to be hanged," Nera replied, "and you've got to hang."

"That's all right," the voice answered, "I don't want to dodge Doom. You could bring me back after I got the drink, and you could hang me up again."

"I don't like the job," said Nera.

"I wouldn't like it myself," the voice replied, "but it would be a charitable act, and a valorous one."

"That is true," said Nera, "and I'll do what you ask."

"For," he continued, "there never was a man in the world before was asked to do the like; and there isn't a man in the world but myself would do it."

Nera then began to climb the tree.

Chapter VI.

"Is this you, decent man?" Nera inquired as he fumbled at a knot.

"It is not," the voice answered. "That's my comrade, and he has been dead for a day and a half."

"This is yourself anyhow," said Nera.

"You're right now," the voice replied.

"I'm afraid," said Nera, as he worked over him. "I'm afraid I shall have to let you fall on the ground; you are too heavy for me to hold with one hand."

"Don't bother about that," said the voice. "I can stand anything except the thirst."

Nera let him drop then, and he got a great fall.

"You'll have to carry me on your back," said the man, "for although I'm not dead enough to be buried I'm too dead to walk."

"I've done that much," said Nera, "and now I'll do whatever I have to do."

He packed the man on to his back and started away looking for a house where a drink could be got.

"What is it like to be hanged?" he asked as he plodded along.

"Nothing is as bad as they make it out," the man answered; "but I'm terribly thirsty, and I can't think of anything else."

They came to a house, and Nera knocked at the door. It was opened by a woman, and the visitor marched in with the man on his back.

The woman gave one look at Nera, and one at the stretched neck and twisted jowl that was waggling on Nera's shoulder, then she gave a low squeal and vanished out of the house.

A man strode to them truculently:

"What are you looking for, gentles?" said he.

Then he caught sight of that fishy eye peering by Nera's ear.

"The devil," said he, and he went through the door in a standing jump.

Three children crawled hastily under a bed in the corner and never another sound came from them. And an old woman, who was sitting by the fire with a mutton-bone in her fist, stared at them with her eyes open and her mouth open, and a long monotonous squawk tumbling off the end of her tongue the way water tumbles off a ledge.

There were three buckets of water standing by the wall. Nera propped his man against the door, and held one of the buckets to his lips. He drank a bucket dry. Then he drank the other two buckets dry.

"That's not a bad drink," said Nera, "and if you're not satisfied 'tis because nothing will satisfy you. Come back to your torment, my soul."

He picked up the malefactor, hunched him on to his back, and went out of the house with him and back to the hill.

As he strung him up he asked:

"Do you feel any better now, my darling?"

"I feel splendid," said the outlaw. "I'll be dead in a jiffey."

Nera left him then, swinging easily and buoyantly, and he took the road back to Cruachan of the Dun Ramparts, for he was impatient to get his prize.

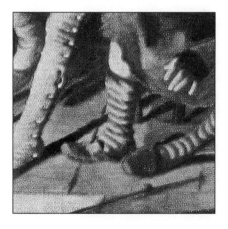

Gay, Ghastly Holiday!

The Fiend's Field. A Legend of the Wrekin (1832)

Anonymous

"This desert soil
Wants not her hidden lustre;
Nor want we skill, or art, from whence to raise
Magnificence."

—Milton

A wild tract of country is that which lies round about, and, in fact, forms the Wrekin; and well did the little dreary, desolate, and isolated hamlet of Wrekinswold merit its appellation. The few scattered cottages of which it consisted, stood on ground whose gradual swell assumed in some places the appearance of hills, but which are absurdly misnamed, when magnified, in school "geography-books," into "mountains." These hills, like many others, were, as well as the country for miles around them, at the period of which we write, a vast expanse of sterile, treeless heath, generally uncultivated; but were attempted to be turned into arable land, ill repaying the labours of the agriculturist, and far too arid to be converted into pasturage. The inhabitants of Wrekinswold were, consequently, a poor and idle race; and, hand in hand with their poverty and idleness, went ignorance and superstition.

Amongst the proprietors and cultivators of land, residing in the vicinity of Wrekinswold, was a man named Howison, who had, it was supposed, amassed a considerable fortune, by successful experiments upon the unpromising district in which stood his habitation. But Howison possessed another treasure—a lovely and

beloved daughter, for whom he had toiled incessantly, and who, it was well known, was destined to inherit the fruits of his labours. This motive had undoubtedly, at first, stimulated the fortunate farmer to those bold agricultural speculations, in which the risk was exceedingly great, but the success, if achieved, splendid; yet, after awhile, losing sight of his original incentive to exertion, the love of lucre, for itself only, took complete possession of his soul, and he became a hardhearted, selfish, and penurious man. The poor have generally, except where they happen to be personally concerned, a great idea that divine retribution will almost immediately overtake the evil-doer; and the neighbours of Howison, who had readily attributed his uncommon prosperity to the peculiar favour of heaven, upon this lamentable change in his disposition, expected nothing less than to witness some terrible manifestation of its wrath; shall we add that their "wish was father to the thought." At length their evil anticipations were destined to be gratified; and not one, but many successive bad seasons caused the farmer's crops to fail, and his cattle to be seized with an infectious disease. Howison was impoverished, but not ruined; and, whilst his avaricious heart was filled with grief, to find that he had lost the fruits of many years' toil, a sudden and happy thought struck him, that his daughter should, at any rate, become the rich lady he had always designed her to be; the only difficulty was how to effect it.

At Wrekinswold resided a young fellow, styled Tony Ryecroft, of whom nobody knew any thing but that he was a very disorderly personage, considered himself a gentleman, dressed like a lounging, slatternly country squire—suffered his neighbours to understand that he was as wealthy as idle; (and far from ordinary was his idleness) but whence came he and his money, or the means whereby he made it, was a mystery—for that make it he must, seemed evident to the boors of Wrekinswold, who could not believe that upon vice and idleness heaven showered blessings hardly obtained by the frugal, virtuous, and industrious. So some fancied that he must be engaged in the smuggling trade; others, more wisely, considering the inland situation of Shropshire, imagined him a shareholder in a mine, or generalissimo of a company of highwaymen; some, again, pronounced him to be "a limb of the law," and others "a limb of Satan," a distinction, be it however observed, without a difference in the apprehension of wiser people than the inhabitants of Wrekinswold.

Tony Ryecroft was an old and ardent admirer of Kate Howison; but the poor girl, by no means captivated with his ruffianly demeanour, slovenly attire, lax principles, and the mystery attached to his birth, connexions, and mode of life, had not only received his addresses with the contumely they merited, but had obtained her father's sanction to a union with her long and well-beloved Walter Burton—that is, as soon as gold should be added to the good and gentle gifts which nature had lavished on him. Howison, with his affairs in an unprosperous condition, now only became anxious to get his daughter off hand as quickly as possible, and recollecting that Tony Ryecroft was a husband for her at any time, (and, as he had always protested, at any price) he scrupled not to declare null and void all stipulations and promises between himself, his daughter, and poor Walter; vowing that he would disinherit her if she did not immediately consent to accept the hand of Ryecroft. In vain Kate wept, pleaded, reasoned, and remonstrated; her father (as fathers frequently are) was inexorable. Poor Kate! to her such severity was new; and sad was the lesson she had now to learn, that adversity could steel the heart of a hitherto fond parent, though an irreligious man, against a faithful and loving child.

It was a blustering evening in autumn: the winds moaned fearfully about the Wrekin, and dark, heavy clouds scudded across the sky. Tony Ryecroft was seated beside a roaring coal fire, in the ancient dilapidated mansion which he called his own, and which had formerly belonged to the Lord of the Wrekin, whose family had let it to Tony Ryecroft, upon his first appearance in the hamlet, at a rent little superior to that by which, from time immemorial, bats, birds, vermin, and reptiles, had tenanted the ruined edifice. Tony, we say, was sitting beside a large pit-coal fire—not dreaming, like the poet who listens in ecstacy to the fierce, wild music of the rushing blast, whilst he conjures up an

Arcadia in the glowing carbone—but busily engaged in watching a large non-descript vessel upon it, in which, apparently, a metallic composition of saffron hue was bubbling and steaming. At no great distance from him stood a table, strewed with lumps of various metals, and a strange assortment of moulds, sand, screws, gimlets, files, gravers, instruments, and combinations of the mechanical powers, for which it would have been difficult for the uninitiated to have found a name or use. Tony, however, was Rosicrucian enough to know very well what he was about; his door was bolted and doubly locked, and he expected no interruption to his pursuits on such a forbidding evening. But a violent ringing at the great gate of his fortalice announced a visitor, and though he had given a strict charge to the old woman, who officiated for him in every male and female capacity, to admit no one, and though he heard her pertinaciously protesting that he was "not at home," yet, to his extreme dismay, he also heard the intruder exclaim, as with heavy strides he approached the door of his sanctum, "Don't tell me about 'not at home;' I know that he is, and I must and will see him."

The intruder now reached Ryecroft's apartment, on the door of which he bestowed many a hearty knock, exclaiming, at intervals, "Why, Tony—Tony Ryecroft—let me in, I say." At last Ryecroft, from within, replied, in a solemn tone, "Bubasticon ilheologysticus! which, being interpreted, good neighbour, means—Demon avaunt!" "I say, Tony," cried the stranger, "please to be putting no tricks upon me. I am neither a demon nor a good neighbour [fairy]; but, as you may know by my voice, if you have an ear left, your old friend Howison." "Passpara iconatham, dentemasticon!" answered Ryecroft, "which is, being interpreted, Welcome, for I know thee! and here thou shalt enter, and thou fearest not."

Tony then said, in his usual manner, unfastening the door, "As you have spoiled all my philosophical work for to-night, and I fear, too, for many succeeding nights, I cannot bid you so cordially welcome as—" "Aye, but you will though, when you know what I've come to say. Faugh! what an odour of burnt tin, or copper, or brimstone, mayhap. Why, Tony, what have you there, simmering on the fire? And what do you mean by these queer instruments? and, above all, what is come to your tongue that you talk so outlandish?"

Ryecroft replied only with a most mysterious look, and re-fastening the door, stole again on tip-toe to his seat. Howison took the chair opposite, and as he held his large, tanned hands within an inch of the fire, whilst his grey curious eye roved stealthily over the apartment and the person of its owner—whose linen trowsers, waistcoat opened at the breast, and uncovered arms, excited on so cold an evening no small surprise—he ventured to ask him, whether the warm work in which he seemed to be engaged were magic?

"Even so," replied Ryecroft, with all the gravity he could command; "but, my excellent friend, start not—the branch of magic in which you now behold me occupied, belongs not to the black art, but is natural magic—the white, or the golden one, which has no kind of connection with the others. Golden, indeed, may I well term it, since it teaches, by the science of divine sublimations and transmutations, how to compound—that is, how to make—Gold!"

"Wheugh!" whistled the astonished and delighted lover of wealth, starting up and seizing our alchymist's hand, which he almost wrung off in the fervour of his transport—"there's some sense in that kind of magic! Ah! Master Ryecroft! I once fancied that I too had made, though in a different way, and with huge toil and trouble, a little of that same gold; but—"

Here poor Howison bent his head over the molten metal until his nose almost touched it; and whether its deleterious fumes, or the overwhelming consideration of Tony's extraordinary power for the accumulation of wealth, deprived him of articulation, is uncertain; but decidedly he found himself unable to conclude his observation. Tony was kind enough partially to relieve him from his embarrassment:

"My good friend, you mean to say that you find gold of late neither so easy to obtain, nor, when once lost, to recover." Howison sighed deeply, and looked perplexed. Tony continued:—"A man can't help bad seasons; even with me, all is not fair weather; for instance, your visit this evening renders vain all the long labours of an entire day. The contents of that vessel are useless to me now."

Consternation and horror were depicted on Howison's countenance at this avowal; he managed to stammer out a few apologies for his unlucky intrusion, and tremulously to inquire the cause of so strange a fatality.

"Why, you see, my dear sir," said Ryecroft, drawing his chair close to Howison's, and assuming one of his best aspects of mystery—"hist! what was that?" looking cautiously round the room, "I hope that no one is present but ourselves." "I hope—I believe so, too," replied his terrified listener, not daring to look behind him, lest his eyes, should encounter the apparition of a wicked Lord of the Wrekin, who was particularly believed to trouble the deserted mansion house, "I fancy, Master Ryecroft, it was only the wind which shrieks to-night."

"Well, sir, it might have been; but, as I was about to remark—when engaged in this little business, I am obliged to be particularly careful, since the White Art has determined enemies in those wicked spirits who are sole agents in the Black Art, and who are sure to trouble me whenever they discover that I am employed in the transmutation of metals. Nay, such is their boldness, that they sometimes intrude upon me, in the form of my most familiar friend; and had you, sir, happened to have been other than you seemed by your voice, you could not have withstood bubasticon itheologysticus. But it is not interruption only from the spiritual world which I have to fear when at my profitable studies, but as there is as much magic in the art of making gold as there is in the shining metal when made, I can only undertake this business under certain conjunctions and influences of the planets; and should mortal shadow cross the heavenly houses, the dominant spirits are offended, and my power lost for the space of seventy hours."

This absurd jargon, which was relished by Howison in exact proportion to its unintelligibility, so exalted Tony in his credulous hearer's estimation, that, after gazing at him for some minutes in silent awe, he ventured to inquire whether so wise a man could not teach him some secret whereby to ensure good crops and sound cattle in future.

"To say the truth, sir," replied Ryecroft, "I have long been thinking of you in this very matter; for, admiring Kate Howison as I do, I cannot unmoved behold adversity overtake her sire; and if I have hitherto, when I knew the means of assisting you laid in my power, held my peace, attribute such conduct to any motive but indifference and unkindness. Perhaps I might dread the charge of impertinent interference in family affairs, which concerned not myself; or, perhaps, I might be aware of certain conditions which, of necessity, I must impose upon him whose fallen fortunes I desired to raise, and which would unhappily seem, in his eyes, to compromise the disinterestedness of my heart."

"Conditions! you mean my daughter's hand! By all that's holy, she shall be yours," exclaimed Howison, in ecstacy; "and, to say the truth, Tony, it was this very matter which brought me here to-night."

"Indeed!" answered the wily Ryecroft, "why, to be candid with you in return, I am not now so anxious about Kate, after her decided rejection of me. But come—my conditions are simply these: that you make over all your property to her whom I once loved; or rather, draw up an instrument which shall cause the revenue of your farm to revert, upon your decease, to him who shall then be her husband."

"It shall be done," cried Howison, in raptures; "what next?"

"If you can certainly assure me of the performance of this condition—"

"I can—I do."

"'Then hearken to what I am going to communicate:—You are aware," he continued, "that Satan, (bubasticon itheologysticus!) as Prince of the Air, is entrusted with the sole command of all tempests, winds, frosts, blights, &c., which, falling upon the earth, injure its fruits and cattle. This power then, ought, as far as is allowable, to be conciliated; and, if he be not, fearful is his vengeance upon the presumptuous mortal who insults him by disregarding his supremacy. In Scotland, therefore, it has been, from time immemorial, a sensible custom, to set apart a small portion, as a rood or two, or half an acre of arable ground, as an offering to the evil spirit, whom, for fear of offending, they designate by some friendly title, as good man, good fellow, &c.; this portion, which is left uncultivated, and, with certain ceremonies in which I am competent to instruct you, consecrated to the demon, is termed the 'Goodman's Croft,' in plain English, 'Fiend's Field.' Now, Master Howison, it has struck me that the late extraordinary losses of a man hitherto so thriving as yourself, can only be referred to your want of respect towards the dark power, who, perceiving you adding acre to acre, purchasing this field, and enclosing that portion of stony, sterile, waste land, without setting apart so much as half an inch for himself, has resented the neglect, you best know how."

"Nothing more likely," answered Howison.

The advice consequent upon this communication was, that Howison should enclose a fresh portion of common, not the old worn ground, and that there should be an annual sacrifice of a black cock and a sheep's heart stuck with pins, in the croft at midnight. The ceremonies of the consecration, Master Ryecroft was, at his leisure, to arrange. Howison then took his leave, sincerely thankful and marvellously enlightened; repeating incessantly, during his dreary homeward walk, (as far as he could count the syllables,) the mysterious exclamation to which the alchymist had attached so magical a meaning.

Kate Howison and Walter now saw with despair, that their hopes were to be frustrated by avarice on one side, and craftiness on the other; and whilst they felt themselves the victims of Ryecroft, they knew that Howison was his dupe. Kate, however, who still retained, in spite of her father's sordid feelings, some little influence over his hard heart, gained, by tears, entreaties, and other all-prevailing female arguments, the respite of one entire year ere her dreaded union with Ryecroft; for, as Howison could not help acknowledging, there was some reason in her observation, that she would then be of age, and he himself would have had an opportunity of proving whether Tony had actually ensured to him the promised prosperity.

It was the evening of the 31st of October, the celebrated vigil of All Saint's Day—more familiarly known, perhaps, as the Scottish and Irish Hallowe'en—when Howison, after frequent conferences with Tony Ryecroft, proceeded to act for, and by himself, according to the adept's instructions. He had lately enclosed a considerable portion of the Wrekinwolds, lying at a distance of about three miles from his home, and behind some of the highest of the hills. The Fiend's Field, a full and fair acre of this acquisition, was situated at its extremity, and was upon this auspicious evening to be consecrated. Howison, who had invited a party of his daughter's young friends, Walter and Ryecroft among them, to burn nuts and try charms with her, drank deep potations of strong ale; and, at a signal given by Ryecroft, soon after the clock had struck eleven, wrapped himself in his great frieze coat, took down his massy oaken cudgel, and sallied forth—joked, of course, by his juvenile guests, who asserted that he was going to dip his shirt-sleeves in the fairy spring beyond the hills.

Heedless of their jests, Howison went on his way, but with an exceedingly heavy heart, thus to quit a warm fire-side, blythe company, and excellent cheer, for a long, dreary, and cold walk over the Wrekinwolds—the wind howling, the rain falling in sullen, heavy drops, the night dark as death, and such a night, too! the witching one of all the year, and its witching hour so nigh! And what was he going to do? unto whom to offer sacrifice? To be sure he did it but as a mere piece of foolish formality, to please Ryecroft; there could be nothing sinful in such a frolic, more than in those simple charms in which he knew, at twelve o'clock, all the gay youths and maidens at the Grange would be engaged.

Thus, alternately a prey to the smitings of conscience and the sophistries which were to heal them, and frequently whistling, singing, and repeating aloud the efficacious scrap of magical lore taught him by Tony, Howison contrived to find his way across hilly, arable, and waste lands, to his new territory. The walls of an old stone building, of which the country people could give no satisfactory account, stood in the portion fenced off for the Fiend's Field. Some believed it to have been a Catholic chapel, dedicated to St. Hubert, the hunter's patron, and thence termed Hubb's House on the Hill; some thought it an ancient watch-tower, whilst, others, referring its origin to the Romans, thought they displayed an extraordinary share of erudition by the conjecture. All, however, agreed that it had been for ages the resort of fairies, apparitions, and witches, who held an annual festival on the Wrekin, though on what night of the year none could positively say, since no person had ever yet been found sufficiently courageous to watch in and about Hubb's House, in order to effect so important a discovery.

The recollection of these traditions, tended by no means to raise the sinking spirits of Howison, whose teeth fairly chattered with affright, and whose limbs almost failed him, as he groped his way into the building, where Ryecroft had assured him he must offer the propitiary sacrifice. The slightest degree of fear was to be deprecated, as liable to incense the being whom he came to conciliate; a circumstance that added to his trepidation. Terror and fatigue, occasioned by the pace at which he had walked to reach the ruin ere the stroke of midnight caused him to sink almost exhausted upon the ground; but, recovering, he took from his pocket a tinder-box and matches, struck a light and set fire to a previously prepared pile of furze, sticks, and fagots, mingled with turf, damp earth, and stones, in order to prevent its immediate combustion. Then, taking from a niche in the ruined wall, the black cock and the heart brought for this sacrifice during the day by Tony and himself, he cast them upon the blazing altar, meaning to utter an invocation taught him for the occasion, when unluckily out slipped by mistake the more familiar phrase, whose signification, according to Ryecroft, was "Demon, avaunt."

Immediately a burst of wild, deriding laughter, so loud that it shook the walls of the crazy building, and seemed echoed and re-echoed by every stone, saluted the ears of Howison, and this had no sooner subsided, than a voice, whose tone seemed to freeze the very blood at his heart, exclaimed, "Fool! Passpara iconathem dentimasticon, thou would'st say. Wherefore am I summoned?" The white curling smoke, which had, upon the firing of the combustible altar, rolled in gross, suffocating volumes around the narrow area enclosed by the ruined walls, having found a vent through the roofless tower as through an ample chimney, now rose majestically upwards in a dense white column, mingled with bright streams of ascending flame; so that Howison was clearly enabled to discern standing before him a black and gigantic apparition, whose dusky countenance was stern and sorrowful, and whose glittering eyes, illumined by the reflection of the burning materials, glowed like living fires. Howison, at length, in faltering accents, gave utterance to the lesson he had studied.

"I, a poor fortune-fallen mortal, have summoned thee, in order to crave for the future fruitful crops and sound cattle; is my sacrifice accepted?"

"Art thou ready," interrupted the power, gloomily, "to fulfil the terms agreed upon by our trusty servant, Anthony Ryecroft?"

The mortal bowed his assent, for terror had sealed his tongue.

"Thy sacrifice is accepted then," pronounced the demon; "see that thou fail not in thy compact, lest when we meet again, for we shall meet again—"

"I know it!" groaned Howison: "upon this same night next year, shall we—"

At this moment the distant church-clock slowly chimed twelve; the blazing altar became suddenly extinct; a hollow rushing sound echoed through the ruin, and Howison, half frenzied, darted from its shade.

Wild, wet, and haggard, at about ten minutes to one, he entered the Grange; his guests were gone, and Kate, beside a cheerful fire, was awaiting her father's return in a mood as cheerful, ready to jest with him upon his secret expedition; but when he rushed in with the wildness of a maniac, and sat with staring eyes fixed on the fire, without uttering a syllable, the poor alarmed girl could only ask him, in broken accents, what he had done, what he had seen. At length she placed in his damp, cold hand, a glass of mulled ale; and, a little refreshed, he replied to her remonstrances, "Go to bed, child—to bed, I say; but remember your father in your prayers, for he may never pray again." And he left his terrified and hapless daughter to muse upon and to mourn the dreadful meaning of his words.

During the ensuing year it was singular that Howison had not the slightest occasion to complain of a bad season, scanty damaged crops, or diseased cattle; he and Ryecroft lived upon terms of extreme intimacy, while Walter Burton and Kate still continued, though more covertly than heretofore, their affectionate intercourse; but some rumours getting afloat that Howison having entered into a compact with the evil power, had consecrated to him that acre of his estate in which stood the old haunted chapel of St. Hubert, the inhabitants of Wrekinswold, though not, as we hinted at the commencement of our tale, the most virtuous peasantry in existence, looked coldly and askance upon him, taking credit to themselves for superior sanctity, because they had not fallen so deeply into the gulf of perdition.

The marriage of Ryecroft and Kate was fixed for the first of November, in the year succeeding that in which the sacrifice was consummated; consequently the anniversary of this event, which was to be observed with similar ceremonies; fell upon the vigil of All-Hallows and of her bridal. A larger party than that which had assembled at the Grange the year preceding, were now met for the double purpose of celebrating the rites of "spritely" Hallowe'en, and the approaching nuptials of one so universally beloved. This party—when Kate beheld her father depart, as he had done exactly a twelvemonth before, on his mysterious nocturnal errand—she strove to detain until his return, conjecturing that his second ramble would not be longer than the first. One o'clock, however, struck, and the rustic company rose to depart; the rival lovers, only, perceiving her anxiety for her father, would not quit her. Ryecroft pressed her much to retire to rest, urging, that as she must rise early in order to prepare for a ceremony which was to take place at eight o'clock, she needed repose. His entreaties were replied to in a tone of bitterness which with Kate was very unusual; and, after an apology from Ryecroft, for having unintentionally offended, the trio maintained a gloomy silence, anxiously listening for the steps of Howison. But nothing stirred to interrupt the awful stillness (which began to press upon the hearts of the alarmed party like a heavy weight) save the dropping embers and the unwearying click of the clock.

The hour of two at length struck, louder, each fancied, than it had ever done before; and Kate, bursting into tears, exclaimed, "One hour longer will I await my father, and, if he return not then, he shall be sought, for harm hath surely happened unto him!" She described his agitation upon his return upon the Hallowe'en past from his nocturnal expedition, which, she now declared her conviction, was undertaken for unhallowed purposes, adding—"And now that we are on the subject, do tell me, Master Ryecroft, what my poor father meant by purchasing a piece of land which still lies fallow, and which, it seems, he never intends to cultivate?"

Tony refused to afford her the slightest information, and his companions witnessed with surprise the ashy paleness of his countenance, and a perplexity, perturbation, and terror, which all his efforts at ease and self possession were inefficient to conceal. He had frequent recourse to some brandy, which, with the remains of the All-Hallowmass supper, still stood on the table, and at last, overcome by the frequency of the application, he fell into a profound slumber.

"Were it not," said Kate, "for my uneasiness respecting my father, I could laugh at the unlover-like figure of that reprobate, and at the trick we have played him. Ah, Walter! how strangely surprised will he be to-morrow when I declare in church—Hark! did you not hear a noise?"

Nothing, in fact, was stirring, yet Kate unfastened the door of the house nearest the road by which she knew her father must return, and looked out. It was a clear, frosty moonlight night, but no Howison appeared; and as the hour passed without his arrival, Burton began, like poor Kate, to forebode the worst; so insisting that she should retire, and suffering Ryecroft to remain where he was and sleep off the effects of the brandy, he set forth alone in quest of the unhappy Howison. Kate threw herself upon the bed in her clothes, and, having for another hour prayed as fervently as she wept bitterly, sunk exhausted into a kind of doze that might rather be termed stupefaction than repose. From this state she was aroused by a violent rapping at her chamber door: it was now full daylight, though the morning was cold and cloudy.

"Kate, my dear girl, for heaven's sake, come here!" exclaimed Walter, as he still knocked and lifted in vain the latch of the bolted door.

This was followed by a mingling of voices, a low deep hum as of consternation and sorrow. With trembling hand, Kate unfastened the door, and Walter, drawing her gently from the chamber, endeavoured in a tender and soothing tone to prepare her mind for the fatal tidings.

"Gracious God!" cried the afflicted girl, "my father—my poor father—is then no more! Speak, is it not so? And Ryecroft is his murderer!"

"Hush, dear Kate, hush! we may not, without cause, thus put any man's life in jeopardy. Ryecroft, suspicious as is his flight from Wrekinswold, was, you know, sitting with us when this lamentable accident befell your poor father; whose body I found at some distance from hence, bearing as you will perceive, when you have sufficient firmness to gaze upon it, every indication of having been destroyed by gunpowder, or something like it."

A neighbour now entered, panting for breath. He brought tidings that Hubb's House was totally demolished—not one stone being left upon another! that fragments of the building were strewn about Goodman's Croft and the field near it, and that all were blackened and burnt, as if the place had been destroyed by an explosion.

"How curious is it," observed Kate, looking up through her tears, after an hour or two had elapsed, "that neither my unhappy parent, nor Anthony Ryecroft, should be here on this eventful morning, to learn that I became your wife three months ago!"

The opinion now entertained was, that Ryecroft had endeavoured to secure immediately that wealth for which alone he desired the heiress of the infatuated Howison; and that only a few hours previous to the marriage, when he might fancy that nothing could delay it, luring his luckless dupe, under superstitious pretences, to a lonely and shunned ruin; in the middle of the night, he there accomplished his destruction; having instigated him to light a pile of combustible materials, which contained, unknown to his victim, a quantity of gunpowder. The rustics of Wrekinswold, however, tenacious of the superstitions of their day and country, affirmed, that as Howison failed to perform the promise, his daughter being already married, the evil one had thought proper to carry off the soul of the unfortunate man in a tempest of sulphur and fire; leaving behind, to ensure the destruction of Ryecroft, the blackened and mangled corpse.

Ryecroft was, in the course of a few days, apprehended and securely lodged in Shrewsbury jail. Being convicted upon another serious and singular charge, he was sentenced to suffer the extreme penalty of the law. An execution having been levied upon the rich Tony for debt, amongst his other property were found certain instruments, engines, and utensils, moulds, and metals, which clearly proved him to belong to a gang of coiners, for whose apprehension the magistrates of Shropshire had been long on the alert. He refused to betray his accomplices in "the divine art of transmutation;" and, to the last, persisted in denying with the most solemn asseverations, any implication in the murder of Howison, save that which had unhappily accrued to him by the fatal termination of a mere youthful frolic, got up, he affirmed, for the purpose of obtaining a wealthy alliance, and of creating a profound idea of his own knowledge and power. Leaving this mysterious subject still in darkness, thus died the crafty Ryecroft. But for some years after the catastrophe of our story, it was a tradition current amongst the inhabitants of Wrekinswold, that annually, upon the eve of All Saint's Day, those who happened to cross the site of Hubb's House at midnight, would behold the apparition of Howison; an elderly man, who appears with vain labour to be gathering and piling visionary stones, which sink down and disperse as soon as collected; when, should the startled wanderer on the Wrekin take courage to ask the phantom who he is and what he does, he will civilly and sadly reply—

"Friend, go thy way, and heap not up riches which thou knowest not who shall inherit. Beware, I say, of the chaff which flitteth away at the breath of the least wind, even as thou perceivest these stones to do, wherewith I strive for ever and for ever to erect an altar to the Goodman of the Croft; and from which I labour through everlasting years—but in vain—to clear the Field of my great master—the FIEND!"

Reality or Delusion? (1895; 1st pub. 1868)

Mrs. Henry Wood

This is a ghost story. Every word of it is true. And I don't mind confessing that for ages afterwards some of us did not care to pass the spot alone at night. Some people do not care to pass it yet.

It was autumn, and we were at Crabb Cot. Lena had been ailing; and in October Mrs. Todhetley proposed to the Squire that they should remove with her there, to see if the change would do her good.

We Worcestershire people call North Crabb a village; but one might count the houses in it, little and great, and not find four-and-twenty. South Crabb, half a mile off, is ever so much larger; but the church and school are at North Crabb.

John Ferrar had been employed by Squire Todhetley as a sort of overlooker on the estate, or working bailiff. He had died the previous winter; leaving nothing behind him except some debts; for he was not provident; and his handsome son Daniel. Daniel Ferrar, who was rather superior as far as education went, disliked work: he would make a show of helping his father, but it came to little. Old Ferrar had not put him to any particular trade or occupation, and Daniel, who was as proud as Lucifer, would not turn to it himself. He liked to be a gentleman. All he did now was to work in his garden, and feed his fowls, ducks, rabbits, and pigeons, of which he kept a great quantity, selling them to the houses around and sending them to market.

But, as every one said, poultry would not maintain him. Mrs. Lease, in the pretty cottage hard by Ferrar's, grew tired of saying it. This Mrs. Lease and her daughter, Maria, must not be confounded with Lease the pointsman: they were in a better condition of life, and not related to him. Daniel Ferrar used to run in and out of their house at will when a boy, and he was now engaged to be married to Maria. She would have a little money, and the Leases were respected in North Crabb. People began to whisper a query as to how Ferrar got his corn for the poultry: he was not known to buy much; and he would have to go out of his house at Christmas, for its owner, Mr. Coney, had given him notice. Mrs. Lease, anxious about Maria's prospects, asked Daniel what he intended to do then, and he answered, "Make his fortune: he should begin to do it as soon as he could turn himself round." But the time was going on, and the turning round seemed to be as far off as ever.

After Midsummer, a niece of the schoolmistress's, Miss Timmens, had come to the school to stay: her name was Harriet Roe. The father, Humphrey Roe, was half-brother to Miss Timmens. He had married a Frenchwoman, and lived more in France than in England until his death. The girl had been christened Henriette; but North Crabb, not understanding much French, converted it into Harriet. She was a showy, free-mannered, good-looking girl, and made speedy acquaintance with Daniel Ferrar; or he with her. They improved upon it so rapidly that Maria Lease grew jealous, and North Crabb began to say he cared for Harriet more than for Maria. When Tod and I got home the latter end of October, to spend the Squire's birthday, things were in this state. James Hill, the bailiff who had been taken on by the Squire in John Ferrar's place (but a far inferior man to Ferrar; not much better, in fact, than a common workman, and of whose doings you will hear soon in regard to his little step-son, David Garth), gave us an account of matters in general. Daniel Ferrar had been drinking lately, Hill added, and his head was not strong enough to stand it; and he was also beginning to look as if he had some care upon him.

"A nice lot, he, for them two women to be fighting for," cried Hill, who was no friend to Ferrar. "There'll be mischief between 'em if they don't draw in a bit. Maria Lease is next door to mad over it, I know; and t'other, finding herself the best liked, crows over her. It's something like the Bible story of Leah and Rachel, young gents, Dan Ferrar likes the one, and he's bound by promise to the t'other. As to the French jade," concluded Hill, giving his head a toss, "she'd make a show of liking any man that followed her, she would; a dozen of 'em on a string."

It was all very well for surly Hill to call Daniel Ferrar a "nice lot", but he was the best-looking fellow in church on Sunday morning—well-dressed too. But his colour seemed brighter; and his hands shook as they were raised, often, to push back his hair, that the sun shone upon through the south-window, turning it to gold. He scarcely looked up, not even at Harriet Roe, with her dark eyes roving everywhere, and her streaming pink ribbons. Maria Lease was pale, quiet, and nice, as usual; she had no beauty, but her face was sensible, and her deep grey eyes had a strange and curious earnestness. The new parson preached, a young man just appointed to the parish of Crabb. He went in for great observances of Saints' days, and told his congregation that he should expect to see them at church on the morrow, which would be the Feast of All Saints.

Daniel Ferrar walked home with Mrs. Lease and Maria after service, and was invited to dinner. I ran across to shake hands with the old dame, who had once nursed me through an illness, and promised to look in and see her later. We were going back to school on the morrow. As I turned away, Harriet Roe passed, her pink ribbons and her cheap gay silk dress gleaming in the sunlight. She stared at me, and I stared back again. And now, the explanation of matters being over, the real story begins. But I have to tell some of it as it was told by others.

The tea-things waited on Mrs. Lease's table in the afternoon; waited for Daniel Ferrar. He had left them shortly before to go and attend to his poultry. Nothing had been said about his coming back for tea: that he would do so had been looked upon as a matter of course. But he did not make his appearance, and the tea was taken without him. At half-past five the church-bell rang out for evening service, and Maria put her things on. Mrs. Lease did not go out at night.

"You are starting early, Maria. You'll be in church before other people."

"That won't matter, mother."

A jealous suspicion lay on Maria—that the secret of Daniel Ferrar's absence was his having fallen in with Harriet Roe: perhaps had gone of own accord to seek her. She walked slowly along. The gloom of dusk, and a deep dusk, had stolen over the evening, but the moon would be up later. As Maria passed the school-house, she halted to glance in at the little sitting-room window: the shutters were not closed yet, and the room was lighted by the blazing fire. Harriet was not there. She only saw Miss Timmens, the mistress, who was putting on her bonnet before a hand-glass propped upright on the mantel-piece. Without warning, Miss Timmens turned and threw open the window. It was only for the purpose of pulling-to the shutters, but Maria thought she must have been observed, and spoke.

"Good evening, Miss Timmens."

"Who is it?" cried out Miss Timmens, in answer, peering into the dusk. "Oh, it's you, Maria Lease! Have you seen anything of Harriet? She went off somewhere this afternoon, and never came in to tea."

"I have not seen her."

"She's gone to the Batleys, I'll be bound. She knows I don't like her to be with the Batley girls: they make her ten times flightier than she should otherwise be."

Miss Timmens drew in her shutters with a jerk, without which they would not close, and Maria Lease turned away.

"Not at the Batleys', not at the Batleys', but with *him,*" she cried, in bitter rebellion, as she turned away from the church. From the church, not to it. Was Maria to blame for wishing to see whether she was right or not?—for walking about a little in the thought of meeting them? At any rate it is what she did. And had her reward; such as it was.

As she was passing the top of the withy walk, their voices reached her ear. People often walked there, and it was one of the ways to South Crabb. Maria drew back amidst the trees, and they came on: Harriet Roe and Daniel Ferrar, walking arm-in-arm.

"I think I had better take it off," Harriet was saying. "No need to invoke a storm upon my head. And that would come in a shower of hail from stiff old Aunt Timmens."

The answer seemed one of quick accent, but Ferrar spoke low. Maria Lease had hard work to control herself: anger, passion, jealousy, all blazed up. With her arms stretched out to a friendly tree on either side,—with her heart beating,—with her pulses coursing on to fever-heat, she watched them across the bit of common to the road. Harriet went one way then; he another, in the direction of Mrs. Lease's cottage. No doubt to fetch her—Maria—to church, with a plausible excuse of having been detained. Until now she had no proof of his falseness; had never perfectly believed in it.

She took her arms from the trees and went forward, a sharp faint cry of despair breaking forth on the night air. Maria Lease was one of those silent-natured girls who can never speak of a wrong like this. She had to bury it within her; down, down, out of sight and show; and she went into church with her usual quiet step. Harriet Roe with Miss Timmens came next, quite demure, as if she had been singing some of the infant scholars to sleep at their own homes. Daniel Ferrar did not go to church at all: he stayed, as was found afterwards, with Mrs. Lease.

Maria might as well have been at home as at church: better perhaps that she had been. Not a syllable of the service did she hear: her brain was a sea of confusion; the tumult within it rising higher and higher. She did not hear even the text, "Peace, be still", or the sermon; both so singularly appropriate. The passions in men's minds, the preacher said, raged and foamed just like the angry waves of the sea in a storm, until Jesus came to still them.

I ran after Maria when church was over, and went in to pay the promised visit to old Mother Lease. Daniel Ferrar was sitting in the parlour. He got up and offered Maria a chair at the fire, but she turned her back and stood at the table under the window, taking off her gloves. An open Bible was before Mrs. Lease: I wondered whether she had been reading aloud to Daniel.

"What was the text, child?" asked the old lady.

No answer.

"Do you hear, Maria! What was the text?"

Maria turned at that, as if suddenly awakened. Her face was white; her eyes had in them an uncertain terror.

"The text?" she stammered. "I—I forget it, mother. It was from Genesis, I think."

"Was it, Master Johnny?"

"It was from the fourth chapter of St. Mark, 'Peace, be still'."

Mrs. Lease stared at me. "Why, that is the very chapter I've been reading. Well now, that's curious. But there's never a better in the Bible, and never a better text was taken from it than those three words. I have been telling Daniel here, Master Johnny, that when once that peace, Christ's peace, is got into the heart, storms can't hurt us much. And you are going away again to-morrow, sir?" she added, after a pause. "It's a short stay?"

I was not going away on the morrow. Tod and I, taking the Squire in a genial moment after dinner, had pressed to be let stay until Tuesday, Tod using the argument, and laughing while he did it, that it must be wrong to travel on All Saints' Day, when the parson had specially enjoined us to be at church. The Squire told us we were a couple of encroaching rascals, and if he did let us stay it should be upon condition that we did go to church. This I said to them.

"He may send you all the same, sir, when the morning comes," remarked Daniel Ferrar.

"Knowing Mr. Todhetley as you do Ferrar, you may remember that he never breaks his promises."

Daniel laughed. "He grumbles over them, though, Master Johnny."

"Well, he may grumble to-morrow about our staying, say it is wasting time that ought to be spent in study, but he will not send us back until Tuesday."

Until Tuesday! If I could have foreseen then what would have happened before Tuesday! If all of us could have foreseen! Seen the few hours between now and then depicted, as in a mirror, event by event! Would it have saved the calamity, the dreadful sin that could never be redeemed? Why, yes; surely it would. Daniel Ferrar turned and looked at Maria.

"Why don't you come to the fire?"

"I am very well here, thank you."

She had sat down where she was, her bonnet touching the curtain. Mrs. Lease, not noticing that anything was wrong, had begun talking about Lena, whose illness was turning to low fever, when the house door opened and Harriet Roe came in.

"What a lovely night it is!" she said, taking of her own accord the chair I had not cared to take, for I kept saying I must go. "Maria, what went with you after church? I hunted for you everywhere."

Maria gave no answer. She looked black and angry; and her bosom heaved as if a storm were brewing. Harriet Roe slightly laughed.

"Do you intend to take holiday to-morrow, Mrs. Lease?"

"Me take holiday! what is there in to-morrow to take holiday for?" returned Mrs. Lease.

"I shall," continued Harriet, not answering the question: "I have been used to it in France. All Saints' Day is a grand holiday there; we go to church in our best clothes, and pay visits afterwards. Following it, like a dark shadow, comes the gloomy Jour des Morts."

"The what?" cried Mrs. Lease, bending her ear.

"The day of the dead. All Souls' Day. But you English don't go to the cemeteries to pray."

Mrs. Lease put on her spectacles, which lay upon the open pages of the Bible, and stared at Harriet. Perhaps she thought they might help her to understand. The girl laughed.

"On All Souls' Day, whether it be wet or dry, the French cemeteries are full of kneeling women draped in black; all praying for the repose of their dead relatives, after the manner of the Roman Catholics."

Daniel Ferrar, who had not spoken a word since she came in, but sat with his face to the fire, turned and looked at her. Upon which she tossed back her head and her pink ribbons, and smiled till all her teeth were seen. Good teeth they were. As to reverence in her tone, there was none.

"I have seen them kneeling when the slosh and wet have been ankle-deep. Did you ever see a ghost?" added she, with energy. "The French believe that the spirits of the dead come abroad on the night of All Saints' Day. You'd scarcely get a French woman to go out of her house after dark. It is their chief superstition."

"What *is* the superstition?" questioned Mrs. Lease.

"Why, *that,* said Harriet. "They believe that the dead are allowed to revisit the world after dark on the Eve of All Souls; that they hover in the air, waiting to appear to any of their living relatives, who may venture out, lest they should forget to pray on the morrow for the rest of their souls."

"Well, I never!" cried Mrs. Lease, staring excessively. "Did you ever hear the like of that, sir?" turning to me.

"Yes; I have heard of it."

Harriet Roe looked up at me; I was standing at the corner of the mantelpiece. She laughed a free laugh.

"I say, wouldn't it be fun to go out to-morrow night, and meet the ghosts? Only, perhaps they don't visit this country, as it is not under Rome."

"Now just you behave yourself before your betters, Harriet Roe," put in Mrs. Lease, sharply. "That gentleman is young Mr. Ludlow of Crabb Cot."

"And very happy I am to make young Mr. Ludlow's acquaintance," returned easy Harriet, flinging back her mantle from her shoulders. "How hot your parlour is, Mrs. Lease."

The hook of the cloak had caught in a thin chain of twisted gold that she wore round her neck, displaying it to view. She hurriedly folded her cloak together, as if wishing to conceal the chain. But Mrs. Lease's spectacles had seen it.

"What's that you've got on, Harriet? A gold chain?"

A moment's pause, and then Harriet Roe flung back her mantle again, defiance upon her face, and touched the chain with her hand.

"That's what it is, Mrs. Lease: a gold chain. And a very pretty one, too."

"Was it your mother's?"

"It was never anybody's but mine. I had it made a present to me this afternoon; for a keepsake."

Happening to look at Maria, I was startled at her face, it was so white and dark: white with emotion, dark with an angry despair that I for one did not comprehend. Harriet Roe, throwing at her a look of saucy triumph, went out with as little ceremony as she had come in, just calling back a general good night; and we heard her footsteps outside getting gradually fainter in the distance. Daniel Ferrar rose.

"I'll take my departure too, I think. You are very unsociable to-night, Maria."

"Perhaps I am. Perhaps I have cause to be."

She flung his hand back when he held it out; and in another moment, as if a thought struck her, ran after him into the passage to speak. I, standing near the door in the small room, caught the words.

"I must have an explanation with you, Daniel Ferrar. Now. To-night. We cannot go on thus for a single hour longer."

"Not to-night Maria; I have no time to spare. And I don't know what you mean."

"You do know. Listen. I will not go to my rest, no, though it were for twenty nights to come, until we have had it out. I *vow* I will not. There. You are playing with me. Others have long said so, and I know it now."

He seemed to speak some quieting words to her, for the tone was low and soothing; and then went out, closing the door behind him. Maria came back and stood with her face and its ghastliness turned from us. And still the old mother noticed nothing.

"Why don't you take your things off, Maria?" she asked.

"Presently," was the answer.

I said goodnight in my turn, and went away. Half-way home I met Tod with the two young Lexoms. The Lexoms made us go in and stay to supper, and it was ten o'clock before we left them.

"We shall catch it," said Tod, setting off at a run. They never let us stay out late on a Sunday evening, on account of the reading.

But, as it happened, we escaped scot-free this time, for the house was in a commotion about Lena. She had been better in the afternoon, but at nine o'clock the fever returned worse than ever. Her little cheeks and lips were scarlet as she lay on the bed, her wide-open eyes were bright and glistening. The

Squire had gone up to look at her, and was fuming and fretting in his usual fashion.

"The doctor has never sent the medicine," said patient Mrs. Todhetley, who must have been worn out with nursing. "She ought to take it; I am sure she ought."

"These boys are good to run over to Cole's for that," cried the Squire. "It won't hurt them; it's a fine night."

Of course we were good for it. And we got our caps again; being charged to enjoin Mr. Cole to come over the first thing in the morning.

"Do you care much about my going with you, Johnny?" Tod asked as we were turning out at the door. "I am awfully tired."

"Not a bit. I'd as soon go alone as not. You'll see me back in half-an-hour."

I took the nearest way; flying across the fields at a canter, and startling the hares. Mr. Cole lived near South Crabb, and I don't believe more than ten minutes had gone by when I knocked at his door. But to get back as quickly was another thing. The doctor was not at home. He had been called out to a patient at eight o'clock, and had not yet returned.

I went in to wait: the servant said he might be expected to come in from minute to minute. It was of no use to go away without the medicine; and I sat down in the surgery in front of the shelves, and fell asleep counting the white jars and physic bottles. The doctor's entrance awoke me.

"I am sorry you should have had to come over and to wait," he said. "When my other patient, with whom I was detained a considerable time, was done with, I went on to Crabb Cot with the child's medicine, which I had in my pocket."

"They think her very ill to-night, sir."

"I left her better, and going quietly to sleep. She will soon be well again, I hope."

"Why! is that the time?" I exclaimed, happening to catch sight of the clock as I was crossing the hall. It was nearly twelve. Mr. Cole laughed, saying time passed quickly when folk were asleep.

I went back slowly. The sleep, or the canter before it, had made me feel as tired as Tod had said he was. It was a night to be abroad in and to enjoy; calm, warm, light. The moon, high in the sky, illumined every blade of grass; sparkled on the water of the little rivulet; brought out the moss on the grey walls of the old church; played on its round-faced clock, then striking twelve.

Twelve o'clock at night at North Crabb answers to about three in the morning in London, for country people are mostly in bed and asleep at ten. Therefore, when loud and angry voices struck up in dispute, just as the last stroke of the hour was dying away on the midnight air, I stood still and doubted my ears.

I was getting near home then. The sounds came from the back of a building standing alone in a solitary place on the left-hand side of the road. It belonged to the Squire, and was called the yellow barn, its walls being covered with a yellow wash; but it was in fact used as a storehouse for corn. I was passing in front of it when the voices rose upon the air. Round the building I ran, and saw—Maria Lease: and something else that I could not at first comprehend. In the pursuit of her vow, not to go to rest until she had "had it out" with Daniel Ferrar, Maria had been abroad searching for him. What ill fate brought her looking for him up near our barn?—perhaps because she had fruitlessly searched in every other spot.

At the back of this barn, up some steps, was an unused door. Unused partly because it was not required, the principal entrance being in front; partly because the key of it had been for a long time missing. Stealing out at this door, a bag of corn upon his shoulders, had come Daniel Ferrar in a smockfrock. Maria saw him, and stood back in the shade. She watched him lock the door and put the key in his pocket; she watched him give the heavy bag a jerk as he turned to come down the steps. Then she burst out. Her loud reproaches petrified him, and he stood there as one suddenly turned to stone. It was at that moment that I appeared.

I understood it all soon; it needed not Maria's words to enlighten me. Daniel Ferrar possessed the lost key and could come in and out at will in the midnight hours when the world was sleeping, and help himself to the corn. No wonder his poultry throve; no wonder there had been grumblings at Crabb Cot at the mysterious disappearance of the good grain.

Maria Lease was decidedly mad in those few first moments. Stealing is looked upon in an honest village as an awful thing; a disgrace, a crime; and there was the night's earlier misery besides. Daniel Ferrar was a thief! Daniel Ferrar was false to her! A storm of words and reproaches poured forth from her in confusion, none of it very distinct. "Living upon theft! Convicted felon! Transportation for life! Squire Todhetley's corn! Fattening poultry on stolen goods! Buying gold chains with the profits for that bold, flaunting French girl, Harriet Roe! Taking his stealthy walks with her!"

My going up to them stopped the charge. There was a pause; and then Maria, in her mad passion, denounced him to me, as representative (so she put it) of the Squire—the breaker-in upon our premises! the robber of our stored corn!

Daniel Ferrar came down the steps; he had remained there still as a statue, immovable; and turned his white face to me. Never a word in defence said he: the blow had crushed him; he was a proud man (if any one can understand that), and to be discovered in this ill-doing was worse than death to him.

"Don't think of me more hardly than you can help, Master Johnny," he said in a quiet tone. "I have been almost tired of my life this long while."

Putting down the bag of corn near the steps, he took the key from his pocket and handed it to me. The man's aspect had so changed; there was something so grievously subdued and sad about him altogether, that I felt as sorry for him as if he had not been guilty. Maria Lease went on in her fiery passion.

"You'll be more tired of it to-morrow when the police are taking you to Worcester gaol. Squire Todhetley will not spare you, though your father was his many-years bailiff. He could not, you know, if he wished; Master Ludlow has seen you in the act."

"Let me have the key again for a minute, sir," he said, as quietly as though he had not heard a word. And I gave it to him. I'm not sure but I should have given him my head had he asked for it.

He swung the bag on his shoulders, unlocked the granary door, and put the bag beside the other sacks. The bag was his own, as we found afterwards, but he left it there. Locking the door again, he gave me the key, and went away with a weary step.

"Goodbye, Master Johnny."

I answered back goodnight civilly, though he had been stealing. When he was out of sight, Maria Lease, her passion full upon her still, dashed off towards her mother's cottage, a strange cry of despair breaking from her lips.

"Where have you been lingering, Johnny?" roared the Squire, who was sitting up for me. "You have been throwing at the owls, sir, that's what you've been at; you have been scudding after the hares."

I said I had waited for Mr. Cole, and had come back slower than I went; but I said no more, and went up to my room at once. And the Squire went to his.

I know I am only a muff; people tell me so, often: but I can't help it; I did not make myself. I lay awake till nearly daylight, first wishing Daniel Ferrar could be screened, and then thinking it might perhaps be done. If he would only take the lesson to heart and go on straight for the future, what a capital thing it would be. We had liked old Ferrar; he had done me and Tod many a good turn: and, for the matter of that, we liked Daniel. So I never said a word when morning came of the past night's work.

"Is Daniel at home?" I asked, going to Ferrar's the first thing before breakfast. I meant to tell him that if he would keep right, I would keep counsel.

"He went out at dawn, sir," answered the old woman who did for him, and sold his poultry at market. "He'll be in presently: he have had no breakfast yet."

"Then tell him when he comes, to wait in, and see me: tell him it's all right. Can you remember, Goody? 'It is all right'."

"I'll remember, safe enough, Master Ludlow."

Tod and I, being on our honour, went to church, and found about ten people in the pews. Harriet Roe was one, with her pink ribbons, the twisted gold chain showing outside a short-cut velvet jacket.

"No, sir; he has not been home yet; I can't think where he can have got to," was the old Goody's reply when I went again to Ferrar's. And so I wrote a word in pencil, and told her to give it him when he came in, for I could not go dodging there every hour of the day.

After luncheon, strolling by the back of the barn: a certain reminiscence I suppose taking me there, for it was not a frequented spot: I saw Maria Lease coming along.

Well, it was a change! The passionate woman of the previous night had subsided into a poor, wild-looking, sorrow-stricken thing, ready to die of remorse. Excessive passion had wrought its usual consequences; a reaction: a reaction in favour of Daniel Ferrar. She came up to me, clasping her hands in agony—beseeching that I would spare him; that I would not tell of him; that I would give him a chance for the future: and her lips quivered and trembled, and there were dark circles round her hollow eyes.

I said that I had not told and did not intend to tell. Upon which she was going to fall down on her knees, but I rushed off.

"Do you know where he is?" I asked, when she came to her sober senses.

"Oh, I wish I did know! Master Johnny, he is just the man to go and do something desperate. He would never face shame; and I was a mad, hard-hearted, wicked girl to do what I did last night. He might run away to sea; he might go and enlist for a soldier."

"I dare say he is at home by this time. I have left a word for him there, and promised to go in and see him to-night. If he will undertake not to be up to wrong things again, no one shall ever know of this from me."

She went away easier, and I sauntered on towards South Crabb. Eager as Tod and I had been for the day's holiday, it did not seem to be turning out much of a boon. In going home again—there was nothing worth staying out for—I had come to the spot by the three-cornered grove where I saw Maria, when a galloping policeman overtook me. My heart stood still; for I thought he must have come after Daniel Ferrar.

"Can you tell me if I am near to Crabb Cot—Squire Todhetley's?" he asked, reining-in his horse.

"You will reach it in a minute or two. I live there. Squire Todhetley is not at home. What do you want with him?"

"It's only to give in an official paper, sir. I have to leave one personally upon all the county magistrates."

He rode on. When I got in I saw the folded paper upon the hall-table; the man and horse had already gone onwards. It was worse indoors than out; less to be done. Tod had disappeared after church; the Squire was abroad; Mrs. Todhetley sat upstairs with Lena: and I strolled out again. It was only three o'clock then.

An hour, or more, was got through somehow; meeting one, talking to another, throwing at the ducks and geese; anything. Mrs. Lease had her head, smothered in a yellow shawl, stretched out over the palings as I passed her cottage.

"Don't catch cold, mother."

"I am looking for Maria, sir. I can't think what has come to her to-day, Master Johnny," she added, dropping her voice to a confidential tone. "The girl seems demented: she has been going in and out ever since daylight like a dog in a fair."

"If I meet her I will send her home."

And in another minute I did meet her. For she was coming out of Daniel Ferrar's yard. I supposed he was at home again.

"No," she said, looking more wild, worn, haggard than before; "that's what I have been to ask. I am just out of my senses, sir. He has gone for certain. Gone!"

I did not think it. He would not be likely to go away without clothes.

"Well, I know he is, Master Johnny; something tells me. I've been all about everywhere. There's a great dread upon me, sir; I never felt anything like it."

"Wait until night, Maria; I dare say he will go home then. Your mother is looking out for you; I said if I met you I'd send you in."

Mechanically she turned towards the cottage, and I went on. Presently, as I was sitting on a gate watching the sunset, Harriet Roe passed towards the withy walk, and gave me a nod in her free but good-natured way.

"Are you going there to look out for the ghosts this evening?" I asked: and I wished not long afterwards I had not said it. "It will soon be dark."

"So it will," she said, turning to the red sky in the west. "But I have no time to give to the ghosts to-night."

"Have you seen Ferrar to-day?" I cried, an idea occurring to me.

"No. And I can't think where he has got to; unless he is off to Worcester. He told me he should have to go there some day this week."

She evidently knew nothing about him, and went on her way with another free-and-easy nod. I sat on the gate till the sun had gone down, and then thought it was time to be getting homewards.

Close against the yellow barn, the scene of last night's trouble, whom should I come upon but Maria Lease. She was standing still, and turned quickly at the sound of my footsteps. Her face was bright again, but had a puzzled look upon it.

"I have just seen him: he has not gone," she said in a happy whisper. "You were right, Master Johnny, and I was wrong."

"Where did you see him?"

"Here; not a minute ago. I saw him twice. He is angry, very, and will not let me speak to him; both times he got away before I could reach him. He is close by somewhere."

I looked round, naturally; but Ferrar was nowhere to be seen. There was nothing to conceal him except the barn, and that was locked up. The account she gave was this—and her face grew puzzled again as she related it.

Unable to rest indoors, she had wandered up here again, and saw Ferrar standing at the corner of the barn, looking very hard at her. She thought he was waiting for her to come up, but before she got close to him he had disappeared, and she did not see which way. She hastened past the front of the barn, ran round to the back, and there he was. He stood near the steps looking out for her; waiting for her, as it again seemed; and was gazing at her with the same fixed stare. But again she missed him before she could get quite up; and it was at that moment that I arrived on the scene.

I went all round the barn, but could see nothing of Ferrar. It was an extraordinary thing where he could have got to. Inside the barn he could not be: it was securely locked; and there was no appearance of him in the open country. It was, so to say, broad daylight yet, or at least not far short of it; the red light was still in the west. Beyond the field at the back of the barn, was a grove of trees in the form of a triangle; and this grove was flanked by Crabb Ravine, which ran right and left. Crabb Ravine had the reputation of being haunted; for a light was sometimes seen dodging about its deep descending banks at night that no one could account for. A lively spot altogether for those who liked gloom.

"Are you sure it was Ferrar, Maria?"

"Sure!" she returned in surprise. "You don't think I could mistake him, Master Johnny, do you? He wore that ugly seal-skin winter-cap of his tied over his ears, and his thick grey coat. The coat was buttoned closely round him. I have not seen him wear either since last winter."

That Ferrar must have gone into hiding somewhere seemed quite evident; and yet there was nothing but the ground to receive him. Maria said she lost sight of him the last time in a moment; both times in fact; and it was absolutely impossible that he could have made off to the triangle or elsewhere, as she must have seen him cross the open land. For that matter I must have seen him also.

On the whole, not two minutes had elapsed since I came up, though it seems to have been longer in telling it: when, before we could look further, voices were heard approaching from the direction of Crabb Cot; and Maria, not caring to be seen, went away quickly. I was still puzzling about Ferrar's hiding-place, when they reached me—the Squire, Tod, and two or three men. Tod came slowly up, his face dark and grave.

"I say, Johnny, what a shocking thing this is!"

"What is a shocking thing?"

"You have not heard of it?—But I don't see how you could hear it."

I had heard nothing. I did not know what there was to hear. Tod told me in a whisper.

"Daniel Ferrar's dead, lad."

"What?"

"He has destroyed himself. Not more than half-an-hour ago. Hung himself in the grove."

I turned sick, taking one thing with another, comparing this recollection with that; which I dare say you will think no one but a muff would do.

Ferrar was indeed dead. He had been hiding all day in the three-cornered grove: perhaps waiting for night to get away—perhaps only waiting for night to go home again. Who can tell? About half-past two, Luke Macintosh, a man who sometimes worked for us, sometimes for old Coney, happening to go through the grove, saw him there, and talked with him. The same man, passing back a little before sunset, found him hanging from a tree, dead. Macintosh ran with the news to Crabb Cot, and they were now flocking to the scene. When facts came to be examined there appeared only too much reason to think that the unfortunate appearance of the galloping policeman had terrified Ferrar into the act; perhaps—we all hoped it!—had scared his senses quite away. Look at it as we would, it was very dreadful.

But what of the appearance Maria Lease saw? At that time, Ferrar had been dead at least half-an-hour. Was it reality or delusion? That is (as the Squire put it), did her eyes see a real, spectral Daniel Ferrar; or were they deceived by some imagination of the brain? Opinions were divided. Nothing can shake her own steadfast belief in its reality; to her it remains an awful certainty, true and sure as heaven.

If I say that I believe in it too, I shall be called a muff and a double muff. But there is no stumbling-block difficult to be got over. Ferrar, when found, was wearing the seal-skin cap tied over the ears and the thick grey coat buttoned up round him, just as Maria Lease had described to me; and he had never worn them since the previous winter, or taken them out of the chest where they were kept. The old woman at his home did not know he had done it then. When told that he died in these things, she protested that they were in the chest, and ran up to look for them. But the things were gone.

Ken's Mystery (1883)

Julian Hawthorne

One cool October evening—it was the last day of the month, and unusually cool for the time of year—I made up my mind to go and spend an hour or two with my friend Keningale. Keningale was an artist (as well as a musical amateur and poet), and had a very delightful studio built on to his house, in which he was wont to sit of an evening. The studio had a cavernous fire-place, designed in imitation of the old-fashioned fire-places of Elizabethan manor-houses, and in it, when the temperature out-doors warranted, he would build up a cheerful fire of dry logs. It would suit me particularly well, I thought, to go and have a quiet pipe and chat in front of that fire with my friend.

I had not had such a chat for a very long time—not, in fact, since Keningale (or Ken, as his friends called him) had returned from his visit to Europe the year before. He went abroad, as he affirmed at the time, "for purposes of study," whereat we all smiled, for Ken, so far as we knew him, was more likely to do anything else than to study. He was a young fellow of buoyant temperament, lively and social in his habits, of a brilliant and versatile mind, and possessing an income of twelve or fifteen thousand dollars a year; he could sing, play, scribble, and paint very cleverly, and some of his heads and figure-pieces were really well done, considering that he never had any regular training in art; but he was not a worker. Personally he was fine-looking, of good height and figure, active, healthy, and with a remarkably fine brow, and clear, full-gazing eye. Nobody was surprised at his going to Europe, nobody expected him to do anything there except amuse himself, and few anticipated that he would be soon again seen in New York. He was one of the sort that find Europe agree with them. Off he went, therefore; and in the course of a few months the rumor reached us that he was engaged to a handsome and wealthy New York girl whom he had met in London. This was nearly all we did hear of him until, not very long afterward, he turned up again on Fifth Avenue, to every one's astonishment; made no satisfactory answer to those who wanted to know how he happened to tire so soon of the Old World; while as to the reported engagement, he cut short all allusion to that in so peremptory a manner as to show that it was not a permissible topic of conversation with him. It was surmised that the lady had jilted him; but, on the other hand, she herself returned home not a great while after, and though she had plenty of opportunities, she has never married to this day.

Be the rights of that matter what they may, it was soon remarked that Ken was no longer the careless and merry fellow he used to be; on the contrary, he appeared grave, moody, averse from general society, and habitually taciturn and undemonstrative even in the company of his most intimate friends. Evidently something had happened to him, or he had done something. What? Had he committed a murder? or joined the Nihilists? or was his unsuccessful love affair at the bottom of it? Some declared that the cloud was only temporary, and would soon pass away. Nevertheless, up to the period of which I am writing it had not passed away, but had rather gathered additional gloom, and threatened to become permanent.

Meanwhile I had met him twice or thrice at the club, at the opera, or in the street, but had as yet had no opportunity of regularly renewing my acquaintance with him. We had been on a footing of more than common intimacy in the old days, and I was not disposed to think that he would refuse to renew the former relations now. But what I had heard and myself seen of his changed condition imparted a stimulating tinge of suspense or curiosity to the pleasure with which I looked forward to the prospects of this evening. His house stood at a distance of two or three miles beyond the general range of habitations in New York at this time, and as I walked briskly along in the clear twilight air I had leisure to go over in my mind all that I had known of Ken and had divined of his character. After all, had there not always been something in his nature—deep down, and held in abeyance by the activity of his animal spirits—but something strange and separate, and capable of developing under suitable conditions into—into what? As I asked myself this question I arrived at his door; and it was with a feeling of relief that I felt the next moment the cordial grasp of his hand, and his voice bidding me welcome in a tone that indicated unaffected gratification at my presence. He drew me at once into the studio, relieved me of my hat and cane, and then put his hand on my shoulder.

"I am glad to see you," he repeated,—with singular earnestness—"glad to see you and to feel you; and to-night of all nights in the year."

"Why to-night especially?"

"Oh, never mind. It's just as well, too, you didn't let me know beforehand you were coming; the unreadiness is all, to paraphrase the poet. Now, with you to help me, I can drink a glass of tamarind-water and take a bit draw of the pipe. This would have been a grim night for me if I'd been left to myself."

"In such a lap of luxury as this, too!" said I, looking round at the glowing fireplace, the low, luxurious chairs, and all the rich and sumptuous fittings of the room. "I should have thought a condemned murderer might make himself comfortable here."

"Perhaps; but that's not exactly my category at present. But have you forgotten what night this is? This is November-eve, when, as tradition asserts, the dead arise and walk about, and fairies, goblins, and spiritual beings of all kinds have more freedom and power than on any other day of the year. One can see you've never been in Ireland."

"I wasn't aware till now that you had been there, either."

"Yes, I have been in Ireland. Yes—" He paused, sighed, and fell into a reverie, from which, however, he soon roused himself by an effort, and went to a cabinet in a corner of the room for the liquor and tobacco. While he was thus employed I sauntered about the studio, taking note of the various beauties, grotesquenesses, and curiosities that it contained. Many things were there to repay study and arouse admiration; for Ken was a good collector, having excellent taste as well as means to back it. But, upon the whole, nothing interested me more than some studies of a female head, roughly done in oils, and, judging from the sequestered positions in which I found them, not intended by the artist for exhibition or criticism. There were three or four of these studies, all of the same face, but in different poses and costumes. In one the head was enveloped in a dark hood, overshadowing and partly concealing the features; in another she seemed to be peering duskily through a latticed casement, lit by a faint moonlight; a third showed her splendidly attired in evening costume, with jewels in her hair and ears, and sparkling on her snowy bosom. The expressions were as various as the poses; now it was demure penetration, now a subtle inviting glance, now burning passion, and again a look of elfish and elusive mockery. In whatever phase, the countenance possessed a singular and poignant fascination, not of beauty merely, though that was very striking, but of character and quality likewise.

"Did you find this model abroad?" I inquired at length. "She has evidently inspired you, and I don't wonder at it."

Ken, who had been heating the tamarind-water, and had not noticed my movements, now looked up, and said: "I didn't mean those to be seen. They don't satisfy me, and I'm going to destroy them; but I couldn't rest till I'd made some attempts to reproduce—What was it you asked? Abroad? Yes—or no. They were all painted here within the last six weeks."

"Whether they satisfy you or not, they are by far the best things of yours I have ever seen."

"Well, let them alone, and tell me what you think of this beverage. To my thinking, it goes to the right spot. It owes its existence to your coming here. I can't drink alone, and those portraits are not company, though, for aught I know, she might have come out of the canvas to-night and sat down in that chair." Then, seeing my inquiring look, he added, with a hasty laugh, "It's November-eve, you know, when anything may happen, provided it's strange enough. Well, here's to ourselves."

We each swallowed a deep draught of the smoking and aromatic liquor, and set down our glasses with approval. The punch was excellent. Ken now opened a box of cigars, and we seated ourselves before the fire-place.

"All we need now," I remarked, after a short silence, "is a little music. By-the-bye, Ken, have you still got the banjo I gave you before you went abroad?"

He paused so long before replying that I supposed he had not heard my question. "I have got it," he said at length, "but it will never make any more music."

"Got broken, eh? Can't it be mended? It was a fine instrument."

"It's not broken, but it's past mending. You shall see for yourself."

He arose as he spoke, and going to another part of the studio, opened a black oak coffer, and took out of it a long object wrapped up in a piece of faded yellow silk. He handed it to me, and when I had unwrapped it, there appeared a thing that might once have been a banjo, but had little resemblance to one now. It bore every sign of extreme age. The wood of the handle was honey-combed with the gnawings of worms, and dusty with dry-rot. The parchment head was green with mould, and hung in shrivelled tatters. The hoop, which was of solid silver, was so blackened and tarnished that it looked like dilapidated iron. The strings were gone, and most of the tuning-screws had dropped out of their decayed sockets. Altogether it had the appearance of having been made before the Flood, and been forgotten in the forecastle of Noah's Ark ever since.

"It is a curious relic certainly," I said. "Where did you come across it? I had no idea that the banjo was invented so long ago as this. It certainly can't be less than two hundred years old, and may be much older than that."

Ken smiled gloomily. "You are quite right," he said; "it is at least two hundred years old, and yet it is the very same banjo that you gave me a year ago."

"Hardly," I returned, smiling in my turn, "since that was made to my order with a view to presenting it to you."

"I know that; but the two hundred years have passed since then. Yes, it is absurd and impossible, I know, but nothing is truer. That banjo, which was made last year, existed in the sixteenth century, and has been rotting ever since. Stay. Give it to me a moment, and I'll convince you. You recollect that your name and mine, with the date, were engraved on the silver hoop?"

"Yes; and there was a private mark of my own there also."

"Very well," said Ken, who had been rubbing a place on the hoop with a corner of the yellow silk wrapper; "look at that."

I took the decrepit instrument from him, and examined the spot which he had rubbed. It was incredible, sure enough; but there were the names and the date precisely as I had caused them to be engraved; and there, moreover, was

166 A HALLOWEEN READER

my own private mark, which I had idly made with an old etching point not more than eighteen months before. After convincing myself that there was no mistake, I laid the banjo across my knees, and stared at my friend in bewilderment. He sat smoking with a kind of grim composure, his eyes fixed upon the blazing logs.

"I'm mystified, I confess," said I. "Come; what is the joke? What method have you discovered of producing the decay of centuries on this unfortunate banjo in a few months? And why did you do it? I have heard of an elixir to counteract the effects of time, but your recipe seems to work the other way—to make time rush forward at two hundred times his usual rate, in one place, while he jogs on at his usual gait elsewhere. Unfold your mystery, magician. Seriously, Ken, how on earth did the thing happen?"

"I know no more about it than you do," was his reply. "Either you and I and all the rest of the living world are insane, or else there has been wrought a miracle as strange as any in tradition. How can I explain it? It is a common saying—a common experience, if you will—that we may, on certain trying or tremendous occasions, live years in one moment. But that's a mental experience, not a physical one, and one that applies, at all events, only to human beings, not to senseless things of wood and metal. You imagine the thing is some trick or jugglery. If it be, I don't know the secret of it. There's no chemical appliance that I ever heard of that will get a piece of solid wood into that condition in a few months, or a few years. And it wasn't done in a few years, or a few months either. A year ago to-day at this very hour that banjo was as sound as when it left the maker's hands, and twenty-four hours afterward—I'm telling you the simple truth—it was as you see it now."

The gravity and earnestness with which Ken made this astounding statement were evidently not assumed. He believed every word that he uttered. I knew not what to think. Of course my friend might be insane, though he betrayed none of the ordinary symptoms of mania; but, however that might be, there was the banjo, a witness whose silent testimony there was no gainsaying. The more I meditated on the matter the more inconceivable did it appear. Two hundred years—twenty-four hours; those were the terms of the proposed equation. Ken and the banjo both affirmed that the equation had been made; all worldly knowledge and experience affirmed it to be impossible. What was the explanation? What is time? What is life? I felt myself beginning to doubt the reality of all things. And so this was the mystery which my friend had been brooding over since his return from abroad. No wonder it had changed him. More to be wondered at was it that it had not changed him more.

"Can you tell me the whole story?" I demanded at length.

Ken quaffed another draught from his glass of tamarind-water and rubbed his hand through his thick brown beard. "I have never spoken to any one of it heretofore," he said, "and I had never meant to speak of it. But I'll try and give you some idea of what it was. You know me better than any one else; you'll understand the thing as far as it can ever be understood, and perhaps I may be relieved of some of the oppression it has caused me. For it is rather a ghastly memory to grapple with alone, I can tell you."

Hereupon, without further preface, Ken related the following tale. He was, I may observe in passing, a naturally fine narrator. There were deep, lingering tones in his voice, and he could strikingly enhance the comic or pathetic effect of a sentence by dwelling here and there upon some syllable. His features were equally susceptible of humorous and of solemn expressions, and his eyes were in form and hue wonderfully adapted to showing great varieties of emotion. Their mournful aspect was extremely earnest and affecting; and when Ken was giving utterance to some mysterious passage of the tale they had a doubtful, melancholy, exploring look which appealed irresistibly to the imagination. But the interest of his story was too pressing to allow of noticing these incidental embellishments at the time, though they doubtless had their influence upon me all the same.

"I left New York on an Inman Line steamer, you remember," began Ken, "and landed at Havre. I went the usual round of sight-seeing on the Continent, and got round to London in July, at the height of the season. I had good introductions, and met any number of agreeable and famous people. Among others was a young lady, a country-woman of my own—you know whom I mean—who interested me very much, and before her family left London she and I were engaged. We parted there for the time, because she had the Continental trip still to make, while I wanted to take the opportunity to visit the north of England and Ireland. I landed at Dublin about the first of October, and, zigzagging about the country, I found myself in County Cork about two weeks later.

"There is in that region some of the most lovely scenery that human eyes ever rested on, and it seems to be less known to tourists than many places of infinitely less picturesque value. A lonely region, too: during my rambles I met not a single stranger like myself, and few enough natives. It seems incredible that so beautiful a country should be so deserted. After walking a dozen Irish miles you come across a group of two or three one-roomed cottages, and, like as not, one or more of those will have the roof off and the walls in ruins. The few peasants whom one sees, however, are affable and hospitable, especially when they hear you are from that terrestrial heaven whither most of their friends and relatives have gone before them. They seem simple and primitive enough at first sight, and yet they are as strange and incomprehensible a race as any in the world. They are as superstitious, as credulous of marvels, fairies, magicians, and omens, as the men whom St. Patrick preached to, and at the same time they are shrewd, skeptical, insensible, and bottomless liars. Upon the whole, I met with no nation on my travels whose company I enjoyed so much, or who inspired me with so much kindliness, curiosity, and repugnance.

"At length I got to a place on the seacoast, which I will not further specify than to say that it is not many miles from Ballymacheen, on the south shore. I have seen Venice and Naples, I have driven along the Cornice Road, I have spent a month at our own Mount Desert, and I say that all of them together are not so beautiful as this glowing, deep-hued, soft-gleaming, silvery-lighted, ancient harbor and town, with the tall hills crowding round it and the black cliffs and headlands planting their iron feet in the blue, transparent sea. It is a very old place, and has had a history which it has outlived ages since. It may once have had two or three thousand inhabitants; it has scarce five or six hundred to-day. Half the houses are in ruins or have disappeared; many of the remainder are standing empty. All the people are poor, most of them abjectly so; they saunter about with bare feet and uncovered heads, the women in quaint black or dark blue cloaks, the men in such anomalous attire as only an Irishman knows how to get together, the children half naked. The only comfortable-looking people are the monks and the priests, and the soldiers in the fort. For there is a fort there, constructed on the huge ruins of one which may have done duty in the reign of Edward the Black Prince, or earlier, in whose mossy embrasures are mounted a couple of cannon, which occasionally sent a practice-shot or two at the cliff on the other side of the harbor. The garrison consists of a dozen men and three or four officers and noncommissioned officers. I suppose they are relieved occasionally, but those I saw seemed to have become component parts of their surroundings.

"I put up at a wonderful little old inn, the only one in the place, and took my meals in a dining-saloon fifteen feet by nine, with a portrait of George I (a print varnished to preserve it) hanging over the mantel-piece. On the second evening after dinner a young gentleman came in—the dining-saloon being public property, of course—and ordered some bread and cheese and a bottle of Dublin stout. We presently fell into talk; he turned out to be an officer from the fort, Lieutenant O'Connor, and a fine young specimen of the Irish soldier he was. After telling me all he knew about the town, the surrounding country, his friends, and himself, he intimated a readiness to sympathize with whatever tale I might choose to pour into his ear; and I had pleasure in trying to rival his own outspokenness. We became excellent friends; we had up a half-pint of Kinahan's whiskey, and the lieutenant expressed himself in terms of high praise of my countrymen, my country, and my own particular cigars. When it became time for him to depart I accompanied him—for there was a splendid moon abroad—and bade him farewell at the fort entrance, having promised to come over the next day and make the acquaintance of the other fellows. 'And mind your eye, now, going back, my dear boy,' he called out, as I turned my face homeward. 'Sure 'tis a spooky place, that grave-yard, and you'll as likely meet the black woman there as anywhere else!'

"The grave-yard was a forlorn and barren spot on the hill-side, just the hither side of the fort: thirty or forty rough head-stones, few of which retained any semblance of the perpendicular, while many were so shattered and decayed as to seem nothing more than irregular natural projections from the ground. Who the black woman might be I knew not, and did not stay to inquire. I had never been subject to ghostly apprehensions, and as a matter of fact, though the path I had to follow was in places very bad going, not to mention a hap-hazard scramble over a ruined bridge that covered a deep-lying brook, I reached my inn without any adventure whatever.

"The next day I kept my appointment at the fort, and found no reason to regret it; and my friendly sentiments were abundantly reciprocated, thanks more especially, perhaps, to the success of my banjo, which I carried with me, and which was as novel as it was popular with those who listened to it. The chief personages in the social circle besides my friend the lieutenant were Major Molloy, who was in command, a racy and juicy old campaigner, with a face like a sunset, and the surgeon, Dr. Dudeen, a long, dry, humorous genius, with a wealth of anecdotical and traditional lore at his command that I have never seen surpassed. We had a jolly time of it, and it was the precursor of many more like it. The remains of October slipped away rapidly, and I was obliged to remember that I was a traveller in Europe, and not a resident in Ireland. The major, the surgeon, and the lieutenant all protested cordially against my proposed departure, but as there was no help for it, they arranged a farewell dinner to take place in the fort on All-halloween.

"I wish you could have been at that dinner with me! It was the essence of Irish good-fellowship. Dr. Dudeen was in great force; the major was better than the best of Lever's novels; the lieutenant was overflowing with hearty good-humor, merry chaff, and sentimental rhapsodies anent this or the other pretty girl of the neighborhood. For my part I made the banjo ring as it had never rung before, and the others joined in the chorus with a mellow strength of lungs such as you don't often hear outside of Ireland. Among the stories that Dr. Dudeen regaled us with was one about the Kern of Querin and his wife, Ethelind Fionguala—which being interpreted signifies 'the white-shouldered.'

The lady, it appears, was originally betrothed to one O'Connor (here the lieutenant smacked his lips), but was stolen away on the wedding night by a party of vampires, who, it would seem, were at that period a prominent feature among the troubles of Ireland. But as they were bearing her along—she being unconscious—to that supper where she was not to eat but to be eaten, the young Kern of Querin, who happened to be out duck-shooting, met the party, and emptied his gun at it. The vampires fled, and the Kern carried the fair lady, still in a state of insensibility to his house. 'And by the same token, Mr. Keningale,' observed the doctor, knocking the ashes out of his pipe, 'ye're after passing that very house on your way here. The one with the dark archway underneath it, and the big mullioned window at the corner, ye recollect, hanging over the street, as I might say—'

"'Go 'long wid the house, Dr. Dudeen, dear,' interrupted the lieutenant; 'sure can't you see we're all dyin' to know what happened to sweet Miss Fionguala, God be good to her, when I was after getting her safe upstairs—'

"'Faith, then, I can tell ye that myself, Mr. O'Connor,' exclaimed the major, imparting a rotary motion to the remnants of whiskey in his tumbler. 'Tis a question to be solved on general principles, as Colonel O'Halloran said that time he was asked what he'd do if he'd been the Dook o' Wellington, and the Prussians hadn't come up in the nick o' time at Waterloo. 'Faith,' says the colonel, 'I'll tell ye—'

"'Arrah, then, major, why would ye be interruptin' the doctor, and Mr. Keningale there lettin' his glass stay empty till he hears—The Lord save us! the bottle's empty!'

"In the excitement consequent upon this discovery, the thread of the doctor's story was lost; and before it could be recovered the evening had advanced so far that I felt obliged to withdraw. It took some time to make my proposition heard and comprehended; and a still longer time to put it in execution; so that it was fully midnight before I found myself standing in the cool pure air outside the fort, with the farewells of my boon companions ringing in my ears.

"Considering that it had been rather a wet evening in-doors, I was in a remarkably good state of preservation, and I therefore ascribed it rather to the roughness of the road than to the smoothness of the liquor, when, after advancing a few rods, I stumbled and fell. As I picked myself up I fancied I had heard a laugh, and supposed that the lieutenant, who had accompanied me to the gate, was making merry over my mishap; but on looking round I saw that the gate was closed and no one was visible. The laugh, moreover, had seemed to be close at hand, and even to be pitched in a key that was rather feminine than masculine. Of course I must have been deceived; nobody was near me: my imagination had played me a trick, or else there was more truth than poetry in the tradition that Halloween is the carnival-time of disembodied spirits. It did not occur to me at the time that a stumble is held by the superstitious Irish to be an evil omen, and had I remembered it it would only have been to laugh at it. At all events, I was physically none the worse for my tumble, and I resumed my way immediately.

"But the path was singularly difficult to find, or rather the path I was following did not seem to be the right one. I did not recognize it; I could have sworn (except I knew the contrary) that I had never seen it before. The moon had risen, though her light was as yet obscured by clouds, but neither my immediate surroundings nor the general aspect of the region appeared familiar. Dark, silent hill-sides mounted up on either hand, and the road, for the most part, plunged downward, as if to conduct me into the bowels of the earth. The place was alive with strange echoes, so that at times I seemed to be walking through the midst of muttering voices and mysterious whispers, and a wild, faint sound of laughter seemed ever and anon to reverberate among the passes of the hills. Currents of colder air sighing up through narrow defiles and dark crevices touched my face as with airy fingers. A certain feeling of anxiety and insecurity began to take possession of me, though there was no definable cause for it, unless that I might be belated in getting home. With the perverse instinct of those who are lost I hastened my steps, but was impelled now and then to glance back over my shoulder, with a sensation of being pursued. But no living creature was in sight. The moon, however, had now risen higher, and the clouds that were drifting slowly across the sky flung into the naked valley dusky shadows, which occasionally assumed shapes that looked like the vague semblance of gigantic human forms.

"How long I had been hurrying onward I know not, when, with a kind of suddenness, I found myself approaching a grave-yard. It was situated on the spur of a hill, and there was no fence around it, nor anything to protect it from the incursions of passers-by. There was something in the general appearance of this spot that made me half fancy I had seen it before; and I should have taken it to be the same that I had often noticed on my way to the fort, but that the latter was only a few hundred yards distant there-from, whereas I must have traversed several miles at least. As I drew near, moreover, I observed that the head-stones did not appear so ancient and decayed as those of the other. But what chiefly attracted my attention was the figure that was leaning or half sitting upon one of the largest of the upright slabs near the road. It was a female figure draped in black, and a closer inspection—for I was soon within a few yards of her—showed that she wore the calla, or long hooded cloak, the most common as well as the most ancient garment of Irish women, and doubtless of Spanish origin.

"I was a trifle startled by this apparition, so unexpected as it was, and so strange did it seem that any human creature should be at that hour of the night in so desolate and sinister a place. Involuntarily I paused as I came opposite her, and gazed at her intently. But the moonlight fell behind her, and the deep hood of her cloak so completely shadowed her face that I was unable to discern anything but the sparkle of a pair of eyes, which appeared to be returning my gaze with much vivacity.

"'You seem to be at home here,' I said at length. 'Can you tell me where I am?'

"Hereupon the mysterious personage broke into a light laugh, which, though in itself musical and agreeable, was of a timbre and intonation that caused my heart to beat rather faster than my late pedestrian exertions warranted; for it was the identical laugh (or so my imagination persuaded me) that had echoed in my ears as I arose from my tumble an hour or two ago. For the rest, it was the laugh of a young woman, and presumably of a pretty one; and yet it had a wild, airy, mocking quality, that seemed hardly human at all, or not, at any rate, to be characteristic of a being of affections and limitations like unto ours. But this impression of mine was fostered, no doubt, by the unusual and uncanny circumstances of the occasion.

"'Sure, sir,' said she, 'you're at the grave of Ethelind Fionguala.'

"As she spoke she rose to her feet, and pointed to the inscription on the stone. I bent forward, and was able, without much difficulty, to decipher the name, and a date which indicated that the occupant of the grave must have entered the disembodied state between two and three centuries ago.

"'And who are you?' was my next question.

"'I'm called Elsie,' she replied. 'But where would your honor be going November-eve?'

"I mentioned my destination, and asked her whether she could direct me thither.

"'Indeed, then, 'tis there I'm going myself,' Elsie replied; 'and if your honor'll follow me, and play me a tune on the pretty instrument, 'tisn't long we'll be on the road.'

"She pointed to the banjo which I carried wrapped up under my arm. How she knew that it was a musical instrument I could not imagine; possibly, I thought, she may have seen me playing on it as I strolled about the environs of the town. Be that as it may, I offered no opposition to the bargain, and further intimated that I would reward her more substantially on our arrival. At that she laughed again, and made a peculiar gesture with her hand above her head. I uncovered my banjo, swept my fingers across the strings, and struck into a fantastic dance measure, to the music of which we proceeded along the path, Elsie slightly in advance, her feet keeping time to the airy measure. In fact, she trod so lightly, with an elastic, undulating movement, that with a little more it seemed as if she might float onward like a spirit. The extreme whiteness of her feet attracted my eye, and I was surprised to find that instead of being bare, as I had supposed, these were incased in white satin slippers quaintly embroidered with gold thread.

"'Elsie,' said I, lengthening my steps so as to come up with her, 'where do you live, and what do you do for a living?'

"'Sure, I live by myself,' she answered; 'and if you'd be after knowing how, you must come and see for yourself.'

"'Are you in the habit of walking over the hills at night in shoes like that?'

"'And why would I not?' she asked, in her turn. 'And where did your honor get the pretty gold ring on your finger?'

"The ring, which was of no great intrinsic value, had struck my eye in an old curiosity shop in Cork. It was an antique of very old-fashioned design, and might have belonged (as the vender assured me was the case) to one of the early kings or queens of Ireland.

"'Do you like it?' said I.

"'Will your honor be after making a present of it to Elsie?' she returned, with an insinuating tone and turn of the head.

"'Maybe I will, Elsie, on one condition. I am an artist; I make pictures of people. If you will promise to come to my studio and let me paint your portrait, I'll give you the ring, and some money besides.'

"'And will you give me the ring now?' said Elsie.

"'Yes, if you'll promise.'

"'And will you play the music to me?' she continued.

"'As much as you like.'

"'But maybe I'll not be handsome enough for ye,' said she, with a glance of her eyes beneath the dark hood.

"'I'll take the risk of that,' I answered, laughing, 'though, all the same, I don't mind taking a peep beforehand to remember you by.' So saying, I put forth a hand to draw back the concealing hood. But Elsie eluded me, I scarce know how, and laughed a third time, with the same airy, mocking cadence.

"'Give me the ring first, and then you shall see me,' she said, coaxingly.

"'Stretch out your hand, then,' returned I, removing the ring from my finger. 'When we are better acquainted, Elsie, you won't be so suspicious.'

"She held out a slender, delicate hand, on the forefinger of which I slipped the ring. As I did so, the folds of her cloak fell a little apart, affording me a glimpse of a white shoulder and of a dress that seemed in that deceptive semi-darkness to be wrought of rich and costly material; and I caught, too, or so I fancied, the frosty sparkle of precious stones.

"'Arrah, mind where ye tread!' said Elsie, in a sudden, sharp tone.

"I looked round, and became aware for the first time that we were standing near the middle of a ruined bridge which spanned a rapid stream that flowed at a considerable depth below. The parapet of the bridge on one side was broken down, and I must have been, in fact, in imminent danger of stepping over into empty air. I made my way cautiously across the decaying structure; but when I turned to assist Elsie, she was nowhere to be seen.

"What had become of the girl? I called, but no answer came. I gazed about on every side, but no trace of her was visible. Unless she had plunged into the narrow abyss at my feet, there was no place where she could have concealed herself—none at least that I could discover. She had vanished, nevertheless; and since her disappearance must have been premeditated, I finally came to the conclusion that it was useless to attempt to find her. She would present herself again in her own good time, or not at all. She had given me the slip very cleverly, and I must make the best of it. The adventure was perhaps worth the ring.

"On resuming my way, I was not a little relieved to find that I once more knew where I was. The bridge that I had just crossed was none other than the one I mentioned some time back; I was within a mile of the town, and my way lay clear before me. The moon, moreover, had now quite dispersed the clouds, and shone down with exquisite brilliance. Whatever her other failings, Elsie had been a trustworthy guide; she had brought me out of the depth of elf-land into the material world again. It had been a singular adventure, certainly; and I mused over it with a sense of mysterious pleasure as I sauntered along, humming snatches of airs, and accompanying myself on the strings. Hark! what light step was that behind me? It sounded like Elsie's; but no, Elsie was not there. The same impression or hallucination, however, recurred several times before I reached the outskirts of the town—the tread of an airy foot behind or beside my own. The fancy did not make me nervous; on the contrary, I was pleased with the notion of being thus haunted, and gave myself up to a romantic and genial vein of reverie.

"After passing one or two roofless and moss-grown cottages, I entered the narrow and rambling street which leads through the town. This street a short distance down widens a little, as if to afford the wayfarer space to observe a remarkable old house that stands on the northern side. The house was built of stone, and in a noble style of architecture; it reminded me somewhat of certain palaces of the old Italian nobility that I had seen on the Continent, and it may very probably have been built by one of the Italian or Spanish immigrants of the sixteenth or seventeenth century. The moulding of the projecting windows and arched doorway was richly carved, and upon the front of the building was an escutcheon wrought in high relief, though I could not make out the purport of the device. The moonlight falling upon this picturesque pile enhanced all its beauties, and at the same time made it seem like a vision that might dissolve away when the light ceased to shine. I must often have seen the house before, and yet I retained no definite recollection of it; I had never until now examined it with my eyes open, so to speak. Leaning against the wall on the opposite side of the street, I contemplated it for a long while at my leisure. The window at the corner was really a very fine and massive affair. It projected over the pavement below, throwing a heavy shadow aslant; the frames of the diamond-paned lattices were heavily mullioned. How often in past ages had that lattice been pushed open by some fair hand, revealing to a lover waiting beneath in the moonlight the charming countenance of his high-born mistress! Those were brave days. They had passed away long since. The great house had stood empty for who could tell how many years; only bats and vermin were its inhabitants. Where now were those who had built it? and who were they? Probably the very name of them was forgotten.

"As I continued to stare upward, however, a conjecture presented itself to my mind which rapidly ripened into a conviction. Was not this the house that Dr. Dudeen had described that very evening as having been formerly the abode of the Kern of Querin and his mysterious bride? There was the projecting window, the arched doorway. Yes, beyond a doubt this was the very house. I emitted a low exclamation of renewed interest and pleasure, and my speculations took a still more imaginative, but also a more definite turn.

"What had been the fate of that lovely lady after the Kern had brought her home insensible in his arms? Did she recover? and were they married and made happy ever after? or had the sequel been a tragic one? I remembered to have read that the victims of vampires generally became vampires themselves. Then my thoughts went back to that grave on the hill-side. Surely that was unconsecrated ground. Why had they buried her there? Ethelind of the white shoulder! Ah! why had not I lived in those days? or why might not some magic cause them to live again for me? Then would I seek this street at midnight, and standing here beneath her window, I would lightly touch the strings of my bandore until the casement opened cautiously and she looked down. A sweet vision indeed! And what prevented my realizing it? Only a matter of a couple of centuries or so. And was time, then, at which poets and philosophers sneer, so rigid and real a matter that a little faith and imagination might not overcome it? At all events, I had my banjo, the bandore's legitimate and lineal descendant, and the memory of Fionguala should have the love ditty.

"Hereupon, having retuned the instrument, I launched forth into an old Spanish love song, which I had met with in some mouldy library during my travels, and had set to music of my own. I sang low, for the deserted street re-echoed the lightest sound, and what I sang must reach only my lady's ears. The words were warm with the fire of the ancient Spanish chivalry, and I threw into their expression all the passion of the lovers of romance. Surely Fionguala, the white-shouldered, would hear, and awaken from her sleep of centuries, and come to the latticed casement and look down! Hist! see yonder! What light—what shadow is that that seems to flit from room to room within the abandoned house, and now approaches the mullioned window? Are my eyes dazzled by the play of the moonlight, or does the casement move—does it open? Nay, this is no delusion; there is no error of the senses here. There is simply a woman, young, beautiful, and richly attired, bending forward from the window, and silently beckoning me to approach.

"Too much amazed to be conscious of amazement, I advanced until I stood directly beneath the casement, and the lady's face, as she stooped toward me, was not more than twice a man's height from my own. She smiled and kissed her fingertips; something white fluttered in her hand, then fell through the air to the ground at my feet. The next moment she had withdrawn, and I heard the lattice close.

"I picked up what she had let fall; it was a delicate lace handkerchief, tied to the handle of an elaborately wrought bronze key. It was evidently the key of the house, and invited me to enter. I loosened it from the handkerchief, which bore a faint, delicious perfume, like the aroma of flowers in an ancient garden, and turned to the arched doorway. I felt no misgiving, and scarcely any sense of strangeness. All was as I had wished it to be, and as it should be; the medieval age was alive once more, and as for myself, I almost felt the velvet cloak hanging from my shoulder and the long rapier dangling at my belt. Standing in front of the door I thrust the key into the lock, turned it, and felt the bolt yield. The next instant the door was opened, apparently from within; I stepped across the threshold, the door closed again, and I was alone in the house, and in darkness.

"Not alone, however! As I extended my hand to grope my way it was met by another hand, soft, slender, and cold, which insinuated itself gently into mine and drew me forward. Forward I went, nothing loath; the darkness was impenetrable, but I could hear the light rustle of a dress close to me, and the same delicious perfume that had emanated from the handkerchief enriched the air that I breathed, while the little hand that clasped and was clasped by my own alternately tightened and half relaxed the hold of its soft cold fingers. In this manner, and treading lightly, we traversed what I presumed to be a long, irregular passageway, and ascended a staircase. Then another corridor, until finally we paused, a door opened, emitting a flood of soft light, into which we entered, still hand in hand. The darkness and the doubt were at an end.

"The room was of imposing dimensions, and was furnished and decorated in a style of antique splendor. The walls were draped with mellow hues of tapestry; clusters of candles burned in polished silver sconces, and were reflected and multiplied in tall mirrors placed in the four corners of the room. The heavy beams of the dark oaken ceiling crossed each other in squares, and were laboriously carved; the curtains and the drapery of the chairs were of heavy figured damask. At one end of the room was a broad ottoman, and in front of it a table, on which was set forth, in massive silver dishes, a sumptuous repast, with wines in crystal beakers. At the side was a vast and deep fire-place, with space enough on the broad hearth to burn whole trunks of trees. No fire, however, was there, but only a great heap of dead embers; and the room, for all its magnificence, was cold—cold as a tomb, or as my lady's hand—and it sent a subtle chill creeping to my heart.

"But my lady! how fair she was! I gave but a passing glance at the room; my eyes and my thoughts were all for her. She was dressed in white, like a bride; diamonds sparkled in her dark hair and on her snowy bosom; her lovely face and slender lips were pale, and all the paler for the dusky glow of her eyes. She gazed at me with a strange, elusive smile; and yet there was, in her aspect and bearing, something familiar in the midst of strangeness, like the burden of a song heard long ago and recalled among other conditions and surroundings. It seemed to me that something in me recognized her and knew her, had known her always. She was the woman of whom I had dreamed, whom I had beheld in visions, whose voice and face had haunted me from boyhood up. Whether we had ever met before, as human beings meet, I knew not; perhaps I had been blindly seeking her all over the world, and she had been awaiting me in this splendid room, sitting by those dead embers until all the warmth had gone out of her blood, only to be restored by the heat with which my love might supply her.

"'I thought you had forgotten me,' she said, nodding as if in answer to my thought. 'The night was so late—our one night of the year! How my heart rejoiced when I heard your dear voice singing the song I know so well! Kiss me—my lips are cold!'

"Cold indeed they were—cold as the lips of death. But the warmth of my own seemed to revive them. They were now tinged with a faint color, and in her cheeks also appeared a delicate shade of pink. She drew fuller breath, as one who recovers from a long lethargy. Was it my life that was feeding her? I was ready to give her all. She drew me to the table and pointed to the viands and the wine.

"'Eat and drink,' she said. 'You have travelled far, and you need food.'

"'Will you eat and drink with me?' said I, pouring out the wine.

"'You are the only nourishment I want,' was her answer. 'This wine is thin and cold. Give me wine as red as your blood and as warm, and I will drain a goblet to the dregs.'

"At these words, I know not why, a slight shiver passed through me. She seemed to gain vitality and strength at every instant, but the chill of the great room struck into me more and more.

"She broke into a fantastic flow of spirits, clapping her hands, and dancing about me like a child. Who was she? And was I myself, or was she mocking me when she implied that we had belonged to each other of old? At length she stood still before me, crossing her hands over her breast. I saw upon the forefinger of her right hand the gleam of an antique ring.

"'Where did you get that ring?' I demanded.

"She shook her head and laughed. 'Have you been faithful?' she asked. 'It is my ring; it is the ring that unites us; it is the ring you gave me when you loved me first. It is the ring of the Kern—the fairy ring, and I am your Ethelind—Ethelind Fionguala.'

"'So be it,' I said, casting aside all doubt and fear, and yielding myself wholly to the spell of her inscrutable eyes and wooing lips. 'You are mine, and I am yours, and let us be happy while the hours last.'

"'You are mine, and I am yours,' she repeated, nodding her head with an elfish smile. 'Come and sit beside me, and sing that sweet song again that you sang to me so long ago. Ah, now I shall live a hundred years.'

"We seated ourselves on the ottoman, and while she nestled luxuriously among the cushions, I took my banjo and sang to her. The song and the music resounded through the lofty room, and came back in throbbing echoes. And before me as I sang I saw the face and form of Ethelind Fionguala, in her jewelled bridal dress, gazing at me with burning eyes. She was pale no longer, but ruddy and warm, and life was like a flame within her. It was I who had become cold and bloodless, yet with the last life that was in me I would have sung to her of love that can never die. But at length my eyes grew dim, the room seemed to darken, the form of Ethelind alternately brightened and waxed indistinct, like the last flickerings of a fire; I swayed toward her, and felt myself lapsing into unconsciousness, with my head resting on her white shoulder."

Here Keningale paused a few moments in his story, flung a fresh log upon the fire, and then continued:

"I awoke, I know not how long afterward. I was in a vast empty room in a ruined building. Rotten shreds of drapery depended from the walls, and heavy festoons of spiders' webs gray with dust covered the windows, which were destitute of glass or sash; they had been boarded up with rough planks which had themselves become rotten with age, and admitted through their holes and crevices pallid rays of light and chilly draughts of air. A bat, disturbed by these rays or by my own movement, detached himself from his hold on a remnant of mouldy tapestry near me, and after circling dizzily round my head, wheeled the flickering noiselessness of his flight into a darker corner. As I arose unsteadily from the heap of miscellaneous rubbish on which I had been lying, something which had been resting across my knees fell to the floor with a rattle. I picked it up, and found it to be my banjo—as you see it now.

"Well, that is all I have to tell. My health was seriously impaired; all the blood seemed to have been drawn out of my veins; I was pale and haggard, and the chill—Ah, that chill," murmured Keningale, drawing nearer to the fire, and spreading out his hands to catch the warmth—"I shall never get over it; I shall carry it to my grave."

The Face in the Glass. A Hallowe'en Sketch. (1891)

Letitia Virginia Douglas

Blythe Hurst's busy tongues wagged an excited buzz of comments when it became known for a fact that the old Manor House in Witches' Walk was taken.

The place had an eerie look, and a reputation for being haunted; but the "new folks" had evinced no curiosity as to its history, else a score of old inhabitants had stood ready to pour the same into their ears, with variations.

The *fact* is, the old Manor House had been the scene of a tragedy, in itself rather pathetic than horrifying. A fair girl had been stricken by lightning on her wedding eve. The stone had gathered so much moss as it rolled that the Manor House in Witches' Walk now boasted a ghost in the likeness of the dead maiden, with magnified horrors of a kindred nature. But the new tenants were not disturbed by the faint, far-off, dark whispers that reached their ears unasked. They brought their own servants with them, and these, too, were of a nature so stolid that they did not appear to be at all in awe of "the ghost." The "new family" consisted of Mr. Arthur Whitting, a humorous writer and something of a recluse—bachelor—and his spinster sister, Miss Florimel, who kept house for her dreamy and unpractical brother.

Mr. Whitting was in the habit of forgetting, so lost was he to all interests not literary, and in all probability he would have forgotten meal-time, so absentminded was he in regard to such trifles, but Florimel was firm on the subject. So it happened that Mr. Whitting had his sister to thank for his excellent health and goodly avoirdupois.

That same determined lady was also in the habit of thrusting her brother out for a "constitutional" regularly after breakfast each morning, deaf to his meek entreaties that he might be allowed to "finish that chapter first." And it was during one of these strolls that he was first awakened to the startling fact that his Manor House was "ha'nted," by the following little occurrence: He passed a field, and stumbled upon worthy Farmer Mayhew.

"You're fr'm the old Manor House, hain't you?" observed Mayhew, with a curious glance of his shrewd gray eyes, from under the big brim of his sun hat.

Mr. Whitting replied that he was.

"Never see anything queer yet o' nights?"

"Any—I beg your pardon?" faltered Mr. Whitting, with a puzzled stare.

"Why, land alive! man, didn't you know the place is ha'nted; has been ever sence a young gal—twin, she was, too, the rector's twin darter, and *powerful* pretty!—was struck dead by lightnin' in the little back room with the vines runnin' all over the winder and the porch under it? No? Well, I'll tell ye—"

And he proceeded to edify the new tenant of the Manor House with a hair-raising chapter of horrors too lengthy to be quoted here.

Mr. Whitting was disturbed, even though he had forced his loquacious informant to a reluctant acknowledgment that "he hadn't seen nothin' himself, and couldn't lay his hand on any one as could *swear they'd* seed it with *their* own eyes, but *everybody* 'lowed—"

"Whew! the sun's getting hot. I must be going," interrupted Mr. Whitting, impatiently. Why couldn't people have let him and his delicious old woodland rat-trap alone? He had left the busy whirl of Philadelphia and come here, thinking to bury himself in the seclusion of a sylvan paradise, where he might pursue his literary labors undisturbed by any whisper from the outside world. And, lo! his beautiful dream was straightway dispelled by the harsh voice of the multitude buzzing its everlasting tattle. "They say," his pet aversion, had even pursued him into these woodland depths!

Mr. Arthur Whitting, the humorist, forgot his pet jokes now. This was no joking matter. If the servants should get tainted with this silly superstition (he recollected, with a start, having seen Stephens cast a nervous glance behind him in the library at dusk last evening), they would be giving notice next, and if there was anything he hated it was having new servants about. They mussed his MSS., mislaid his books, put him out of temper, and drove his plots out of his head. They *shouldn't* take fright. They should be coerced into sense if not coaxed, the first sign of shying they showed.

Half an hour later, Mr. Whitting, hot with his energetic homeward tramp, although a crisp October breeze was blowing, burst into the kitchen and confronted Stephens.

"Here, you! listen to what I tell you, now, and see you heed it, or *I'll make you;* do you hear? No matter what silly babble you may hear from these country gawks, don't you believe it—it's nonsense."

"About the—the—ghost, sir?" faltered Stephens, in a whisper, with a sheepish look behind at the yawning cellar-way.

Mr. Whitting laid a forcible hand on the fellow's coat-collar by way of a gentle reminder.

"You blockhead! if I ever see you looking like that again I'll—I'll *shake you!* You're old enough to know better. No giving notice, mind! if you threaten to leave this I'll lock you up. You can tell your wife the same thing *from me!* I'm not going to have my household demoralized by a lot of idle talk."

"All—all—right, sir!" sputtered Stephens, when he had at last succeeded in extricating his coat-collar from his employer's energetic grip, and had placed a safe distance between himself and that irate gentleman.

While Mr. Whitting was talking Miss Florimel entered the room.

"Why Arthur!" she cried, "what has disturbed you?"

Arthur deigned not to enlighten her then, but plunged at once into a vigorous plan of his own for setting his household an example.

"Florimel, my dear," he said, "I am thinking of changing my sleeping apartment. I shall take the little chamber in the wing—the back one on the ground floor, with the porch outside and the vines running all over the window. I observe that my ceiling leaks, and I certainly discover a draught. Be good enough to have the room thrown open and aired to day. I shall occupy it tomorrow night."

Mr. Whitting had rented the Manor House as the last occupants left it—furnished. The rector, its owner, had placed it in the hands of an agent immediately after the sad accident that befell his daughter, and had taken his family abroad.

Miss Whitting looked at her brother, under the impression that he had gone suddenly out of his senses. Stephens, too, was staring, but with the glare of horror added to the amazement in his eyes.

It had not occurred to Mr. Whitting that the next night was that deliciously-horrible gala night of the spooks, Hallowe'en.

Stephens quaked in his shoes as he lighted his master to the ground floor chamber at nine o'clock, and the latter turned a disapproving eye on his trembling hands as the spluttering candle they held quivered nervously, and the fellow stared superstitiously into the black gulf beyond the rays of light.

"You may go," said Mr. Whitting, coldly.

When he was alone he speedily lost himself in his book. The effect he had worked for was produced; or, rather, would be produced when he stepped forth whole and sound from the "ha'nted" room the next morning, and the news should have gone abroad on Maria's loquacious tongue that the master hadn't "seen anything queer there,"—nor even been disturbed by an unquiet dream. Then people would begin to feel ashamed of themselves, and maybe they would let him live out the remainder of his lease in quiet. Mr. Whitting's interest in the chamber, or the subject of which it was the keystone, did not extend beyond the impression he wished to make on his servants in thus sacrificing his comfort to destroy a popular bugaboo. He turned to his work with a sigh of relief, and speedily forgot his surroundings.

So absorbed was he that he did not hear Miss Whitting's low tap at the door until it was repeated more emphatically, and her voice said through the keyhole: "Arthur, if you have not yet retired, open the door; I have something for you."

When he had obeyed, he was confronted by his sister and a dainty tray of smoking pippins, their plump cheeks shriveled to darkest tan, with the white foam of the roasted meat just showing here and there on their shining skins. A plate of baked chestnuts and a jar of home-brewed ale completed the contents of that festive tray.

The *litterateur* opened his eyes in astonishment. There was but one night in all the year when he was wont to indulge in a midnight feast, and that particular night was observed as religiously by the brother and sister as though it had been the festival of some saint. For they had been born on a New England farm, and had been trained to love that "night in the lonesome October" when nuts, apples, games, and ghost-stories hold the tapis by common consent.

"Have you clean forgotten that this is Hallowe'en?" prattled Miss Florimel, cheerily. "Why, Art! what a sleepyhead you are growing to be, with your everlasting books and ink-pots—in your old age, I was going to say; but forty-eight is *young*. I'm fifty-five myself, and see how I have to exert my faculties for us both! You ought to be ashamed!—we haven't missed keeping Hallowe'en in at least forty-five years—*you* haven't, that is. I've kept it ever since I could remember, and—There now, *do* close that book, and sit down and toast your feet by the fire, and drink the ale while it's warm. Good-night, dear."

Mr. Whitting blew out his candle and pulled the curtain aside, to let in the bright moonlight. But the thick vine-tendrils outside, still loaded down with their luxurious leafage of crimson and freckled gold, barred the way, so that only a gleam of silvery light struggled through into the inner darkness. They had probably forgotten to air the room as he had ordered, and so the vines had been overlooked. There was a suspicious dimness in the glass as seen by the uncertain light, too, which suggested dust—the bachelor's pet abhorrence. He drew a long track down the obscured pane with his forefinger. Yes, the glass was thick with it. Ugh! No matter. To-morrow he would order Maria here with buckets and brooms; and in the meantime he would soon rid himself of those superabundant vines, so as to get a little more light on the subject. No sooner thought of than done. He threw up the sash, and, penknife in hand, began the work of destruction. In ten minutes' time not a tendril remained clinging to the window, through which a flood of fairest moonlight poured, subdued a little by the thick veil of dust.

Suddenly, as he lingered there looking out upon the pleasant landscape, he was conscious of a faint, dim profile between himself and the outer world.

He rubbed his eyes, and looked again intently. It was gone—no, the faintest shadow of a shape still remained, like a thought undefined.

He snatched his flannel pen-wiper off the desk, and hastily rubbed it over the dusty glass, that he might see more clearly. Then he quickly threw up the sash, and stepped out on to the little porch beneath. He could have sworn that some one—a woman—had stood there, with her profile turned toward him, stiff and immovable as a creature turned to stone. Where had she gone? He stepped off the low porch, and moved softly round to the rear of the house. But only the cool night wind sighing a lonely lubbaby [sic] to the crisped leaves was there. Not a moving thing in sight.

"Pshaw!" he muttered to himself, with an impatient laugh at "his folly," "has the silly tattle of the country turned *my* brain, too, I wonder?" And he turned sharply about, stepped into the room again, and shut the glass down; resolutely undressed, and sprang into bed.

But soon that unpleasant consciousness of a mysterious presence intruded on the would-be sleeper again, this time strongly.

With a low exclamation of disgust at himself and everything in general, he raised himself upon his elbow and looked toward the window, with difficulty restraining a positive start as he did so, for, clearer than before, it appeared again—a distinct face and figure, apparently standing just outside the window-pane, in a position sidewise to him. The face, beautiful in profile, yet sphinx-like in its calm solemnity, almost to expressionlessness, shone clear out as a face done in cameo, amongst a surrounding halo of hair, the whole—woman, hair, and gown—colorless with a kind of lambent whiteness that was only semi-opaque. Soft and indistinct shone through the shape the bright outer world; the hills; the forest shadows.

Mr. Whitting could not have told, so unreal was the whole experience, even while its spell was on. He leaned a little forward to see the eyes. *Were* they open? Only on the faces of sleeping children was that expression of utter oblivion to be seen. This was not the face of a child, but that of a young maiden, just budding into womanhood. There was not the faintest change of attitude. There it stood, stock-still, with hands clasped before it; not like a maiden indulging in pensive thoughts, as she stands in idle mood; not in an attitude of assumed stiffness, like one posing for effect; but with an air of solemn indescribableness [sic], like a creature turned to stone by some sudden bolt hurled from the hand of a swift Fate.

A feeling that he could not have put in words swept over Mr. Whitting. We have demonstrated that he was not a superstitious man; yet he actually shuddered, to his own immediate disgust. For the next moment he had thrown the feeling off and bounded to the window, with his dressing gown thrown about his shoulders, confident that, in his own words, "some one of those fool-idiots was playing a confounded Hallowe'en joke on him, because he had shown his contempt of their foolish ghost-rubbish."

The fact that the figure had mysteriously disappeared by the time he had reached the sash and thrown it up, only strengthened this conviction and stirred up Mr. Whitting's latent ire, as he closed the window again and crept shiveringly back to bed; but not to lie down and slumber. One backward glance at the window showed him the still figure in its place again, distinct as ever.

"I'll see how long this thing will last," quoth Mr. Whitting, grimly, to himself. "If she can stand it mooning out there in the cold, with a thin frock on, surely so can I stand it in here. We'll see who gives up first."

And fixing himself comfortably, Mr. Whitting glued his wide-awake eyes upon the serene profile, and waited. Yet, through the slow hours of the night, that sphinx never moved. Goodness! would this last all night—or rather, all morning? For the clock was striking again now—one—two—three! The creature's fondness for a joke must certainly be extreme to carry her this length, or she was mad!

He threw on his dressing-gown and sprang to the window again; and again she, or it, was gone.

Perplexed and angry at having lost his night's sleep, Whitting sat down, with the calmness of despair, to "see it out."

The cheerful voice of a distant chanticleer ushered in the pale gray light of dawn. The moon's sickly pallor mingled with it; dissolved into it; yielded itself up to annihilation, and it was day.

For a brief half-hour Mr. Whitting yielded to tired nature's demands, and dozed off into forgetfulness. When he awoke, the bright first rays of the rising sun were streaming in upon him. The mysterious profile at the window was gone.

Dressing himself, hurriedly, he stepped out into the fresh air, and carefully looked about for the lightest trace of footsteps; but there were none.

Miss Florimel laughed cheerfully when he related his experience, and declared "it was the nuts and ale, and things." They had disturbed her own digestion a little, she admitted, but had not carried her the length of seeing ghosts.

Mr. Whitting was not convinced. He was vehement and angry; not at Miss Florimel, but "at that confounded agent for misrepresenting his old spook-hole," and at those vague individuals who had dared to "put up a joke on him."

It was the agent's business to protect his tenants against annoyance of this species. He decided, against Florimel's discreet counsel, to complain to the agent, to protest, and otherwise vent his indignation.

So his morning walk was directed toward Blythe Hurst, with a purpose. The agent heard his story in silence.

"Last week, he said, briefly, "the owner of the Manor, the rector, returned from abroad. He is on his way to visit friends in Boston, and has stopped with us for a few days in order that his daughter, who is not very strong, may get completely rested before continuing the journey. I had best let him hear your complaint—he will explain. Ah! there is Miss Benton now. Miss Frances will you tell your papa there is a gentleman here to speak to him, please.

A young woman had come languidly out upon the porch from an adjoining room. She had not noticed, probably, that there was a stranger in the parlor, which also opened on the wide porch with long French windows. So she had carelessly taken up her station in front of the latter, standing with profile turned toward them, her hands loosely clasped in front of her, looking away toward the distant hills.

The face was fine and fair; but pale, either from ill health or one of those immobile, placid temperaments which never betray a thought through the medium of the features by so much as a tinge of color. A mass of loose blonde hair framed the profile. Still as a statue the girl stood until the agent's voice roused her from her apparent lethargy. The likeness was complete! Whitting was startled—so startled that he felt himself actually grow pale. For this, with a ghostly difference, was the very picture that had kept him awake all night.

There *must* be some lucid explanation of it all; though *how* [to] explain what he had seen? The dull semi-opaque shadow—the clear profile; the lambert colorlessness—were absent here; this was a girl of flesh and blood. The other—well! he would probe to the bottom of the mystery ere he left this house. Now or never. He was determined on that. His own perplexity and helplessness had one effect only, it made him angry with himself and everybody. He was in no mood to be trifled with now; and, by Jove! if this pale-faced automaton with the white hair and expressionless face thought to play upon his superstition, by prowling about her old home masquerading as a ghost to frighten the tenants off, she should pay for her prank—he would tell her father! he would—he would sue the agent! he would move! he would—would— "Please, will you step into the other room? Papa is not feeling very well this morning, and is lying down," said a soft, timid voice at his elbow. The agent had vanished. Whitting stood there alone, looking foolish enough, no doubt, with the flush and frown of anger adding their unbecoming emphasis to the deep sunburn he had lately acquired, owing to Florimel's foolish whim of making him tramp for miles in the open air every morning after breakfast.

"Ah!" he murmured sarcastically on the impulse of the moment, "this is the young lady, I presume, who had such a vast amount of fun at my expense by haunting my window on Hallowe'en. I trust you didn't catch cold, *and that you enjoyed it more than I did!*"

A deep wave of crimson surged over the girl's pale face; a look of incredulous amazement, of haughty anger, followed in its train.

"I!" she faltered, making a little gesture with her hand—a gesture of scorn and hurt dignity.

"*I* haunt your window, man! *I!*" The scorn expressed in that soft, contemptuous tone of slow disdain would have cut a less sensitive man to the quick; especially her way of saying '*man*'—"as though she had been speaking to her coachman," quoth Mr. Whitting to himself, crestfallen.

Ere he had time to rally to the attack a deep voice called from the other room:

"Frances, my love!"

"Coming, papa!"

Miss Benton deigned to turn her flashing eyes—Heaven knows there was no lack now of expression in the angry face she turned upon him!—in his direction, while her straight mouth writhed in indescribable curves of contempt as she imperiously waved him into her father's presence.

"Papa," she began at once, leaving no loophole for attack to poor Mr. Whitting, "this man—your Manor tenant—comes here with a strange complaint. He says—he dares to say—that I masqueraded before his window last night *as a ghost,* or something!"

"My daughter, my daughter, do not be hasty. You forget the—" and the white-haired old rector drew his daughter to his side and murmured something.

To Whitting's amazement the expression of haughty anger and insulted pride instantly faded from the girl's face, giving place to one of pensive sadness, as when one recalls some tender memory inseparable from sorrow.

She gave him one glance as she passed him swiftly in leaving the room, and he fancied that there were tears shining in the soft blue eyes.

"Sir," said the old rector, courteously, "you sleep in the little ground-floor bedroom in the back wing, do you not? But I know you do, else you had not been annoyed."

Whitting explained his reason for the transfer.

"Then let me solve the problem for you in a few words," resumed the old rector, in tones of gentle emotion.

"A few years ago I lived in the old manor-house with my wife and my twin daughters. My children were born there, and they had never known any other. I brought my wife there a bride—I buried her there.

"One of our daughters gave her heart to a worthy man, and they were shortly to be married, when, quite unexpectedly, he was summoned to Europe to attend the dying-bed of a relative. He cabled home, however, that he would surely be back in time for the 30th, which had been the original date set for the wedding, so that no change need be made on the cards. The night before the 30th he wired from New York: 'Will be with you early in the morning.' And my child's happiness was complete. As she was in somewhat delicate health, being at all times constitutionally fragile, she retired early to her chamber that night—the small back one on the ground floor—in order that she might gather fresh strength for the morrow. There came up that night one of those sudden, violent thunder-storms so common here in the summer-time. As she stood dreamily beside her little window, looking out through the pane at the grandeur of the storm—the crashing branches and bending trees—a fearful flash of vivid, blue sheet lightning suddenly enveloped the whole world in blinding brightness, flaring full upon her face and figure, and, by some curious freak, photographing both indelibly on the glass! . . . But my child uttered one piercing shriek and fell to the floor—*dead.*"

The speaker's voice died away in a tremulous whisper, and for one moment there was deepest silence in the room. All of Whitting's indignation had vanished. At length he said, respectfully: "But why was the pane of glass never removed? *That* would be a very easy mode of getting rid of this annoyance to your future tenants who may *not* know the story, but may object—may even be frightened off by *it* if they be of a superstitious turn."

"Because my poor wife pleaded that the wonderful picture of our child painted upon the glass by the hand of God, as it were, might never be destroyed or removed. 'It would be almost sacrilege to touch it,' she said. 'Let it always stay. Promise! Never a mortal artist could have given us as true a picture of our beloved. It is as though her spirit came back to visit us.'

"The strangest part of it is, the face of my daughter cannot be seen from the outside of the window by broad daylight, or at close quarters, except vaguely. I would never," he concluded, "have consented to leave the old place even temporarily had my own health not failed as well as that of my surviving child. And I hesitated to put it at the disposal of strangers, but could not well afford to go abroad leaving it lying idle. However, I hope soon to re-enter my old home to leave it no more."

A month later the Manor House received another family into its capacious recess—the old rector and his child came home to live. But Mr. Whitting did not move; for shortly thereafter the two families became one. And the beautiful face in the glass still looks out at twilight upon the pleasant hills, while it's counterpart in the flesh smiles at Whitting across the cosy tea-table in another room.

Man-Size in Marble (1893)

Edith Nesbit

Although every word of this story is as true as despair, I do not expect people to believe it. Nowadays a "rational explanation" is required before belief is possible. Let me then, at once, offer the "rational explanation" which finds most favor among those who have heard the tale of my life's tragedy. It is held that we were "under a delusion," Laura and I, on that thirty-first of October; and that this supposition places the whole matter on a satisfactory and believable basis. The reader can judge, when he, too, has heard my story, how far this is an "explanation," and in what sense it is "rational." There were three who took part in this: Laura and I and another man. The other man still lives, and can speak to the truth of the least credible part of my story.

I never in my life knew what it was to have as much money as I required to supply the most ordinary needs—good colors, books, and cab-fares—and when we were married we knew quite well that we should only be able to live at all by "strict punctuality and attention to business." I used to paint in those days, and Laura used to write, and we felt sure we could keep the pot at least simmering. Living in town was out of the question, so we went to look for a cottage in the country, which should be at once sanitary and picturesque. So rarely do these two qualities meet in one cottage that our search was for some time quite fruitless. We tried advertisements, but most of the desirable rural residences which we did look at proved to be lacking in both essentials, and when a cottage chanced to have drains it always had stucco as well and was shaped like a tea-caddy. And if we found a vine or rose-covered porch, corruption invariably lurked within. Our minds got so befogged by the eloquence of house-agents, and the rival disadvantages of the fever-traps and outrages to beauty which we had seen and scorned, that I very much doubt whether either of us, on our wedding morning, knew the difference between a house and a haystack. But when we got away from friends and house-agents, on our honeymoon, our wits grew clear again, and we knew a pretty cottage when at last we saw one. It was at Brenzett—a little village set on a hill over against the southern marshes. We had gone there, from the seaside village where we were staying, to see the church, and two fields from the church we found this cottage. It stood quite by itself, about two miles from the village. It was a long, low building, with rooms sticking out in unexpected places. There was a bit of stone-work—ivy-covered and moss-grown, just two old rooms, all that was left of a big house that had once stood there—and round this stone-work the house had grown up. Stripped of its roses and jasmine it would have been hideous. As it stood it was charming, and after a brief examination we took it. It was absurdly cheap. The rest of our honeymoon we spent in grubbing about in second-hand shops in the country town, picking up bits of old oak and Chippendale chairs for our furnishing. We wound up with a run up to town and a visit to Liberty's, and soon the low oak-beamed lattice-windowed rooms began to be home. There was a jolly old-fashioned garden, with grass paths, and no end of hollyhocks and sunflowers, and big lilies. From the window you could see the marsh-pastures, and beyond them the blue, thin line of the sea. We were as happy as the summer was glorious, and settled down into work sooner than we ourselves expected. I was never tired of sketching the view and the wonderful cloud effects from the open lattice, and Laura would sit at the table and write verses about them, in which I mostly played the part of foreground.

We got a tall old peasant woman to do for us. Her face and figure were good, though her cooking was of the homeliest; but she understood all about gardening, and told us all the old names of the coppices and cornfields, and the stories of the smugglers and highwaymen, and, better still, of the "things that walked," and of the "sights" which met one in lonely glens of a starlight night. She was a great comfort to us, because Laura hated housekeeping as much as I loved folklore, and we soon came to leave all the domestic business to Mrs. Dorman, and to use her legends in little magazine stories which brought in the jingling guinea.

We had three months of married happiness, and did not have a single quarrel. One October evening I had been down to smoke a pipe with the doctor—our only neighbor—a pleasant young Irishman. Laura had stayed at home to finish a comic sketch of a village episode for the *Monthly Marplot.* I left her laughing over her own jokes, and came in to find her a crumpled heap of pale muslin weeping on the window seat.

"Good heavens, my darling, what's the matter?" I cried, taking her in my arms. She leaned her little dark head against my shoulder and went on crying. I had never seen her cry before—we had always been so happy, you see—and I felt sure some frightful misfortune had happened.

"What *is* the matter? Do speak."

"It's Mrs. Dorman," she sobbed.

"What has she done?" I inquired, immensely relieved.

"She says she must go before the end of the month, and she says her niece is ill; she's gone down to see her now, but I don't believe that's the reason, because her niece is always ill. I believe someone has been setting her against us. Her manner was so queer—"

"Never mind, Pussy," I said; "whatever you do, don't cry, or I shall have to cry too, to keep you in countenance, and then you'll never respect your man again!"

She dried her eyes obediently on my handkerchief, and even smiled faintly.

"But you see," she went on, "it is really serious, because these village people are so sheepy, and if one won't do a thing you may be quite sure none of the others will. And I shall have to cook the dinners, and wash up the hateful greasy plates; and you'll have to carry cans of water about, and clean the boots and knives—and we shall never have any time for work, or earn any money, or anything. We shall have to work all day, and only be able to rest when we are waiting for the kettle to boil!"

I represented to her that even if we had to perform these duties, the day would still present some margin for other toils and recreations. But she refused to see the matter in any but the greyest light. She was very unreasonable, my Laura, but I could not have loved her any more if she had been as reasonable as Whately.

"I'll speak to Mrs. Dorman when she comes back, and see if I can't come to terms with her," I said. "Perhaps she wants a rise in her screw [salary]. It will be all right. Let's walk up to the church."

The church was a large and lonely one, and we loved to go there, especially upon bright nights. The path skirted a wood, cut through it once, and ran along the crest of the hill through two meadows, and round the churchyard wall, over which the old yews loomed in black masses of shadow. This path, which was partly paved, was called "the bier-balk," for it had long been the way by which the corpses had been carried to burial. The churchyard was richly treed, and was shaded by great elms which stood just outside and stretched their majestic arms in benediction over the happy dead. A large, low porch let one into the building by a Norman doorway and a heavy oak door studded with iron. Inside, the arches rose into darkness, and between them the reticulated windows, which stood out white in the moonlight. In the chancel, the windows were of rich glass, which showed in faint light their noble colouring, and made the black oak of the choir pews hardly more solid than the shadows. But on each side of the altar lay a grey marble figure of a knight in full plate armour lying upon a low slab, with hands held up in everlasting prayer, and these figures, oddly enough, were always to be seen if there was any glimmer of light in the church. Their names were lost, but the peasants told of them that they had been fierce and wicked men, marauders by land and sea, who had been the scourge of their time, and had been guilty of deeds so foul that the house they had lived in—the big house, by the way, that had stood on the site of our cottage—had been stricken by lightning and the vengeance of Heaven. But for all that, the gold of their heirs had bought them a place in the church. Looking at the bad hard faces reproduced in the marble, this story was easily believed.

The church looked at its best and weirdest on that night, for the shadows of the yew trees fell through the windows upon the floor of the nave and touched the pillars with tattered shade. We sat down together without speaking, and watched the solemn beauty of the old church, with some of that awe which inspired its early builders. We walked to the chancel and looked at the sleeping warriors. Then we rested some time on the stone seat in the porch, looking out over the stretch of quiet moonlit meadows, feeling in every fibre of our beings the peace of the night and of our happy love; and came away at last with a sense that even scrubbing and blackleading were but small troubles at their worst.

Mrs. Dorman had come back from the village, and I at once invited her to a *tête-à-tête*.

"Now, Mrs. Dorman," I said, when I had got her into my painting room, "what's all this about your not staying with us?"

"I should be glad to get away, sir, before the end of the month," she answered, with her usual placid dignity.

"Have you any fault to find, Mrs. Dorman?"

"None at all, sir; you and your lady have always been most kind, I'm sure—"

"Well, what is it? Are your wages not high enough?"

"No, sir, I gets quite enough."

"Then why not stay?"

"I'd rather not"—with some hesitation—"my niece is ill."

"But your niece has been ill ever since we came."

No answer. There was a long and awkward silence. I broke it.

"Can't you stay for another month?" I asked.

"No, sir. I'm bound to go by Thursday."

And this was Monday!

"Well, I must say, I think you might have let us know before. There's no time now to get any one else, and your mistress is not fit to do heavy housework. Can't you stay till next week?"

"I might be able to come back next week."

I was now convinced that all she wanted was a brief holiday, which we should have been willing enough to let her have, as soon as we could get a substitute.

"But why must you go this week?" I persisted. "Come, out with it."

Mrs. Dorman drew the little shawl, which she always wore, tightly across her bosom, as though she were cold. Then she said, with a sort of effort—

"They say, sir, as this was a big house in Catholic times, and there was a many deeds done here."

The nature of the "deeds" might be vaguely inferred from the inflection of Mrs. Dorman's voice—which was enough to make one's blood run cold. I was glad that Laura was not in the room. She was always nervous, as highly-strung natures are, and I felt that these tales about our house, told by this old peasant woman, with her impressive manner and contagious credulity, might have made our home less dear to my wife.

"Tell me all about it, Mrs. Dorman," I said; "you needn't mind about telling me. I'm not like the young people who make fun of such things."

Which was partly true.

"Well, sir"—she sank her voice—"you may have seen in the church, beside the altar, two shapes."

"You mean the effigies of the knights in armour," I said cheerfully.

"I mean them two bodies, drawed out man-size in marble," she returned, and I had to admit that her description was a thousand times more graphic than mine, to say nothing of a certain weird force and uncanniness about the phrase "drawed out man-size in marble."

"They do say, as on All Saints' Eve them two bodies sits up on their slabs, and gets off of them, and then walks down the aisle, *in their marble*"—(another good phrase, Mrs. Dorman)—"and as the church clock strikes eleven they walks out of the church door, and over the graves, and along the bier-balk, and if it's a wet night there's the marks of their feet in the morning."

"And where do they go?" I asked, rather fascinated.

"They comes back here to their home, sir, and if anyone meets them—"

"Well, what then?" I asked.

But no—not another word could I get from her, save that her niece was ill and she must go. After what I had heard I scorned to discuss the niece, and tried to get from Mrs. Dorman more details of the legend. I could get nothing but warnings.

"Whatever you do, sir, lock the door early on All Saints' Eve, and make the cross-sign over the doorstep and on the windows."

"But has anyone ever seen these things?" I persisted.

"That's not for me to say. I know what I know, sir."

"Well, who was here last year?"

"No one, sir; the lady as owned the house only stayed here in summer, and she always went to London a full month afore the night. And I'm sorry to inconvenience you and your lady, but my niece is ill and I must go on Thursday."

I could have shaken her for her absurd reiteration of that obvious fiction, after she had told me her real reasons.

She was determined to go, nor could our united entreaties move her in the least.

I did not tell Laura the legend of the shapes that "walked in their marble," partly because a legend concerning our house might perhaps trouble my wife, and partly, I think, from some more occult reason. This was not quite the same to me as any other story, and I did not want to talk about it till the day was over. I had very soon ceased to think of the legend, however. I was painting a portrait of Laura, against the lattice window, and I could not think of much else. I had got a splendid background of yellow and grey sunset, and was working away with enthusiasm at her face. On Thursday Mrs. Dorman went. She relented, at parting, so far as to say—

"Don't you put yourself about too much, ma'am, and if there's any little thing I can do next week, I'm sure I shan't mind."

From which I inferred that she wished to come back to us after Hallowe'en. Up to the last she adhered to the fiction of the niece with touching fidelity.

Thursday passed off pretty well. Laura showed marked ability in the matter of steak and potatoes, and I confess that my knives, and the plates, which I insisted upon washing, were better done than I had dared to expect.

Friday came. It is about what happened on that Friday that this is written. I wonder if I should have believed it, if anyone had told it to me. I will write the story of it as quickly and plainly as I can. Everything that happened on that day is burnt into my brain. I shall not forget anything, nor leave anything out.

I got up early, I remember, and lighted the kitchen fire, and had just achieved a smoky success, when my little wife came running down, as sunny and sweet as the clear October morning itself. We prepared breakfast together, and found it very good fun. The housework was soon done, and when brushes and brooms and pails were quiet again, the house was still indeed. It is wonderful what a difference one makes in a house. We really missed Mrs. Dorman, quite apart from considerations concerning pots and pans. We spent the day in dusting our books and putting them straight, and dined gaily on cold steak and coffee. Laura was, if possible, brighter and gayer and sweeter than usual, and I began to think that a little domestic toil was really good for her. We had never been so merry since we were married, and the walk we had that afternoon was, I think, the happiest time of all my life. When we had watched the deep scarlet clouds slowly pale into leaden grey against a pale-green sky, and saw the white mists curl up along the hedgerows in the distant marsh, we came back to the house, silently, hand in hand.

"You are sad, my darling," I said, half-jestingly, as we sat down together in our little parlour. I expected a disclaimer, for my own silence had been the silence of complete happiness. To my surprise she said—

"Yes. I think I am sad, or rather I am uneasy. I don't think I'm very well. I have shivered three or four times since we came in, and it is not cold, is it?"

"No," I said, and hoped it was not a chill caught from the treacherous mists that roll up from the marshes in the dying light. No—she said, she did not think so. Then, after a silence she spoke suddenly—

"Do you ever have presentiments of evil?"

"No," I said, smiling, "and I shouldn't believe in them if I had."

"I do," she went on; "the night my father died I knew it, though he was right away in the North of Scotland." I did not answer in words.

She sat looking at the fire for some time in silence, gently stroking my hand. At last she sprang up, came behind me, and, drawing my head back, kissed me.

"There, it's over now," she said. "What a baby I am! Come, light the candles, and we'll have some of these new Rubinstein duets."

And we spent a happy hour or two at the piano.

At about half past ten I began to long for the good-night pipe, but Laura looked so white that I felt it would be brutal of me to fill our sitting room with the fumes of strong cavendish.

"I'll take my pipe outside," I said.

"Let me come, too."

"No, sweetheart, not to-night; you're much too tired. I shan't be long. Get to bed, or I shall have an invalid to nurse to-morrow as well as the boots to clean."

I kissed her and was turning to go, when she flung her arms round my neck and held me as if she would never let me go again. I stroked her hair.

"Come, Pussy, you're over-tired. The housework has been too much for you."

She loosened her clasp a little and drew a deep breath.

"No. We've been very happy to-day, Jack, haven't we? Don't stay out too long."

"I won't, my dearie."

I strolled out of the front door, leaving it unlatched. What a night it was! The jagged masses of heavy dark cloud were rolling at intervals from horizon to horizon, and thin white wreaths covered the stars. Through all the rush of the cloud river, the moon swam, breasting the waves and disappearing again in the darkness. When now and again her light reached the woodlands they seemed to be slowly and noiselessly waving in time to the swing of the clouds above them. There was a strange grey light over all the earth; the fields had that shadowy bloom over them which only comes from the marriage of dew and moonshine, or frost and starlight.

I walked up and down, drinking in the beauty of the quiet earth and the changing sky. The night was absolutely silent. Nothing seemed to be abroad.

There was no scurrying of rabbits, or twitter of the half-asleep birds. And though the clouds went sailing across the sky, the wind that drove them never came low enough to rustle the dead leaves in the woodland paths. Across the meadows I could see the church tower standing out black and grey against the sky. I walked there thinking over our three months of happiness—and of my wife, her dear eyes, her loving ways. Oh, my little girl! My own little girl; what a vision came then of a long, glad life for you and me together!

I heard a bell-beat from the church. Eleven already! I turned to go in, but the night held me. I could not go back into our little warm rooms yet. I would go up to the church. I felt vaguely that it would be good to carry my love and thankfulness to the sanctuary whither so many loads of sorrow and gladness had been borne by the men and women of the dead years.

I looked in at the low window as I went by. Laura was half lying on her chair in front of the fire. I could not see her face, only her little head showed dark against the pale blue wall. She was quite still. Asleep, no doubt. My heart reached out to her as I went on. There must be a God, I thought, and a God who was good. How otherwise could anything so sweet and dear as she have ever been imagined?

I walked slowly along the edge of the wood. A sound broke the stillness of the night, it was a rustling in the wood. I stopped and listened. The sound stopped too. I went on, and now distinctly heard another step than mine answer mine like an echo. It was a poacher or a wood-stealer, most likely, for these were not unknown in our Arcadian neighbourhood. But whoever it was, he was a fool not to step more lightly. I turned into the wood, and now the footstep seemed to come from the path I had just left. It must be an echo, I thought. The wood looked perfect in the moonlight. The large dying ferns and the brushwood showed where through thinning foliage the pale light came down. The tree trunks stood up like Gothic columns all around me. They reminded me of the church and I turned into the bier-balk, and passed through the corpse-gate between the graves to the low porch. I paused for a moment on the stone seat where Laura and I had watched the fading land-scape. Then I noticed that the door of the church was open, and I blamed myself for having left it unlatched the other night. We were the only people who ever cared to come to the church except on Sundays, and I was vexed to think that through our carelessness the damp autumn airs had had a chance of getting in and injuring the old fabric. I went in. It will seem strange, per-haps, that I should have gone half-way up the aisle before I remembered—with a sudden chill, followed by as sudden a rush of self-contempt—that this was the very day and hour when, according to tradition, the "shapes drawed out man-size in marble" began to walk.

Having thus remembered the legend, and remembered it with a shiver, of which I was ashamed, I could not do otherwise than walk up towards the altar, just to look at the figures—as I said to myself; really what I wanted was to assure myself, first, that I did not believe the legend, and, secondly, that it was not true. I was rather glad that I had come. I thought now I could tell Mrs. Dorman how vain her fancies were, and how peacefully the marble figures slept on through the ghastly hour. With my hands in my pockets I passed up the aisle. In the grey dim light the eastern end of the church looked larger than usual, and the arches above the two tombs looked larger too. The moon came out and showed me the reason. I stopped short, my heart gave a leap that nearly choked me, and then sank sickeningly.

The "bodies drawed out man-size" *were gone,* and their marble slabs lay wide and bare in the vague moonlight that slanted through the east window.

Were they really gone? or was I mad? Clenching my nerves, I stooped and passed my hand over the smooth slabs, and felt their flat unbroken surface. Had someone taken the things away? Was it some vile practical joke? I would make sure, anyway. In an instant I had made a torch of a newspaper, which happened to be in my pocket, and lighting it held it high above my head. Its yellow glare illumined the dark arches and those slabs. The figures *were* gone. And I was alone in the church; or was I alone?

And then a horror seized me, a horror indefinable and indescribable—an overwhelming certainty of supreme and accomplished calamity. I flung down the torch and tore along the aisle and out through the porch, biting my lips as I ran to keep myself from shrieking aloud. Oh, was I mad—or what was this that possessed me? I leaped the churchyard wall and took the straight cut across the fields, led by the light from our windows. Just as I got over the first stile, a dark figure seemed to spring out of the ground. Mad still with that certainty of misfortune, I made for the thing that stood in my path, shouting, "Get out of the way, can't you!"

But my push met with a more vigorous resistance than I had expected. My arms were caught just above the elbow and held as in a vice, and the raw-boned Irish doctor actually shook me.

"Would ye?" he cried, in his own unmistakable accents—"would ye, then?"

"Let me go, you fool," I gasped. "The marble figures have gone from the church; I tell you they've gone."

He broke into a ringing laugh. "I'll have to give ye a draught to-morrow, I see. Ye've bin smoking too much and listening to old wives' tales."

"I tell you, I've seen the bare slabs."

"Well, come back with me. I'm going up to old Palmer's—his daughter's ill; we'll look in at the church and let me see the bare slabs."

"You go, if you like," I said, a little less frantic for his laughter; "I'm going home to my wife."

"Rubbish, man," said he; "d'ye think I'll permit of that? Are ye to go saying all yer life that ye've seen solid marble endowed with vitality, and me to go all me life saying ye were a coward? No, sir—ye shan't do ut."

The night air—a human voice—and I think also the physical contact with this six feet of solid common sense, brought me back a little to my ordinary self, and the word "coward" was a mental shower bath.

"Come on, then," I said sullenly; "perhaps you're right."

He still held my arm tightly. We got over the stile and back to the church. All was still as death. The place smelt very damp and earthy. We walked up the aisle. I am not ashamed to confess that I shut my eyes: I knew the figures would not be there. I heard Kelly strike a match.

"Here they are, ye see, right enough; ye've been dreaming or drinking, asking yer pardon for the imputation."

I opened my eyes. By Kelly's expiring vesta I saw two shapes lying "in their marble" on their slabs. I drew a deep breath, and caught his hand.

"I'm awfully indebted to you," I said. "It must have been some trick of light, or I have been working rather hard, perhaps that's it. Do you know, I was quite convinced they were gone."

"I'm aware of that," he answered rather grimly; "ye'll have to be careful of that brain of yours, my friend, I assure ye."

He was leaning over and looking at the right-hand figure, whose stony face was the most villainous and deadly in expression.

"By Jove," he said, "something has been afoot here—this hand is broken."

And so it was. I was certain that it had been perfect the last time Laura and I had been there.

"Perhaps some one has tried to remove them," said the young doctor.

"That won't account for my impression," I objected.

"Too much painting and tobacco will account for that, well enough."

"Come along," I said, "or my wife will be getting anxious. You'll come in and have a drop of whisky [sic] and drink confusion to ghosts and better sense to me."

"I ought to go up to Palmer's, but it's so late now I'd best leave it till the morning," he replied. "I was kept late at the Union, and I've had to see a lot of people since. All right, I'll come back with ye."

I think he fancied I needed him more than did Palmer's girl, so, discussing how such an illusion could have been possible, and deducing from this experience large generalities concerning ghostly apparitions, we walked up to our cottage. We saw, as we walked up the garden-path, that bright light streamed out of the front door, and presently saw that the parlour door was open too. Had she gone out?

"Come in," I said, and Dr. Kelly followed me into the parlour. It was all ablaze with candles, not only the wax ones, but at least a dozen guttering, glaring tallow dips, stuck in vases and ornaments in unlikely places. Light, I knew, was Laura's remedy for nervousness. Poor child! Why had I left her? Brute that I was.

We glanced round the room, and at first we did not see her. The window was open, and the draught set all the candles flaring one way. Her chair was empty and her handkerchief and book lay on the floor. I turned to the window. There, in the recess of the window, I saw her. Oh, my child, my love, had she gone to that window to watch for me? And what had come into the room behind her? To what had she turned with that look of frantic fear and horror? Oh, my little one, had she thought that it was I whose step she heard, and turned to meet—what?

She had fallen back across a table in the window, and her body lay half on it and half on the window-seat, and her head hung down over the table, the brown hair loosened and fallen to the carpet. Her lips were drawn back, and her eyes wide, wide open. They saw nothing now. What had they seen last?

The doctor moved towards her, but I pushed him aside and sprang to her; caught her in my arms and cried—

"It's all right, Laura! I've got you safe, wifie."

She fell into my arms in a heap. I clasped her and kissed her, and called her by all her pet names, but I think I knew all the time that she was dead. Her hands were tightly clenched. In one of them she held something fast. When I was quite sure that she was dead, and that nothing mattered at all any more, I let him open her hand to see what she held.

It was a grey marble finger.

A Hallowe'en Party (1896)

Caroline Ticknor

The writer smiled complacently as he penned the following lines: "Mr. J. Turner Dodge regrets that a previous engagement will prevent him from accepting Mrs. Horton's very kind invitation for Hallowe'en." Then he cheerfully directed an envelope, and after extracting a stamp from his letter-case, he caught up his hat and went forth to mail his note at once.

As the lid of the letter-box clicked after the descending "regret," J. Turner Dodge gave an audible sigh of relief and briskly retraced his steps to his rooms in Beck Hall. His return was hailed by his special crony, Charles Manhattan, who had come in to consult him about some vital question regarding athletics.

"What are you so pleased about?" his friend inquired, as he entered; "you look as if you had just received an extra check from the old man."

"I've been doing up my society correspondence," laughed the other; "by the way, are you going to do anything special next Monday night?"

Manhattan took out a small engagement-book and scanned it. "No, nothing for Monday night," he replied.

"Well, then, you have a pressing engagement to go to the theatre with me; we'll go anywhere you say. Now set it down and underline it three times, and put 'supper afterwards' in a big parenthesis."

After Manhattan had gone, his friend sat for some time gazing thoughtfully at the frost-nipped plants in the box outside of his window. A casual observer would have said that he was critically inspecting the condition of the drooping geraniums, but, in reality, at that moment he was totally unconscious of the existence of the vegetable creation.

J. Turner Dodge was inwardly reviewing his first Hallowe'en party; it was just a year ago that he had received an invitation from some suburban friends to spend that witching evening at their pleasant country house.

He knew the people only slightly, and the invitation seemed rather a formal one, but "Hallowe'en" sounded decidedly attractive. It savored of old-fashioned games and dances (of which his knowledge was very limited), and of thrilling ghost stories whispered to a spellbound circle about a blazing wood-fire. Therefore Dodge accepted the invitation immediately, undismayed by the fact that he must take a trip out of town, and he found himself looking forward to the prospective party with no little pleasure.

"They never have anything of the sort in New York," he remarked to his friend Thornton, who roomed near him; "nothing but the same old tiresome things over and over again."

That young gentleman grunted unsympathetically.

"It may be the same old thing with a different label, my boy; at the last Hallowe'en party I went to, we played progressive euchre all the evening. There is the booby prize," he concluded, pointing to a many-colored drum suspended from his gas-fixture, and bearing the appropriate motto, "Something that you *can* beat."

This was a bit disheartening to Dodge, but he consoled himself with the thought that he always had pretty good luck at progressive euchre, after all.

He was in a particularly happy frame of mind on the eventful evening. The football team had been doing fine work all the afternoon, and he had been able to cut a large number of recitations successfully; then, his new dress suit had just come out from the tailor's and it fitted him perfectly. It had arrived exactly in the nick of time, he meditated, as his old one was really too shabby to be seen in. If Dodge had been a girl he would have gazed at himself in the mirror long and with undisguised admiration; being only a man, however, he merely glanced carelessly at his glossy-coated reflection a couple of times with tolerable complacency.

The first damper upon his high spirits he sustained when he reached the railway station, for as he strolled leisurely in to take the eight o'clock train, he was greeted by the announcement that the train had gone. "Eight o'clock train goes at seven minutes of, now," the man at the gate informed him with evident satisfaction; "just changed last Wednesday; next train goes at eight-thirty."

Dodge went back and bought copies of *Life, Judge,* and *Puck,* and frowned over the jokes; after he had read them all, he discovered that it was only quarter-past eight, and then he went out and walked up and down in front of the closed gate; he wondered if it was a card-party, and pictured them playing three at one table, or getting in some unwilling elderly member of the family who didn't know the game, to torture the other players. He could see the unhappy substitute dragged from the quiet enjoyment of an evening paper, throwing down the left bower, and then hurriedly exclaiming: "Oh, I beg your pardon, I never can remember that is a trump."

Dodge was aroused from his meditations by the sound of the last bell, which bespoke the departure of the eight-thirty train, and, dashing through the gate, he jumped aboard just as the train began to move out of the station.

He was the last guest to arrive, and as he descended to greet his hostess, he became aware of the fact that the young people were enjoying a game of blind man's buff; he also noticed that he was apparently the only man present attired in a dress suit; the perception of this fact did not tend to put him greatly at his ease, but he nevertheless endeavored to enter into the game with great enthusiasm, the result of this being his immediate capture, after which he was blindfolded and left to dash wildly about with his arms extended in the air. He fell over chairs and crickets, and struck his head against the sharp corners of bookcases and jutting cabinets laden with bric-à-brac, while the fun ran high and everybody danced about and jeered at him, and the other fellows jerked his coat tails.

By the time he had captured somebody it was announced that everybody was to adjourn to the kitchen for some magnificent fun. There were chestnuts to be roasted, apples to be pared, and endless other delightful things to be done.

In the centre of the kitchen stood a tub half-filled with water. "How jolly, we are going to bob for apples!" somebody cried out.

"Have you ever tried it, Mr. Dodge?" a sprightly young girl at his elbow asked, seeing him look curiously at the wash-tub.

He replied that he had not. "Oh, Mr. Dodge has never bobbed for apples!" she exclaimed; "we must make him begin."

"Thank you, but I think I'll let somebody else show me first," he protested, determined not to indulge, if he could possibly help it.

"Yes, Mr. Dodge had better not try it in his dress suit," put in some thoughtful member of the company; and after that, there was nothing left for him to do but to insist upon bobbing for the kind of fruit which he specially disliked, to prove that his dress suit was only an old one, which he would rather spoil than not. He was instructed that the floating apples were to be extracted from the water by the victim's teeth, and intent upon not seeming disagreeable, he ducked his head desperately into the tub and splashed and spluttered with the others. "Fortune favors the brave," and showers them with things they do not want, and this, without doubt, accounted for Dodge's well-deserved success, for he finally succeeded in extracting a much bitten apple with which he emerged dripping and wrathful, but determined not to show the white feather, even if he were asked to dance in a coal-bin.

Then followed apple act number two; this time an apple was suspended from a string, and all jumped wildly in the air after it, as if the loss of a couple of front teeth was a secondary consideration compared with the pleasure to be derived from securing a bite of that apple. Dodge and a fellow opposite him jumped for it at the same moment, and the result was a violent collision which nearly broke both their noses.

Next, some one produced a candle which was to be blown out, and the girls took turns standing upon a chair and holding it up at arms length, while the young men jumped vigorously up and down, trying to extinguish it with frantic puffs. Dodge, being not very tall, exerted himself manfully until he was fairly covered with candle wax, but he blew the candle out and nearly upset the chair, young lady and all, at the same time.

After this, they experimented with a bowl of flour and a ring, and Dodge was, of course, the unlucky one to take up the ring with his teeth from the midst of the suffocating white particles, of which he inhaled a sufficient quantity to almost choke him to death.

One of the young ladies found a dish-cloth to dust him off with, and was so kind about helping him to dispose of the superfluous flour that he was led to commit the folly of running around to the cellar door on the sly, when she started down the stairs with a looking-glass and candle.

Several of the fellows called after him that there were three steps down into the cellar, but he did not hear them, and tumbled down all three; the sudden crash frightened the young lady dreadfully, and she dropped her looking-glass and candle, and proceeded to fall down the remainder of the cellar stairs, turning her ankle, so that Dodge had the satisfaction of carrying her up the whole flight. This would have been quite romantic if he had not discovered that she was engaged to one of the other men, who had intended going around to the cellar door himself, until Dodge cut in ahead of him; moreover, she was very angry because the looking-glass was broken, and said that she should now have nothing but bad luck for seven years.

By this time, the chestnuts which had been put on the top of the stove burned up, instead of popping as they should have done, and it was discovered that nobody had thought to cut the necessary slits in them. This filled the kitchen with black smoke, which set everybody coughing, although they all declared these little mishaps were half the fun. Dodge wondered when the other half was going to begin, as he tried to remove from his knees the traces of his encounter with the cellar steps, with a sooty brush which he found hanging near the stove.

Then it was suggested that one of the most satisfactory things to do was to fill one's mouth with water and run around the house; this was a sure way of summoning one's fate in spiritual form. Dodge was so glad to fill his lungs with a little fresh air after breathing in an atmosphere of chestnuts in a state of cremation for twenty minutes, that he volunteered to make a circuit of the house among the first. He started off briskly into the wet grass, regardless of his patent leathers, and was making remarkably good time when he was suddenly stopped by an intervening clothes-line, which caught him under the chin and threw him heavily to the ground. He went quietly back to the house, thinking that if a rope around his neck was to be his fate it was not necessary to mention the lamentable fact, and he had the satisfaction of seeing the next man measure his length in the same way. Number two, however, had not the sense to keep quiet about it, but called out loudly, and applied several uncomplimentary adjectives to the clothes-line, thereby spoiling any subsequent fun in that direction.

Being all thoroughly chilled by this time, they went back and cracked nuts and pared apples, and threw the peel over their shoulders; and one girl that he had taken a special dislike to, insisted that her peel formed a perfect D, "did anybody's name that she knew begin with a D?" she inquired. Nobody could think of anybody whose name began with that letter, and Dodge tried to back quietly into the china closet, but just then somebody looked at him and giggled, and then all the others took in the situation and looked away from him, so as not to make him feel conscious, and began to talk about something else, while he blushed and tried to pretend that his interest in cracking nuts had prevented his hearing the previous conversation.

Later they went back into the dining-room, and had lemonade and more apples and nuts, and all said how much nicer this simple, informal kind of thing was, than any stereotyped supper. Dodge was almost starved, but he contented himself with paring another apple, and then chopping it up into small pieces and distributing it over his plate. The crowning event was a Hallowe'en cake, which contained a ring, a bodkin, a piece of money, and other appropriate tokens.

Dodge got the thimble in his slice, and nearly swallowed it by mistake, he was so hungry; he tried to make believe that he thought this a capital joke, but he refrained from eating any more of the cake, feeling sure that he had already unwittingly swallowed the button, which all were anxiously searching for, and which nobody could seem to find.

A silvery stroke from an adjacent clock warned him that it was time to depart, and he rose, thankfully, to say good-night.

"I shall always remember my first Hallowe'en party," he protested, as he tore himself away from the festivities, amid regrets that he must hurry off so soon.

The silvery-toned clock turned out to be five minutes slow, but, by running all the way to the station, Dodge managed to swing himself on to the platform of the rear car of the departing train, at the risk of breaking his neck. When he reached the city, he wearily entered the railroad cafe, and indulged in an oyster stew; it was a poor one, and the oysters therein seemed to have clung persistently to their shells, and faithfully retained fragments thereof, but Dodge meditated, philosophically, that he might as well swallow oyster shells as buttons.

As he was hurrying to recitation next morning, he met Thornton on the steps. "How was the party?" he called out; "anything like what you have in New York?"

"No, thank heaven," Dodge responded, "we may be awfully degraded there, but we haven't fallen quite so low yet."

These were the recollections that rose before the mind's eye of J. Turner Dodge, as he gazed at the withered geraniums in his window-box.

A couple of days later Manhattan dropped in to see him, remarking: "Oh, I say, when I got back to my room the other day, I found an invitation from Mrs. Horton for Hallowe'en, and I accepted, so we'll have to have our theatre-party some other night. I knew it wouldn't make any difference to you, and, moreover, I thought you might be going to the party yourself."

"No, I declined on account of a previous engagement with you."

"Oh, come now, Dodge, I know better than that."

"Well, then, I haven't been educated up to Halloween parties. There are some tastes that can't be acquired, you know; you must be born with them, like the love of Boston baked beans."

"Oh, you're too New Yorky for anything; don't you know that these jolly informal things are twice as much fun?"

"Yes; but I'm satisfied with half as much fun; you can have my other half."

"I believe you think you won't get anything to eat."

"I know better than that; they'll have apples pared, and drawn and quartered, and suspended, and submerged, and named, and numbered, and gnawed; and chestnuts, and bodkins, and buttons, and lots of lovely things; but, in spite of all that, I prefer to be excused from parlor and kitchen gymnastics, they're too great a strain upon my nervous system."

"All right, I'll mention that fact to them, if they inquire about you."

"Thank you, I wish you would; and if they pin you down more particularly," Dodge concluded, "you can say to them that the truth was I'd just got in my new football rig, and I couldn't bear to spoil it."

Clay (1916)

James Joyce

The matron had given her leave to go out as soon as the women's tea was over and Maria looked forward to her evening out. The kitchen was spick and span: the cook said you could see yourself in the big copper boilers. The fire was nice and bright and on one of the side-tables were four very big barm-bracks. These barmbracks seemed uncut; but if you went closer you would see that they had been cut into long thick even slices and were ready to be hand-ed round at tea. Maria had cut them herself.

Maria was a very, very small person indeed but she had a very long nose and a very long chin. She talked a little through her nose, always soothingly: *'Yes, my dear,'* and *'No, my dear.'* She was always sent for when the women quarrelled over their tubs and always succeeded in making peace. One day the matron had said to her:

'Maria, you are a veritable peace-maker!'

And the sub-matron and two of the Board ladies had heard the compli-ment. And Ginger Mooney was always saying what she wouldn't do to the dummy who had charge of the irons if it wasn't for Maria. Everyone was so fond of Maria.

The women would have their tea at six o'clock and she would be able to get away before seven. From Ballsbridge to the Pillar, twenty minutes; from the Pillar to Drumcondra, twenty minutes; and twenty minutes to buy the things. She would be there before eight. She took out her purse with the silver clasps and read again the words *A Present from Belfast.* She was very fond of that purse because Joe had brought it to her five years before when he and Alphy had gone to Belfast on a Whit-Monday trip. In the purse were two half-crowns and some coppers. She would have five shillings clear after paying tram fare. What a nice evening they would have, all the children singing! Only she hoped that Joe wouldn't come in drunk. He was so different when he took any drink.

Often he had wanted her to go and live with them; but she would have felt herself in the way (though Joe's wife was ever so nice with her) and she had become accustomed to the life of the laundry. Joe was a good fellow. She had nursed him and Alphy too; and Joe used often say:

'Mamma is mamma but Maria is my proper mother.'

After the break-up at home the boys had got her that position in the *Dublin by Lamplight* laundry, and she liked it. She used to have such a bad opinion of Protestants but now she thought they were very nice people, a lit-tle quiet and serious, but still very nice people to live with. Then she had her plants in the conservatory and she liked looking after them. She had lovely ferns and wax-plants and, whenever anyone came to visit her, she always gave the visitor one or two slips from her conservatory. There was one thing she didn't like and that was the tracts on the walls; but the matron was such a nice person to deal with, so genteel.

When the cook told her everything was ready she went into the women's room and began to pull the big bell. In a few minutes the women began to come in by twos and threes, wiping their steaming hands in their petticoats and pulling down the sleeves of their blouses over their red steaming arms. They settled down before their huge mugs which the cook and the dummy filled up with hot tea, already mixed with milk and sugar in huge tin cans. Maria superintended the distribution of the barmbrack and saw that every woman got her four slices. There was a great deal of laughing and joking during the meal. Lizzie Fleming said Maria was sure to get the ring and, though Fleming had said that for so many Hallow Eves, Maria had to laugh and say she didn't want any ring or man either; and when she laughed her grey-green eyes sparkled with disappointed shyness and the tip of her nose nearly met the tip of her chin. Then Ginger Mooney lifted up her mug of tea and proposed Maria's health while all the other women clattered with their mugs on the table, and said she was sorry she hadn't a sup of porter to drink it in. And Maria laughed again till the tip of her nose nearly met the tip of her chin and till her minute body nearly shook itself asunder because she knew that Mooney meant well though, of course, she had the notions of a common woman.

But wasn't Maria glad when the women had finished their tea and the cook and the dummy had begun to clear away the tea-things! She went into her little bedroom and, remembering that the next morning was a mass morning, changed the hand of the alarm from seven to six. Then she took off her working skirt and her house-boots and laid her best skirt out on the bed and her tiny dress-boots beside the foot of the bed. She changed her blouse too and, as she stood before the mirror, she thought of how she used to dress for mass on Sunday morning when she was a young girl; and she looked with quaint affection at the diminutive body which she had so often adorned. In spite of its years she found it a nice tidy little body.

When she got outside the streets were shining with rain and she was glad of her old brown waterproof. The tram was full and she had to sit on the little stool at the end of the car, facing all the people, with her toes barely touching the floor. She arranged in her mind all she was going to do and thought how much better it was to be independent and to have your own money in your pocket. She hoped they would have a nice evening. She was sure they would but she could not help thinking what a pity it was Alphy and Joe were not speaking. They were always falling out now but when they were boys together they used to be the best of friends: but such was life.

She got out of her tram at the Pillar and ferreted her way quickly among the crowds. She went into Downes's cake-shop but the shop was so full of people that it was a long time before she could get herself attended to. She bought a dozen of mixed penny cakes, and at last came out of the shop laden with a big bag. Then she thought what else would she buy: she wanted to buy something really nice. They would be sure to have plenty of apples and nuts. It was hard to know what to buy and all she could think of was cake. She decided to buy some plumcake but Downes's plumcake had not enough almond icing on top of it so she went over to a shop in Henry Street. Here she was a long time in suiting herself and the stylish young lady behind the counter, who was evidently a little annoyed by her, asked her was it wedding-cake she wanted to buy. That made Maria blush and smile at the young lady; but the young lady took it all very seriously and finally cut a thick slice of plumcake, parcelled it up and said:

'Two-and-four, please.'

She thought she would have to stand in the Drumcondra tram because none of the young men seemed to notice her but an elderly gentleman made room for her. He was a stout gentleman and he wore a brown hard hat; he had a square red face and a greyish moustache. Maria thought he was a colonel-looking gentleman and she reflected how much more polite he was than the young men who simply stared straight before them. The gentleman began to chat with her about Hallow Eve and the rainy weather. He supposed the bag was full of good things for the little ones and said it was only right that the youngsters should enjoy themselves while they were young. Maria agreed with him and favoured him with demure nods and hems. He was very nice with her, and when she was getting out at the Canal Bridge she thanked him and bowed, and he bowed to her and raised his hat and smiled agreeably; and while she was going up along the terrace, bending her tiny head under the rain, she thought how easy it was to know a gentleman even when he has a drop taken.

Everybody said: 'O, here's Maria!' when she came to Joe's house. Joe was there, having come home from business, and all the children had their Sunday dresses on. There were two big girls in from next door and games were going on. Maria gave the bag of cakes to the eldest boy, Alphy, to divide and Mrs [sic] Donnelly said it was too good of her to bring such a big bag of cakes and made all the children say:

'Thanks, Maria.'

But Maria said she had brought something special for papa and mamma, something they would be sure to like, and she began to look for her plumcake. She tried in Downes's bag and then in the pockets of her waterproof and then on the hallstand but nowhere could she find it. Then she asked all the children had any of them eaten it—by mistake, of course—but the children all said no and looked as if they did not like to eat cakes if they were to be accused of stealing. Everybody had a solution for the mystery and Mrs Donnelly said it was plain that Maria had left it behind her in the tram. Maria, remembering how confused the gentleman with the greyish moustache had made her, coloured with shame and vexation and disappointment. At the thought of the failure of her little surprise and of the two and four-pence she had thrown away for nothing she nearly cried outright.

But Joe said it didn't matter and made her sit down by the fire. He was very nice with her. He told her all that went on in his office, repeating for her a smart answer which he had made to the manager. Maria did not understand why Joe laughed so much over the answer he had made but she said that the manager must have been a very overbearing person to deal with. Joe said he wasn't so bad when you knew how to take him, that he was a decent sort so long as you didn't rub him the wrong way. Mrs Donnelly played the piano for the children and they danced and sang. Then the two next-door girls handed round the nuts. Nobody could find the nut-crackers and Joe was nearly getting cross over it and asked how did they expect Maria to crack nuts without a nut-cracker. But Maria said she didn't like nuts and that they weren't to bother about her. Then Joe asked would she take a bottle of stout and Mrs Donnelly said there was port wine too in the house if she would prefer that. Maria said she would rather they didn't ask her to take anything: but Joe insisted.

So Maria let him have his way and they sat by the fire talking over old times and Maria thought she would put in a good word for Alphy. But Joe cried that God might strike him stone dead if ever he spoke a word to his brother again and Maria said she was sorry she had mentioned the matter. Mrs Donnelly told her husband it was a great shame for him to speak that way of his own flesh and blood but Joe said that Alphy was no brother of his and there was nearly being a row on the head of it. But Joe said he would not lose his temper on account of the night it was and asked his wife to open some more stout.

The two next-door girls had arranged some Hallow Eve games and soon everything was merry again. Maria was delighted to see the children so merry and Joe and his wife in such good spirits. The next-door girls put some saucers on the table and then led the children up to the table, blindfold. One got the prayer-book and the other three got the water; and when one of the next-door girls got the ring Mrs Donnelly shook her finger at the blushing girl as much as to say: *O I know all about it!* They insisted then on blindfolding Maria and leading her up to the table to see what she would get; and, while they were putting on the bandage, Maria laughed and laughed again till the tip of her nose nearly met the tip of her chin.

They led her up to the table amid laughing and joking and she put her hand out in the air as she was told to do. She moved her hand about here and there in the air and descended on one of the saucers. She felt a soft wet substance with her fingers and was surprised that nobody spoke or took off her bandage. There was a pause for a few seconds; and then a great deal of scuffling and whispering. Somebody said something about the garden, and at last Mrs. Donnelly said something very cross to one of the next-door girls and told her to throw it out at once: that was no play. Maria understood that it was wrong that time and so she had to do it over again: and this time she got the prayer-book.

After that Mrs Donnelly played Miss McCloud's Reel for the children and Joe made Maria take a glass of wine. Soon they were all quite merry again and Mrs Donnelly said Maria would enter a convent before the year was out because she had got the prayer-book. Maria had never seen Joe so nice to her as he was that night, so full of pleasant talk and reminiscences. She said they were all very good to her.

At last the children grew tired and sleepy and Joe asked Maria would she not sing some little song before she went, one of the old songs. Mrs Donnelly said 'Do, please, Maria!' and so Maria had to get up and stand beside the piano. Mrs Donnelly bade the children be quiet and listen to Maria's song. Then she played the prelude and said 'Now, Maria!' and Maria, blushing very much, began to sing in a tiny quavering voice. She sang *I Dreamt that I Dwelt,* and when she came to the second verse she sang again:

'I dreamt that I dwelt in marble halls
With vassals and serfs at my side
And of all who assembled within those walls
That I was the hope and the pride.

I had riches too great to count, could boast
Of a high ancestral name,
But I also dreamt, which pleased me most,
That you loved me still the same.'

But no one tried to show her her mistake; and when she had ended her song Joe was very much moved. He said that there was no time like the long ago and no music for him like poor old Balfe, whatever other people might say; and his eyes filled up so much with tears that he could not find what he was looking for and in the end he had to ask his wife to tell him where the corkscrew was.

PART III.

Plays

The Disappointment: or, The Forces of Credulity

(1796; 1st performance scheduled 1767)
Andrew Barton
[Excerpt, Act II., scene ii.]

Characters

Humorists:

Rattletrap, a supposed conjurer
Spitfire, assistant to Rattletrap
Quadrant, Hum & Parchment
 (in cahoots with Rattletrap)

Dupes:

Raccoon, an old debauchee
Trushoop, a cooper
Washball, an avaricious old barber
M'Snip, a tailor

The Place of Action, near the Stone Bridge.
Scene opens and discovers Rattletrap, *dress'd in his magic Habit, with a dark Lanthorn and candle;* Spitfire, *with a dark Lanthorn and Candle;* Quadrant, *with a Magnet, Rod and Wand; a Chest, and a figure representing the Head and Shoulders of* Blackbeard.
Rattle.

Well that's right—the holes I see are made.
Spit.
Yes, I've not been idle since you left me.
Quad.
We must lose no time 'tis near eleven o'clock.
(They poke in the chest two or three rusty pieces of silver.)
Come, come bury it at once.
(They all assist and bury the chest.)
Rattle. *(to Spitfire.)*
Now we've nothing more to do, than to see you safe in your hole—step down, step down, and mind when I give you the signal, throw fire balls—and when they come to a sight of the chest, push up the figure—now besure you act the devil, as if you were going to deceive the devil himself; and we'll reward you devilishly well.
Spit.
And the devil take me if I don't.
(Spitfire goes down the hole, and takes the figure, and the lanthorn and candle with him.)
Quad.
Now I think we're right—we're ready to receive them—and if our devil plays his part well, I think we shall make a devilish merry night of it. He, he, he. Egad here's some of them. *(he halloos)* Canoe.
(They answer without Canoe Canoe.)
Enter Hum and Parchment, hallooing Canoe.
Rattle.
Where are the rest of you?
Parch.
They're all coming; I heard them as we came down the Hill.
(Different voices without hallooing canoe, one after another, they on the stage answering them with the same word)
Enter Washball, Trushoop, M'Snip and Raccoon, *with Pick axe, Spades and Spit shouldered.*
Wash.
I tore my shins unaccountably, coming thro' the briar.
Trus.
Fait and I tumbled up the hill, 'till I got my fut in the boggs and if I hadn't held fast by the vater, I'd be drown'd.
Rac.
Don't mind gentlemen—what is de broken shin, or de cold foot compar'd wid de prospect of dese riches.

M'Sn.

By my fault I charg'd my fel with twa bottles, to leeghten me nawse; and that's a bonny geed? in a dark neete—and for fare of meeting woth any Icoondrils, I'se brought my andra under my cot—as gude stuff as e'er was made in aw Scotland.

Rattle.

Well gentlemen, are we all here?

(He calls them over by their names.)

(All say) We're all here Mr Rattletrap.

Rattle.

Keep silence gentlemen—by the calculation I made this morning, by the Satellites it must be some where near this place. *(He sets his magnet.)*

Rac.

Dis seems a likely place broder Ham, now let us hab a good heart.

Hum.

Let me beg of you brother Raccoon, not to be too fierce, I am fearful your courage will get the better of your prudence.

Rattle.

Not a word, not a word gentlemen—the magnet works this way—pray be silent—where's my rod? *(Quadrant gives him the rod and he works it.)* It draws excessive strong this way. I feel myself interrupted by invisibles—I can scarcely keep the rod in my hands—there—now I have it—it draws this way.

Rac.

Dis is de critical moment gentlemen, now gentlemen.

Hum.

You've too much courage brother Raccoon, pray be advis'd.

Rattle.

Silence—I'm near the place—the rod points to this spot—I'm near the center—I know the rod to be good: I've try'd it's virtue—'Twas cut on All-Hallow's Eve, at twelve o'clock at night, with my back to the moon: and the Mercury injected while the sap was running.

Trus.

By the holy stone: I believe he was born in the moon.

Rattle.

Not a word gentlemen. *(He draws a circle with his wand, and speaks these words)* Diapaculum interravo, testiculum stravaganza.

Trus.

By my showl! my dear, and he speakes halgebra to it.

Wash.

Oh dear! oh dear—you'll spoil all.

(Rattletrap goes round the circle and sticks twelve pieces of iron wire in the periphery; each wire having a piece of paper cut out in form of a star on its head. As he sticks them down he names the twelve signs of the Zodiack.)

Rattle.

Aries, Taurus, Gemini, Cancer, Leo, Virgo, Libra, Scorpio, Sagitarius, Capricornus, Aquarus, Pisces—make no noise else you'll disturb Jupiter, who is the most wakeful planet: he is now in his first sleep. *(He puts on a large pair of spectacles)* Let me see, it's now twelve o'clock—the moon is near her southing—Jupiter is in a sound sleep, a good omen.

Rac. *(to Hum.)*

What does he say? Upiter—is Upiter a lucky omium, broder Hum?

Hum.

Don't speak, don't speak, good brother Raccoon, pray don't—let me intreat you.

Rattle.

(Calls Washball, Trushoop, M'Snip and Raccoon.) Take off your cloaths gentlemen? *(They pull off their coats and jackets)* and stand within this circle. *(He places Hum, Quadrant, and Parchment without the circle at different posts and says)* Keep a good look out—canoe's the word, don't forget it—now run down the spit, and try this place Mr. Washball.

Wash.

(thrusts down the spit and crys out)

I feel it—I feel it—it strikes against something!

All-Hallow-Eve (1817)

James Hogg
[Excerpts from Act II, ii and Act III, ii]

[It is Halloween. A group of young villagers including the beautiful country maiden Gelon are gathered to have their fortunes read by two local weird women, Nora and Grimald. Nora is the shill—she arranges fake auguries in cahoots with local criminals—but her sister Grimald truly believes herself to possess dark power. Lord Hindlee, rich and powerful, loves Gelon, but Gelon loathes him. In the first excerpt Gelon is distracted at the very moment the image of her future husband appears, and begs the weird sisters for a second chance to see him. In Act III, scene ii, Gelon returns to the witches' cottage to try her prophecy again. Hindlee, maddened by demonic vision, appears, and Gelon, mistaking him for the image of her future husband, is devastated. Gil Moules is Hogg's term for the devil.]

Characters:

Gelon: a country maiden
Nora: a weird woman
Grimald: a weird woman
Hindlee: Lord of the land

Act II., scene ii.
[Excerpt]
Enter Gelon.
Nora.
Ha! here's our own sweet Gelon, with her sleeve
Well wash'd and wrung, and ready for the spell.
Is't the left sleeve that lies across the heart?
If not, 'tis worthless.—Aye, this is the thing!
Now, note we well what comes.—There's something strange
Connected with your fortune, Gelon.—
Here let us stand with lifted hand;
Sister, give the high command.
Grim.
King of the night-wind, come away.—
Come not like gier or ouphen gray;—

Come not like crazed or eildron wight;—
Come in youthful guise bedight,
Most pleasant to this maiden's sight!—
While thus I wave my charmed wand,
Come at this fair maid's command.
Gel.
Whoever is my true-love to be,
Come and turn over this sleeve for me.
(While they are waiting attentively, a slight noise is heard; and while they are attending to that, enter one, habited like Lord Hindlee, who turns the sleeve quickly, and goes off at the other side. They see him only as he retires.)
Grim.
Kempy's come, and also gone!
My power is to myself unknown!
There was a man, and there is none,
And the place is a void that he stood upon!
Gel.
Who was he? or what like?—Did'st see his face?
Grim.
But indistinctly, for I see not well.
How grew your strange neglect?
Gel.
I cannot tell.
O bring him back, I'll scan him o'er and o'er.—
Bring him again, dear Grimald.
Grim.
A twelvemonth you must wait ere that may be.
Gel.
A twelvemonth!—'tis an age!—I cannot bear it.
O, Grimald—Nora, call him; he will come.
Grim.
No, no—No more.
He will not come but most reluctantly.
Gel.
O you are cursed, and cruel, both of ye.
My fancy's all on tiptoe, and my mind
Stretch'd on the rack.— Sure you will pity me.
Grim.
Art thou a Christian?
Gel.

Certes; how darest thou ask?
Grim.
He will not come again! or, if he do,
The vision's fraught with danger. True, I can
Force him, by spells of potent gramarye,
To rise again, if thou darest wait the issue.
Gel.
There is not aught I will not brave t'allay
This thirst inquisitive.—I have no fear
Of form that I must love.—Nay, on my life,
I'd give all in this world I can call mine
To gain the chance I've lost.
Grim.
Then be it so;
When thy comrades go,—
Long ere the cock begins to crow,—
Unlatch the door and come to me;
But note thou well when the time must be.
When the cricket sings beyond the hearth,
And the little glow-worm pearls the earth;—
When Charles of Norway has lash'd his wain
Around by the west, and the north again,
To plow the gleam of the eastern main;—
When the seven stars the midnight have driven
Across the crown of the hoary heaven,
And hang like an ear-ring studded bright
Upon the left cheek of the night;—
When Moules, in mantle of silver gray,
Rides on the belt of the starry ray,
Or sits on the clough of the milky-way;
Then come to me, and thou shalt see
The man that is thy lord to be.
(Exit Gelon.)

Act III., Scene ii.
[Excerpt]

The Witches' Cot.
Discovers Grimald, Nora, and Gelon, standing by a Fire, at which is placed a
Waxen Image.

Gel.
Are these unearthly orgies done?
Grim.
Scarce begun!—Scarce begun!—
Come, sing one other strain with me,
To charm the spirit of destiny.
(They sing slowly and wild.)
Where art thou? Where art thou?
Busy Spirit, where art thou
Weaving the fates of mortals now?
Where art thou? &c.
Grim. (Speaks.)
Where art thou? Where art thou?
Busy Spirit, where art thou
Weaving the fates of mortals now?
Art thou beneath the ocean wave,
Scraping the sea-weeds from the grave
Where the merry sailor must shortly lie?
Or art thou gone to bustle and ply
Where flaring standards flap the sky,
Working thy baleful web of woe,
Or binding wreaths for the hero's brow?
Or art thou gone to heaven above,
Away to the waning star of love,
To skim the dew-web from the tree,
Of which the golden skene shall be
That guides the lover's destiny?
Or watchest thou the stripling's bed,
Or the couch where maiden beauty is laid,
With dreams their feelings to suborn,
And sprinkle from thy living urn
The kindred spark that long shall burn?
Spirit! wherever thou may'st be,
Or gone to the caves beneath the sea,
Or flown the wild sea-rock to haunt
And scare the drowsy cormorant;
Whether thou rangest vale or steep,
Or watchest mellow beauty's sleep,
The monarch's throne, or the field of death,
The world above, or the world beneath,

We ask thy welcome presence here,
Come—Come—Appear—Appear.
(Pause.)
I see thee not—I cannot see
The slightest shade or drapery
Of fate's own herald, known to me.
O come like a feeling, or come like a sound,
Or come like an odour along the ground;
Come like a film of floating blue,
Or come like the moss-crop's slightest flue,
Or glimmering rack of the midnight dew.
We wait thee motionless and dumb—
Come, O gentle Spirit! come.
(Pause.)
Oh me! there is trouble and torsel here;
Some countervailing spirit is near,
Who will not let the gye appear.
Sister, go to the door and see;
Note the sound that comes from the tree,
And the vapour that sleeps on the midnight lea.
Note if the shred of silver grey
Floats o'er the belt of the starry ray,
Or streams in the cleft of the milky-way.
And look between the north and the east
For the star above the mountain's crest
That changes still its witching hue,—
Note if it's green, or red, or blue.
(Exit Nora.)
This is a night of mystery!
Maiden, say a hymn with me.
(They sing soft and slow.)
Thou art weary, weary, weary!
Thou art weary and far away!
Hear me, gentle Spirit, hear me!
Come before the dawn of day!
Thou art weary, &c.
Re-enter Nora.
Say, bodes the night's eye well or ill?
Nora.
I heard a small voice from the hill;

The vapour is deadly, pale, and still.
A murmuring sough is on the wood,
And the little star is red as blood.
Moules sits not on his throne to-night,
For there is not a hue of the grizly light;
But in the cleft of heaven I scan
The giant form of a naked man;
His eye is like the burning brand,
And he holds a sword in his right hand.
Grim.
All is not well!
By dint of spell,
Somewhere between the heavens and hell,
There is this night a wild deray,
The spirits have wandered from their way!
And the purple drops shall tinge the moon
As she wanders through the midnight noon;
And the dawning heaven shall all be red
With aerial blood by angels shed.
Be as it will,
I have the skill
To work by good, or to work by ill.
(They prick the Image alternately with sharp bodkins.)
Take that for pain!
Nora.
And that for thrall!
Grim.
And that for conscience, the worst of all!
If spirits come not, mortals shall!
Another chaunt, and then, and then,
From the but or from the ben,
Spirits shall come or christian men.
(They chaunt.)
Where is Gil-Moules,
Where is Gil-Moules,
Works he not save when the tempest howls?
Where is Gil-Moules, &c.
Grim. (Speaks.)
Sleep'st thou, wakest thou, lord of the wind?
Mount thy steeds and gallop them blind,

Leave the red thunder-bolt lagging behind;
And the long-tail'd fiery dragon outfly,
The rocket of heaven, the bomb of the sky;
Over the dog-star, over the wain,
Over the cloud and the rainbow's mane;
Over the mountain and over the sea,
Haste, haste, haste to me! *(They pierce the Figure alternately.)*
Take that for trouble!
Nora.
And that for smart!
Grim.
And that for the pang that seeks the heart!
Nora.
That for madness!
Grim.
And that for thrall!
And that for conscience, the worst of all!
(Here Lord Hindlee enters furiously, half-naked—he runs his Sword through the Breast of the Figure and overturns it—then, in distracted mood, breaks away, leaving his Sword sticking in the Image.—Pause.)
Grim. (With raptures.)
Hail to thee! hail to thee, Spirit of might!
I judged thee deft, and I judged aright!
But ah! I knew not half thy might!
Not half so high had been my wonder
If thou had'st cleft the earth asunder,
And risen thyself from out the cell
In any shape of earth or hell!
But that the sons of men, submiss
Should leave their couch of happiness;
That knights and kings should quit their rest,
And trace the night at thy behest,
I knew it not! O, Spirit high,
Thine are the workings of destiny!—
Bless thee, fair lady of Hindlee towers,
(Kneeling to Gelon.)
These hills, these vales, and all are yours.
Nora.
Great joy and peace to thine and thee,
True love and high felicity;

No more our own dear Gelon Græme,
But Lady Hindlee shall be thy name.
Gel.
Ah me! I fear there is great offence;
I wish that I were safely hence!
Grim.
No evil thing shall thee perplex,
Thou hast a spirit above thy sex,
Above the common race of man—
What pity thou art Christian!
Thou can'st not soar in time of need
To deal with spirits or with the dead!
Or cause these mighty beings rise,
These great controuling energies!
O high should be thy gifted meed
Would'st thou renounce that shallow creed.
Gel.
Let me be gone!
If I had known
The half of what I have look'd upon,
I had never come here at midnight lone!

Balder (1887; written 1848-1853)

Sydney Dobell
[Excerpt, Part I., scene xiv., soliloquy]

Balder.—One can be brave
At noon, and with triumphant logic clear
The demonstrable air, but ne'ertheless,
Sometimes at Hallowe'en when, legends say,
The things that stir among the rustling trees
Are not all mortal, and the sick white moon
Wanes o'er the season of the sheeted dead,
We grow unreasonable and do quake
With more than the cold wind. The very soul,
Sick as the moon, suspects her sentinels,
And thro' her fortress of the body peers
Shivering abroad; our heart-strings over-strung,
Scare us with strange involuntary notes
Quivering and quaking, and the creeping flesh
Knows all the starting horrors of surprise
But that which makes them, and for that, half-wild,
Quickens the winking lids, and glances out
From side to side, as if some sudden chance
Of vision, some unused slant of the eye,
Some accidental focus of the sight
O' th' instant might reveal a peopled world
Crowding about us, and the empty light
Alive with phantoms. Doubtless there are no ghosts;
Yet somehow it is better not to move
Lest cold hands seize upon us from behind
Or forward thro' the dim uncertain time
Face close with paly face. My ominous dream
Leaves me in shuddering incredulity
As logically white.

By Cupid's Trick. A Parlor Drama for All Hallowe'en (1885)

Griffith Wilde

Dramatis Personae.

Ethel Barton
Amy Sellers, *her friend*
Aleck Barton, *Amy's lover*
Mark Waring, *Aleck's friend*

SCENE: A cosy [sic] sitting-room. Ethel and Amy seated reading, and at fancy-work.
Amy. (reading):
"Wi' merry songs, and friendly cracks,
I wat they did na weary;
An' unco tales, an' funnie jokes,
Their sports were cheap an' cheery;
Till buttered so'uns wi' fragrant lunt,
Set a' their gabs a-steerin';
Syne, wi' a social glass o' strunt,
They parted off careerin'
Fu' blythe that night."
(Closes the book)
What a picture that is of Hallowe'en night! It was just such a night as this, Ethel, only those good Scotchmen whom Burns writes about were more and merrier than we two "lone, lorn females." How strange it seems for us to be here alone in this great house on this night of all others. Do you feel nervous, dear?

Ethel. (biting off a thread) Not at all! Why should I?

Amy. (rising, goes to the window) Oh, I don't know. It seems sort of lonely, and—and I wish Aleck had come back.

Ethel. (playfully) Oh, nonsense! Amy, I am afraid you are very much in love with my brother.

Amy. Well, and haven't I a perfect right to be? I shouldn't be engaged to him, if I didn't love him.

Ethel. Of course not. I am sure I am very glad of it, only I never thought of him as a hero of romance. *(Sighs.)*

Amy. *(teazingly)* I suppose not. Your head is too full of some one else.

Ethel. *(reproachfully)* That's unkind, Amy. I never thought you would throw up my folly to me. I know just as well as you do that it was madness for me to think of a man whose name I never knew, who thought of me only as a charity visitor in a hospital! *(Wipes her eyes)* I shall never see him again; he is dead to me indeed, but I shall never love another.

Amy. *(coming forward penitently)* Forgive me, dear. I did not mean to tease you. Don't weep, Ethel. Fate may not be wholly unkind to you. Some day you may be happy yet.

Ethel. *(drying her eyes)* No! I have given love up forever. He is dead and I know that the thought of him is utter madness. Be happy, Amy, in the love that falls to your lot. My heart is dead and I shall bury it out of sight on the day when I marry Mark Waring.

Amy. Ethel! You are not going to throw yourself away on this stranger?

Ethel. If he asks me—yes! My uncle has set his heart upon our union. Why should I oppose it? It makes no difference to me now. *(Sighs again)*

Amy. *(in distress)* You mustn't talk so, dear. Come; cheer up. It is All Hallowe'en. This is the last night of all others to be blue. Can't we have some fun, even if Aleck and his friend can't join us?

Ethel. I am rather glad they didn't come, except on your account, Amy. It is rather dull for you in this gloomy old house.

Amy. *(cheerily)* Oh, I am all right. Don't bother about me. *(Walks about)* It is snowing, Ethel. This is just an ideal Hallowe'en. Can't we try some tricks? Come!

Ethel. *(wearily)* If you like.

Amy. It is nearly twelve o'clock. *(Walking to the fire)* We must find some excuse for such late hours. I'll tell you what, Ethel! If you will put out the lights and eat an apple before this looking glass, I'll walk around the house with my mouth full of water.

Ethel. Not in all this storm!

Amy. (gleefully) Why not? *(Sings)*
"What care I for weather
When Love and I together
Face the gath'ring storm!"
Ethel, dear, I expect to hear the name of my future husband called as I turn the corner.

Ethel. By whom, pray? There's not a soul about the place.

Amy. Nevertheless, I shall hear it, and, when I do, I shall spit the water out and say: "Now and forever, Amen!"

Ethel. (smiling) What a little goose you are, Amy. Suppose you should hear some other name than Aleck's?

Amy. (soberly) I should stop my ears. But how could I? I'm engaged to Aleck, and of course I shall marry him.

Ethel. Then what's the use of trying any of these silly tricks?

Amy. Just for fun. Come; it is five minutes of twelve. I'll give you an apple. *(Runs out)*

Ethel. (alone) I may as well please her; but it seems like mockery to trifle so with fate. Oh, my lost, my unknown lover! When I entered upon the duties of a hospital reader, how little I thought that they were to bring me in contact with the greatest happiness and misery of my life!
(Re-enter Amy with an apple and a glass of water)

Amy. Here it is! Quick! The clock is going to strike. Put the lights out. *(Takes a mouth full of water)*

Ethel. (turning out the lights) You'll get your death, Amy.

(Amy shakes her head and goes out waving her hand. Clock strikes twelve. Ethel

takes the apple and walks toward the mirror. Door opens and a gentleman, covered with snow, enters the room.)

Mark Waring. (shaking himself) This is better luck than I expected. I thought they'd all be gone to bed. There was a light here a moment ago. (Goes toward the fire) It's awfully cold! I thought we'd never get here. *(Bumps into Ethel who is eating her apple before the mirror)* Hello! I—I beg your pardon!

(Ethel turns around and screams.)

Ethel. (covering her face with her hands, starts back) It is his spirit! Oh, I am punished for my folly. In heaven's name, leave me!

Mark. (excitedly) Do my eyes deceive me, or does this dim light cheat me with a vision of happiness! Lady, speak to me! Are you not she who, when I lay sick and alone in a strange city and was taken to St. Mary's Hospital, came to me like an angel from heaven, soothing my fever with sweet dreams of love and happiness? Are you not she whom I lost and mourned so bitterly—speak?

Ethel. (trembling) I—I—oh, is it possible that you are here? They told me you were dead!

Mark. (taking her hand) A man's identity is often lost in a great hospital. My number was confounded with another's but I am here—alive and well—to tell you that I have thought of you night and day since you left me. To-night I came here, hopeless, yielding to my uncle's wish and ready to marry his niece.

Ethel. You! Then you are Mark Waring?

Mark. I am. And you? Tell me, dearest, by what name shall I call you that love cannot divine?

Ethel. I am Ethel Barton.

Mark. Can such things be in real life? Dearest, I have loved you so long! Oh, if you will, may I make my uncle's wish my own? Will you marry me? *(Takes her in his arms)*

Ethel. Gladly now!

(He kisses her. Enter Amy and Aleck covered with snow.)

Amy. I have found him, Ethel! Just as I turned the corner of the house I heard some one say, "Aleck, there's a light in the window!" I spit the water out and said, "Now and forever, Amen!" and then—

Aleck. She ran right into my arms. Goodness! How dark it is in here. *(Sees the tableau)* Hello! Mark is that you?"

Mark. (coming forward) Yes. It is I. I have made quick work of it, you see, old boy. Your sister has promised to marry me.

Aleck. Well! I should say you had. In five minutes you introduce yourself to a girl, propose, and are accepted. That's better than I did—eh, Amy?

Ethel. But Mr. Waring and I have met before. I—I was once reader in a hospital where he lay sick.

Aleck. Oh! Then you have found your sister of mercy, Mark?—the fairy you used to rave about.

Amy. (hugging Ethel) And this is he? Oh, Ethel! It is like a story book.

Mark. Yes. Your sister is the woman I fell in love with, Aleck. Congratulate me! *(They shake hands)*

Amy. You'll never call my Hallowe'en tricks silly again, will you, dear?

Ethel. Never, Amy! This night is Hallowed, indeed.

Aleck. After this, I'll believe in the Fates. It was a blind piece of luck, our catching the late train down. And who'd have thought that Mark would turn out a hero?

Ethel (shyly) I should.

Aleck (to Amy) My dear, I think a little solitude would do them good. Don't you think we'd better leave them alone?

[The Curtain]

The Immortal Hour (1911)

William Sharp
[Excerpt]

[Etain is the daughter of a fairy king. Eochaidh Airem is High King of Ireland and needs a wife. They fall in love, marry, and are happy until Midir, a fairy, comes to claim Etain. Midir was Etain's husband in the fairy world, and lost her when a spell rendered them apart. Midir challenges Eochaidh to a battle of chess and wins; as a reward, he asks for a kiss from Etain. Eochaidh is honor-bound to grant the request but fears Midir will steal Etain. Eochaidh surrounds the two with his best and bravest warriors, but Midir wraps Etain in his arms and together they disappear up the smoke-hole. Shortly, two swans circle overhead linked with chain of gold.

At the moment of this excerpt, Etain slips from the Eochaidh's mortal world to Midir's world of Fairy. It is Samhain, the only night of the year the mist lifts from the mounds and men and fairy folk trespass in each other's worlds.]

Eochaidh:
Etain, speak!
What is this song the harper sings, what tongue
It this he speaks? for in no Gaelic lands
Is speech like this upon the lips of men.
No word of all these honey-dripping words
Is known to me. Beware, beware the words
Brewed in the moonshine under ancient oaks
White with pale banners of the mistletoe
Twined round them in their slow and stately death.
It is the Feast of Sáveen.   [Samhain]

Etain:
All is dark
That has been light.

Eochaidh:
Come back, come back, O love that slips away!

Etain:
I cannot hear your voice so far away:
So far away in that dim lonely dark

Whence I have come. The light is gone.
Farewell!

Eochaidh:
Come back, come back! It is a dream that calls,
A wild and empty dream! There is no light
Within that black and terrible abyss
Whereon you stand. Etain, come back, come back,
I give you life and love.

Etain:
I cannot hear
Your strange forgotten words, already dumb
And empty sounds of dim defeated shows.
I go from dark to light.

Midir: (Slowly whispering)
From dark to light.

Eochaidh:
O, do not leave me, Star of my Desire!
My love, my hope, my dream: for now I know
That you are part of me, and I the clay,
The idle mortal clay that longed to gain,
To keep, to hold, the starry Danann fire,
The little spark that lives and does not die.

Etain:
Old, dim, wind-wandered lichens on a stone
Grown grey with ancient age: as these thy words,
Forgotten symbols. So, Farewell: farewell!

Midir:
Hasten, lost love, found love! Come, Etain, come!

Etain:
What are those sounds I hear? The wild deer call
From the hill-hollows: and in the hollows sing,
Mid waving birchen boughs, brown wandering streams:
And through the rainbow'd spray flit azure birds
Whose song is faint, is faint and far with love:

O, home-sweet, hearth-sweet, cradle-sweet it is,
The song I hear!

Midir: (Slowly moving backward)
Come, Etain, come! Afar
The hillside maids are milking the wild deer;
The elf-horns blow: green harpers on the shores
Play a wild music out across the foam:
Rose-flusht on one long wave's pale golden front,
The moon of faery hangs, low on that wave.
Come! When the vast full yellow flower is swung
High o'er the ancient woods wherein old gods,
Ancient as they, dream their eternal dreams
That in the faery dawns as shadows rise
And float into the lives and minds of men
And are the tragic pulses of the world,
Then shall we two stoop by the Secret Pool
And drink, and salve our sudden eyes with dew
Gathered from foxglove and the moonlit fern,
And see...
(Slowly chanting and looking steadfastly at Etain)
How beautiful they are,
The lordly ones
Who dwell in the hills,
In the hollow hills.
They have faces like flowers,
And their breath is wind
That stirs amid grasses
Filled with white clover.
Their limbs are more white
Than shafts of moonshine:
They are more fleet
Than the March wind.
They laugh and are glad
And are terrible:
When their lances shake
Every green reed quivers.
How beautiful they are,
How beautiful,
The lordly ones
In the hollow hills.

PART IV.

Hallowoddities

6008 Hallow e'en party. Bobbing for apples.
Copyright 2000 by C. H. Graves.

6009 Hallow e'en party. An Intruder.
Copyright 1900 by C. H. Graves.

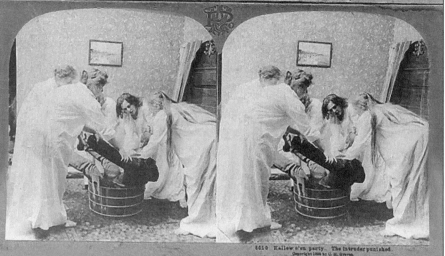

6010 Hallow e'en party. The Intruder punished.
Copyright 1900 by C. H. Graves.

The Method of Making a Magic Staff

Albertus Parvus Lucius
—Reprinted in F. Edward Hulme, *Natural History Lore and Legend,* London, 1895. Hulme cites the text from *Albertus Parvus Lucius' Little Book on the Arcane Marvels of Nature,* a medieval Latin manuscript.

Gather, on the morrow of All-Saints, a strong branch of willow, of which you will make a staff, fashioned to your liking. Hollow it out, by removing the pith from within, after having furnished the lower end with an iron ferule. Put into the bottom of the staff the two eyes of a young wolf, the tongue and heart of a dog, three green lizards, and the hearts of two young swallows. These must all be dried in the sun between two papers, having been first sprinkled with finely pulverized saltpetre. Besides all of these, put into the staff seven leaves of vervain, gathered on the eve of St. John the Baptist, with a stone of divers colours, which you will find in the nest of the lapwing, and stop the end of the staff with a panel of box, or of any other material you please, and be assured that this staff will preserve you from the perils which too often befall the traveller, either from robbers, wild beasts, mad dogs, or venemous animals. It will also procure you the goodwill of those with whom you lodge.

Dittay [Indictment] **Against Christen Michell**

—Trial testimony from Scottish historical records for 1597, reprinted in *Miscellany of The Spalding Club*, Vol. I, Aberdeen, 1841.

ITEM, Vpon Allhallowevin last bypast, at xii houris at evin or thairby, thow, accumpaniet with the said vmquhill Jonet Wischert, vmquhill Issobell Manteath, vmquhile Thomas Leis, Bessie Thom, Issobell Barroun, with a certan of vther witches and sorceraris, com to the Fische Croce of this burght vnder the conduct of Sathan, present than with yow, playing on his forme of instrumentis befoir yow, ye all dansit about the Fische Croce and about the Meillmercat a lang space, the said vmquhile Thomas Leis, being ringleader of that devilische danse. And this thow can nocht deny. In signe quhairof, the Devill gaf the a nip on the bak of thy richt hand, for a mark that thow was ane of his numer.

Account from the Church of St. Malvay in the Lewis Isles, Scotland

Martin Martin
—From Martin's study of the Lewis islands, circa 1695, published in *A Description of the Western Islands of Scotland.*

They were in greater Veneration in those days than now: it was the constant Practice of the Natives to kneel at first sight of the Church, tho at a great distance from 'em, and then they said their *Pater-noster. John Morison of Bragir* told me, that when he was a Boy, and going to the Church of St. *Mulvay,* he observed the Natives to kneel and repeat the *Pater-noster* at four miles distance from the Church. The Inhabitants of this Island had an ancient Custom to sacrifice to a Sea-God, call'd *Shony* at Hallow-tide, in the manner following: The Inhabitants round the Island came to the Church of St. *Mulvay,* having each Man his Provision along with him; every Family furnish'd a Peck of Malt, and this was brew'd into Ale: one of their number was pick'd out to wade into the Sea up to the middle, and carrying a Cup of Ale in his hand, standing still in that posture, cry'd out with a loud Voice, saying, *Shony, I give you this Cup of Ale, hoping that you'll be so kind as to send us plenty of Sea-ware, for inriching our Ground the ensuing Year:* and so threw the Cup of Ale into the Sea. This was perform'd in the Night time. At his Return to Land, they all went to Church, where there was a Candle burning upon the Altar; and then standing silent for a little time, one of them gave a Signal, at which the Candle was put out, and immediately all of them went to the Fields, where they fell a drinking their Ale, and spent the remainder of the Night in Dancing and Singing, *etc.*

The next Morning they all return'd home, being well satisfy'd that they had punctually observ'd this Solemn Anniversary, which they believ'd to be a powerful means to procure a plentiful Crop. Mr. *Daniel* and Mr. *Kenneth Morison,* Ministers in *Lewis,* told me they spent several Years, before they could persuade the vulgar Natives to abandon this ridiculous piece of Superstition; which is quite abolish'd for these 32 Years past.

Cabbage Thumping

—Eyewitness account published by Hugh Miller in *Scenes and Legends of the North of Scotland,* 1835.

The Scottish Halloween, as held in the solitary farm-house and described by Burns, differed considerably from the Halloween of our villages and smaller towns. In the farm-house it was a night of prediction only; in our towns and villages there were added a multitude of wild mischievous games which were tolerated at no other season. . . . After nightfall, the young fellows of the town formed themselves into parties of ten or a dozen, and breaking into the gardens of the graver inhabitants, stole the best and heaviest of their cabbages. Converting these into bludgeons, by stripping off the lower leaves, they next scoured the streets and lanes, thumping at every door as they passed, until their uncouth weapons were beaten to pieces. When disarmed in this way, all the parties united into one, and providing themselves with a cart, drove it before them, with the rapidity of a chaise and four, through the principal streets. Wo to the inadvertent female whom they encountered! She was instantly laid hold of and placed aloft in the cart,—brothers, and cousins, and even sons, it is said, not unfrequently assisting in the capture; and then dragged backwards and forwards over the rough stones, amid shouts, and screams, and roars of laughter.

Journal Entry by Victoria, Queen of Great Britain

October 31, 1866-1867

While we were at Mrs. Grant's we saw the commencement of the keeping of Halloween. All the children came out with burning torches, shouting and jumping. The Protestants generally keep Halloween on the old day, November 12, and the Catholics on this day; but hearing I had wished to see it two years ago, they all decided to keep it to-day. When we drove home we saw all the gillies coming along with burning torches, and torches and bonfires appeared also on the opposite side of the water. We went up stairs to look at it from the windows, from whence it had a very pretty effect.

On the same day in the following year, viz., Thursday, October 31, 1867, we had an opportunity of again seeing the celebration of Halloween, and even of taking part in it. We had been out driving, but we hurried back to be in time for the celebration. Close to Donald Stewart's house we were met by two gillies bearing torches. Louise got out and took one, walking by the side of the carriage, and looking like one of the witches in "Macbeth." As we approached *Balmoral,* the keepers and their wives and children, the gillies and other people met us, all with torches; Brown also carrying one. We got out at the house, where Leopold joined us, and a torch was given to him. We walked round the whole house, preceded by Ross playing the pipes, going down the steps of the terrace; Louise and Leopold went first, then came Janie Ely and I, followed by every one carrying torches, which had a very pretty effect. After this a bonfire was made of all the torches, close to the house, and they danced reels whilst Ross played the pipes.

Jack o Lantern Lights

—Oral history of Abram C. Hardin, recorded by Harold J. Moss for the Federal Writer's Project of the U.S. Government, 1938. Hardin saw the lights in Iowa, where he lived until 1875.

The strange Jack o Lantern Lights in Iowa were always a mystery to me. They seemed to move thru the air, about ten feet above the earth. It was a soft light red glow and moved slowly.

People naturally had all kinds of ideas about them. Some thought they were spirits or symbols, others that they were some sort of life from deep in the earth. Some tried to follow them expecting to be led to some strange spot, where old Spanish or Indian treasure lay hidden. They were a good sign or a bad sign according to the one who watched them. It was an unearthly glow but this was partly because of their unusual motion. People would say they were nothing but an overworked imagination but they were real to me. I can only explain them as pockets of luminous gas which escaped from some of the coal shafts and floated away. They would appear and disappear. But they remained more or less a mystery.

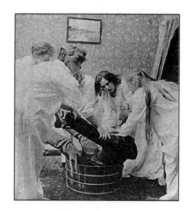

On Preparing a Corpse in Ireland

Jeremiah Curtin
—Published in *Tales of the Fairies and of the Ghost World collected from Oral Tradition in South-West Munster,* 1895.

The burial customs of Ireland are very interesting because they throw light on beliefs concerning another life—beliefs that were once universal on the island and are held yet in a certain way by a good many people. There is much variety in the burial customs of the whole country, but I can refer only to one or two details which are observed carefully in the peninsula west of Killarnney.

When the coffin is ready to be taken to the grave the lid is nailed down, but when it is at the edge of the grave the nails are drawn and placed one across another on the lid, which is left unfastened.

In arranging the corpse in the coffin the feet are generally fastened together to keep them in position. This is done frequently by pinning the stockings each other; but however done, the fastening is removed before burial and the feet are left perfectly free. The corpse is not bound in any way or confined in the coffin. That it is held necessary to free the feet of the corpse is shown by what happened once in Cahirciveen. A man died and his widow forgot to remove the pins fastening his stockings to each other. The voice of the dead man came to the woman on the night after the funeral, telling her that his feet were bound, and to free them. Next day she had the grave opened, took the pins from the stockings, and left the feet untrammelled.

It is believed as firmly by some people that the dead rise their graves time after time, each by himself, independently, as it is by others that all men will rise ages hence at one call and be judged for their deeds simultaneously. Besides the separate movements of each dead person we have the great social apparition on the night of All Saints, when the dead come to the houses of their friends and sit by the fire, unseen of all save those who are to die within the coming year. In view of this visit a good fire is made, the room is swept carefully, and prayers are repeated.

When I inquired why the nails were drawn from the coffin and bonds removed from the corpse with such care, some persons said that it was an old superstition, others that it was an old custom, and others still that it was done to give the dead man his freedom.

The Death Singers

Anatole le Braz
—Report of All Souls' Eve customs in Brittany, published in *The Living Age*,
January 2, 1897

Exactly on the stroke of midnight, they went by. In an interval of stillness between two great gusts of wind, their voices rose in a forlorn lament: the quavering accents of old men, mingling with the tones, crystalline or nasal, as might be of women and youths. The old men droned,—

> You lie abed, and take your ease!
> The poor Souls do so, never more!
> You spread your limbs, and are at peace;
> The Souls move on from door to door.
>
> Five boards, and one white sheet they have,
> A wisp of straw beneath the head,
> Five foot of earth to fill the grave
> These are the riches of the dead!

They went on to speak in the name of the Souls, identifying themselves with them. They told of the dread solitude, the long anguish, the manifold tortures of the place of expiation. They reproached the living with their inconstancy, and showed them, against the early day when they too must die, the spectre of universal ingratitude and everlasting regret.

The women and young men knocked first upon the window-panes and then sang:—

> Out, bare-foot, on the naked ground,
> All who live and are sane and sound!
> Jesus calls you to wake and pray
> For the Souls that have passed away!

I had never in my life listened to so despairing a lament. The accent of the old men in particular fairly froze the heart with anguish. It came like a shriek of terror, a heart-rending appeal out of the very abyss of mortality.

I must confess that I experienced a sense of relief, when the funeral musicians finally withdrew, and the wind got up and swept away into space the echo of their strain.

Gruesome Halloween Joke. Tombstones from a Dealer's Yard Scare a Patchogue Household

—New York Times, November 2, 1900

Patchogue, L.I. Nov. 1—When Ira B. Terry awoke this morning and looked out of his window he saw a sight that astonished him. Tombstones were to be seen in every direction. He called his wife, and when she saw what appeared to be a graveyard outside of the house she gave a cry of alarm. A number of school teachers board with Mrs. Terry, and they joined in a chorus of screams and ejaculations when they saw the spectacle.

Mr. Terry was inclined to be angry at first, but when he recalled the fact that last night was Halloween, a night devoted to pranks of all kinds, he laughed and his wife and the young teachers joined in.

Mr. Goldsmith, the owner of the marble yard from which the tombstones had been taken during the night, was not so much inclined to regard the matter in the light of a joke. His men had a busy day carrying back the stock to the yard. He says boys could not have perpetrated the joke, as the work of removing some of the tombstones would have been far too much for their strength.

Five Women Lost in Swamp. Without Food or Sleep They Wandered About Thirty-Six Hours

—*New York Times,* October 25, 1907

Exeter, Me., Oct. 24—A party of five women, Ella Hill, Nina Buswell, Ethel Burrill, Minnie Avery, and Mrs. George Prescott, who started Wednesday morning to hunt evergreen for a Halloween party were found at 8:30 o'clock to-night in the centre of a dense swamp of 30,000 acres in which they had wandered about, completely lost, for 36 hours, with out food or sleep. All of the women were so weak and exhausted from exposure and fright as to need a physician's attention, and two, Miss Avery and Miss Hill, are ill.

When the women did not return at 6 o'clock last night a searching party of 100 villagers was formed and all night long they formed a human chain and with flaring torches patrolled the swamp which is full of dense thickets and treacherous bogholes. The shouts of the searching party caught the ears of the exhausted women at nightfall to-night and they managed to make their way to their rescuers.

The Witches' Hallowmass Ride

J. Maxwell Wood
—Published in *Witchcraft and Superstitious Record in the South-western District of Scotland.* Dumfries, 1911.

On such a night the very elements themselves seemed in sympathy. The wind rose, gust following gust, in angry and ever-increasing intensity, till it hurled itself in angry blasts that levelled hat-rick and grain-stack, and tore the thatched roof from homestead and cot, where the frightened dwellers huddled and crept together in terror. Over and with higher note than the blast itself, high-pitched eldritch laughter, fleeting and mocking, skirled and shrieked through the air. Then a lull, with a stillness more terrifying than even the wild forces of the angry blast, only to be almost immediately broken with a crash of ear-splitting thunder, and the flash and the glare of forked and jagged flame, lighting up the unhallowed pathway of the "witches' ride."

The journey itself; or rather the mode of progression in passing to the "witch gathering," was itself steeped in "diabolerie" of varying degree. The simple broomstick served the more ordinary witch for a steed. Another vehicle was the chariot of "rag-wort" or ragweed, "harnessed to the wind"; for sisters of higher rank, broomsticks specially shod with the bones of murdered men, became high mettled and most spirited steeds; but the possession of a bridle, the leather of which was made from the skin of an unbaptised infant, and the iron bits forged at the "smithy" of the Evil One himself; gave to its possessor the power of the most potent spell.

NOTES

PART I. POEMS

The Flyting Betwixt Montgomerie and Polwart

The "Flyting" belongs to a style of comedic writing usually composed by two poets engaged in a no-holds-barred insult contest. These entertainments—for they were meant to be performed—were popular with everyone from the poorest to royalty. Montgomerie's "Flyting" is of note because it includes one of the earliest literary mentions of All Hallows Eve in association with witches, fairies, the devil, even ravens, as well as all manner of odious sights, smells, and diseases.

Witches were very much in the consciousness of Scots in Montgomerie's time. During the witch hunt (concentrated in the sixteenth and seventeenth centuries), an estimated 4000 Scottish souls were accused of witchcraft ("The Survey of Scottish Witchcraft," Goodare et. al., 2003). Of those, approximately half were executed. Compared to nearby Ireland, where most reports find only a handful of executions, or England, which had four times the population of Scotland but executed one-third the number of people (Levack, *The Witch-Hunt in Early Modern Europe,* 1995: 202), Scotland's death toll is extreme. It's no wonder witches turn up in the literature of Scotland. That they get attached to Halloween may be due to the collision of a Calvinist Reformation with the country's Celtic and Catholic past. John Calvin denounced trafficking with the dead—such as divination—as witchcraft, and All Souls' Day as the invention of a hallucinating monk. There is no purgatory in Protestantism, and, according to Calvin, if there are beings out at night—whispering secrets of the future, returning home, leading good folks astray—they can only be doing the devil's work. Historian Ronald Hutton writes that a good bit of superstitious belief about Halloween comes from half-remembered Catholic rituals transmuted into games and private beliefs handed down through the generations.

A Halloween Chant—The Midnight Flitting of the Corpse and Tomás MacGahan

Yeats called this "still the weirdest of Irish folk tales." The Flitting tale is much older than its 1915 publication in *One Hundred Ulster Songs (Céad de Cheoltaibh Uladh)*. It is an Irish ballad written down sometime between the mid-seventeenth and early nineteenth century and influenced by both Irish Bardic schools (where students composed conservative, traditional poetry) and contemporaneous folk poems set to harp music (Keefe, *Irish Poems*).

Halloween

Robert Burns included these notes with his poem:

1. [All Hallow Eve, or the eve of All Saints' Day] is thought to be a night when witches, devils, and other mischief-making beings are abroad on their baneful midnight errands; particularly those aerial people, the fairies, are said on that night to hold a grand anniversary.

2. Certain little, romantic, rocky, green hills, in the neighbourhood of the ancient seat of the Earls of Cassilis.

3. A noted cavern near Colean (Culzean) house, called the Cove of Colean; which, as well as Cassilis Downans, is famed, in country story, for being a favorite haunt of fairies.

4. The famous family of that name, the ancestors of Robert, the great deliverer of his country, were Earls of Carrick.

5. The first ceremony of Halloween is pulling each a *stock*, or plant of kail. They must go out hand in hand, with eyes shut, and pull the first they meet with. Its being big or little, straight or crooked, is prophetic of the size and shape of the grand object of all their spells—the husband or wife. If any *yird*, or earth, stick to the root, that is *tocher*, or fortune; and the taste of the *custock*, that is, the heart of the stem, is indicative of the natural temper and disposition. Lastly, the stems, or, to give them their proper appellation, the *runts*, are placed somewhere above the head of the door; and the Christian names of the people whom chance brings into the house are, according to the priority of placing the runts, the names in question.

6. They go to the barn-yard, and pull each, at three different times, a stalk of oats. If the third stalk wants the tap-pickle, that is, the grain at the top of the stalk, the party in question will come to the marriage-bed anything but a maid.

7. When the corn is in a doubtful state, by being too green, or wet, the stack-builder, by means of old timber, etc., makes a large apartment in his stack, with an opening in the side which is fairest exposed to the wind: this he calls a Fause-house.

8. Burning the nuts is a famous charm. They name the lad and lass to each particular nut as they lay them in the fire; and accordingly as they burn quietly together, or start from beside one another, the course and issue of the courtship will be.

9. Whoever would, with success, try this spell, must strictly observe these directions: Steal out, all alone, to the *kiln,* and darkling, throw into the *pot* a clue of blue yarn; wind it in a new clue off the old one; and, toward the latter end something will hold the thread; demand, *Wha hauds?* i.e., who holds? an answer will be returned from the kiln-pot, by naming the Christian and surname of your future spouse.

10. Take a candle and go alone to a looking-glass; eat an apple before it, and some traditions say you should comb your hair all the time; the face of your conjugal companion *to be* will be seen in the glass, as if peeping over your shoulder.

11. Steal out unperceived and sow a hand-ful of hemp-seed, harrowing it with anything you can conveniently draw after you. Repeat now and then, "Hempseed, I saw thee, hemp-seed, I saw thee; and him (or her) that is to be my truelove, come after me and pou thee." Look over your left shoulder, and you will see the appearance of the person invoked in the attitude of pulling hemp. Some traditions say, "come after me and shaw thee," that is, show thyself; in which case, it simply appears. Others omit the harrowing, and say: "come after me and harrow thee."

12. This charm must likewise be performed unperceived and alone. You go to the *barn,* and open both doors, taking them off the hinges, if possible; for there is danger that the *being* about to appear may shut the doors, and do you some mischief. Then take that instrument used in winnowing the corn, which in our country dialect we call a *wecht,* and go through all the attitudes of letting down corn against the wind. Repeat it three times, and the third time an apparition will pass through the barn, in at the windy door and out at the other, having both the figure in question and the appearance or retinue marking the employment or station in life.

13. Take an opportunity of going, unnoticed, to a *Bear-stack* [stack of bere or bigg, a kind of barley] and fathom it three times round. The last fathom of the last time you will catch in your arms the appearance of your future conjugal yoke-fellow.

14. You go out, one or more (for this is a social spell), to a south running spring or rivulet, where "three lairds' lands meet," and dip your left shirt sleeve. Go to bed in sight of a fire, and hang your wet sleeve before it to dry. Lie awake, and somewhere near midnight an apparition, having the exact figure of the grand object in question, will come and turn the sleeve, as if to dry the other side of it.

15. Take three dishes; put clean water in one, foul water in another, and leave the third empty. Blindfold a person, and lead him to the hearth where the dishes are ranged; he (or she) dips the left hand: if by chance in the clean water, the future husband or wife will come to the bar of matrimony a maid; if in the foul, a widow; if in the empty dish, it foretells with equal certainty no marriage at all. It is repeated three times, and every time the arrangement of the dishes is altered.

16. Sowens, with butter instead of milk on them, is always the *Halloween Supper.*

Burns' poem did for Halloween what Clement Clarke Moore's "A Visit From St. Nicholas" (better known as "The Night Before Christmas") did for Christmas; it etched a picture of the holiday in the public's imagination. Because of the importance of Burns both in his own day and for over one hundred years afterwards, here's a brief background of his "Halloween."

The Protestant Reformation bludgeoned pre-sixteenth century Scottish culture. Protestant sympathizers destroyed abbeys and cathedrals, the Scots language splintered into a series of dialects, and, eventually, the people were divided into Lowland (Protestant, more attached to England, more prosperous) and Highland (Gaelic/Celtic/Catholic). Most native poets of that time set their verses in classical lands such as France, Italy, or Greece, and removed any Scottishness from them to reach a broader audience of English readers. But the 1707 Union of Parliaments (most Scots fought against it) sparked a desire to preserve Scots culture before it disappeared entirely. Allan Ramsay (1684?-1758) resurrected the custom of setting poetry in a Scottish landscape, and began a Scottish vernacular revival early in the eighteenth century. Robert Fergusson's (1750-1774) poems in dialect were extremely popular. In fact, writing in Scots dialect could almost be seen as countercultural—anti-classical, anti-Anglican, and anti-British—a stance that said, "You can take our money and our lands but you'll never get our souls." "Halloween" has more dialect than any other Burns poem, even if, as scholars point out, it's not actually Scots (the language is what contemporary poet Seamus Heaney calls "art speech," a combination of oral and written Scots, English, slang, and poetics). Because it takes as its subject the daily life of rural Scots and captures Scottish customs reputedly on the verge of extinction, Burns' "Halloween" became instantly popular.

Burns did not invent folkways for his poem; there are non-literary documents that allude to these and other Halloween charms. Scottish court testimony from 1707, for example, records the trial of a man called Deuart, who had been accused of charging money for divining the whereabouts of lost items. The prosecutor demands: "Whether did you use such charms afore

Hallow-een as throwing nuts in the fire, sowing seeds up and down the house, and herbs to every corner, going backwards from the fire to the door, round the close backwards, up the stairs backwards, and to your bed backward?" Deuart replies: "Yes." (Wood, *Witchcraft and the Superstitious Record,* 133). These charms are not exclusively Scottish, either. In Irish poet Brian Merriman's "Midnight Court" (1780), the female protagonist laments how Irish men refuse to marry, and chronicles everything she's done to find a husband: "I would put my distaff in the lime kiln / I'd secret my yarnball in Reynold's mill / I'd scatter seed on the crown of a street / I'd stick a cabbage beneath the sheet, / From the recital it's clear I don't miss a trick / To see if I could get help from Old Nick." (J. Noel Fahey translation)

With "Halloween," Burns humorously satirizes the superstitions of southwestern Scotland. If there is a moral, and Burns wasn't really of the school that wrote moralistic poems, it is this: no one can know the future, you just have to take life as it comes. Initial reviewers were mixed on the poem. In February 1787, the *English Review* scolded, "A mixture of the solemn and burlesque can never be agreeable." It didn't much matter. "Halloween" was first published July 13, 1786, in the edition of *Poems, chiefly in the Scottish Dialect* now known as the Kilmarnock Burns. There were around 600 copies of the book, and they sold out quickly. More editions were published in Edinburgh and London, followed by New York and Philadelphia. George Washington owned a copy of *Poems,* as did the author of *The Legend of Sleepy Hollow,* Washington Irving. By the nineteenth century, there were Scottish clubs reciting "Halloween" annually, and Scots poets in Canada penning Burnsian verses that urged their countrymen to remember Halloween. Burns' *Poems* was eventually translated into dozens of languages including Korean (1961), Esperanto (1926), and Romanian (1925).

Burns credits his mother's maid for the charms in the poem. Many literary critics believe he owes a lot to Scots poets Allan Ramsay and Robert Fergusson (particularly Fergusson's "Hallow-Fair"), and James Grant Wilson suggests Burns may have borrowed both his subject and tone from a poem of countryman John Mayne's, below. All critics agree on this: Burns was not the first to use Halloween—or Scots rural life—as poetic material, but he did it best. His influence can be felt even today in the Burns Nights celebrated on the poets' birthday, January 25th, and to some extent in the current revival of interest in vintage Halloween images, literature, and crafts.

Halloween

John Mayne
[Excerpt. *Ruddiman's Weekly Magazine,* November 1780; the original poem was 12 stanzas]

Ranged round a bleezing *ingle-side,*   [fireside]
Where *nowther cauld* nor hunger bide,   [neither cold]
The farmer's house, wi' secret pride,
Will a' convene.

Placed at their head the gudewife sits,
And deals round apples, pears and *nits,*   [nuts]
Syne tells her guests how, at *sic* bits,   [Then; such places]
Where she has been,
Bogles hae *gart* folk *tyne* their wits   [made; lose]
At Halloween.

A' things prepared in order due,
Gosh guide's! what fearfu' pranks ensue!   [Good gosh!]
Some i' the *kiln-pat* thraw a *clue,*   [lime kiln; clew/ball of yarn]
At *whilk, bedeen,*   [which; quickly]
Their sweethearts at the far-end *pu',*   [pull]
At Halloween.

But 'twere a *langsome* tale to tell   [tedious]
The *gates* o' *ilka* charm and spell;   [ways; every]
Ance *gaun* to saw hemp-seed himsel'   [gone]
Puir Jock M' Lean
Plump in a filthy peat-pot fell,
At Halloween.

Half-felled wi' fear, and *drookit weel,*   [well-drenched]
He frae the mire dought hardly *spiel;*   [climb]
But frae that time the silly *chiel*   [fellow]
Did never *grien*   [long]
To cast his *cantrips* wi' the *Deil,*   [charms/incantations; Devil]
At Halloween.

Tam Lin

"The Tayl of the young Tamlene" can be found in *The Complaint of Scotland* published in 1549. Francis Child, who produced a five-volume collection of ballads (1882-1898), believes the story of Tam Lin shares motifs with much older Scandinavian ballads, and traces it back 2500 years to a Cretan legend. Child includes nine slightly variant versions of Tam Lin; some are collected from memory, some from printed manuscripts. The names change (Janet to Margaret, for example), and the smaller details change, but the story stays pretty much the same. Halloween is the end of the year, and if Janet doesn't rescue Tam Lin from the fairy queen, she'll have lost her chance for eternity, or at the very least, for another seasonal cycle.

That the fairies came out on Halloween was legend; that they stole babies, wives, and even handsome young men was a part of folk belief so vivid that in 1586, a Scots woman named Alison Pearson was put to death for believing her cousin, William Simpsoune, was taken by the fairies and came back from hell each year.

The verses reprinted here are from James Johnson's Scots *Musical Museum,* contributed by Robert Burns.

St. Swithin's Chair

In Scott's novel *Waverley; or 'Tis Sixty Years Since,* St. Swithin's Chair is a craggy peak known in local superstition for "curious particulars." The young and lovely Miss Rose sings the verses at afternoon tea to entertain her guests, then explains:

> I am sorry to disappoint the company, especially Captain Waverley, who listens with such laudable gravity; it is but a fragment, although I think there are other verses, describing the return of the Baron from the wars, and how the lady was found "clay-cold upon the grounsill ledge."

To_____. Ulalume: A Ballad

This version of "To_____. Ulalume: A Ballad" was published anonymously in *The American Whig Review* and includes an ending stanza that does not appear in revised versions.

Superstition, The Wood Water, Hallowe'en, The Eve of All Saints, The Jack-o'-Lantern, The Owlet

Madison Julius Cawein was a prolific writer born in Kentucky to German parents. He was best known as a nature poet, but wrote an unusually large number of Halloween-related poems.

All Souls

Edith Wharton was a master of the ghost story, and, in fact, this poem has the same title as the subtle, psychologically unnerving short story "All Souls." Women writers both in America and Great Britain wrote—and read—the majority of nineteenth- and early twentieth-century ghost stories, as they had eighteenth-century Gothic novels that inspired the genre. However, ghost stories were most often associated with Christmas. As Jerome K. Jerome wrote in *Told After Supper* (1891): "It is a genial, festive season, and we love to muse upon graves, and dead bodies, and murder and blood. For ghost stories to be told on any other evening than the evening of the twenty-fourth of December would be impossible . . ."

Victorian Magazine Poetry

Repeal of a newspaper tax in England in 1855, new printing technology, the spread of literacy, and the advent of leisure time all contributed to a boom of British periodicals during the second half of the nineteenth century. American magazines emulated their predecessors in both style and content. Some of them, such as *Harper's, Atlantic Monthly, The Delineator,* and *Godey's Lady's Book* regularly ran Halloween features, so that stories, illustrations, sheet music, and poetry made their way into the homes of a growing middle class. Victorian and Edwardian Halloween magazine and newspaper poetry was full of Burns-like charms and folklore, romance, and longing for those who had passed on: love and death.

Nineteenth-century Canadian poets who tried their hand at a Halloween poem usually acknowledged their debt to Robert Burns: "The Bard who sleeps in Dumfries' clay, / Were he but to the fore to-day, / What think you would he sing or say / Of our new-found Canadian way / Of keeping Hallowe'en?" (Thomas D'Arcy McGee, "Hallowe'en in Canada—1863"). They often used the holiday in service of Caledonian chauvinism—writing poems wrapped around a plea to keep Halloween, or more directly, to keep true to Scotland: "Ne'er be Fenian fules amang ye, / Stick to country, kirk, and Queen; / And wherever ye may wander, / Aye keep up auld Hallowe'en." (Alexander McLachlan, "Hallowe'en," 1888).

PART II. STORIES

The Child That Went With the Fairies

J.S. Le Fanu's work dominated nineteenth-century supernatural fiction. The literary ghost story, many agree, was perfected in the middle decades of the nineteenth century in magazine fiction.

Red Hanrahan

"Everyone is a visionary if you scratch him deep enough. But the Celt is a visionary without scratching," wrote Yeats in his introduction to *Irish Fairy and Folk Tales.* Yeats often dug through Irish saga literature to shape the content and characters of his stories, "Red Hanrahan" among them. Irish laws, family trees, magic lore, histories, and stories were originally preserved by Irish poets in memorized poems. Fearing information would be lost, medieval monks inscribed the information and embellished it with Latin poetry and the classics. The idea that time passes differently in the fairy world occurs in this preserved saga literature, as does the practice of being hospitable on Samhain. In the "Wooing of Etain," for example, Samhain is referred to as "a day of peace and amity between the men of Ireland." Yeats' tavern patrons welcome Hanrahan on Samhain in the very same spirit of brotherhood.

All Souls' Eve in Lower Brittany

The narrative excerpted—the story of Nann and Michael—is part of a much longer article submitted to *The Living Age* magazine as a report, rather than a work of fiction. Le Braz' storytelling skill, however, makes the piece more than journalism. For those with an interest in Breton death customs—older than Irish and even more colorful—the complete "All Souls' Eve in Lower Brittany" contains more short pieces.

The Feast of Samhain

James Stephens (along with Yeats) was part of the Irish literary renaissance, an artistic movement that revived Irish folklore and legends in order to connect modern Ireland with an ancient literary past. Stephens employed saga narrative in *The Feast of Samhain* but added his originality, transcendental thinking, and humor. Chapters I through VI introduce the character of Nera from *The Book of Leinster* (circa 1160). Scholars date the Nera story from the ninth century.

Victorian Halloween Stories

As they did with poetry, many periodicals reliably published Halloween stories throughout the nineteenth century and into the twentieth. Their plots are similarly contrived around love charms. Take, for example, "The Hallow-e'en Sensation at Guv'nor Dering's" (1888), in which a dainty heroine challenges the forces of Halloween to reveal her soulmate as she heads to the bottom of dark cellar stairs. She disappears in the "gloomy, yawning mouth" and is lost to all but clever Percival Dering, who (metaphorically) goes through hell and back to find her. In "Clara Lawson; or, The Rustic Toilet," by N.C Brooks *(The Lady's Book,* April 1836), a pretentious, Europhile aunt ("an antiquated maiden lady on the wrong side of fifty") tries to force a match between her niece and a blowhard pretending to be a Royal Professor from London. It turns out the Professor is already married, and townsfolk conspire to set up a Halloween divination trick wherein a fiery image of Satan chases him from the darkness of a cave into the arms of his abandoned, and angry Irish wife. "Hallowe'en" by Helen Elliott *(Godey's,* November, 1870) tells the story of a young woman whose husband is thought to be among the dead of the Civil War. She is coerced into doing the trick of the yarn—"You take the end of this worsted in your hand, and roll the ball into the dark, and your true love will lift it."—only to see her flesh-and-blood husband at the tail-end of the unwound ball of yarn, not dead, but a victim of mistaken identity.

Occasionally a ghost would slip into a Victorian Halloween romance, often to give guidance or provide vindication. "A Legend of All-Hallow Eve" by Georgiana S. Hull *(Harper's Magazine,* November 1879) features a ghost of a grandmother who visits a haunted room on All Hallows—the one night, according to the narrator, the unhappy dead return home. The tale is set in Scotland (as are many Victorian Halloween stories, giving the impression that the holiday is exclusively from the land of Burns). On All Saints Day, the heroine, Miss Cameron, philosophizes:

> While we sleep, the house-place swarms with the poor ghosts. This is their penance and expiation for deeds done in the flesh, until the soul in the fullness of perfection shall enter into possession of the divine. The false witness, the profligate, the murderer, the unforgiving, the miser, the sensualist, the uncharitable—it may be their hell to thus come back one night in the year, stung by an avenging Nemesis, until, their penance done, they are wafted over the Styx. The good ghosts sleep, and are troubled with no waking.

The ghost of grandmother is troubled only because the financial accounts are amiss. Once they are put right and the lines of inheritance straightened up, all may rest in peace.

Nineteenth-century readers gobbled up ghost stories. Victorians were fascinated by death (and its attendant mourning customs, fashions, and objects) and curious about the spirit world. Scholars Wendy Kolmar and Lynette Carpenter *(Ghost Stories by British and American Women)* posit that ghost stories also offered solace to thousands who'd lost family in the American Civil War. People needing consolation found reassurance in spirits, as proof of life after death.

Clay

The original title of this short story was "Christmas Eve." Joyce had drafted it with the invitational "Celtic Christmas" issue of *The Irish Homestead* in mind but he did not submit it. "Clay" was eventually published as a Halloween story in *The Dubliners*.

In Irish superstition, it is bad luck not to finish a song, and Maria does not finish hers. In the game of the three bowls played in "Clay," choosing the clay bowl usually augers death.

PART III. PLAYS

The Disappointment

Andrew Barton is likely the pseudonym of Thomas Forrest. The comic ballad opera was scheduled for production in 1767 (and is generally thought to be the first American opera) but was canceled because the play's satirical treatment of Philadelphia society offended some. The first performance was not given until 1937 in New York (as *Treasure Hunt),* and the second and third during the United States bicentennial (1976). The opera is supposedly based on an actual event and pokes fun at the eighteenth-century passion for treasure hunting. Piracy was a reality at the time, as was Captain Blackbeard (a.k.a. Edward Teach), who terrorized the Virginia and North Carolina coasts.

Historians haven't yet turned up many Halloween references from colonial times in America. But the fact that the playwright included a reference to the divining rod "cut on All Hallow's Eve" implies that, in Philadelphia at least, an audience would have understood the joke. This makes sense in light of census figures that reveal that a substantial number of American immigrants during the colonial period came from Ulster (Foster, *Modern Ireland* p. 216), and that many of them settled in Pennsylvania. The Ulster immigrants, critical to the development of colonial America, were not Irish, but a group we have come to refer to as "Scotch-Irish," mainly Protestant Scots who had emigrated from northern Ireland.

The Immortal Hour

Sharp's play is based on "The Wooing of Etain," fragments of which date from the eighth century. In Irish pseudo-history, Etain's mortal husband, Eochaid Airem, became high king of Ireland in about 134 B.C.

William Sharp also wrote as Fiona Macleod.

BIBLIOGRAPHY

Sources of Anthology Texts

John Kendrick Bangs, "Hallowe'en," *Harper's Weekly* (November 5, 1910) n.p.

Andrew Barton, Esq., Act II, scene ii, *The Disappointment: or, The Force of Credulity. A New American Comic-Opera of Two Acts.* Second edition. Philadelphia: Frances Shallus, 1796.

Joel Benton, "Hallowe'en," *Harper's Weekly* 39 (December 7, 1895): 1069.

Darl Macleod Boyle, "All Souls' Eve," *Where Lilith Dances.* New Haven: Yale University Press, 1920.

Anatole le Braz, "All Souls' Eve in Lower Brittany," *The Living Age* 212 (January 2, 1897): 419.

Robert Burns, "Halloween," *The Complete Poetical Works of Robert Burns.* New York: Thomas Y. Crowell and Co., Publishers, 1900.

Madison J. Cawein, "Superstition," *A Voice on the Wind and Other Poems by Madison J. Cawein.* Louisville: John P. Morton and Co., Publishers, 1902.

_____, "The Wood Water," *The Vale of Tempe, Poems by Madison J. Cawein.* New York: E.P. Dutton and Co., 1905.

_____, "The Eve of All-Saints"; Vol. I.; "Hallowe'en," Vol. V., *The Poems of Madison Cawein.* Boston: Small, Maynard and Co., 1908.

_____,"The Jack-o'-Lantern," *The Giant and the Star. Little Annals in Rhyme.* Boston: Small, Maynard and Co., 1909.

_____,"The Owlet," *Poems by Madison Julius Cawein.* New York: The MacMillan Company, 1911.

Arthur Cleveland Coxe, *Halloween. A Romaunt.* Second edition. Hartford: H.S. Parsons and Co., 1846.

Allan Cunningham, *The Maid of Elvar. A Poem. In Twelve Parts,* Part I. London: Edward Moxon, 1832.

Jeremiah Curtin, "John Cokeley and the Fairy," *Tales of the Fairies and of the Ghost World collected from Oral Tradition in South-West Munster.* Boston: Little, Brown and Company, 1895.

"Dittay Against Christen Michell," *Miscellany of The Spalding Club,* Vol. I., Aberdeen: Printed for the Club, 1841.

Sydney Dobell, "Balder," Part I., scene xiv, *The Poems of Sydney Dobell,* Vol. II. London: Walter Scott, Limited, 1887.

Letitia Virginia Douglas, "The Face in the Glass. A Hallowe'en Sketch," *Godey's Lady's Book* 123 (October 1891): 332.

Joseph Sheridan Le Fanu, "The Child That Went With the Fairies," anonymous in *All The Year Round, A Weekly Journal* 62 (February 5, 1870): 228.

"The Fiend's Field. A Legend of the Wrekin," *The Lady's Book* V. (August 1832): 81.

"Five Women Lost in Swamp," *New York Times* (October 25, 1907): 1.

John Galt, "The Ferry House. A Scottish Tale of Halloween," *The Literary Life and Miscellanies of John Galt.* Vol. II. Edinburgh: Wm. Blackwood; London: T. Cadell, 1834.

Theodosia Garrison, "A Ballad of Halloween," *New York Times* (October 21, 1900): 23.

"Gruesome Halloween Joke," *New York Times* (Nov. 2, 1900): 3.

Abram C. Hardin and Harold J. Moss, *American Life Histories: Manuscripts from the Federal Writers' Project, 1936-1940.* American Memory Project of the Library of Congress, http://memory.loc.gov/ (accessed January, 2004).

Julian Hawthorne, "Ken's Mystery," *Harper's New Monthly Magazine* 67 (November 1883): 925.

James Hogg, Act II, scene ii; Act III, scene ii, "All-Hallow-Eve," *Dramatick Tales.* Vol. I. Edinburgh: James Ballantyne and Co. for Longman, Hurst, Rees, Orme and Brown, 1817.

James Joyce, "Clay," *The Dubliners.* New York: B. W. Huebsch, 1916.

Robert Dwyer Joyce, "The Fire That Burned So Brightly"; "The Spalpeen," *Ballads of Irish Chivalry: Songs and Poems.* Boston: P. Donahoe, 1872.

Joan Keefe, transl., "A Halloween Chant—The Midnight Flitting of the Corpse and Tomás MacGahan," *Irish Poems: from Cromwell to the Famine. A Miscellany.* Lewisburg: Bucknell University Press and London: Associated University Presses, 1977.

Patrick Kennedy, "Black Stairs on Fire," *Legendary Fictions of the Irish Celts.* Second edition. London and Bungay: Richard Clay and Sons, Limited, 1891.

W. M. Letts, "Hallow-e'en, 1914," *The Spires of Oxford and Other Poems.* New York: E.P. Dutton and Co., 1918.

H.P. Lovecraft, "Hallowe'en in a Suburb," *The Ancient Track: The Complete Poetical Works of H.P. Lovecraft,* ed. S. T. Joshi. Night Shade Books, 2001.

James Russell Lowell, "The Black Preacher. A Breton Legend," *The Atlantic Monthly* 13 (April 1864): 465.

Albertus Parvus Lucius, "The Method of Making a Magic Staff," *Albertus Parvus Lucius' Little Book on the Arcane Marvels of Nature.* Reprinted in F. Edward Hulme, *Natural History Lore and Legend.* London: Bernard Quaritch, 1895. [Same text, with minor variation, included as note in Henry Wadsworth Longfellow, *The Poems,* Vol. V, "Christus: A Mystery," Part II (The Golden Legend) in Act V., as a note to Lucifer's line: "Were it not for my magic garters and staff / And the goblets of goodly wine I quaff, / And the mischief I make in the idle throng, / I should not continue the business long.]

Martin Martin, *A Description of the Western Islands of Scotland.* Second edition. London: A. Bell et. al., 1716. Facsimile.

Hugh Miller, *Scenes and Legends of the North of Scotland.* Edinburgh: Adam and Charles Black, 1835.

Alexander Montgomerie, "Montgomeries Answere to Polwart," excerpted from "The Flyting Betwixt Montgomerie and Polwart," *The Poems of Alexander Montgomerie,* ed. James Cranstoun, L.L.D. Printed for the Scottish Text Society. Edinburgh and London: William Blackwood and Sons, 1887.

Edith Nesbit, "The Vain Spell," *Songs of Love and Empire.* Westminster: Archibald Constable and Co., 1898.

_____, "Man-Size in Marble," Gaslight etext, http://gaslight.mtroyal.ca/ (accessed January, 2004). Reprinted from *Grim Tales.* London: A.D. Innes, 1893.

Emma A. Opper, "The Charms," *Munsey's Magazine* 30 (November 1903): 285.

Vicomte de Parny, "The Ghost," *Flowers of France: The Classic Period: Malherbe to Millevoye: Representative Poems of the 17th and 18th Centuries,* translated by John Payne. London: Villon Society, 1914.

Edgar Allan Poe, "To_____. Ulalume: A Ballad," anonymous in *The American Whig Review* 6 (December 1847): 599.

Sir Walter Scott, "St. Swithin's Chair," *Waverley: or 'Tis Sixty Years Since.* Edinburgh: Adam and Charles Black, 1855.

William Sharp (as Fiona Macleod), "The Immortal Hour," *Poems and Dramas.* New York: Duffield and Co., 1911.

Dora Sigerson Shorter, "All Souls' Night"; "The One Forgotten," *The Collected Poems of Dora Sigerson Shorter.* London: Hodder and Stoughton, 1907.

James Stephens, "The Feast of Samhain," *In the Land of Youth.* New York: The MacMillan Co., 1924.

"Tam Lin," *English and Scottish Popular Ballads edited from the collection of Francis James Child,* ed. Helen Child Sargent and George Lyman Kittredge. Boston: Houghton Mifflin and Co., 1904.

Caroline Ticknor, "A Hallowe'en Party," *A Hypocritical Romance and Other Stories.* Boston: Colonial Press, C.H. Simonds and Co., 1896.

Lettie C. VanDerveer, "De Ole Moon Knows"; "When the Woodchuck Chuckles," *Hallowe'en Happenings.* Boston: Walter H. Baker Company, 1921.

Queen Victoria, *More Leaves from the Journal of A Life in the Highlands.* New York: John W. Lovell and Company, 1884.

Edith Wharton, "All Souls," *Artemis to Actaeon and Other Verse.* New York: Charles Scribner's Sons, 1909.

Griffith Wilde, "By Cupid's Trick. A Parlor Drama for All Hallowe'en," *Godey's Lady's Book and Magazine* (November 1885): 499.

Mrs. Henry Wood, "Reality or Delusion?" *Johnny Ludlow,* First Series. London: Richard Bentley and Son, 1895.

J. Maxwell Wood, *Witchcraft and Superstitious Record in the South-western District of Scotland.* Dumfries: J. Maxwell and Son, 1911.

W.B. Yeats, "Red Hanrahan," *Stories of Red Hanrahan The Secret Rose Rosa Alchemica.* New York: The MacMillan Co. 1914.

General Reference

Oscar Fay Adams, October; November, *Through the Year with Poets.* Boston: D. Lothrop and Co., 1886.

Nina Auerbach, *Private Theatricals: The Lives of the Victorians.* Cambridge, MA: Harvard College, 1990.

Margaret Beetham and Kay Boardman, ed., *Victorian Women's Magazines.* Manchester, U.K.: Manchester University Press, 2001.

John Brand, "Allhallow Even," *Observations on Popular Antiquities. A New Edition with the Additions of Sir Henry Ellis.* London: Chatto and Windus, 1900.

Katharine Briggs, *A Dictionary of British Folk-Tales in the English Language,* Part B., Folk Legends. Vol. 2. Bloomington: Indiana University Press, 1971.

Robert Burns, *The Songs and Poems of Robert Burns.* London: T.N. Foulis, 1913.

William Carleton, *Tales and Sketches Illustrating the Character, Usages, Traditions, Sports and Pastimes of the Irish Peasantry.* Dublin: James Duffy, 1845.

Andrew Carpenter, ed., *Verse in English from Eighteenth-Century Ireland.* Cork: Cork University Press, 1998.

Lynnette Carpenter and Wendy K. Kolmar, ed., *Haunting the House of Fiction: Feminist Perspectives on Ghost Stories by American Women.* Knoxville, TN: University of Tennessee Press, 1991.

———, ed., *Ghost Stories by British and American Women.* A selected, annotated bibiliography. New York: Garland Reference Library of the Humanities, 1998.

Madison J. Cawein, *The Cup of Comus Fact and Fancy.* New York: Cameo Press, 1915.

———, *Shapes and Shadows.* New York: R.H. Russell, 1898.

Robert Chambers, *The Romantic Scottish Ballads, their epoch and authorship.* London: W. and R. Chambers, 1859.

Michael Cox and R.A. Gilbert, ed., *Victorian Ghost Stories, An Oxford*

Anthology. Oxford: Oxford University Press, 1991.

David Daiches, *Robert Burns.* London: Andre Deutsch Ltd., 1966.

Alan Dent, *Burns in His Time.* London: Nelson, 1966.

Patrick Fitzgerald and Steve Ickringill, ed. *Atlantic Crossroads: Historical Connections Between Scotland, Ulster and North America.* Newtownards: Colourpoint, 2001.

R.F. Foster, *Modern Ireland 1600-1972.* London: A. Lane; New York: Viking Penguin, 1988.

Delancey Ferguson, *Pride and Passion. Robert Burns.* New York: Oxford University Press, 1939.

Julian Goodare, ed., *The Scottish Witch-Hunt in Context.* Manchester, U.K: Manchester University Press, 2002.

_____, Lauren Martin, Joyce Miller and Louise Yeoman, "The Survey of Scottish Witchcraft," http://www.arts.edu.ac.uk/witches (archived January, 2004, accessed January, 2004).

Jerald C. Grave and Judith Layng, ed. *The Disappointment: or The Force of Credulity* (1767). Madison, WI: A-R Editions, Inc., 1976.

Patrick Griffin, *The People With No Name: Ireland's Ulster Scots, America's Scots Irish, and the Creation of a British Atlantic World, 1689-1764.* Princeton, NJ: Princeton University Press, 2001.

Ronald Hutton, *The Pagan Religions of the Ancient British Isles.* Oxford: Blackwell, 1991.

_____, *The Stations of the Sun, A History of the Ritual Year in Britain.* Oxford: Oxford University Press, 1996.

Jerome K. Jerome, *Told After Supper.* London: Leadenhall Press; New York: Scribner and Welford, 1891.

James Hogg, *The Collected Works of James Hogg,* Stirling/S.C. Research Edition. Edinburgh: Edinburgh University Press, 2001.

Douglas Hyde, *A Literary History of Ireland.* New York: St. Martin's Press, 1980.

P.W. Joyce, *A Social History of Ancient Ireland.* Vol. I. New York and London: Benjamin Blom, 1968.

Brian P. Levack, *The Witch-Hunt in Early Modern Europe.* Second edition. London: Longman Group Ltd., 1995.

F. Marian McNeill, *The Silver Bough*. Vol. 3: A Calendar of Scottish National Festivals Hallowe'en to Yule. Glasgow: Wm. Maclellan, 1961.

Sean O'Faolain, trans. "Summer is Gone," *An Anthology of Irish Literature*. Vol. I., David H. Greene, ed. New York: New York University Press, 1974.

Cóilín Owens, "'Clay' (1): Irish Folklore," *James Joyce Quarterly* 27 (Winter 1990): 337.

Seamus Perry, "Elegant, Unnatural Scots," *Times Literary Supplement* (May 9, 2003): 11.

Ann Radcliffe, *The Castles of Athlin and Dunbayne; A Highland Story*. London: J. Jones, 1821.

John D. Ross, *The Story of the Kilmarnock Burns*. Stirling, U.K.: Eneas MacKay, 1933.

Sir Walter Scott, *Minstrelsy of the Scottish Border*. London: Thomas Tegg, 1839.

Joanne Shattock and Michael Wolff, ed., *The Victorian Periodical Press: samplings and soundings*. Toronto: Leicester University Press, University of Toronto Press, 1982.

Jeanne Sheehy, *The Rediscovery of Ireland's Past: The Celtic Revival, 1830-1930*. London: Thames and Hudson, 1980.

Helena M. Shire, Alexander Montgomerie, *A Selection from His Songs and Poems*. Oliver and Boyd for the Satire Society, 1960.

Butler Waugh, "Robert Burns' Satires and the Folk Tradition: 'Halloween,'" *South Atlantic Bulletin* (November 1967):10.

W. G. Wood-Martin, *Traces of the Edler Faiths of Ireland*. Vol. II. London: Longman's, Green and Co., 1902.

Additional Halloween Reading

Mrs. Samuel M. Alexander, "The Dumb Cake. A Charm of Hallowe'en," *Godey's Lady's Book* 91 (November 1875): 420.

"All Hallows Eve in Wales," *The Living Age* 3 (November 30, 1844): 310.

Osborn Bergin and Richard Irvine Best, ed. and trans., "The Tochmarc Etaine" [The Wooing of Etaine], *The Book of Leinster*, Vol. I. Dublin: Rees and Rees, Dublin Institute for Advanced Studies, 1954-1983.

William Black, "A Hallowe'en Wraith," *The Magic Ink, Collection of British Authors,* Vol. 2839. Leipzig: Bernhard Tauchnitz, 1892.

James Bowker, "All Hallow's Night," *Goblin Tales of Lancashire.* London: W. Swan Sonnenschein and Co., circa 1878.

N.C. Brooks, A.M., "Clara Lawson; or the Rustic Toilet," *Godey's Lady's Book* 12 (April 1836): 145.

Robert Burns, "Tam o' Shanter"; "Twa Dogs"; "Tam Glen," *The Complete Poetical Works of Robert Burns,* ed. Wm. Ernest Henley. Cambridge Edition. Boston: Houghton Mifflin and Co., 1897.

Robert Williams Buchanan, "The Northern Wooing," *The Complete Poetical Works of Robert Buchanan.* Vol. I. London: Chatto and Windus, 1901.

Hezekiah Butterworth, "Captain Tut-Tut-Tuttle and the Miracle Clock. A Hallowe'en Reformation," *In Old New England, The Romance of A Colonial Fireside.* New York: Appleton and Co., 1895.

Will Carleton, "The Bearded Lady's Story," in "The Festival of the Freaks," *City Festivals.* New York: Harper, 1892.

William Carleton, "A Shanagh on Hallow-Eve," *Carleton's Country,* ed. Rose Shaw. Dublin: Talbot Press Ltd., 1930.

Madison J. Cawein, "The House of Fear," *Shapes and Shadows.* New York: R.H. Russell, 1898.

———, "After Autumn Rain," *New Poems.* London: G. Richards, 1909.

———, "Intimations of the Beautiful," *Poems.* New York: The Macmillan Company, 1911.

Robert Chambers, "Halloween," *The Book of Days: A Miscellany of Popular Antiquities in Connection With the Calendar.* Philadelphia: J.B. Lippincott Co., 1891.

Rose Terry Cooke, "All Saints' Eve," *The Atlantic Monthly* 46 (December 1880): 739.

Helen Gray Cone, "A Hallowe'en Frolic," *St. Nicholas Magazine* 20 (November 1888): n.p.

John Cartwright Cross, "Halloween; or, The Castles of Athlin and Dunbayne. A New Grand Scotch Spectacle," *Ballets, Spectacles, Melo-Dramas, etc. Performed at the Royal Circus.* Vol. II., 1809.

Jeremiah Curtin, ed. "St. Martin's Eve," *Tales of the Fairies and of the Ghost World.* Boston: Little Brown and Company, 1895.

John Davidson, "All Hallow's Eve," *Fleet Street Ecologues and Other Poems.* London: Grant Richards, 1909.

Emily Dickinson, "#281/'Tis so appalling—," *The Poems of Emily Dickinson,* ed. Thomas H. Johnson. Cambridge, Mass.: Belknap Press of Harvard University Press, 1955.

Helen Elliott, "Hallowe'en," *Godey's Lady's Book* 81 (November 1870): 439.

J.A. Fergusson, "The Scarecrow. A Hallowe'en Fantasy in One Act," *One Act Plays of To-Day,* 5th Series, sel. by J.W. Marriott. London: George G. Harrap and Co., Ltd., 1931.

Robert Fergusson, "Hallow-Fair," *English Poetry 1700-1780,* ed. David W. Lindsay. New Jersey: Rowman and Littlefield, 1974.

S. Annie Frost, "Ethel's Charm at Hallowe'en," *Godey's Lady's Book* 85 (October 1872): 342.

———, "Hallowe'en at Farmdale," *Godey's Lady's Book* Vol. 87 (October 1873): 350.

Lady Augusta Gregory, ed. and trans., "Midhir and Etain," *Gods and Fighting Men: The Story of the Tuatha de Danaan and of the Fianna of Ireland.* London: John Murray, 1905.

Gerald Griffin, "Holland Tide," *The Aylmers of Bally-Alymer.* Dublin: James Duffy, 1827.

"The Hall of Fame, Hallowe'en A.D. 2000" *New York Times* (October 31, 1900): n.p.

Daisy Baker Hay, "Mammy Explains Hallowe'en. A Play for Hallowe'en." Denver, CO: Eldridge Entertainment House, 1927.

William Cuyler Hosmer, "Halloween," *Later Lays and Lyrics.* Rochester, NY: D.M. Dewey, 1873.

Georgiana S. Hull, "A Legend of All-Hallow Eve," *Harper's Magazine* 59 (November 1879): 833.

Douglas Hyde, "The Piper and the Puca," *Fairy and Folk Tales of Ireland,* ed. W.B. Yeats. Gerrards Cross: Colin Smythe, 1977.

Edward Jerningham, *Honoria, or the Day of All Souls, a poem.* London: J. Robson, 1782.

Mrs. Burton Kingsland, "A Jolly Hallowe'en Party," *Ladies Home Journal* (October 1902): n.p.

George Lafenestre, "Night Visits," *Flowers of France; the Latter Days, Ackermann to Warnery Representative Poems of the 19th and 20th Century,* trans. John Payne. Vol. I. London: Villon Society, 1913.

J. Bell Landfear, "A Harvest Drill," *The Delineator* (October, 1897): 464.

William Augustine Leahy, *The Wedding Feast: a Tragic Drama in Three Acts with a Prologue, Hallowe'en.* Boston, circa 1896.

Fred J. Lissfelt, "Halloween," *The Dutchman Died, and other tales of Pittsburgh's Southside.* Pittsburgh: University of Pittsburgh Press, 1992.

George MacDonald, "Uncle Cornelius His Story," *Victorian Ghost Stories, An Oxford Anthology,* ed. Cox and Gilbert, Oxford: Oxford University Press, 1991.

Donald A. Mackenzie, "A Lost Lady," *Tales from the Moors and the Mountains.* London and Glasgow: Blackie and Sons, Ltd., 1931.

Seamus MacManus, "Hallow-Eve in Ireland," *The Delineator* (November 1909): 409.

Walter de la Mare, "The Song of Shadows"; "The Ride-by-Nights," *Poems 1901 to 1918 by Walter de la Mare.* London: Constable and Company, Ltd., 1920.

———— "All Hallows," *The Connoisseur and Other Stories.* London: W. Collins Sons and Co., 1926.

Rosamond Marriott-Watson, "All Souls Day," *Harper's New Monthly Magazine* 91 (July 1895): 226.

George Martin, "Hallowe'en in Canada; and How it Settled a Domestic Quarrel," *Marguerite; or, the Isle of Demons and Other Poems.* Montreal: Dawson Bros., Publishers, 1887.

John Mayne, "Maggy Maclane," *The Poets and Poetry of Scotland,* ed. James Grant Wilson. New York: Harper and Brothers, Publishers, 1876.

Thomas D'Arcy McGee, "Halloween in Canada," *The Poems of Thomas D'Arcy McGee.* New York: D. and J. Sadlier and Co.; Boston: P.H. Brady, 1869.

James McIntyre, "St. Andrew and Halloween," *Musings on the Banks of the Canadian Thames.* n.p., 1884.

Alexander McLachlan, "Hallowe'en; *Poems and Songs by Alexander McLachlan.* n.p., 1888.

Brian Merriman, "The Midnight Court," trans. J. Noel Fahey. http://www.uhb.fr/Languages/Cei/midcrt.htm/ (archived 1998, accessed January 2004)

"Merry Social Evenings," *Ladies Home Journal* (October 1902): 20.

R.K. Munkittrick, "A Halloween Wish," *Harper's Weekly* 44 (October 27, 1900): 1010.

Michael J. Murphy, "The Love Charm," *My Man Jack. Bawdy Tales from Irish Folklore.* Co. Kerry, Ireland: Brandon Book Publishers Ltd., 1989.

Francis Neilson, "Sin-Eater's Hallowe'en, a fantasy in one act and two scenes." New York: B.W. Huebsch, Inc., 1924.

Virginia Olcott, "On All Souls' Eve. A play of wonders for Hallowe'en," *Holiday Plays for home, school and settlement.* New York: Moffat, Yard and Co., 1917.

Elizabeth Robinson, "A Novel Halloween," *Harper's Bazaar* 38 (1904): 1092.

Saxon, ed., "The Girnin Wean" and "Riddled in the Reek," *Galloway Gossip. Sixty Years Ago; Being a series of articles illustrative of the Manners, Customs and Peculiarities of the Aboriginal Picts of Galloway.* Choppington, Northumberland: Robert Trotter, 1877.

William Sharp, "Halloween. A Threefold Chronicle," *Harper's New Monthly Magazine* 73 (November 1886): 842.

Henry Shoemaker, "Halloween"; "All Soul's Night"; "Merrithew," *Juniata Memories.* Philadelphia: John Joseph McVey, 1916.

James Stephens, Ch. XI.-XIII., "The Boyhood of Fionn," *Irish Fairy Tales.* New York: The MacMillan Co., 1934.

A.G.T., "All-Hallowe'en," *Godey's Lady's Book* 97 (October 1878): 301.

Elizabeth Phipps Train, "The Hallow-e'en Sensation at Guv'nor Dering's," *Godey's Lady's Book* 117 (October 1888): 301.

Edith Wharton, "All Saints," *Artemis to Actaeon.* New York: Charles Scribner's Sons, 1909.

_____, "All Souls'" Collected Stories, 1911-1937, ed. Maureen Howard. New York: Penguin Putnam, 2001.

Charles Williams, *All Hallow's Eve*. Grand Rapids, MI: Wm. B. Eerdman's Publishing Co., 1981.

W. B. Yeats, "All Souls' Night," *The New Republic* (March 9, 1921): 46

_____, ed., "The Three Wishes"; "The Piper and the Puca"; "A Dream," *Irish Fairy and Folk Tales*. New York: The Modern Library, 2003.